KNIGHTMARE ARCANIST

SHAMI STOVALL

CAPITAL
• STATION BOOKS •

KNIGHTMARE ARCANIST

FRITH CHRONICLES #1

Published by
CS BOOKS, LLC

This is a work of fiction. Names, characters, places, and incidents either are the product of author imagination or are used factiously, and any resemblance to actual persons, living or dead, business establishments, events, or locales, is entirely fictional.

Cover Design: Darko Paganus

Editor: Erin Grey, Sallianne Hines

IF YOU WANT TO BE NOTIFIED WHEN SHAMI STOVALL'S NEXT BOOK RELEASES, PLEASE VISIT HER WEBSITE OR CONTACT HER DIRECTLY AT: s.adelle.s@gmail.com

ISBN: 978-0-9980452-2-1

To John, for being the first to see.
To Beka, for making this possible.
To Gail and Big John, for all the support.
To Zoe, for being an awesome beta reader.
To all my writing buddies, this couldn't happen without you.
And finally, to everyone unnamed, thank you for everything.

THE DAY OF PHOENIXES

I outlined a fresh grave for the cemetery as bells rang from the isle's tower, signifying the start of the celebrations. The soil reeked of ammonia and rot, but the crisp morning breeze washed the scent away, dispersing it over the ocean. I removed my shirt, allowing the wind to cool me while I worked.

Every ten years, the people on the Isle of Ruma gathered to watch the fledgling phoenixes bond with a few chosen mortals. Lamplighters did their duty despite the glorious sunshine, each lamp's fire representing the flames of phoenixes. Merchants cleared their horses and carts from the main road in anticipation of the crowds.

This was my second Day of Phoenixes. A decade ago, on my fifth birthday, I missed the bonding ceremony to attend my father's trial. He was convicted of murder, but because he hadn't been born on the island, he was taken to the mainland for final judgement. That was the last time I saw him.

Although the last Day of Phoenixes had been inauspicious, I intended to change that. Once I had finished digging a shallow grave, I would make my way into town.

I slammed the shovel's head into the dirt and scooped deep. The cemetery sat near the edge of the island, far from those gathering to observe the hopeful students trying to win the favor of the phoenixes.

Tradition stated that anyone who handled sewage, waste, and dead bodies wasn't allowed to attend the bonding ceremony, which was just my luck. After my father was sent away, I could've been given to any profession for apprenticeship. I could've gone to the carpenter and learned the craft of woodworking, or I could've gone to the silversmith and learned the art of fine metal work, but misfortune hounded me like a shadow. I was given to the gravekeeper, slated to dig corpse-holes until the end of time, forever exiled from the festivities.

I still intended to go. Even if it meant ignoring the traditions of the isle—something unheard of on our tiny spit of land—no one could stop me from proving myself to a phoenix. No one.

I scooped another mound of dirt and tossed it to the side.

"You look deep in thought, Volke," my fellow corpse-hole apprentice, Illia, said. "What're you planning?"

"I'm waiting for the trials to begin."

"And then what?"

"You'll see."

Illia sat in the shade of a cypress tree, her legs crossed and her chin in both hands. Most people hated the thought of sitting on graves, since it was supposed to bring bad luck, but Illia wasn't like most people. She leaned back on a headstone and exhaled as the ocean wind rushed by, catching her wavy brown hair and revealing the scars on the side of her face.

She held a hand over the marks, like she always did. The

2

moment the wind died down, she pulled some of her hair around to cover her scars, hiding the old knife wounds that had taken her right eye.

I finished one half of the grave and huffed.

Illia and I lived in a tiny cottage on the edge of the cemetery, apprenticed to Ruma's sole gravekeeper. We both held the glorious title of *gravedigger*. Like me, she had no family. Well, we had each other, and Gravekeeper William, but he hardly counted.

For ten years, Illia and I had considered ourselves brother and sister, and siblings always know each other's mood. Illia displayed all the telltale signs of irritation—narrowed eye, rarely blinking, her mouth turned down in a slight frown. She hated the fact I was keeping secrets from her. If I didn't explain myself quick, she'd exact her revenge.

"I don't want to become the next gravekeeper," I said as I threw a mound of dirt off to the side.

With an eyebrow sarcastically raised, Illia asked, "So you're going to impress a phoenix and leave this place, is that it?"

"That's right."

"Only two phoenixes were born this year," she said, wagging her finger. "And the schoolmaster has already picked his two favored disciples to win the right to bond. No one wants you to take a phoenix from either of those try-hards."

"I don't care." I scooped out another clump of dirt, my grip on the shovel so tight it hurt. "Bonding with a phoenix is too important. Besides, no one on this isle likes me anyway. Why should I start caring about their opinions now?"

"Hmph. I should've known you'd say that."

Of course. Anyone who bonded with a mystical creature,

like a phoenix, became an *arcanist*—a powerful wielder of sorcery, capable of great magic based on the creature they bonded to.

Arcanists were the pinnacle of society, the most influential people, and revered by everyone. Some arcanists could control the weather, or devastate armies, or make the land fertile. Even the weakest and laziest of arcanists were well-thought-of and important members of powerful guilds, shepherding humanity to greatness with a mere flick of their wrists.

What I wouldn't give to become an arcanist. They were things of legend.

More significant than a gravedigger, anyway.

"You're not the only one with plans today," Illia said. She waited a minute before adding, "Aren't you going to ask me what I'll be doing during the bonding ceremony?"

I shoveled another chunk of dirt, taking some weeds with it. "All right. Tell me. What will you be doing?"

"It's a secret."

She stood and brushed herself off with a few gentle pats to her dress. Then she crossed her arms and stared at me, no doubt waiting for me to pester her about the secret just so she could say, *see how annoying it is when you do it*?

"I'm sure you'll have fun doing whatever it is you have planned," I said with a shrug.

"You're not the only one who wants to become an arcanist, *Volke*," she replied, saying my name as though it were venom. "But there might be easier ways than embarrassing yourself in front of everyone."

I finished carving the outline of the grave, determined not to be sucked into asking her what she meant. I had too many things on my mind to get into an argument. Besides, I knew she was right. It was irksome being excluded from

4

secrets, especially by family. But I didn't want to run the risk of her trying to dissuade me.

Another round of bells sounded in the distance. I threw my shovel to the side and turned toward the cemetery cottage. "I have to go. Whatever you do, don't get into trouble."

Illia replied with a smile. "Never."

Something about her sarcastic tone told me she had trouble planned, but there wasn't any time to go into it. I jogged into the cottage, ran up the rickety stairs, and then dashed straight into my room. It was technically a storage closet that Gravekeeper William had converted into a sleeping space so that Illia and I wouldn't have to share the second bedroom.

The cramped room fit my cot, a chair, and a trunk for my clothes. That was it.

I squeezed myself in, ripped off my dirty trousers, and then dressed in a clean white shirt and black pants. Although I owned nothing fancy—everything in my trunk had been Gravekeeper William's at some point—I still wanted to make an effort. The phoenixes bonded with individuals they liked the most after the Trials of Worth were over. I needed to impress them, and I couldn't do that with grave dirt on my clothes.

Once dressed, I combed my disheveled hair, even though it never cooperated. For some reason, it always puffed out and tangled at the ends, defying gravity just to make me look foolish. And the blackness of it—an inky hue taken straight from the midnight hour—wasn't common on the isles. Everyone else had red or blond hair, so other kids made fun of me.

Coal head. Ink brush. They weren't clever kids—any dumber and you'd have to water them twice a week—they were just mean. No one harassed me after I grew tall, however. Six feet meant I stood out in the group, and not in a wimpy way.

When I finished the last of my brushing, my hair puffed back out.

Satisfied I had made myself halfway presentable, I laced up my boots and headed downstairs to the kitchen. I grabbed a small canteen of water and the cleanest rag we owned before rushing out the front door.

The vast ocean sparkled in the distance, so blue it put the sky to shame. The winds brought waves, but nothing strong enough to reach far inland—just the melody of water lapping across the white sand beaches.

With the breeze in my face, I ran down the dirt road until I came to the cobblestone streets of the city. I pushed my way through the crowds of people swarming toward the town square.

Our small island didn't have much flatland, so the one city—creatively named *Ruma*, like the island—was the only place to live. The two-story houses were smooshed together, most with stores downstairs and homes above. Despite the congested living arrangements, people went out of their way to keep the place lively. Potted flowers, colored cobblestone for the roads, wrought-iron fences in the shape of fish for the balconies—Ruma had a special beauty waiting in every nook and cranny.

The crowds made their way to the Pillar to watch the bonding trials begin.

The Pillar—nothing more than a sheer column of pointed rock jutting straight up into the sky—was well over one hundred and twenty feet tall. It could be seen from anywhere on the island, the reddish stone shimmering in the sunlight. A single tree grew at the top, its branches forever swaying in the ocean winds, its roots laced over the rock, its fruit rare and delicious.

That sole charberry tree was what had attracted the first phoenixes to our island centuries ago. The spicy fruit tasted like a chili pepper, but sweeter and juicier. Phoenixes loved them.

The base of the Pillar was the starting location for the Trials of Worth—the tasks given to the wide-eyed hopefuls wanting to prove their value to the phoenixes. I continued through the crowd, my head tilted back, my gaze locked on the Pillar. A staircase wrapped around the column of rock, all the way to the top.

"Hey," someone yelled as I shoved my way deeper into the excited masses. "Isn't that one of the gravedigger kids?"

I ignored the remark, sidestepped the slow-moving families, and nimbly maneuvered through a group of schoolchildren. If I bonded with a phoenix, I wouldn't have to stay here anymore and listen to their whispers. All new arcanists traveled to the mainland to join a guild for training.

A third round of bells chimed, and my pulse quickened with each step. I didn't want to be late for the trials.

The whole population of Ruma packed the streets, shoulder to shoulder. No one missed the Day of Phoenixes unless they were specifically excluded, like the garbage men. Everyone wore their best attire, children tossed red flower petals, and the theater troupe wore costumes made of bird feathers while they pranced around pretending to be phoenixes. It took all of my willpower not to crane my head to get a better look at as I ran by.

"—and today is a day of glory," the schoolmaster's voice boomed across the town square.

Schoolmaster Tyms was a naturally loud individual—

Gravekeeper William described him as *a regular blowhard in love with his own voice.*

I slipped between two elderly men and stayed off to the side, making sure to remain in the shadows cast by the morning sun. Hundreds of people crowded the center of town, but their gazes never turned in my direction. They all kept their attention on a wooden stage near the Pillar —a platform only a few feet off the ground—where Schoolmaster Tyms stood squarely in the middle, his arms raised.

Whenever he glanced in my direction, I ducked. Schoolmaster Tyms didn't care for anyone except those who attended his lectures, and he especially hated those with "unsavory" professions.

"I've mentored two extraordinary people," Tyms said. "Both are talented beyond their years and worthy of a phoenix."

He walked to the edge of the stage, lifting his arms even higher, his wrinkled face pulled back in an unnatural smile. I had seen corpses do a better job at conveying emotion.

But I didn't stare at him for long because on either side of him, perched on ornate bird stands, were two phoenixes.

I stood transfixed, taking in their lustrous scarlet feathers and golden eyes. They had the build of herons, delicate and sleek, but every time they moved, soot fell from them and drifted to the ground. Fire flashed underneath their wings as though their whole bodies were made of flame. Their tails hung down two feet and twisted a bit at the end, like a peacock.

They were young, not even a year old, but that was old enough for them to leave the island. Mystical creatures didn't reach maturity unless they were bonded to a person —I was certain they were giddy for the ceremony as well.

"We're honored to be here today," one phoenix said, her voice sing-song and brilliant.

The other added, "We can't wait to see our potential partners." He lifted his head as he spoke, his voice soft but distinct.

I wanted to hold one in my arms and feel the warmth of their magic coursing through my body, but touching a phoenix was forbidden. Only once they bonded with a person were they allowed to be handled.

The phoenixes tilted their heads as two individuals walked forward. The two were around my age, fifteen, the age of adulthood. They wore robes of glistening white, tied at the waist with silver ropes made of silk. Fancy outfits made on the mainland, betraying their wealth.

Tyms motioned to the rich newcomers. "On this Day of the Phoenixes I've selected Zaxis Ren and Atty Trixibelle to take part in the trials."

Of course *they* would be picked. Ever since we were kids, they were always favored by the schoolmaster.

I cursed under my breath as Zaxis walked to the base of the Pillar.

He stopped under the metal archway, a century-old artifact which had been shaped into a phoenix and gilded. The arch signified the start of the trial. Anyone who passed beneath it would become a participant.

Zaxis smiled at the crowd with the smuggest expression a human could muster. His red hair shimmered in the sunlight and fluttered about with the wind. It wasn't long enough to tie back, and I took a small amount of pleasure in watching him clumsily pat it down every few seconds, only for a stray hair to poke him in the eye again.

Zaxis's family, the Ren House, stood at the front of the crowd, their personal soldiers keeping the "riffraff" a couple feet back. They cheered for Zaxis and threw flower petals. I had never been cheered for anything, yet all he did was *show up*. Life wasn't fair sometimes.

"Thank you," Zaxis said as he flashed a toothy smile. "Thank you. Once I'm bonded with a phoenix, I'll make all of Ruma proud with my many accomplishments. I'll become the world's most renowned arcanist, loved by all."

I balled my hands into fists and gritted my teeth. He already assumed a phoenix would choose him *and* that he would make one of the world's greatest arcanists? Of course he did—he wasn't expecting any competition.

Then Atty stepped forward, and the crowds hushed.

Unlike Zaxis, whose insufferable attitude knew no bounds, Atty held herself with regal sophistication. Her long blonde hair, tied in a neat braid, didn't twirl in the winds. She held her head high, her slender neck adorned with a silver necklace depicting a charberry tree. I had always admired her poise and grace, like a pauper admires a member of royalty, even when I was young.

If things had been different—if I wasn't a gravedigger— maybe I could've courted Atty. No doubt she would be disgusted to have someone like me approach her now. But once I bonded with a phoenix, perhaps I'd have the courage.

"Thank you, Schoolmaster Tyms," Atty said, her voice a sweet relief after a long day's work. "It's a privilege to prove myself worthy of a phoenix. If I become an arcanist, I swear to dedicate myself to becoming a helpful ruler, one all of Ruma can be proud of."

Atty's family, the Trixibelle House, owned most of the buildings on the island. They sat on nearby balconies, each of them poised on chairs and cushions, cheering for Atty, along with everyone else on the island.

Although I wanted a phoenix for myself, *I* almost joined

in on the clapping. Her answer was perfect, and when the phoenixes exchanged glances, I knew they thought the same.

No one else stepped forward.

While other people *could* offer themselves to the phoenixes, it was frowned upon. The schoolmaster knew best, or so they said—for centuries the keepers of knowledge were deemed the wisest and most capable of determining who would become the best arcanists. It was tradition. And for the last few decades, the schoolmaster hadn't even made it a competition. He simply chose the exact number of students equal to phoenixes, ensuring his recommendation carried more weight than gold.

And the Isle of Ruma knew the importance of picking the right people to become arcanists. If the competition was open to everyone, someone with ill intents could gain vast magical power. The schoolmaster was supposed to weed them out and put forward only the best, most deserving people. That was why no one else entered the competitions. *Following traditions is the way of the isles!* Our island's motto.

But even if I was noble of spirit, Atty and Zaxis studied and trained eight hours a day under the care of Schoolmaster Tyms. Everyone else, myself included, had work and chores. Atty and Zaxis were lucky. I wasn't. How could I ever hope to match their knowledge and skills?

That didn't matter, though. I wouldn't make excuses. The phoenixes could, in theory, bond with anyone they found worthy. And I would show them just how worthy I was by passing each of the three trials.

"Once our hopefuls walk through the archway," Tyms said, gesturing to the gold phoenix arch, "they will officially become participants in the trials. For the first task, each hopeful must walk up all one hundred and twelve steps of the Pillar to the charberry tree. Then they will pick a fruit to present to the phoenixes and return down the stairs."

Every Day of Phoenixes had the same three trials. The charberry tree was the first. Only one stairway led to the tree —the spiral stairway made of stone steps that wrapped around the Pillar. The steps were hundreds of years old and worn smooth from use. Oh, and no railing, which was why I never felt safe standing on them, as falling from anything past the tenth step meant serious injury, possibly death.

"And with that, you may begin," Tyms shouted.

Both Atty and Zaxis bowed to the crowd before turning and walking through the archway.

This was it.

My moment.

I ran through the crowd, pushing people out of the way when I needed to, even knocking over a few men of the Ren Family as I dashed toward the arch. My heart beat so hard I almost didn't hear people screaming for me to stop.

"Hey!" a woman barked.

"What's he doing?" someone else shouted.

"Stop him!"

But before anyone could grab me, I raced through the archway, dashing past Atty and Zaxis.

"What do you think you're doing, Volke?" Zaxis growled. "Good-for-nothing gravediggers can't enter the trials!"

I had my foot on the first step of the Pillar when I glanced over my shoulder. "I already passed under the archway. That makes me a participant."

"What? That's not allowed!" Zaxis glanced over his shoulder. "Right, Master Tyms?"

Tyms blubbered and flailed his arms. "How dare you, Volke! You walk back through that archway this instant. You're disgracing all of Ruma with your disrespect!"

I ran up the steps, taking them two at a time despite the lack of railing.

Today I would prove myself to a phoenix. I would prove myself to all of Ruma.

I was more than just a gravedigger.

I wouldn't stop. Not now, not ever.

TRIALS OF WORTH

"Volke!" Zaxis shouted. "Damn you, get down here!"

Gasps from the townsfolk got caught in the ocean breeze as Zaxis lifted his white robes and ran up the stairs after me. I didn't glance back. Zaxis had been one of those not-so-clever kids who used to make my life difficult, including chasing me around. If I didn't focus, he would catch up to me. So I took the steps three at a time, muttering *don't fall, don't fall* as I climbed higher and higher above the crowd.

The stonework of the steps had writing etched into them, and I glanced at the words as I went.

They were the virtues of the arcanist—the traits arcanists should display to lead humanity into an age of greatness. Arcanists were role models, after all. Paragons of mankind. Anyone who hoped to bond with a phoenix needed to memorize the steps backward and forward, so every day after I finished working for Gravekeeper William, I went to the steps and practiced. Evening after evening. No day skipped, not even during the worst of weather, for ten whole years.

The first stone step read: *Integrity. Without it, we cannot have trust.*

The second stone step read: *Passion. Without it, we grow complacent.*

The third stone step read: *Discipline. Without it, we are not the masters of our destiny.*

It went on for all one hundred and twelve steps.

Charity. Strategy. Sacrifice. Bravery. Loyalty. Respect. Perseverance. Humility. Wisdom.

I knew them all. Each step, each phrase.

Well, that wasn't entirely true. I knew all of them but the last two—the last two steps had been destroyed long ago, leaving nothing more than jagged rocks. Anytime I asked the people in town what they were, no one ever answered. Either they didn't know or they didn't want to speak with me. I suspected it had more to do with the latter.

Halfway up the steps, the cheering of the crowds grew distant. I could still hear a mix of boos and shouts, but I pushed them from my mind. My legs grew stiff, and I gulped down air. Zaxis gained on me, his huffing and puffing loud enough for me to easily keep track of his location. The spiral stairway wrapped around the column-like mountain, giving me a great view of Ruma from one shore to the other. The green water, clear down to its sandy bottom, almost took my breath away.

When I reached the top, I inhaled deep, but my lungs still felt shredded and unable to inflate. I had never run to the top of the Pillar before, and I knew I would never do it again. My body couldn't handle it.

I forced myself to continue to the charberry tree. Zaxis was close on my heels, his steps heavy, betraying his exhaustion. Maybe he said something, I wasn't sure. He sounded like a ravenous dog about to sink its teeth into a fresh kill, though.

The charberries hung from the branches, swollen with juice and ready to fall. Each one shone in the sunlight, their glossy crimson skin a thing of beauty. I reached up and plucked one from the tree, the delicate outside almost bruising from the pressure of my touch. In one swift motion, I wrapped the charberry in my cloth and tied it to my belt.

"What—" Zaxis inhaled and then wheezed, "—do you think you're doing?" He stopped and placed his hands on his knees, his head hung.

"I'm competing," I replied, breathless.

"You can't... do that."

"Who's gonna stop me?"

"You won't take a phoenix from me." He huffed. "I've worked my whole life to get one. *I* deserve it."

"We'll see, won't we," I said.

Zaxis snapped his gaze to mine, the dark green of his eyes alight with rage. "I'll throw you off this damn cliff myself."

He lunged, and I stepped around the massive trunk of the charberry tree, dodging his grasp. The roots grew over the rock of the Pillar, creating an awkward terrain of limbs that threatened to trip me no matter where I stepped. Zaxis leapt over the roots and came at me again, but I already had what I came for.

I jumped off the edge of the Pillar and landed eight steps down on the stairway, my knees flaring in pain when I didn't brace myself correctly. Then I staggered on, a slight smile on my face despite the weakness in my legs. Nothing would stop me. I would make it. I would.

While I wanted nothing more than to fly down the steps and make it back to the town square as fast as possible, I slowed to allow for my stamina to recover. Halfway back, I nearly collided with Atty.

She glanced up at me, stopped, and then stepped to the side, her back to the wall of rock. She kept her hands clasped together in front of her and stood with perfect posture. I even straightened a bit when I stepped by, trying to imitate her regal confidence. After I passed, Atty resumed her walking, taking one step at a time, no haste or frustration to her gait, conducting herself as though nothing out of the ordinary had happened.

On the last ten steps I walked with my shoulders back and my head high. While the denizens of Ruma stared with wide eyes, some wore scowls and others had small smiles. As far as I knew, no one had ever barged their way into the Trials of Worth before. At least I was unique. Always a silver lining.

A table had been placed in the middle of the wooden stage. I sauntered over, stepped up onto the stage, and went straight to the table. Before I placed my charberry on top, I pulled out my canteen of water and washed off the berry until it glistened. Once finished, I placed it on the table and took a step back, proud of the fist-sized berry I managed to pluck before I ran back down the steps.

Both the phoenixes stared at my offering, their gold eyes flitting from me, to the charberry, and then back to me.

"Delicious," the girl phoenix murmured.

The boy nodded. "Yes. Delectable."

Zaxis jogged down the last of the steps and ran straight for the stage. He hopped up and shot me a heated glare as he placed his charberry next to mine. In his haste he forgot to wash it, so it appeared dirty, but his berry was obviously bigger.

"You won't win," Zaxis muttered under his breath as he

stepped back to wait for the phoenix's judgment. "The phoenixes can probably smell the corpse dirt on you."

I replied with a smile.

He ground his teeth in response.

Tyms stood at the opposite end of the stage, his face red and his lips nothing more than a thin line of anger. He glowered at me the entire time, never saying a word. According to tradition, I was officially in the running to bond with a phoenix, and there was little anyone could do about it.

The crowd cheered and pointed to the top of the Pillar. Zaxis and I craned our heads back to catch a glimpse of Atty descending the steps with a charberry in hand. Since there was nothing to do but wait, I kept my gaze on her the entire way, impressed by her patience and grace. When she finally reached the bottom, she brought her fruit up onto the stage and placed it on the table next to mine.

She had washed hers as well, and it was even larger than Zaxis's. If anything, it looked too perfect—like a fantastical painting given life. I wondered how long she had searched through the branches of the tree to find exactly what she was looking for.

"Now we shall see who brought back the most appealing fruit," Tyms said with a sweeping motion of his arm. He pointed to Atty's. "Will it be the succulent berry, picked with care?" He pointed to Zaxis's. "Will it be this juicy berry, perfectly ripe in all regards?" Then he gestured to mine with a flick of his wrist. "Or will it be the merely adequate offering?"

Ha! *Merely adequate offering.* How blatantly biased could he get?

Both phoenixes stretched their wings and took flight, a burst of fire whooshing with each flap as they sailed overhead. The festival goers clapped and pointed, some even swaying together in a semi-dance as the birds circled around. Soot rained onto the streets, but no one in Ruma minded. They all knew phoenix soot wouldn't harm them.

Whichever berry the phoenixes chose would determine which participant of the trials gained favor.

The girl phoenix swooped down and snatched up Atty's fruit in one beautiful streak of flame. The city burst into instant celebration, the cheers so loud they shook the cobblestone under the stage. Atty smiled and waved, never breaking her calm demeanor.

Then the masses hushed themselves and waited.

The second phoenix circled around, and I held my breath. Whose would he pick? Even if he didn't pick mine, there were still two trials left for me to prove myself. I could recover. Nothing to worry about. I had just waited ten years for this moment. No pressure.

No. Pressure.

Sweat dappled my skin with each passing moment.

Damn. There was a lot of pressure.

What if the phoenix hated my rude gesture? What if he thought me arrogant and unworthy? What if both the phoenixes were secretly laughing at me for even trying? I was probably making a fool of myself, and I didn't even realize it.

I balled my hands into fists and forced my thoughts to come to a halt.

I couldn't worry now. I had already made my choice.

Then the phoenix descended. It grabbed my charberry with its talons and flew back into the air on a breeze of heat and flame. Every last piece of me wanted to leap into the air but I contained my delight.

Yes! Finally! I took in breath, unable to control my smile.

The citizens of Ruma didn't share my enthusiasm, however.

A wave of murmuring spread through the crowd like a ripple on the water. Words of discontent floated up one at a time, the onlookers growing bolder with each statement.

"Is it even fair that he's here?" a woman asked.

A man replied, "I can't believe the phoenixes were impressed by someone like him."

"Isn't he the son of *that murderer*?"

"Oh, you're right. Dreadful. Someone like him should never become an arcanist."

I hated it when people commented on my father, but I held my breath and didn't acknowledge their words.

Tyms marched across the wooden stage, his face so red it shifted into a shade of purple. No doubt he would pass out at any second.

The phoenixes landed back on their perch and slurped down their charberries.

I wanted to ask them which charberry was tastier, in an attempt to beat Atty at *something*, but I kept my question to myself. Tradition stated that none of the participants were to speak with the phoenixes until the final trial, and while I had broken a lot of traditions today, I didn't want to make myself completely unlikeable.

"The second trial is of knowledge," Tyms said, spittle sprinkling out with each forced word. He looked his age when he shouted—I could practically see the last of his brown hair turning white. "The first question will go to Volke."

No cheering. No applause. Children sat on the roofs of houses, deep frowns on their faces. The people on the streets continued whispering, their stares more intense than ever.

I stepped forward, prepared for any examination. In the past, the schoolmaster would ask questions about the history of Ruma, the history of arcanists, or the meaning of the steps leading up to the charberry tree. I studied the steps by looking at them, and Gravekeeper William had books on the subjects of history and arcanists.

Although I had doubts, I lifted my head. "I'm ready."

"Who was our island's sixth keeper of the coin, and how many years did he serve us?" Tyms demanded.

What an obscure and specific question. Although I had reviewed many of the past questions, nothing had been *this* difficult. Tyms had it out for me, I already knew, but I didn't think he would be so blatant about it.

Still, I had studied our island's leaders in preparation. Illia even helped with the process. She created a mnemonic for remembering all the rulers of the island—a poem, so to speak, that mostly rhymed, but not all the time. Ruma didn't have many positions of office, so there were less than fifty people to memorize, even when counting all the keepers of coin.

Under my breath I whispered our poem, "We *swam* to the island with Mr. Mayor *Lamb*, who kept his coin beyond his *height* with a lady named Freda *White*." While I continued until I reached the sixth set of rulers, Tyms grew more impatient, his jaw clenching tight.

"Have you suffered a stroke, boy?" he yelled.

"And the *herd* kept Mr. Mayor *Bird* away from the *shovel* and loyal coin keeper—" I took a breath and spoke louder, "—Brisby *Hovel*. That was the sixth keeper of the coin and he served for six years."

Tyms sneered. The crowd remained silent, but the few who knew the answer nodded and pointed. I had gotten it correct, which meant Tyms had to move on to the next participant.

"Hmph." Tyms turned away. "Next will be Atty."

"I'm ready," she said.

Cheers. Applause. General worship that lasted a good ten seconds before everyone tired themselves out.

Tyms asked, "Who was our island's founder?"

I almost laughed. *Who was our island's founder?* His name was Gregory Ruma—his name was where we got our island's name. A small child would know the answer without a second's thought. I almost wanted to call Tyms out on his favoritism, but again, I kept quiet.

"Our island's founder was none other than Master Arcanist Gregory Ruma," Atty responded.

"Very good." Tyms smiled and then turned to Zaxis. "Are you prepared for your question?"

"I've been ready my whole life," Zaxis replied.

More cheering, but less than with Atty. No doubt the citizens of Ruma were disappointed Zaxis hadn't beaten me outright.

"Which mystical creature did Gregory Ruma bond to?"

"A leviathan," Zaxis said without a second's hesitation.

Again Tyms had given another ridiculously easy question. Everyone knew the wondrous tales of Ruma and his leviathan. The two sailed from island to island, establishing ports and discovering all sorts of strange lands never before documented. Ruma fought pirates, raided ruins, and even fell in love, all while on the high seas. He was an arcanist beyond compare.

I adored the stories about Gregory Ruma. Maybe one day I would be just like him.

"That's correct," Tyms said. Then he turned his glower

back to me. "Young arcanists must know our island's oath. It is a requirement for bonding."

"I'm aware," I said.

"Can you recite every step up the Pillar? Without paper or prompt?"

"I can."

My statement got the crowd murmuring again. Would I beat Zaxis a second time? If I did, it was all over. The phoenixes tended to bond with the person who had won their favor twice in a row, and if Tyms kept giving me the most difficult questions, he would unwittingly make me look the most impressive. Well, as long as I answered them correctly.

"Then recite the thirty-seventh step," Tyms said.

I forced a smile, still aware of the scrutiny, not only from the town, but the phoenixes. "Compassion. Without it, we make the world a crueler place."

The hushed response from the people of Ruma clawed at my confidence. I knew I got the correct answer, yet they still glowered as though I was somehow cheating. A few pointed and others whispered about the need for a blindfold.

Really though—a blindfold? What did they think I was reading off? Tyms's face?

"And the eightieth step?"

Typically the schoolmaster went between the participants, asking them one question at a time, but Tyms hadn't turned away from me. He continued staring, his glare a permanent fixture to his expression.

"Bravery," I replied. "Without it, we cannot act in the face of fear."

"What about the one hundred and twelfth step?"

I caught my breath and waited. Then I narrowed my

eyes and said, "It's been destroyed. It's been gone for over a decade."

"That's no excuse," Tyms snapped. "You said you could recite every step, so let's hear it."

Unable to breathe, I mulled over his request a thousand times in a matter of seconds. I didn't know. I never knew. There was nothing to recall. Nothing for my mind to latch onto. What did he want from me? How could he get away with asking an impossible question?

"There is no answer," I said, more defiant than I wanted. "The step doesn't exist."

Tyms's wrinkled face finally twisted from a frown into a genuine smile. The red drained from his cheeks as he lifted his bushy white eyebrows straight toward his receding hairline. "Zaxis, can you recite the one hundred and twelfth step?"

"Justice," Zaxis replied, his voice as smug as the expression on his face. "Without it, we cannot differentiate from revenge."

Tyms turned to me. "Do you know the hundred and eleventh step?"

Again, of course I didn't. It was just as destroyed as the last. "I don't know," I said through clenched teeth.

"Atty." Tyms snapped his fingers.

"Mercy," Atty replied. "Without it, we cannot help others find redemption."

Tyms held his arms up. "Well, there you have it. Volke, you misspoke about your talents, you're clearly not as educated as your peers, and you attempted to hide your shortcomings through arrogance. For shame."

"Wait a minute," I said as I took a step forward. Then I stopped myself, the pounding of my heart deafening me to the agitated crowd. "How do Atty and Zaxis know about the last two steps? How would anyone know that? I asked around town—no one knew what those steps said!"

"Atty and Zaxis attended my lectures," Tyms said.

"So, you're the only one who knows of those missing steps? Then of course I couldn't—"

"If you were serious about proving yourself worthy, you would've found the time, and coin, to attend, wouldn't you? Excuses are not becoming of an arcanist, young man. Clearly you have a long way to go."

Tyms tossed the edge of his robes to the side in a dramatic swirl as he turned on his heel and walked back across the stage.

But I wouldn't be stopped by such weak games.

Despite the collective gasp from the citizens of Ruma and the angry growls of Zaxis, I stepped forward, right into the center of the stage. Only people who attended Tyms's lectures could be arcanists? No. That shouldn't be how it worked.

"It's not fair," I said. "I did everything I could on my own. Ask me any other question—about the island, about magic, about mystical creatures—I can still prove myself!"

Tyms glared. "If you're this upset, perhaps you aren't mature enough to participate in the competition. Go home, boy."

"What about the lesson on the sixth step? *Tenacity. Without it, we fail at life's most important tasks.* I refuse to quit."

A sea of eyes watched our confrontation, especially the golden eyes of the phoenixes.

"Fine," Tyms spat. "I didn't want to embarrass you, but you've left me no choice."

Embarrass me? I readied myself for a difficult question, my mind raking through every story I had ever heard—

every whisper of famous arcanists—preparing for an answer to leave Tyms, and the phoenixes, with no doubts about my worth.

"You will *never* become an arcanist," Tyms said. "It doesn't matter how many stairs you stare at, or how fast you can pluck a fruit from a tree branch, or how much of Ruma's history you know. You're the son of two criminals. Both your mother and your father were blackhearts. Fiends!"

Silence fell over the island. Even the wind stopped, as though the world held its breath after the declaration. I swear my heart seized for a moment.

When people bonded with mystical creatures, they became arcanists, whereas when mystical creatures bonded with people, they became *eldrin*.

Eldrin drew energy from the soul of their bonded person —that was how creatures aged and matured. The stronger and more capable the person, the more magical and powerful the eldrin became. Which meant the arcanist could wield stronger and more potent magic. Together they formed a unique bond that strengthened both participants.

But drawing power from a person's soul meant the eldrin became more like the person they were bonded to.

If a stubborn man with an anger issue bonded with a phoenix, the phoenix would slowly become a stubborn and angry bird. If a woman with a gentle disposition bonded with a phoenix, the bird of flame would become gentle in turn.

It was another reason to have a Trial of Worth. The creatures would get a feel for the personality of their human before deciding—before becoming more like them.

No one wanted to become more criminal in behavior and thought. No mystical creature wanted to bond to someone with a soul that would corrupt them. They wanted pure souls of innocence, optimism, good work ethic, and hope. Criminals were dishonest, selfish, and wicked.

"I'm not a criminal," I said in a small voice.

"Everyone knows it runs in the blood," Tyms said matter-of-factly. "Do you want proof? Look at how you conducted yourself today. No respect for the traditions of the island. No respect for your schoolmaster or your peers. All of your actions are evidence of your true nature. Do we want your flippant attitudes infesting our phoenixes and giving all of Ruma a bad name?"

The citizens of Ruma voiced loud opinions. Boos added to the mix, becoming a cacophony of disgust all aimed in my direction. Even the phoenixes huffed and held a quiet conversation between themselves, no longer giving me any of their attention.

"Your worthless mother was a thief who abandoned her family," Tyms continued. "And your heinous father a murderer." He threw a hand up into the air. "After they were sentenced, no one would take you but the gravekeeper, and even now you run wild through the streets, doing whatever you please!"

Every word cut deep. I scooted back to the edge of the stage, my chest tight, my vision tunneling. I hated when people brought up my mother and father. I wasn't them! Why did I carry their shadow? Why couldn't I escape it? Even when I thought people had forgotten me entirely, someone always brought it up again. And then they all looked at me as though I were a seed of evil ready to blossom into malevolence at any second.

Was breaking the traditions of the island just the first steppingstone to a life of crime? I wanted to prove myself. No one would give me a chance otherwise. What else should I have done?

But everyone always made the same argument. Good kids came from proper households and families. Pickpockets and thugs were the product of terrible parenting or no parents whatsoever.

"I..." It took me a moment to gather my courage. "But I want to be a noble arcanist. Someone righteous and—"

"If that's what you wanted, you should have done the right thing," Tyms interjected. "You should have done your duty to the island and stayed with the gravekeeper. Actions speak louder than words, boy! And your words about being noble are a terrible lie, trying to conceal who you really are."

People in the crowd threw stones. I shielded my head and stumbled back. Tyms continued speaking, but I no longer heard the words. Then the phoenixes returned their attention to me, their glowering and ruffled feathers a clear sign.

They had made their decision. My soul was tainted. They didn't need any more trials to know I was unworthy.

Neither of them would bond with me now.

Go home, boy, that was what Tyms said. The words haunted me.

I jumped down from the stage, and the citizens of Ruma parted, creating a path, their boos eating at the last shreds of my resolve. Unable to look anyone in the eye, I kept my head down and ran back to the cottage on the edge of the cemetery.

3

SECOND CHANCE

I sat at the edge of the island, staring out over the ocean as though I were at the end of the world. The moon reflected off the restless waters. Waves splashed across the sands of the shore. Stars dotted the sky. Despite the beauty of nature glittering all around me, I couldn't appreciate it.

Sometimes it felt as though life were beating me into a role I didn't choose.

Did I have to become a gravekeeper? Was that my fate? Was fighting against it just making me unhappy? Should I give up and accept everything everyone expected of me? The booing and shouting of the crowd were tattooed in my memory, permanently inked.

I had waited for ten long years, keeping my head down, doing what I needed to during the day and reading at night. When the kids my age went out and played, I studied. When the kids my age made friends and contacts, I only ever interacted with Illia and Gravekeeper William. When other kids learned the trades of their family, I toiled at a profession everyone scorned.

I had nothing but my dream to become an arcanist.

And now it was gone.

"Volke."

I didn't need to turn around. I would recognize Illia's voice no matter the circumstance.

But I couldn't bring myself to face her, not even when she took a seat next to me, her legs dangling over the ocean. The edge of the rock made for a perfect balcony overlooking the waves. It was why I came to this spot—to clear my thoughts with the white noise of the ocean all around me.

Illia leaned close, trying to meet my gaze, but I turned away. I already knew what she was going to say. *I told you so.* If I was lucky, she would gloat for a few minutes, get it all off her chest, and then leave me with my thoughts. But I wasn't lucky, so I braced myself for a long tirade about my actions.

Illia placed a hand on my knee. "I'm so sorry," she whispered.

Her pity hurt more than gloating.

"Don't," I growled. But I couldn't bring myself to push away her hand. "Just... tell me I was being foolish. Tell me I acted like an idiot. Tell me... it was silly to think I could ever become someone I wasn't."

"You weren't foolish," Illia said. Then she smacked my knee. "But you're being foolish now!"

Shocked, I turned to face her. Illia stared at me with a hard expression. She had mastered a half-sympathetic, half-scolding glare, staring up at me through her eyelashes, her eyebrows set low.

Although she typically hid her scarred face, she didn't move when the wind caught her hair. The scarring only added to the seriousness of her expression and her words. I glanced away from the long knife cuts, blocking out the empathic pain as I forced myself not to imagine what it must have been like to lose an eye to pirates.

"How am I being foolish right now?" I asked.

"Moping around. Blaming yourself for everything that happened. You need to pick yourself up and try again."

"Ha," I said with a huff. "Right. Atty and Zaxis already bonded with the phoenixes. Or are you saying I should wait *another ten years* just so I can get chased from town a second time? Sorry, Illia. I'm not interested."

It wouldn't matter. Tradition stated only those coming of age could prove their worth to a phoenix. Men and women under the age of twenty or so. Sure, maybe I could run through the arch again, but would the phoenixes even listen to a man who failed so hard the last Day of the Phoenixes? I doubted it. Plus, I was certain no one would ever forget about my past ever again. I would forever be known as *the son of criminals*. The heart of a villain beat in my chest, apparently.

Illia crossed her arms. "So that's it? You're gonna give up and stay a gravedigger your whole life?"

"What else am I going to do?"

"Become an arcanist, of course."

I genuinely laughed for a moment before letting out a long sigh. "If only it were that easy."

"It can be. If you want it enough."

"Uh-huh. I'm not five. Reality works a little different."

"I'm being serious."

"Look," I said. "If you're playing games to cheer me up, it's not working. Just leave me alone."

Illia scooted closer to me. Then she glanced over her shoulder, her gaze drifting across the evening terrain. Everyone in Ruma went to bed with the sun, leaving the island still and quiet. The streetlamps remained lit, and the cloudless night provided plenty of moonlight, but there was no one to see or greet.

"I wasn't at the trial ceremony because I was busy," Illia whispered. She reached into the pocket of her dress and pulled out three pieces of paper. "I told you I had a plan to become an arcanist, remember?"

I lifted an eyebrow. "Are you going to tell me now?"

"Well, while the whole town was out to watch trials, I snuck into the schoolmaster's quarters and stole this." She handed over the paper, a sly smile on her face.

"Why?"

"I overheard the schoolmaster talking to some of the fishermen about that ship that went missing a few weeks ago. Apparently they found it crashed in the Endless Mire. Some of the fishermen even said they saw mystical creatures around the wreckage."

I took the paper. "And what is this?"

"It's all the reports from the fishermen."

With the moon as my light, I sat up straight and read the paper, confirming Illia was correct. No one knew what the missing boat had been transporting, but apparently it had been magical supplies and creatures. The fishermen had reported numerous sightings of odd creatures using magic, though none of them had many details. One thought he saw a white squirrel, another thought he saw a unicorn, and the last said there was a swamp creature in the mire, watching him go about his business.

Mystical creatures, no matter the type, were intelligent and capable of speech, even if they were shaped as beasts. Why would three of them live on the outskirts of society? Why didn't they try to reach town after the shipwreck? Maybe they were hurt or they didn't know the area well enough to travel. Or perhaps they were still young. Mystical creatures who had yet to bond typically stayed child-like forever—the magic they gained from an arcanist their only way to mature.

Why hadn't anyone gone to rescue them?

"Schoolmaster Tyms wrote the mainland," Illia said. "He's asked an arcanist to come collect the creatures."

"Why? What if he convinced one to bond with him? Then *he* could become an arcanist." And there were no traditions on the island about bonding with random creatures, only phoenixes.

"Didn't you finish reading the fishermen's report?" Illia asked as she jabbed the paper. "Look. One said he was attacked with magic when they tried to get their boats close. Apparently the mystical creatures are confused and lashing out. Well, the fishermen didn't say that, but I'm pretty sure that's what's happening."

Attacked? That didn't sound good.

"I bet you Tyms didn't go out there because he's too scared and doesn't want to look weak in front of everyone on the island. He's the *magic expert*, after all. Can you imagine him trying to bond with something and then getting rejected? He would be a laughingstock. No one would go to his lectures."

The upsides of becoming an arcanist were so many I was surprised anyone would pass it up. Then again, fighting a mystical creature was dangerous. They had powerful magic, and Tyms didn't.

"Why do you think *we'll* be able to approach the creatures?" I asked.

Illia tapped the side of her head with her pointer finger. "I think anyone with the moxie to barge into the trial ceremonies has the guts to face a few disgruntled creatures."

"What about you?"

She smiled. "I think anyone with the moxie to break into

the schoolmaster's quarters also has the guts to face a few disgruntled creatures."

I was almost at a loss for words as I ran an unsteady hand through my black hair. "Illia... how did you even find out about these fisherman reports?"

"I snoop around," she said. "And Tyms was talking about it to one of his assistants. He thinks he can get a reward from arcanists on the mainland if he manages to help them collect the missing mystical creatures. He'll probably ask the arcanist to give him something to bond with. Something docile—something he can handle."

"Oh, yeah?"

"Hm. Maybe a griffon or something."

"A griffon would never bond with someone like *Tyms*."

We both shared a laugh as a large wave crashed against the rocks below us.

What kind of creatures were in the Endless Mire? The magical power of an arcanist was determined by the mystical creature they bonded to. The more powerful their eldrin, the more powerful the arcanist. Phoenixes and griffons were things of legend, and the magic they provided their arcanist was on a higher scale than those who bonded with weaker creatures, like fairies or will-o-wisps. A phoenix arcanist could create a firestorm worth of flame, while a will-o-wisp arcanist could create a campfire at most.

Illia and I could go out and find a random white squirrel in the wilderness, but the creature likely wouldn't be anything powerful. A weak arcanist was still an arcanist, though. Better than becoming a gravedigger.

"Volke, this is a once-in-a-lifetime opportunity," Illia said. "The boat from the mainland comes in two days, and you know it'll be carrying an arcanist looking to collect those creatures. We have to act now if we're going to have a chance."

I nodded along with her words. It *was* a once-in-a-lifetime opportunity. Ruma didn't have any mystical creatures on it other than phoenixes.

"When should we leave?" I asked.

"Before sunrise. While everyone is sleeping off the celebrations." She smiled. "Hey, once we become arcanists we'll get to leave the island, just like Atty and Zaxis. Doesn't that excite you?"

"Yeah."

"We'll be just like Gregory Ruma! Just think about it. Traveling the world, helping people, discovering new lands —it'll be an adventure."

Again, I nodded. She was right. We couldn't pass up this opportunity, and we couldn't dawdle. I would become an arcanist one way or another, even if it meant a risky trek into the mire to confront random, and potentially agitated, mystical creatures.

Illia jumped to her feet and held out her hand. I took it and stood, my whole body shaking. I couldn't stop thinking about our new plan. We could do this.

"Thank you for this," I said as I handed Illia back the paper.

She jogged toward the cottage, a bright smile on her face. "What would you do without me?"

4

GRAVEKEEPER WILLIAM

Gravekeeper William had once been a naval officer, and he ran our cottage like it was one of the many boats he used to command. The place was clean from stern to bow, right down to the grain of wood. He kept all the doors and cupboards securely closed, like he was afraid of the cottage taking a tumble through the ocean. Everything had a place and everything in its place—that was his motto.

And that, along with William's obsessive need to keep an exact schedule, made it difficult to get away with anything.

Illia and I packed a few things for our trek in silence. The far southern end of the island was known as the Endless Mire for its swamp-like waters, mud, and vegetation. I didn't have much to pack, so I took it all, but I worried about not having the right tools for our travels. My boots had holes in them, and Illia's socks were unraveling. Trudging through the Endless Mire would result in us being soaked to the core in a matter of moments.

With my sack of clothes in hand, I stepped out of my tiny room and into the hall. The floorboards creaked. I held still, silently cursing myself. If he heard us, William would surely wake and stop us from heading out simply because the Endless Mire wasn't the safest location on the island. He wasn't the kind of man who appreciated unnecessary risks.

His room was at the other end of the hall, cold and dark. Nothing stirred, no matter how long I waited. After another thirty seconds, I continued to the staircase. Illia stood at the bottom, a satchel slung over her shoulder, a candle in her other hand. I walked downstairs, skipping a step I knew would squeak, and met her with a smile.

She motioned to the front door, but as I went to grab the handle, I heard a loud and gruff, "Ahem."

My shoulders bunched at my neck. I already knew. There was no need to turn around, just a terrible sense of dread at the impending conversation.

What could I say to William that would convince him I needed to go?

"Thought I wouldn't notice, didn't ya?"

Illia whirled around, her candle held high. "We're both adults according to the island rules." She straightened her posture. "We can come and go as we please without your permission."

"If you really thought that, why're you sneaking around?"

William stepped from the darkness of the kitchen door into the flickering light of the candle. I was six feet tall, one of the tallest people around, but he stood a good six inches above me. In truth, everything about him was larger than life—protruding gut, thick arms, tree trunk legs. He kept his face clean, though. A habit from his time as a naval officer.

"You don't understand," Illia said as she smoothed the hair over the right side of her face, hiding all her twisted blemishes. "We need to leave. Volke and I don't want to be—"

"Enough," he said.

Illia stopped herself cold.

Then William exhaled. "Come 'ere you two."

We moved away from the door. My heart beat hard against my ribs. If William tried to keep us here, what would I do? Would I fight him, the man who cared for me the last ten years? Would I give in and stay his apprentice? My whole being wanted to run from the cottage and head straight for my destiny, but honor told me I should at least hear him out.

William patted his gut. "It may not look it, but I was once a young man too. I know what it's like to get in trouble, but runnin' away isn't gonna solve anything."

"We're not running away," Illia immediately replied.

"Uh-huh. Well, whatever you're doin', I wouldn't recommend strollin' through town. Everyone on this island is damn upset. I've heard an earful of it."

"It's not Volke's fault! He didn't deserve any of that treatment during the ceremony. He's never committed a crime! All he's done is study to become—"

"I know that," William snapped. After a deep inhale, he continued at a calmer tone. "I've watched you two for years: Volke studying, you snooping around. But listen now, while I quietly hoped you two would catch a breeze of good luck, the fact is that reality's harsh. You've made enemies of the Ren and Trixibelle families. All of them."

I gritted my teeth and nodded along. He was right. They probably considered me tantamount to a thief for trying to take a phoenix from Zaxis or Atty.

"And I'm your caretaker. I'm sure I'll hear about it for years to come."

"I'm sorry," I forced myself to say.

"Hush, boy. I'm not done."

I met his gaze, confused by his attitude. There wasn't much heat in his words, and he spoke almost with an apologetic tone.

William placed his large hands on his hips. "Your actions have consequences. Not just for you, but everyone else."

"Yes, sir," I said.

Illia nodded. "I understand."

"But that doesn't mean I want either of you to give up," William said.

I caught my breath. "What?"

"Every parent wants a better life for their kids. No one wants to be a gravekeeper—even *I* didn't start this way. I lived a life on the oceans, fighting sea monsters with the good ol' boys. I contributed to the world, even if I wasn't as amazing as an arcanist. You kids need that, too. A chance to do what you're destined to do."

The words sunk into my mind, but all I could picture was my father. Did he want a better life for me? Then why did he kill that other man in cold blood? But that didn't matter. I wasn't my father. His actions were his own.

Then another part of William's speech finally hit me. He considered himself a parent? *To me?* Even though everyone on the island hated my existence?

Illia stepped forward and smiled. She threw her arms around William's wide gut. I stood awkwardly off to the side, shifting my weight from one foot to the other until William grabbed me by the shoulder and pulled me into the group embrace.

"Thank you," Illia said, her voice strained. "You've always been like a father."

William patted us both on the back. "Calm down, lass. It's not like you two are disappearing anytime soon. We've still got plenty of time to find some way for you to live out your destiny."

My heart sank, and I bit back my words. Should we tell him about the Endless Mire? Perhaps he wouldn't worry about us now that we were adults. I opened my mouth to explain, but Illia shot me a glance. *Don't*, she mouthed, so I faked a cough and rubbed at the back of my neck as I broke away from the hug.

She was probably right. William wouldn't be pleased with us running around the mire, and we couldn't afford to squander this opportunity. Better to ask for forgiveness than permission—at least in this situation.

"You don't mind that we're going to leave?" Illia asked.

William let go of her. Then he sighed. "I think you'll be fine. But I do worry about you, especially in these dark times."

Illia and I exchanged questioning glances.

"Dark times?" she asked. "Everything is peaceful here."

"Aye. On the Isle of Ruma." William stared at the floor, the shadows flicking over his face, hiding his emotions. "Sometimes I feel like this island is trapped in a bubble of time. So quiet and peaceful. But you two need to look out. There's an occult plague sweeping across the lands, killing people and twisting magic into something vile. Ruma's never seen it, thank the heavens, but I remember dealing with it back in the day."

I had heard of a plague from the whispering seamen who stopped at the docks, but I never had the time to investigate their stories. Plus, the Isle of Ruma was separated from everything else, so it never mattered.

An occult plague? What did it do? How was it spreading?

40

"Arcanists can handle a plague," Illia said matter-of-factly.

"Don't be so cocky, lass," William said as he turned his gaze back to us. "That plague has taken its toll on apprentice and master arcanists alike. It'll destroy everything, given the chance."

I nodded.

Arcanists were heroes and protectors. They used their magic to make the world a better place. Well, in theory. There were also pirate arcanists in the world and arcanists who never amounted to anything. Not all of them could be heroes, but I liked to imagine they could be.

My chest tightened, and I squared my shoulders.

That was how I would prove the world wrong about me. I would save them. I would fight whatever plague or pirate came for them. I would show them all I had the soul of a knight and not a criminal.

William motioned to the staircase. "You two get some sleep. I know things seem bleak right now, but everything will look better in the morning. I'll have a talk with that blowhard Tyms."

"Really?" Illia smiled, but I knew she didn't feel it.

It was her fake smile. Something she wore to trick people into thinking she was excited.

But William didn't seem to notice. "There are other Trials of Worth on other islands. Or maybe there's a ceremony on the mainland. We'll have to see. Perhaps you two can prove yourselves to some mystical creatures yet."

"That sounds amazing. Right, Volke?"

I forced a nod. "It sounds like a good plan."

We gave William our best *good nights* and then headed up the stairs. He walked into the kitchen and lit the fire for the stove, no doubt preparing to make himself breakfast before the sunrise.

The moment he was out of sight, Illia grabbed my arm and rushed me to her room. Although I complained about getting stuck with a storage room, Illia didn't have it much better. She had a bed and a trunk, but every wall was lined with William's bookshelves. It was the only place he had to store his books. Fortunately, Illia didn't mind living with leather-bound brothers and sisters.

She took me to the far wall and opened the window. "C'mon. We need to leave before he goes outside."

The sizzling of fats on a skillet echoed throughout the cottage. William would never allow us to slink out of town. We either went now, while he was distracted, or not at all.

"Okay," I said. "Let's go."

Illia slid over the sill and onto the woodshed just below her window. Then she scooted to the edge and hopped down to the ground. Once she had dusted herself off, she glanced up and motioned for me to follow.

I stepped over the sill, slid down the roof of the woodshed, and leapt down to the ground, my legs buckling once I hit. I had forgotten how sore I was from running straight up the Pillar. It took me a second of sucking in air to regain feeling from the knees down.

Illia stifled a laugh. "Can you walk?"

"Of course," I snapped as I forced myself to stand, even though it burned. It burned so bad. But I didn't want her to see that. I was an adult now. I had to act like it.

"Good," she said. "Because we should hurry."

Illia made her way south as the sky shifted from black to purplish-blue, the sun waking from its long rest.

Before I chased after her, I turned to the woodshed and searched for William's axe. I couldn't find it, though—

William always put it back in its place, of course—but I did spot his shovel. It had a sharpened point so I took that instead. Although I didn't know how to wield a weapon, I wanted *something*, just in case things went poorly.

With the shovel in hand, I jogged after Illia. She waited for me across the cobblestone road, her one visible eyebrow raised. "A shovel?"

"Preparation," I said. "Without it, we leave our fate to chance."

Illia rolled her eye. "I hate it when you quote that damn Pillar."

"Those are the values all arcanists should strive for."

"Maybe I want to make my own values. I certainly don't need a centuries-old staircase to do it for me."

"But those steps have good advice."

"Urg." Illia motioned to the road with an angry wave of her hand. "Forget it. C'mon."

We continued without any more words between us. We had to skirt around town to make it to our destination. The quiet roads of Ruma made for quick and pleasant travel, and soon the anxiety of getting caught left me. Who would stop us now?

"Hey!" someone barked. "Where do you think you two are goin'?"

5

THE ENDLESS MIRE

Illia and I froze.

A terrible chill ran from my head to my feet. If we told anyone where we were going, Tyms would have us publicly punished, perhaps even branded. That was what had happened to my mother. She got caught stealing, and a brand was burned into her wrist to forever mark her as a criminal. Would Tyms do it to a pair of troublemakers? I wouldn't put it past him.

"You two look like you're sneaking off somewhere. Admit it."

I recognized the nasally whine of the voice.

Lyell Ren. Zaxis's younger brother.

I turned around, holding back a sneer.

Lyell sauntered out from the darkness between two buildings, his hands in the pockets of his tailored trousers. He had recently turned thirteen, but he looked a few years older due to his height and wiry frame. His oily red hair, thin and tied back, didn't help his odd appearance. Puberty had hit him like a tsunami and he was still trying to recover.

"Mind your own business," Illia said. "Gravekeeper William knows we're out and that's all that matters."

I motioned to the dank alley he had slithered out of. "What're *you* doing out at this hour?"

He didn't even need to answer. I spotted chalk coating the knees of his pants. He had been vandalizing the buildings with his terrible graffiti—a delinquent activity everyone always assumed I was responsible for.

He huffed. "I'm out for a walk."

"Shouldn't you be celebrating with your brother?"

"Ugh," Lyell said with a groan. "He's more insufferable than ever now that he has his stupid phoenix."

Even Lyell disliked Zaxis? The information almost got me laughing.

Since we were the same age, Zaxis and I often ran into each other. He loved flaunting all his good fortune and reminding me gravediggers had to handle corpses. If a drop of water disappeared every time he spoke down to me, we'd all be living in a desert.

At least I wasn't the only one who found him irritating.

Illia grabbed my elbow and turned back toward our path. "It's best to just ignore him, Volke. C'mon. Let's go."

"Where are you two off to?" Lyell asked.

"Like I said, it's none of your business."

"Well, if you won't tell me, maybe I should go inform Tyms you're up to your usual suspicious activity."

I dug my heels into the cobblestone and came to a halt. I was certain Tyms wanted me dead after what I did during the Day of Phoenixes, and that meant he would take every opportunity to make my life a living nightmare, even if I never admitted my intentions. Illia must have felt the same way because she turned to me, her one eye searching my gaze, a frown on her face.

"We're going to the Endless Mire," I said without glancing back at Lyell. "William wants us to gather a few herbs and we're going to camp at the edge." I hefted my sack and shovel to emphasize my impromptu story.

Lyell snorted. "Oh. So, you're tucking your tail and running, huh? Don't want to face anyone after that *embarrassing* stunt you pulled at the ceremony?"

I gritted my teeth and said nothing. He could believe whatever he wanted to believe, so long as he left me alone.

"Let's just go," Illia muttered as she tugged my elbow again. "We don't owe him any more explanations."

We turned away and continued out of the city proper, following the roads until they transformed from cobblestone to dirt. I glanced over my shoulder, surprised to see Lyell trailing behind us, his hands still in his pockets. If I yelled, he would cause a fuss, and if I broke his nose, everyone in town would only take it as evidence of my deepseated violent nature. So I kept my mouth shut and silently hoped Lyell would just grow bored and leave.

The rhythmic song of the ocean soothed my irritation. William said currents were the lifeblood of the world and that the waves were the pumping of nature's blood. Such intriguing images fueled my imagination as a child. I fell in love with the beach. Even the endless cries of the gulls put me at ease.

The sun rose, breaking the last of the darkness. Although yesterday had been everything I feared, the glow of a new day reassured me. I could still become an arcanist. I could still prove myself.

"My father says gravediggers are the ones who make coffins," Lyell said. "Or does the gravekeeper do that?"

He was closer to us than before. The grate of his voice brought back all of my frustrations.

"That's right," Illia said. "What of it?"

"Well, is it hard?"

"No."

"Doesn't blood get all over the wood?"

Illia glanced over her shoulder and huffed. "Corpses don't bleed. Gravekeeper William measures out the body, Volke cuts the wood to match the measurements, and I affix the hinges and carve in all the decorations. It's not complicated."

Lyell jogged to our side and crossed his arms tight over his chest. "You shouldn't take that tone with me. I'm going to become a phoenix arcanist one day, just like Zaxis. Plus, if you're nice to me now, maybe I'll let you accompany me to the mainland as my handmaiden."

"You aren't going to bond with a phoenix," I said. "In ten years, you'll be twenty-three. Too old for the ceremony then. Tyms had the chance to advance you, even though you're a little young, but he skipped over you because he liked Zaxis better."

I didn't need to add that last sentence, but it was true.

Lyell huffed and mumbled something under his breath. I ignored him and picked up my pace. The Endless Mire wasn't far and I figured Lyell would leave once we reached the soggy wetlands.

The sun continued rising into the sky, half-hidden by fluffy white clouds. Although I enjoyed the patches of shade, the clouds could always shift from pleasant to malicious, blackening in a matter of moments and threatening us with rain. I kept my eye on them, but it wasn't like I could do much if the weather decided my trek needed to be even more difficult.

Then we came to the edge of the Endless Mire and stopped to look around.

Red mangrove trees filled the area with their bright scarlet trunks and vibrant jade leaves. Their roots branched out above the ground, creating a tent of tangled wood before disappearing beneath the murky water. Although the ocean waters were clear enough to see ten feet down without problem, the Endless Mire reminded me of mud. Bugs scuttled across the surface, toads hid themselves in the grime, and snakes dangled from the red branches of the mangrove trees.

"This place is disgusting," Lyell said as he wrinkled his nose.

Illia sighed. "Leave, then. We didn't ask you to follow us."

"Uh, I'm probably more educated than the two of you combined, thank you very much." Lyell smiled as he walked around us. "I've studied with Tyms for six years now. If anyone can identify herbs, it's me."

"We don't need help from a child."

Lyell shot Illia a glare. "Ya know, someone with a face as ugly as yours shouldn't be so rude."

Although her hair was already covering the scars, Illia quickly slid a trembling hand over her face.

I grabbed Lyell by the collar of his shirt and jerked him close. "What in the name of the abyssal hells is your problem?" I growled.

"What?" he said. "She started it." He ripped himself from my grasp and brushed himself off. "My father says the same thing. If Illia had been nicer when she came to Ruma, maybe someone else besides the gravekeeper would've taken her as an apprentice. But nope. She was ill-mannered *and* disgusting."

"*Lyell.*" My fingernails dug into my palms, and I gave serious thought to smacking Lyell across the face with

William's shovel. But then I took a few calming breaths and remembered the steps of the Pillar. "Didn't you say you studied with Tyms for six years?"

"That's right," Lyell answered matter-of-factly.

"Do you know what the tenth step up the Pillar says?"

"Ugh. Even you want to give me lessons?" He stared up into the green leaves of the mangrove trees. "Fine. It's respect. Without it, we make fast enemies of our acquaintances."

"And what about the thirty-seventh step?"

"Compassion. Without it, we make the world a crueler place."

I rolled my hand, hoping he would put one and two together. Lyell stared at me for a moment, narrowing his eyes until he finally snorted back a laugh.

"You're not clever enough to understand what those steps mean," he said with a dismissive wave of his hand. "What about step fifty? Honesty. Without it, we cannot learn the truth about ourselves. I was just being *honest*, Volke. That's what arcanists do. They tell the truth, even when it hurts."

Illia turned away, her hand never leaving her face. "It doesn't matter," she whispered to me. "Let's just get into the mire. Lyell isn't worth our time." She leapt up onto the red roots of the mangrove trees and walked across their sturdy tangles to avoid getting her boots wet.

I had known Illia for close to a decade. Maybe she was ill-mannered as a child, but her family had been killed by pirates just weeks before her arrival in Ruma. Of course she had been upset. And the scars... She always clung to the shadows, just out of sight, snooping around the island and listening in on conversations that no one would have with an ugly little girl.

I stepped onto the first root, but Lyell held me back.

"Wait," he said. "I didn't know you two were going deep into the mire."

"That's where the best herbs are," I said with a false apologetic tone.

Why had he followed us to begin with? Didn't he have somewhere else to be? Anywhere else? What I would've given for him to go back home.

"Ah!"

Both Lyell and I snapped our attention to Illia. She slipped and fell into the knee-deep waters of the mire, her one eye wide and fixed to the branches above her.

I threw down my sack of clothes. "Illia?" I trudged through the mud until I reached her side.

"Look!" She pointed.

I glanced up. A bright white creature sat perched on a crimson branch, sticking out like snow in the dead of summer. It wasn't a squirrel—it appeared more like a ferret—with brilliant blue eyes and silver stripes down its back.

Illia got to her feet, her dress half-covered in brown grime.

"Is that a mystical creature?" Lyell asked as he walked over. Well, he wasn't really walking. He lifted his leg high with each step, making sure his foot came out of the thick water before moving forward. At one point his boot got sucked off his foot, and he struggled to find it with a sneer on his face. "I can't believe it. A mystical creature *here*, of all places?"

"Hello," Illia called up to the white ferret. "My name is Illia. What's yours?"

The tiny creature, no bigger than my forearm, tilted its head from side to side. At first, I didn't think it would respond. Then it rubbed at its face like only rodents could and replied, "Are human parents trying to kill off their children through negligence nowadays? You three really shouldn't be here unsupervised."

Although he spoke with an air of sophistication, his squeaky little voice made it hard to take anything he had to say seriously. I stifled a laugh.

"Volke and I are adults," Illia said. "But not Lyell. He was just going home. Right, Lyell?"

"What?" Lyell said once he reached us. "Why would I go home now? Do you see that? It's a mystical creature! In the flesh!"

"Yeah. Maybe you should hurry home and report it to your father."

"What? N-no!" He straightened himself and then glanced up at the ferret. "Bond with me, creature. I'm a member of the Ren family. I'm educated, talented, and my brother is already an arcanist."

"I won't bond with a child," the ferret said.

"What? But—"

The ferret shook his head. "No exceptions."

It didn't surprise me. Mystical creatures became more like the person they bonded to, and children often haven't grown into their true selves yet. Plus, no one wanted to become immature or childish, so most mystical creatures waited to bond with individuals only after their coming of age. Lyell still had a couple years to go.

Knowing the ferret wouldn't bond with him also sent a flood of relief through my body. The last thing I wanted was to lose another arcanist opportunity to the Ren family.

"I want to bond with you," Illia said, completely ignoring Lyell's incredulous look. "I think we would be perfect together."

The ivory ferret rubbed at his nose. "Bond with you, huh?"

"That's right."

"Hm. I see." He bounded to the edge of the branch and hopped up and down. "While I want nothing more than to leave this wretched mire, I can't just bond with any ol' random person."

Illia glanced around and then cocked her good eyebrow. "Well, I'm not just *anyone*. I'm the talented individual who discovered your whereabouts. I'm your rescuer."

The ferret chirped as he hopped. But then he stopped and stroked his tiny chin with one of his paws. "I suppose you did find me. Though, to be fair, I was heading out of the mire myself. Finding me doesn't prove much. Oh, I know! We'll have a ceremony of worth. It's only proper, after all. You have to prove yourself to me."

"Anything," Illia replied.

The ferret bounded across the branch again, his run a mix of jumping and scurrying. Then he stopped at the far end of the limb—the closest he could get to Illia, though he was still three feet above her head—and he stared down with a rodent smile.

"But how shall I determine your worth?" he asked. "I don't want to watch you parade around in the mud. Physical feats aren't as impressive to me as wits and cunning. Oh! I have an idea. We should have a contest of character. You should impress me with tales of your past."

Illia nodded and then flashed me a quick smile. I replied in kind, almost giddy to the point of laughing. We were doing it! We had met a stray mystical creature, and now we would become arcanists! This really was an opportunity of a lifetime!

"Did you two know about this *thing*?" Lyell asked with a

huff. "Is that why you came out here? There are no herbs, are there?"

"Keep it down," I said.

"Why? So one of you can bond with a pathetic little creature?" He held up his hands, trying to measure the ferret by closing one eye and squinting. "It's so tiny. Look at it. It doesn't have the magical power of a phoenix. You'll be one of the weakest arcanists of all time."

The ferret chirped and gave Lyell a blue glare. "Ha! This is why I would never bond with a child. You have no idea what you're talking about." The ferret puffed out his fur, a little ball of white, making himself look larger. "I'm amazing, if I do say so myself."

"Seriously, what is it?" Lyell frowned. "I've never even heard of a creature that looks like that. It's not a griffon or a unicorn or anything recognizable. It's probably a bastard cousin of some water rat sailors always complain about."

Again, I held back a laugh as the ferret arched his back in cat-like fashion and flashed his teeth. They were all sharp, sure, but no bigger than my fingernails.

With an adorable growl, the ferret said, "You should count yourself lucky you're young! If I had to show my *real* power to you, there'd be nothing left." His squeaking became extra ridiculous with his anger.

Lyell snickered and crossed his arms.

After a calming breath, the ferret smoothed back its impossibly white fur. "For your information, I'm a *rizzel*. Very rare. Very powerful. More so than a *unicorn* or a *phoenix*, at any rate."

"I've never heard of a rizzel."

"Hm. Maybe you aren't as smart as you thought."

"Pfft," Lyell said. "You're just saying that you're amazing so we don't leave you out in this swamp. I bet no one ever wanted to bond with you, and that's why you're out here living like an actual animal."

Although it was obvious Lyell was just saying things because he was angry about being rejected, I knew his statements held merit. There were mystical creatures no one ever wanted to bond with, mostly because they were so much hassle or because the magic they offered was harmful to everyone around. Some bog spirits produced noxious gas, making bonding an impossibility. Maybe that was why these creatures were on the ship that crashed—they were transporting dangerous goods no one wanted.

Was that the case with a rizzel? I had never heard of one before. Ever. And I had read plenty of books on William's shelves. Then again, there were hundreds of thousands of mystical creatures, some big, some small, some numerous, some rare—some were even extinct. I couldn't be expected to know them all.

Ignoring Lyell altogether, Illia stepped forward. "When I was a little girl, I escaped from a pirate ship. Does that prove my character enough?"

The rizzel settled down for a moment and stroked his chin. "Hm. Maybe. How did you escape?"

With unmitigated enthusiasm, Illia smiled and held up her hands. "It was the dead of night." Her dramatic tone caught everyone's attention. Even Lyell stopped his scoffing to listen. She continued, "I had been the pirates' prisoner for two days, but they didn't think a little girl would pose much threat. They let me wander around the hold, away from their treasures, but foolishly close to their stocks of oil."

Illia pantomimed sneaking around. "So, while most of the crew slept, I spilled the oil and set it on fire." She threw her arms up in a demonstration of whooshing fire. "The pirates were so frantic they were tripping over each other in their haste to quell the flames."

"This actually happened?" Lyell asked.

"Shh," I hissed.

The rizzel motioned Illia to continue. "And then what happened?"

"The pirates were distracted," Illia said. "So I dove into the water." She clapped her hands together once. I flinched at the loud *snap*, and so did the rizzel. "We were close to shore, and I had always been a good swimmer, so I didn't fret. I made my way to the beach and called for help."

Lyell stepped closer. "And?"

"And then the pirates were chased away by a local arcanist," Illia said with a hint of pride in her voice. "Which is why I want to become an arcanist. I want to protect people from the pirates of the world. I want—" she stopped herself for a moment as her hand went back under her hair and over the scars of her face, "—I want to make the world a safer place."

The rizzel clapped his little ferret hands together. "Yes, yes! What a tale. You escaped using your wits and won the day. I'm impressed!"

Although Illia had never told me the details of her escape—I always thought it inappropriate to ask—I believed every word. Maybe other people would've cried or given up in the hopeless situation of a pirate cargo hold, but Illia wasn't like that. Even after they cut her eye away. She never gave up.

I wanted to have that kind of determination.

The rizzel turned to me, its blue eyes searching mine. "And what about you?"

"Me?" I shook my head. Illia had been the one to engage first. It seemed dishonorable to attempt to take the opportunity of bonding away from her. "I didn't say I was part of the ceremony."

"True. But someone has to compete against her or else it's not a real competition."

Illia turned to me, her expression neutral, but her tightly balled fists told me she didn't want to fight with me over anything. I knew because I felt the same way. It was one thing to prove myself to a mystical creature over Zaxis or Lyell—or anyone from the Ren family, to be frank—but I could never imagine besting Illia after everything she had done to bring us here.

"Will you bond with a criminal's son?" I asked the rizzel.

He shook his head. "Probably not."

"Then... it doesn't matter. My mother was a thief and my father a murderer." Although it pained me to utter every word, I knew it was for the best. This way there would be no contest.

"Not even the phoenixes would bond with him," Lyell chimed in. "My father said he's as disrespectful as she is ugly." Then he jutted a thumb in Illia's direction and laughed.

She pressed her lips together and said nothing. Although I hated Lyell more and more, my mind wouldn't stop dwelling on the situation.

A random mystical creature in the mire felt I would somehow inherit my parent's wicked ways. Was I really doomed to be like them? Everyone was so convinced, what hope did I have of finding anything to bond with?

The rizzel swished his tail from side to side. "Well, since we have no other contestants... and because I'm tired of waiting here in the mire for that arcanist to return... you're the winner." He stood on his two back legs and patted his chest. "You may call me Nicholin."

"Hold on," Illia said. "You're waiting for an arcanist?"

"What does it matter?" Nicholin huffed. "He was supposed to take me and a few others to a new island, but he crashed the boat instead! Then he said we can't leave the mire because of a plague or some nonsense and took off. He was a nutter, that one. I haven't seen him for some time."

Him and a few others? It had to be the other mystical creatures the fishermen reported on. But the reports also said the creatures were dangerous and lashed out. Nicholin wasn't like that. He seemed the exact opposite, actually—desperate for company and ready to leave. Perhaps the fishermen had run into a different creature?

Nicholin shook his head. "But that doesn't matter now. I'm ready to bond, and I'm confident we'll make a great team."

Illia stepped forward and held out her hand. "I think we will too."

The rizzel leapt from the tree and landed on her arm with the grace of a falling leaf. Then he scurried to her shoulders and wrapped himself around the back of her neck.

Nicholin glowed a soft white that intensified until the area around us was engulfed in a flash of light. I covered my eyes and took a step back. Then the light faded.

6

WHITE HART

I llia turned to me and smiled. Her forehead bore the mark of all arcanists, a seven-pointed star.

The star represented a person's soul—their source of magic. At first the star was small and pale, but as an arcanist developed their magic and became stronger, the star became more prominent. And each star had a picture of the arcanist's eldrin—even Illia's star had a rizzel woven around it, its ferret-like body twisting around the points and its face smiling in mischief.

Once bonded, an arcanist and eldrin shared their magic. Arcanists offered their soul to fuel their powers, and an eldrin determined the types of magic used. Phoenixes gave their arcanists fire and healing, but what would a rizzel do?

I admired Illia's star for far too long.

"I can't believe it," she whispered to me as she rubbed at the mark. "It's like a dream."

"I'm happy for you," I said, my chest tight.

I meant it. But...

What if none of the other mystical creatures bonded with me? Would Illia leave Ruma with Zaxis and Atty?

Would she... leave me behind? This could be our last few days together, and here I was celebrating.

I couldn't bear to voice my concerns. I didn't want to dampen her moment or the mood. I needed to stay strong. The fifteenth step on the Pillar said as much. *Optimism. Without it, we lose ourselves to misery.* I needed to remain focused and hopeful. There would be a mystical creature somewhere in the Endless Mire who would want to bond with me.

There had to be.

"So there are other mystical creatures out here?" Lyell asked.

Nicholin nodded. "Two others were on the boat with me, but they weren't the friendliest of sorts, so we went our separate ways."

Without another word, Lyell stomped through the mire, trudging to the heart of the mangrove trees, never glancing back. I watched him go for a moment before turning back to Illia.

"We can't let him wander too far on his own," she said.

"He'll be fine." I secretly hoped he would get stuck in a sinkhole, but I wasn't about to say anything.

"What if he bonds with one of the others?"

I sighed. "I'll go after him in a second. I just wanted to ask what it felt like. Being an arcanist, I mean."

Illia stroked Nicholin's ivory fur. "Well, I'm still me, but... it's like there's a new part of me I never knew before. Like growing a third arm." She grimaced and then shook her head. "That wasn't the best analogy, but it's kinda like that. Having a new limb. Or maybe a new sense."

Nicholin nodded. "Yes! Together we create something new. And your soul is so strong! I lucked out when you stumbled into the mire, that's for sure. I was starting to worry I'd die here... all alone." He squeaked and nuzzled against Illia's neck. "But now that we're together, we're partners! You're my arcanist, and I'm your eldrin."

She laughed and nodded along with his words. "Yes. Exactly."

"I'm going to go after Lyell," I said as I motioned to his hustling form off in the distance.

"I want to stay here and chat with Nicholin for a moment, okay?"

"Sure. Just don't take too long. Now that you're an arcanist, you need to protect us."

Illia gave me a salute. "I'll do my best."

I headed for Lyell. He wasn't hard to catch up to, not when I used the red mangrove trees as leverage. I couldn't hop onto the roots, not when my boots were slick with mud and water, but the trees were still sturdy enough to use as a guide.

"Don't try to stop me," Lyell hissed when I got close. "I can't believe you knew about these creatures and said nothing!"

"Would you have said anything?"

"O-of course!"

I scoffed. "You could say something right now."

"Obviously I'm going to bond with something before you get your gravedigger hands on it!"

"Hm."

"What're you doing, anyway?" Lyell said as he motioned to the mire. "None of these creatures are going to bond with someone like you. And I'll make sure they know your past if you try to stop me from finding one!"

I gripped my shovel tight. If I wanted, I could stop him in his tracks, but that wasn't becoming of an arcanist. What would Gregory Ruma do? The tales of him and his leviathan always had a clever ending. Tricking pirates. Making friends of enemies. Solving complex puzzles. I had to be like him.

"Well, what're *you* going to do?" I asked. "None of the mystical creatures will bond with a child."

Lyell stopped his stomping and glared. "I look old enough."

I placed my hand on his shoulder. "Listen. How about we make a deal? I won't tell the creatures how old you are, and you won't tell them about my parents. See? And there are at least two creatures out here. We can both benefit if we cooperate."

Lyell jerked his shoulder away. "Ha! I'm not going to lie. Then the creatures will never bond with me."

"I didn't say *lie about it*. Just *don't mention it*. Those are two entirely different things."

"Fine." He crossed his arms. "We won't mention details about one another. But I get the better of the creatures, whatever we find."

"Deal."

It really didn't matter to me anymore. All I could think about was Illia leaving for the mainland. I had to be on the boat with her—I had to become an arcanist.

Although she still hadn't joined us, I pressed forward. I almost felt embarrassed that she was an arcanist and I wasn't. I was older, after all. Only by a few months, but still. And what if we found something that rejected me? I didn't want to make a fool of myself in front of everyone like I had at the Day of Phoenixes.

Sloshing through the mire had left my feet cold and slimy. I gritted my teeth and tried to think of something else, but the slippery feeling was hard to ignore. And the bugs. The bugs were the worst. William had a lavender and peppermint rub that kept all kinds of bugs at bay, but I hadn't thought to bring it.

I cursed my foolishness under my breath.

"Hey," Lyell said, his gaze down. "Do you really think I'll be too old for a phoenix next bonding ceremony?"

I didn't know how to reply. It was obvious to me he wouldn't be allowed to join, but what good would it do me to rub it in his face? I probably shouldn't have said it to begin with.

"Lyell," I began. But nothing insightful came to me. Not even the Pillar offered an appropriate nugget of wisdom to deal with this kind of situation.

Lyell huffed. "N-never mind. Forget I said anything. I'll bond with something, just you see."

Without warning, as though storm clouds had blotted out the sun, the mire grew dark. Lyell and I stopped in our tracks and glanced around the area. Shadows thickened, obscuring the path we had taken to get here. Even the chirp of crickets went quiet as the world became eerie and still.

"What's going on?" Lyell asked.

"I don't know," I said as I held my shovel close.

A mound of mud rose from the water, no taller than two feet.

Lyell jumped behind me and pointed, even though it was impossible to miss.

The mound remained nothing more than a glob of twigs, mud, and rocks. It undulated a bit when it spoke.

"Travelers," it said with a dark and curt voice. A bubble rose out of the mud and popped, punctuating its speech. "Why have you come to this place?"

Was it some sort of swamp spirit? Perhaps it was a *bunyip*—a swamp guardian—or a *grootslang*—a mystical creature who supposedly created mires and bogs—but since it was covered in mud, it was hard to say for sure.

"You can have this one," Lyell whispered. He gave the odd creature a sneer. "It looks like something you should bond with."

I held back my sarcastic commentary and stepped forward.

Anything was better than staying on Ruma as a gravedigger.

"We heard there were mystical creatures in the mire, and we came to bond," I said.

The mound of mud didn't reply.

I continued, "I, uh, would be honored if you considered me."

"I am not looking to bond with anyone. A lifetime of failures has led me here. I'd rather dwell on my mistakes in solitude."

When it started to sink back beneath the surface of the water, I held out a hand.

"W-wait, please hear me out. I think I could help you. We could help each other."

Lyell snickered. "I can't wait to tell Zaxis you groveled to a swamp thing."

"Why?" the mound asked. "Why do you want to bond with a mystical creature?"

"To become an arcanist, of course," I said.

"Why?" it asked again. "Why do you seek to become an arcanist?"

Lyell stepped around me and said, "Who *wouldn't* want to become an arcanist?"

The mound waited a moment. Then it replied, "I can bond with anyone. If you want to become an arcanist simply because everyone else wants it, then you are nothing more than a sad imitation of others, an easily replaced duplicate with a dream as shallow as these waters. Why should I make your goals my own? If you can't give me a proper answer, then bonding is out of the question and I will return to my self-imposed isolation. So I'll ask again. Why do you want to become an arcanist?"

Although the mound bubbled and undulated, it spoke with such a regal presence that I found myself questioning what it really was. A simple swamp creature? Or was it disguised as a swamp thing and really something else? Either way, I wanted to be truthful and upfront, but I also wanted to impress it.

I hesitated. Should I be completely honest? A part of me wanted to reveal everything and see how it reacted.

"I was born to criminals," I muttered.

Lyell snapped his attention to me, his eyes wide.

"That doesn't answer my question," the mound said. "Your lineage doesn't matter. Your choices and actions are your own. All I want to know is why you sought to bond."

I could hardly believe it. This mystical creature didn't care about my bloodline? It was a miracle and a blessing rolled into one. This had to be the creature I was destined to bond with!

"I want to prove to the world I'm not who they think I am," I said, straightening my posture. "That's why I want to become an arcanist."

"Truthfully?"

"Yes. If I'm an arcanist, I can show the world I'm not a criminal. I'll have the power to prove everyone wrong."

"Feh," the mound said, a large bubble popping at the same time and releasing gas. "Those who seek power for power's sake soon find themselves in hell. You don't need to become an arcanist to prove to the world you're not a villain, you need only to avoid villainous activities." The mound half-sank back into the water. "Seek me out when you have a real reason to become an arcanist." It slid the rest of the way, disappearing from sight.

I clenched my jaw and fought back the urge to yell.

Why was I never good enough? I thought being truthful would be appreciated, but perhaps lying would've been best all along. I should have just said what everyone wanted to hear. If I was going to be punished for being a criminal, why not benefit from criminal activity? Why not lie to all the creatures in the mire and bond with one through trickery? At least then I would have something instead of *nothing*.

I ran a hand through my hair, clawing at my scalp.

The darkness thinned and disappeared, leaving Lyell and I standing in the midafternoon light streaming through the emerald leaves above.

Lyell belted out a round of laughter, even going so far as to smack his knees in delight.

"Not even a gross pile of swamp mud would take you!" he said between heavy chuckles. "It turned you down! Just like that! Zaxis will love this story!" He devolved into more laughter, so amused by my defeat I swear he wasn't getting enough air to breathe.

I silently hoped he would pass out and drown in the foot-deep waters.

Filled with regret and unending frustration, I turned to seek out Illia. She always knew what to say to get me out of my spiral of depression. And maybe her new rizzel would have some insight into the situation. Perhaps Nicholin could convince the swamp thing to hear me out a second time.

I couldn't give up hope.

I couldn't.

"Did I *hear* you say... you wanted *power*?"

The awkward cadence of the sentence left me unnerved —it sounded like someone trying to speak for the first time, only instead of sounds, it was a full-blown sentence, and they didn't truly understand what they were saying or even how to say it correctly.

I slowly turned around, my eyebrows knit together, until I caught sight of the speaker.

A mystical creature.

A giant snowy stag—a legendary white hart.

White harts were deer as large as a stallion, with gold antlers that curved up and around. All tales about them spoke of their stealth and ability to hide in plain sight, despite their massive size and power. The beast stood only ten feet from us and I hadn't detected it at all. Invisibility? I didn't know. But it had clearly been close enough to hear our conversation.

"You're looking to bond... *aren't*... you?" the white hart asked.

Again, his words were so unnatural, they were hard to understand.

And he didn't open his eyes. They were tightly shut, almost sunken in. The beast hung his head, as if he was going to drink from the mire water, but he never did.

"A white hart," Lyell whispered. He pushed me aside and stepped forward. "I'm looking to bond!"

White harts were probably just as powerful as a phoenix. Was it one of the mystical creatures from the boat wreck? I thought the fishermen had seen a unicorn, but perhaps they mistook the ivory pelt of the white hart as the sign of a unicorn.

The white hart took two steps forward, its legs jerking with an unnatural gait.

Something wasn't right, and each second that passed I

grew colder and more aware of my ever-increasing heart-beat. I had never seen a creature move or talk like this white hart. Ever.

"I could... hear your *thoughts*," the stag said. "When you... spoke. To my friend."

Lyell took a step back and gave me a questioning glance. "Why is it talking like that?" he whispered.

"I don't know," I whispered back.

The white hart lifted his head. "Volke."

I shivered. "Y-yes?" How did it know my name?

"Your wish... has been answered. Bond with me. I will... *we will*... have the power to show everyone in town. We can... prove to all of Ruma... what you really are."

I caught my breath, my mind locking up with indecision. The white hart didn't look right. He didn't sound right. But I liked his words. And he was willing to bond, right now. No questions. No judgments.

"It's not fair... what they did," the beast continued. It took another step forward, its movements still forced and jerky. "It's not fair... that they cast you aside... Not *fair*... that undeserving men... get *phoenixes*... while you wait on... the fringes of society."

I fiddled with my shovel and nodded. It wasn't fair.

Should I bond with him? I wanted to. I wanted to stroll into town with a creature just as mighty as a phoenix and show them all up. But the swamp creature's words echoed in my thoughts. It was right. I already wasn't a criminal, so why, then, did I want to bond? Surely I had a reason beyond petty revenge, but why couldn't I articulate it?

Bonding with the white hart didn't feel right. He might have what I want, but something was off. I couldn't ignore that for my own selfish gains.

"Hey," Lyell said. Again, he sloshed forward, his shoulders squared. "I'm here too. Volke is half the man I am."

"Ah, you... Lyell Ren... *forgotten child*... You won't ever get. A phoenix. Too young for one now... too old for one in the future... Perhaps... you and I... *should show your family how powerful you are*."

No.

No, no, no.

I didn't know what was happening, but I knew it was wrong. I took Lyell by the shoulder and pulled him back.

"We need to leave," I whispered.

"No." He slipped from my grasp and walked closer to the strange beast. "The white hart is right. I am the forgotten child. I deserve a mystical creature, just like my older brother. I'm going to bond with it."

"Lyell. It's sick and not acting right. Get away from it."

"You're just jealous," he snapped. "You had your chance, but you wasted it." Then he held out his hand. "Bond with me, white hart. I'm ready."

The beast opened his eyes all the way, as wide as they would go until they were perfect circles.

I froze, my heart pounding in my ears.

The white hart's eyes were like dead fish eyes. They shook—jiggled, really—as though struggling not to pop out of the sockets. Bulging outward, they swiveled around with no rhyme or reason to where the head was facing.

And then he smiled. I didn't know deer mouths stretched so far upward, but it did, expressing emotion like only a madman could.

"Look out!" I shouted as I yanked Lyell by the collar of his tailored shirt.

"*Come back*," the white hart said with a giggle.

The beast lunged, his golden antlers thrusting forward

to gore us both. I swung with my shovel and took a chunk of flesh from its face, but instead of crying out in pain or screaming, the monster deer reared back on its hind legs and laughed.

"Bond with me!" He cackled as he slammed down into the mire, splashing me and Lyell with mud, some of which got in my eye. "Bond with me... or I'll have you begging for death!"

When the monster lunged again, I pushed Lyell out of the way, but the grime in my vision stole my ability to react properly. The antlers caught my hip and leg, gouging a furrow of blood and muscle. I yelled and stumbled backward, but I managed to keep my footing. I swung with the shovel again, harder than I had ever swung anything before.

I clipped the beast across the eyes, slicing one open and chipping the skull underneath.

Still, the white hart laughed.

"Volke," Lyell shouted, breathless.

"Run," I said. "Get away. Hurry! Before he uses his—"

When I glanced back, the white hart was gone.

No, not gone. Invisible. Nearby. Using his magic to conceal himself and strike from the shadows of the mangrove trees.

7

KNIGHTMARE

L yell stood frozen, a look of abject terror cemented on his face.

I sloshed to his side, took him by the arm, and continued back the way we came. I couldn't feel the injury on my hip or leg, but the scarlet blood that soaked my trousers and drizzled into the water wasn't helping me remain focused.

"Yes, *run*," the white hart said with a giggle, his voice close, though I couldn't see him. "Then one of you can *die tired*."

When the monster attacked, he revealed himself, appearing out of nowhere, right by my side. I shoved Lyell out of the way and got caught by another pointed antler, this time ripping my shirt and goring my forearm. I yelled, half from surprise and half from the heated sting of the injury.

At this rate, we were going to die.

The white hart leapt back, laughing louder than before, his antlers red with my blood. He disappeared again. Not even the water rippled with his movement—something about his magic made it impossible to detect.

Lyell trembled. "You... y-you saved me."

I grabbed his arm and glanced around the area.

The mangrove trees. Their roots grew like tents above the ground, creating sheltered spaces. I rushed over to a large grouping and pushed Lyell toward one. "In," I commanded. "We need to put things between us and the white hart."

My voice remained remarkably steady for how panicked my thoughts were. Where was the creature? How long did we have? Where was Illia? Was there a way to call for help?

Lyell squeezed into the roots and hid under the tree. I held my shovel ready, knowing the white hart wouldn't appreciate our actions. Sure enough, the beast appeared again, this time on his hind legs, ready to trample me.

I swung the shovel as I dove to the side. The sharpened tip sliced the ribs of the beast, drawing blood enough to mar the beauty of his pelt. The creature' diamond-hard hooves missed me by mere inches. Murky water splashed everywhere.

"You're fools for refusing me," the white hart shouted. "*Ingrates!* I am more powerful than you can imagine! I'm becoming perfect! *I'm transforming!*"

I had never heard of a mystical creature as insane as the white hart. His eyes swirled, and I realized then that the one I had sliced had healed. Actually, all of it had healed as though I had done nothing this entire fight. The incessant laughter only added to my dread. What could I possibly do to defeat this beast?

The white hart slammed his hooves on the roots of the tree, splitting one into splinters. Then it gored at the roots, breaking them apart with his antlers, inching closer to Lyell with each powerful swing.

"H-help!" Lyell shouted, his voice breaking. "Volke! Don't leave me!"

Although I had become sluggish, my injured body on the verge of quitting, I stepped forward and swung my shovel into the beast's shank. I took another chunk of flesh, but the monster didn't even turn around. The white hart smashed farther into the tree, already halfway through.

I wasn't going to kill the beast with a damn shovel, that much I knew.

"He's just a kid," I said. "It's me you want!"

The white hart huffed and let out a single laugh. Then he turned to face me, his smile somehow widening, distorting the creature's deer face into something straight out of a nightmare.

"Come closer," he whispered.

There were certain things in the world people instinctually knew were bad—falling from great heights, fire, snakes... and the way this monster whispered.

I stepped forward regardless. I had to keep its attention. Lyell would never survive the creature's onslaught if I abandoned him. At least I had a weapon. That was what I kept telling myself, anyway.

The white hart gave me his full attention, turning away from the tree and cackling.

"Lyell," I said. "Go. Stay under the trees."

"But it'll kill you!"

"*Go*. I'll handle this."

Lyell nodded and squeezed himself through another set of roots. He continued toward the edge of the mire. *I'll handle this*, I said, like I had any damn clue what I was doing. But sometimes a show of confidence, even if it was all a farce, could make the difference.

The white hart didn't glance back at Lyell. Instead, he advanced toward me, his toothy smile never waning.

"Bond with me," he said. "Or I... kill the forgotten child."

72

I took a step back. "What? No trial of worth?" I quipped.

The monster laughed.

Then he disappeared.

"A trial of worth? *Yes*! We need... one."

When the white hart reappeared, he flipped around and kicked me square in the chest with one of his massive hooves. I don't know how long I lost my sight or consciousness, but the next thing I knew I was underwater, my body in so much pain I couldn't move—I wasn't even capable of inhaling, so drowning was out of the question.

I regained control of my body one limb at a time until I flailed and pulled myself out of the mud by the roots of a mangrove tree. Still, I couldn't breathe. Instead, I hacked and wheezed, my lungs squeezing themselves harder and harder.

"You didn't die," the white hart said with a giggle. "Congratulations. That means you passed the *test*. Now, bond with me, maggot. I need... more... magic... to become perfect."

I couldn't stand. I couldn't find my shovel. Heck, I could barely see, my vision fading in and out.

The white hart drew closer and touched my shoulder with his smile-twisted snout. Then he glowed a brilliant white. A feeling washed over me—like something raked at my insides, demanding to connect, an icy grip on my soul—and although I had never felt it before, I knew it had to be the offer to bond. But I had the option to reject, I could feel that too.

I really didn't know what to do. The white hart had proven himself insane and violent—nothing like any mystical creature I had ever read about—so whatever he wanted, I figured the outcome would only lead to more insanity and violence. I couldn't let that happen. I couldn't let him get "more magic" and "become perfect" or whatever he really wanted. I had to keep the monster's attention so that Lyell could fully escape, perhaps even tell Illia what had happened.

Even if it meant my life.

I mean, that was what true arcanists did, wasn't it? They fought until the bitter end. They gave their lives to ensure the world was protected from monsters like this.

Bravery. Without it, we cannot act in the face of fear.

I had to keep fighting. Just a little bit longer.

I rejected the white hart's offer to bond.

The monster stopped glowing, but he didn't stop laughing.

"Wrong decision," he said with glee.

He thrust forward and gored me with his antlers. It was hard to feel anything, and my vision slid in and out. Maybe a few points went straight through my chest, I don't know. The next thing I remember was opening my eyes under the murky water, the haze of dirt and grime all I could see.

I pulled myself up into a sitting position, my whole body trembling as I leaned against the roots of a mangrove tree. The white hart clopped around, splashing water the entire time, and my heart seized in my chest. I closed my eyes.

It was going to kill me.

The light faded and darkness swept between the trees, blanketing the mire in a zone of shadow. A mound of mud rose from the water just as I lost the last bit of my sight. Was it the other mystical creature? I couldn't even find the strength to voice the question.

"Corrupted beast," some dark and imposing voice echoed between the trees. "You lost yourself to the plague and now you're nothing more than a monster."

The white hart responded with a howl of laughter.

"Finally come to show yourself, knightmare? I'll see... you *broken!*"

"You can't even remember your name, can you?"

"*Fight me, wretch!*"

"Your suffering ends here, old friend."

A cold rush of wind. Then a splash of water.

No more laughter.

I forced myself to take a ragged breath, my whole body awash in agony as though on fire. The darkness receded, allowing me to see once more, but at first I thought I was hallucinating.

The white hart had been sliced into pieces—the head, the body, the hind legs—all separated and gushing foul blood and intestines into the waters of the Endless Mire. Bits of him twitched, but there was no healing such outrageous injuries. He was dead and vivisected.

I closed my eyes.

What could have done such a thing?

Something walked through the mire waters and stopped at my side. I shuddered. Was it the thing that killed the white hart?

"I stood by and did nothing," the voice said, more melancholy than before. "Forgive me. I did not want to get involved. I should have acted sooner."

I coughed up water. I felt tired. I wanted to sleep.

"Your determination impressed me. I thought you were a child in the body of a man, seeking power to harm others as they had harmed you. But your true nature revealed itself in your battle."

My true nature? I wished I could speak, but I didn't have the strength.

"A power hungry fiend would've taken the white hart's offer to bond," the voice continued. "A coward would have left Lyell to die and saved himself. A weak-willed sycophant would have bonded with the white hart the moment his life was threatened. But a true knight stands firm in the face of overwhelming darkness."

My heart beat weaker and weaker each passing second. Soon it wouldn't have the blood necessary to continue. Hot tears mixed with the dirt streaked across my face.

"I was once bonded," the voice said. "My arcanist was killed, however, leaving me fragmented and lost. I don't want to watch you fade away, but I cannot abandon my revenge either. Bond with me and your new magic will stitch your broken body together enough to save your life."

Bond? Right now?

"But know this," the voice continued. "If you bond, you agree to help me in my quest for vengeance. I will see my old arcanist's murderer brought to justice. And if you get in my way, I'll cut you down as well."

Again, I felt a presence flood my being. Something calming and resolute. Gripping at my soul.

An offer to bond.

And this time I took it.

"I am a knightmare. You may call me Luthair."

After that I lost consciousness.

"Volke! *Volke!* Wake up."

I opened my eyes and stared into the jade canopy of mangrove trees overhead. With each new breath I felt better than before. After a few moments I sat up, my body sore, but not wrecked.

"Thank the heavens."

Illia knelt next to me, smiling wide as she stroked my

hair. I glanced around, groggy. Had I been sleeping? It was hard to tell. I was on a patch of dirt a few feet from the insect-infested waters of the mire. How had I gotten here?

"I was so worried," Illia said as she threw her arms around my neck and hugged me. "Lyell told me all about the white hart. I can't believe you're okay. He made it sound as though you were already dead."

"Where is Lyell?" I asked.

"I told him to go back to town. I thought... Well, I thought you would be in trouble so I told him to get Tyms and William." She frowned. "I'm sorry, Volke. I didn't want to tell them, but I figured they should know if you were in danger."

"It's fine."

Illia grabbed my hand with both of hers and squeezed tight.

I glanced up and met her gaze. Despite the fact everyone in town would know what we had done, she smiled wide.

"We did it," she whispered. "We're both arcanists."

I stared at the mark on her forehead, still impressed with the detail and design of the magical badge. And she said we were both arcanists? The memories of the voice in the swamp came back to me bit by bit. I reached up and stroked my forehead. The seven-pointed star was etched into my flesh with shallow furrows, the picture of a sword and cape laced throughout the design.

I really was an arcanist.

"Illia," a squeaky voice cried out. "I got what you asked for, but it's not the season for these."

Nicholin bounded across the red tree branches, a bundle of plants in one paw. He leapt from the nearest tree and hit the dirt with a feather-touch grace that left no footprints.

"Here," he said. "For the injuries."

Illia took the plants. They were an assortment of lava weeds—a type of vegetation that numbed pain when made into a paste. As apprentice gravekeepers, Illia and I had our fair share of cuts and bruises from making coffins or gathering wood. Lava weeds always took the sting away.

Nicholin stared at my forehead for a long moment and then crossed his little ferret arms over his fluffy chest. "Hm! I see you bonded with Luthair. Surprising, considering what happened to his last arcanist."

Illia glanced around. "Where is Luthair? I haven't seen a mystical creature since we found Volke. Luthair wouldn't leave him defenseless, would he?"

"Definitely not. And don't fret, Luthair is here with us, hiding in the shadows like he always does. Isn't that right, Luthair? Or are you still pretending to be a swamp spirit so people leave you alone?"

I held my breath as I waited. Where was he?

The shadows around us moved and snaked about, finally coalescing into an inky object. It twisted upward and created an ebony suit of heavy plate armor with a sword—gauntlets, sollerets, a chest piece, tassets to protect the legs and hips—complete with a black cape lined in red.

Even if I wanted to breathe, I couldn't. It was only after seeing Luthair that I remembered I had read passages in William's books about knightmares—walking suits of armor made from shadows and terror, or so the tales said. They were rare and their numbers dwindling, but here stood Luthair.

While I continued to stare, I took in more details. Luthair appeared cracked and scuffed. His cape was tattered at the end and littered with holes. The sword scabbard hanging at the waist seemed thin and worn.

Illia stood and stared at the knightmare with her one good eye as wide as I had ever seen it.

"You're a knightmare," she said. "From those old stories!"

Luthair nodded, his helmet seemingly attached to the rest, though there was no body within the suit of armor.

She stepped forward and slowly reached out a hand. Before she touched Luthair's cape, she hesitated. "May I?"

Again, Luthair nodded.

Illia stroked the cape, her fingers lingering on the holes and ragged edges. "You were once bonded?"

"Yes."

"I thought most eldrin died with their arcanist."

"Most die protecting their arcanist. Some kill themselves afterward from the grief."

"Didn't you say you wouldn't die until you caught your arcanist's murderer?" Nicholin asked. "That's what you said on the boat."

"I will never forgive that man," Luthair stated, cold and almost detached. "I will have his blood on my blade before I give up on life, that much I promise."

Illia lifted her one visible eyebrow and then turned to me. She stared, her eye expressing more emotion than a thousand words. Worry and doubt—she didn't like the icy declaration of revenge—but I couldn't get around it. I had agreed to that mission when I accepted the bonding.

"It's okay," I said to her. "That's what arcanists do in the first place, right? They stop murderers and pirates from committing any more crimes. Whoever killed Luthair's last arcanist needs to be brought to justice, one way or another."

"Just be careful," Illia whispered. "You don't want to end up like the last arcanist."

"I won't. It's not like we have to chase him down right away." I turned to Luthair. "Right?" I couldn't even wield magic yet. I hoped Luthair didn't intend to sail away from the island, sword in hand.

Luthair shook his helmet—but the dark void within didn't move, and there were no eyes or physical body to be seen.

"You must master your magic," he said. "I won't lose another arcanist to that fiend."

Nicholin huffed. "We don't need to brood about it right now, do we? We should celebrate! You found a new arcanist. That's good, right? Well, so long as you aren't driven to madness."

"I will retain my wits, if only to see justice done."

I rubbed at my forehead as I recalled all the stories of mystical creatures who bonded twice. Because eldrin absorbed the personalities of their arcanists, bonding with multiple people could lead to irrational behavior and odd habits. Plus, the magic they gave their new arcanist was never the same. Sometimes it was worse, or made it harder to wield powers.

It meant I would probably have a difficult time mastering magic since I was the second arcanist bonded to Luthair. While that wasn't the most ideal situation, I was still beyond overjoyed. I was an arcanist, even if I would be hampered by a "secondhand" eldrin.

Nicholin leapt onto Illia's shoulders and curled himself around her neck.

It occurred to me then that all three of the mystical creatures from the shipwreck were rare and valuable. A knightmare, a white hart, and a rizzel—one so rare and elusive I had never even heard of it.

"You all traveled together?" I asked as I glanced between Nicholin and Luthair. "On the same boat? Are you all related somehow?"

"We were escaping the plague," Nicholin replied. "That's when Luthair's arcanist was killed. We were loaded onto a boat, but there was so much fighting and confusion that we left without half our crew. When the storms hit, there wasn't much we could do about it."

The plague.

Even the offhanded mention got my heartrate back to a panicked level. My encounter with the white hart left a lasting impression and knowing it was the result of the occult plague gave me a whole new appreciation for the illness. It drove the white hart mad. Laughing mad. And power hungry. Would it do that with all mystical creatures? Would it affect both arcanists and eldrin?

Illia placed her hand on my head. "Are you able to walk, Volke? Here. Let me apply some of that lava weed."

"No," I said as I forced myself to my feet. "We should go before the whole town panics."

Luthair had been right. The magic that coursed through my body had stitched up the wounds, just like how the white hart had healed himself from my shovel attacks.

I took a moment to admire my torn and bloody clothing. It appeared as though I had been shredded by a pack of wild dogs, but my skin underneath was merely bruised and scraped. My ribs hurt—in the exact spot the white hart had kicked me—but I suspected the worst of it would be gone in a few days.

And once again, I was struck with an uplifting and emotional thought.

Finally, after all the waiting, I would leave the Isle of Ruma.

As an arcanist.

A knightmare arcanist.

8

FAREWELLS

Our walk back to town occurred in comfortable silence. Illia stroked Nicholin, and I admired the way his fur shimmered in the daylight. When I glanced around, I realized Luthair had disappeared. He wasn't invisible, like the white hart. Instead, he had the ability to merge into the shadows themselves. Even my own shadow moved a bit more than I did, betraying Luthair's presence.

Illia had been right. After the bonding, it felt like I possessed a new part of me that I somehow always had, but never realized. I didn't know how to wield my magic, yet a piece of me knew I could. It was like discovering smells for the first time—the world took on a whole new dimension.

I wanted to speak with Luthair and Nicholin, but my mind and body were worn out from the fighting. I needed proper rest. Only then would I have the energy to discover the answers.

The afternoon sun shone down by the time we made it back to town. The citizens of Ruma waited outside their homes, everyone from the farmers to the tanners. When we reached the cobblestone roads, we were given a funeral's welcome. No one spoke to us. They watched with intent gazes as we made our way back to the cottage.

"Not a friendly place," Nicholin muttered. "Haven't these people ever seen an arcanist before? There should be celebrations. And dancing. And delicious foods."

Illia patted his head. "Those things aren't for us."

"Hmpf! Maybe in your past life, but you're different now. I'm outraged. You should be outraged too." Nicholin squeaked and grumbled, his tail swishing back and forth at a fierce rate.

We rounded the corner onto the last path to the cottage. People pointed and whispered, but still, no one spoke to us.

Gravekeeper William stood outside, his arms crossed. Schoolmaster Tyms hovered close by, his face so red it was as prominent as the Pillar. No doubt they were discussing our situation.

When Illia and I got close, all conversation came to a halt. Although the pain from my fight had waned, a dull ache remained. I straightened my posture regardless, ready to face Tyms with all the confidence I could muster.

"You made it home," William called out. We rushed to his side, and Illia threw her arms around him in a tight embrace. "Illia, my girl." Then he looked me over, his gaze fixated on the dried blood. "Volke, what happened?"

"It's a long story," I said.

"What is this?" Tyms asked, his voice set to *yell*. "We were told there were monsters in the Endless Mire! The town's guards and fishermen are heading straight for the mire as we speak!"

"The monster is dead," I said.

Tyms opened his mouth to continue, but he stopped cold when his beady eyes glanced up at my forehead. Then he turned to Illia and took a step back, his mouth slack, and his eyes wide.

"You two," he murmured. "I can't believe it. You've become arcanists!"

William nodded. "Lyell did say Illia had bonded."

"Preposterous. Absolutely unheard of. You three children never should have been allowed into the Endless Mire!"

"Illia and Volke are adults."

"Pah! Adults by mere hours! Infants still in thought and behavior!"

Did Tyms have to shout everything he said? The trumpet he had for a windpipe never rested.

It took a full minute of Tyms's incoherent blubbering before he finally calmed himself enough to speak again. Without a word to me or Illia—not even *are you okay?*—he turned to William.

"Did you put your apprentices up to this? Did you tell them about the mystical creatures out in the Endless Mire?"

"I would never put my apprentices in danger," William said. "I had no idea where they were until Lyell came hollerin'."

"What a tale you weave, but no fool in the abyssal hells would ever believe it."

"Are you callin' me a liar?"

"Everyone knows these two don't deserve to become arcanists! They haven't paid the proper dues!"

William glanced around the street. Although our cottage was set apart from the rest of the buildings, people were still close by, watching. They pointed at Nicholin perched on Illia's shoulders. If William and Tyms continued to argue outside, the conversation would be all over town.

"Let's go inside," William said. "We can discuss everything there."

Tyms huffed and dramatically threw his robes to the side as he walked into the cottage. William, Illia, and I followed after him. Once we were all situated in the kitchen, Tyms wheeled on me.

"Tell me what happened."

"With the white hart?" I asked.

"With your eldrin, boy! How did you become an arcanist?"

"Well, I fought a white hart, and when it was about to kill me, there was—"

Tyms laughed a single sarcastic laugh, cutting me off. "Already your story contradicts Lyell's. What was that you said on my stage yesterday? You wanted to be a noble arcanist? You can start by telling the truth."

"Wait, what did Lyell say?"

"He said the white hart wanted to bond with him, but then you interfered with the bonding and agitated the creature."

"What?" I balked.

"It gets worse! When the white hart refused to bond with the likes of you, it devolved into a fight. You wanted to kill the creature before it could bond with anyone else! You were threatening it!"

This complete inaccuracy of the events left me speechless. Sure, the white hart wanted to bond, but he was obviously insane, and even Lyell ended up running from him rather than bonding.

I took a step back and ran a hand through my hair, desperately trying to understand why Lyell would spin such a crazy tale. Was it just to make me look ill-tempered and crazy? Or did he have a specific reason?

"That's not what happened," Illia said.

Tyms turned his glare on her. "Oh? Then why don't you give us your account of the story."

Illia glanced to the floor. "Well, I didn't actually see what happened."

"Ha! Then what business do you have saying Lyell's story is untrue?"

"Because that's not how Volke acts. I know him. William knows him."

"Volke wouldn't have attacked a white hart simply because it didn't bond," William said.

Tyms stomped around the kitchen, his huffing and puffing reaching fairytale levels. Then he motioned to the door. "The Ren family has asked that the island prosecute the boy based on Lyell's testimony. If Volke's an arcanist because he stole the opportunity from Lyell, then the Ren family has a case to be made. Years ago, we drowned people in the bay who bonded with phoenixes outside of the trials. This is the same thing."

William shook his head. "You can't be serious."

"No one is going to drown Volke," Illia said with an edge of defiance in her voice. Nicholin hunched his back, his fur standing on end as he hissed.

"Yeah," Nicholin added. "If Illia doesn't want him dead, then I don't want him dead either!"

Despite the shouting and William's deepening frown, Tyms headed for the front door. Before he grabbed the handle, the shadows shook the cottage and rattled the windows. Everyone caught their breath, and a terrible silence followed. Luthair formed from the darkness and rose up, seemingly from the floor, many pieces of his shadowy armor coming together to form a single entity.

"I won't allow it," he said, his dark voice echoing in the small space.

Tyms jumped back and nearly tripped over a chair in his haste.

"By the stars," he muttered, his eyes wide. "It's full grown."

I had never seen a knightmare so I didn't know what one should look like before bonding. The phoenixes on our island started small, the size of a heron. Eventually, as eldrin, they matured into giants of the sky.

Was Luthair grown? It made sense, considering he already had an arcanist who passed away.

Tyms shook his head. "This will never do. Even if we kill the boy to give his mystical creature to Lyell, it'll be for nothing. A full grown creature like this had to have been bonded before. Bonding a second time makes for a terrible arcanist. Bonding a third time is nearly impossible."

"It matters not," Luthair said. "I will not bond to Lyell. I saw him for what he was—a child who had yet to mature. He refused to see the white hart as a dangerous monster until it was too late."

"You're saying you saw it?" Tyms asked. "When the white hart attacked?"

"I saw everything. Lyell ran, and Volke fought the plague-ridden beast to allow him time to escape."

"Plague-ridden?"

"Indeed."

Tyms melted back into an incoherent mess. He paced the small portion of our kitchen, mumbling the entire time about plagues and mystical creatures. To my surprise, he bit his knuckles to quell his nervous babbling. I never thought of him as a man who fretted like a fussy mother hen searching for her chicks, but his trembling hands couldn't be hidden.

"This changes everything," he whispered. "I will tell the Ren family. There won't be any need for prosecution."

William walked to Tyms' side and patted him on the shoulder. "Tyms, is everything all right? Ya know I'm here if you need something."

"The presence of plague is different. We can't allow these creatures to stay."

"These ones?" William glanced between Nicholin and Luthair. "They're not plague-ridden."

"It doesn't matter."

"Then what—"

"Your apprentices need to go." Tyms motioned in the cardinal direction of the ports. "They need to train away from our island. I'll make arrangements for them to travel with Atty and Zaxis."

When Tyms headed for the front door a second time, Luthair stepped to the side. His shadow armor rang with a dull clink, similar to metal, but colder and distinct. Tyms rushed out of the cottage without a glance back.

I never thought I would feel anxiety about leaving the Isle of Ruma.

On the contrary, I had dreamed about it for years. Who wouldn't want to leave? Small, secluded, overly obsessed with tradition, uneventful—and everything was worse because I was relegated to the sidelines.

But the island was all I knew. Sure, I had traveled to nearby places, and I had spoken to some sailors from far off locations. It wasn't the same, though.

I sat on the edge of the cliff again, waiting for the sun to rise on my final day. Perhaps I would never return—that was what Tyms said, anyway. He wanted me and Illia gone forever. Better than being drowned in the bay, I suppose. There was my silver lining.

"Luthair," I said.

The moonlight shadows stirred, like crows fluttering just at the edge of my peripherals. He didn't reply with words, but I knew he had acknowledged my statement.

"Why do you think Lyell lied about what happened in the mire?"

The shadows swirled around me, creating a second silhouette next to me on the grass. "If someone has a choice between blaming themselves for their failures or blaming others, rarely do people choose themselves."

"Yeah, I guess." I sighed. "It must have been an easy lie. They've never liked me."

"Who?"

"Everyone, really, but I meant the Ren family. My father killed a member of their family ten years back. It was Lyell and Zaxis's uncle. I'm not surprised they would call for my death just because one of their kids said I stopped him from bonding."

"You've no need to dwell on this problem. I won't let them kill you, and we will leave within a few hours' time."

"Luthair."

"Yes, my arcanist?"

The title brought my thoughts to a halt. I still almost couldn't believe it. I loved the sound. I would be called Arcanist Volke from here on out.

"Uh," I began. "Do you know what the mainland will be like?"

"I've been to the capital, Fortuna, on many occasions.

The vast number of people often overwhelms me. It won't be long until you have a master to help guide you through your magic training, however, and a master will surely want you to travel the world. Fortuna will not be your final home."

"Really? Travel the world?"

"You cannot see the whole tapestry if you stare at a single thread."

The thought of traveling the world brought more anxiety than just leaving the island. Where would I go? Who would I be with? Would I ever call a place home again? The uncertainty ate at my confidence, but at the same time fueled my wanderlust.

Would I travel the seas, like Master Arcanist Gregory Ruma? He sailed on boats, rode with sea dragons, and flew the skies on magical clouds. He jumped from one adventure to the next, never worrying about where he called home.

One of his stories said he claimed his home was wherever his friends were.

I needed to be more like him. And if I traveled the world, I guess I would be more like him.

It was a dream come true.

"I'm looking forward to the adventure," I said, my anxiety releasing its grip on my chest.

Luthair shifted back into the far evening shadows. "Be careful, my arcanist. Adventures can lead to dangerous corners."

"You'll be with me, Luthair. And Illia too. We can handle dangerous situations."

The whole isle gathered for our departure.

Well, they didn't gather for *my* departure. They gathered for Atty and Zaxis. Both of them, with their beautiful phoenixes, waved to the crowds as they rode carriages to the docks. And just like at the trials, both were clothed in white robes with silver belts. Every part of them, including their eldrin, glittered in the early morning sunlight.

I hadn't slept. I couldn't. Not when my mind refused to stop thinking about the future.

It was starting. My new life.

"You okay?" Illia asked as we walked along the road behind the carriages.

I wiped sweat from my brow, my arcanist mark catching the worst of it. "I'll be fine. The Pillar has advice for this too. Adaptability. Without it, we break at the slightest change."

"There you go with the wisdom steps again."

"I studied them for an entire decade. They're part of me now."

Illia sighed. "Trust me, I'm aware."

Nicholin stood on her shoulder and waved his paws to the crowds. While we weren't cheered as much as Atty and Zaxis, people did throw flower petals our way as we headed for the boats. It was nice—if I closed my eyes, I could even fantasize the upbeat music from the theater troupe was meant for me and me alone.

William walked behind us, the tallest man in the sea of people. I was the second tallest, though.

People pointed at Nicholin as he hopped up and down.

"That's right," he said. "I *am* amazing, thank you!" He tapped Illia's shoulder with his tail. "See? This is the adoration I was expecting!"

Illia rolled her eye and chuckled. "I think they're just curious about you."

"Well, I am super rare. And I have *panache*. That's even more uncommon than being a rizzel."

Illia laughed out loud.

The citizens of Ruma didn't crowd the docks. They waited on the dirt and stone of the island, never stepping onto the planks, all out of tradition. Only the new arcanists were to walk to the boat. It was the final strut to show off their new eldrin and bid everyone a final farewell.

Sometimes there were speeches, but mostly it was just waving.

The carriages stopped and allowed Atty and Zaxis off. They walked together, blowing kisses to their family and smiling to everyone else. They walked all the way to our boat—the Sapphire Tide—a barque vessel with three masts and fifteen sails. I had seen several before; they were popular with merchants. I almost couldn't hear the crowd cheering over the beat of my excited heart.

Atty and Zaxis showed off their phoenixes before walking up the gangplank. Servants had already loaded their luggage the night before. Illia and I had to carry our belongings. It wasn't difficult, considering how little we had.

Before we stepped foot on the dock, William held us back.

"Wait, you two," he said.

Illia hugged him. "We'll be back. No matter what Tyms says."

He chuckled. "That's my girl."

"Thank you," I said before my throat tightened with sentiment. "For everything. You've been like a—"

William grabbed me and squeezed me in tight with Illia, his arms large enough to wrap around us all. Nicholin squirmed between us, his squeaking in my ears.

"Hey, hey," he said. "My fur is beautiful and easily ruffled!"

"No one could've asked for better apprentices," William said. "I'm glad you two have become arcanists, but remember to protect each other, ya hear? We're family and I want to see my family safe and sound when they come to visit."

"Of course," I muttered into his tunic.

Illia sniffled and bit back a crack in her voice. "We'll be fine. You worry too much."

William released us and then pulled three objects from his trouser pocket. He handed us each a letter sealed with wax. I turned it over, curious.

"Becoming an arcanist is just the first step," he said. "Now you have to find a master to apprentice with you. This is a letter of recommendation."

"For what?" I asked.

"New arcanists join guilds to apprentice with. That's where you'll find a master willing to teach you. Atty and Zaxis will have contacts on the mainland, but this is all I can offer you two."

"Thank you."

Illia held her letter close. "Is it for a specific guild?"

"Aye," William said. "The Frith Arcanist Guild. I worked with them when I was a naval officer. They're good people, and I've spoken with the guildmaster on several occasions. Her name is Liet Eventide. Hand her these letters."

"We will," Illia said.

"You'll like it there. Gregory Ruma was one of the founding arcanists."

"R-really?" I asked.

"That's right. It's famous, that guild. Lots of talented arcanists have come out of it."

William tossed me a pouch. I caught it and enjoyed the jingle of coins within.

"It's not much," he said. "So use it wisely."

I nodded.

We all gave each other a final round of hugs before heading toward the boat. To my surprise, the citizens of Ruma cheered as Illia and I walked the short distance across the dock planks. Were they happy we were leaving? Or did they really want us to succeed as arcanists?

"Volke! Wait!"

Gasps rang out as Lyell dashed from the crowd and onto the dock. Some people even booed him, despite the fact he was a member of the Ren family. I couldn't believe he had the audacity to show his face in front of me after all the lies he spouted.

Illia and I waited. If he started shouting his tall tales for the crowd, I'd toss him into the ocean.

Lyell jogged to my side, and I tensed.

"Here," he said between heavy breaths. He handed me a small box with his family's insignia stamped into the wood. I took the box, the object palm-sized. Lyell never met my gaze. He stared at the dock beneath his feet, his eyebrows knit together. "I... I wanted to thank you."

His statement chilled my anger. "Lyell?"

"My father never would've understood the truth. He would've wanted me to bond no matter what." Lyell huffed as his shoulders slumped. "I... Well, I just couldn't stand to have him angry with me, and—"

"It's okay," I said with half a smile. "I'm a jealous nobody who couldn't stand all your success, right? Everyone on the island knows it."

Lyell rubbed at his face. "Volke. I—" Then his voice cracked, and he couldn't finish his sentence.

In that moment, I actually kinda liked Lyell. He wasn't as insufferable as I had thought.

"What's going on?" Zaxis shouted from the gangplank. He stormed down, his green eyes flashing with anger. Even his phoenix swirled around, his soot raining down on the dock.

When he got close, his arcanist mark became visible under the widow's peak of his red hair. A phoenix with its wings spread was interwoven with the seven-pointed star etched into his forehead.

Lyell shook his head. "Nothing. Good luck, Zaxis. Illia. Volke." He dashed away into the crowd, leaving me with his box.

Illia took my elbow. "It's time."

"Yeah," I said. "No more delays. Let's go."

9

THE MAINLAND

The Sapphire Tide glided across the waves with a speed and grace far superior to that of the smaller skiffs I had ridden in the past. I leaned over the edge to get a better look at the water splashing against the port side hull. The smell of salt invaded my nose.

A smile crept across my face when I remembered my first boat trip with Gravekeeper William. He was a naval officer through and through and demanded I learn all the proper terms for a boat. Port meant left, starboard meant right, a jib was a triangular sail—and when I called the anchor a *stopping hook* he nearly had a heart attack. After that, he launched into a terminology tirade that lasted four hours.

I already missed him.

In order to distract myself, I withdrew Lyell's box from my trouser pocket. The lightweight container didn't have a lock, just a latch secured with a metal pin. I removed the pin and opened it up.

Inside I found a letter and three gold leafs. I stared at the contents for a prolonged moment, admiring the glitter of the coins. Leafs were the currency on the mainland—a circular coin with an oak leaf-shaped hole in the center. I had seen copper leafs and silver leafs, but never gold. William had given us ten simple silver coins, the currency used on most islands, and while that was nice, it didn't even compare to one gold leaf.

I suspected one gold leaf was worth fifty silver island coins.

After the shock of the money wore away, I opened the letter.

Volke,

I am truly sorry. I hope you'll be able to forgive my lie about what happened in the Endless Mire. You saved my life, and even as I spun my tale to my father, I knew it wasn't right. I figured you had died and that my tale wouldn't harm you, but when you returned an arcanist, I couldn't go back on my word lest my father throw me from the house.

Please forgive me one day. These coins should help you on the mainland.

I don't have any right to ask you this, but could you please keep an eye on Zaxis? My parents think he can do no wrong, but I know better.

. . .

I know a guild will accept you. Just find a talented master arcanist in that guild you can apprentice with.

Lyell Ren

I folded the letter and returned it to the box. Although we had never been friends, I resolved to write Lyell once I had time and paper to do so. Lyell and William—I wanted to hear from them both.

A chorus of gasps brought me back to the present. I turned and found the sailors gathered around Atty and her phoenix. She smiled and waved her hand. An arc of flame sailed into the air, the red blaze lasting a few seconds before disappearing on the ocean winds.

"Amazin'," one sailor said.

Another nodded. "She's had her phoenix for less than a week and already she's wieldin' magic? Talented, she is. One to keep an eye on."

"Uh, that's hardly impressive," Nicholin said.

Illia and her rizzel stood on the opposite side of the boat. Atty and the sailors turned in her direction, their eyebrows raised, some scratching their heads.

Nicholin swished his tail and clapped his paws together. "My arcanist is way more talented, thank you very much."

"Well, that's just subjective opinion," Illia said.

"Ha! So modest. Show them your magic."

"I don't think it's necessary."

"C'mon! I already made the declaration. They're all waiting."

"Please do," Atty chimed in. She smiled and waved Illia over. "I'd love to see what you and your, um, what is your creature again? I'm sorry, I've never read anything about it."

"I'm a rizzel," Nicholin replied. "That's right. In the flesh."

"Ah. Yes. Please, Illia. Let's see your rizzel magic."

I didn't like the tone in her voice. It bordered on sarcastic, but maybe I was reading into it. Atty had never been anything but lady-like and pleasant—she wasn't one of the jerks who made fun of Illia for her scars.

The sailors nodded and gave Illia their full attention. Although she held her ground, Illia slid a hand over the scarred half of her face. With her other hand she reached into a nearby barrel and withdrew a green breadfruit.

I held my breath, unsure what she would demonstrate. What did rizzels do, exactly? Fire was expected for phoenixes, right along with their substantial healing powers, but what a rizzel could do was a mystery to me.

Illia held up the breadfruit with her fingers straight, propping it up like a stand.

The ocean waves and the cawing of gulls were the only sounds for miles. Everyone watched and waited with bated breath.

Then she brought her fingers together, as if to crush the fruit, but instead it disappeared in a puff of sparkles. Half a second later, the breadfruit appeared a foot away on the deck, popping into existence with a *snap* and another round of glittering dust.

The sailors responded with a collective gasp.

She had teleported the breadfruit! I almost said it aloud, as shocked as I was. Though it wasn't very far, and she looked like she had to concentrate fully to make it happen, it was still impressive. How many mystical creatures had *teleportation* as a part of their portfolio? Not many.

Atty didn't react. She kept the same smile as before, her thoughts about the demonstration hidden by her mastery of expression. Her phoenix flew to her side, and she held out her arm to provide a perch. It was only then that I noticed the leather guard over her forearm to protect from the black talons.

"Impressive," Atty said. "Perhaps you and I should seek the same arcanist to apprentice under."

Illia replied with a curt nod. "Maybe."

"Ha," Nicholin said with a snort. "I think Illia could net herself the best arcanist in the land if she wanted. No need to hold herself back with whoever you're going with."

Illia placed her hand on Nicholin's face, half-smothering him by gripping at his little ferret mouth. He squirmed while she turned away and waved to the sailors. "Well, I'm going to rest before we arrive at the mainland. It was a pleasure seeing your magic, Atty."

"Likewise," she replied.

The sailors clapped and whispered amongst each other as Illia retreated to the opposite side of the boat. Once the commotion died down, the sailors returned to their posts, but an air of excitement lingered in their boisterous conversation. Atty took her phoenix and walked to the bow, her long blonde hair fluttering in the wind.

A thought struck me. Perhaps I should approach her. I could tell her I had always admired her, and her use of magic impressed me. What would I say after that? Maybe I would say: *I haven't mastered any magic, isn't that hilarious? I'm such a loveable sad sack!*

Yup. That would get her heart beating fast.

"Luthair," I said.

The shadows around my feet stirred, but he didn't form.

"Do you think I can wield magic like Atty?" I asked.

"You may try, my arcanist."

"Well, uh, how do I do that?" I held up my hands and stared at my palms.

"I am no instructor. The way you wield magic will always be different than the way I wield it. I was born to exist with this power, whereas you must channel it."

Channel it?

I concentrated on my hands as though they were the mouth of a river connecting with the ocean. Could the magic run through me like water? I tried to imagine something happening—like the shadows coalescing at my fingertips—but I wasn't entirely sure what I would be able to do.

I narrowed my eyes, tightening my focus.

A terrible pain flooded my right arm from the elbow to the wrist, like a knife had been stabbed between the bones. I grunted and grabbed at my forearm, my whole body trembling. The shadows on the deck of the boat shifted for a moment, as though the sun had changed position in the sky, but nothing else resulted from my efforts.

The agony lingered for a few seconds before disappearing entirely.

"Are you all right?" Luthair asked from beneath my feet.

I nodded. "Yeah... yeah. I'm fine. It just stung."

"My magic was forged and refined with the soul of my previous arcanist. It won't be compatible when it flows through your body."

I knew that. Second-bonded mystical creatures always had that problem, but a part of me wondered if it would be a permanent problem. Would there come a time when I got used to the odd magic flowing through me? Or when my soul changed Luthair more than his old arcanist had?

A growing fear took root in my thoughts. Such burning pain for a tiny show of magic—and not even a useful showing! Moving shadows was a parlor trick at best. I would be a circus arcanist and nothing more.

Still an arcanist, though. I had to keep that in mind. But not good enough to approach Atty. What would I even do? Show off my shifting-the-shadows-two-inches-to-the-right powers? If it ever got too hot, I could save everyone with an emergency patch of shade. What a hero.

I exhaled, allowing my breath to take my worries with it.

Maybe, if I found a talented instructor, I could overcome the limitations of my eldrin's past. But who would take someone with a handicap such as mine?

It took two days of sailing to reach the mainland.

Atty and Zaxis kept to themselves. Illia and I did the same. Our two groups never interacted, like there was some sort of unspoken agreement everyone inherently understood and accepted. And each time I gave Atty a fleeting glance, Zaxis offered me a cold glare. For some reason, I think he thought I was looking at *him*. Nothing could be further from the truth. I wished he would've fallen off the side of the boat, to be frank.

In my fantasies, I pulled him from the ocean with amazing shadow powers while he was choking on sea water. Atty would walk over and ask me where I had learned such amazing abilities. I'd tell her it just came to me because I'm naturally talented, and then we'd share a dinner.

It was a pleasant daydream.

I rested on my cot, knowing we were close to our destination, my anticipation preventing any rest and relaxation. "Luthair, how long do you think it'll take me to master magic?"

"It took my last arcanist two years to move from a novice to a journeyman arcanist, and then another five to become a master arcanist." His voice echoed in the tiny room within the ship's hold. "I never saw him reach grandmaster. He died before then."

"Sorry to hear that." But I didn't want to stop the conversation. "Being a master arcanist didn't save him from his killer?"

"No."

Although I had made a promise to Luthair to help catch this villain, I did worry. My use of magic on the boat confirmed my fears. Magic would be difficult to learn. And then I would have to fight the same killer who got Luthair's last arcanist.

To distract myself, I wondered how long Gregory Ruma took to develop his magic.

"We're comin' into port," one of the sailors shouted. "Passengers, grab your things! We'll be unloadin' after you've departed."

I snatched up my sack and slung it over my shoulder. Luthair followed me through the darkness, slithering by undetected. Illia stayed close to my side as we walked up on deck. Nicholin remained on her left shoulder, his head high and his gaze searching.

The city of Fortuna shone in the morning sun, windows glistening in the light, kites fluttering in the wind. The city seemed to be built around, and on top of, a giant hill. Buildings lined the flatlands around the base, and roads led up to the step-like terraces of the massive hill, allowing for even more homes and farmland. At the top stood a massive clock tower, complete with bells and a representation of the stars in the night sky etched on a steel dais—a gigantic machine to keep track of the celestial changes throughout the year.

I held my breath as I took it all in, never blinking despite the ocean winds.

"Wow," Illia breathed. "It's so amazing."

I nodded. "Yeah."

Zaxis and Atty walked to our side of the boat, their belongings carted along by two sailors.

"Never seen this place before?" Zaxis asked me.

I shook my head.

"Yeah. Your gawking says it all."

"You've been here?" I asked.

"Of course. Unlike you, I've traveled all around this region. Many times."

"What's that called?" I pointed to the clock, ignoring his pompous attitude.

"The Astral Tower," Zaxis said matter-of-factly. "Fancy, right? The arcanists who rule Fortuna live in that building. People in town say they keep watch over everything with their clairvoyant creatures."

"What's that island?" Illia asked. She pointed out into the ocean, to a large island with a single manor house built atop it. "I've never seen it on any maps."

"Island?" Zaxis turned and stared. For a moment he said nothing, his nonplussed expression an amusing change from his default smug. "I... don't think I've ever seen that island there before."

It was a substantial island, complete with gardens, a series of trees, a glittering pond, and a stone wall painted with murals of mystical creatures. It was hard to miss. How had Zaxis never seen it?

"I've never seen it either," Atty added.

We all stared at the mystery island as the Sapphire Tide settled into port. Other ships and their sails quickly blocked our view, but the enigma still intrigued me. Islands didn't pop up out of nowhere. If the sailors hadn't been so busy tying down the boat, I would've inquired further. I decided to wait, however. The allure of the city quickly became the only thing I could think about.

Once the gangplank was lowered, Illia, Zaxis, Atty, and I disembarked from the ship.

The crowded ports of Fortuna were five times the size of Ruma. No—even that was too small—maybe twenty times the size of Ruma. People hustled and bustled from one end to the other, and at least sixteen other ships floated idly next to the piers, each ranging in size and type.

We walked as a group toward the gates. People parted after they got a good look at our foreheads and the majestic phoenixes on Atty's and Zaxis's arms. Arcanists were revered, even in the capital, and the giddy whispers that followed us got me smiling. At least they weren't pointing in scorn or throwing things.

No one here knew I was the son of criminals. I would have a clean slate.

"Where can we find the Frith Guild?" Illia asked as she smoothed some of her hair over the damaged portion of her face. "William never gave us an address."

"All arcanist guilds are registered in the guildhall," Zaxis said, curt. "You should've known that before coming here."

"Obviously I didn't."

"Heh."

I held up my letter of recommendation as I stepped between them. "Is that where we take this?"

Zaxis scoffed. "Really? Are you such an uneducated bumpkin that you don't know how the world works?"

"*Zaxis*," Atty said.

Her one word got him grinding his teeth.

Although I had spent my childhood days dreaming of

becoming an arcanist, I hadn't thought about the guilds or professions I would join once I had bonded. Zaxis just wanted to torment us, but he did have a point. We should've known where to go long before arriving in Fortuna. Picking a guild and finding a master arcanist to study under was a monumental task and decision. If we picked a terrible master, it could take us years of extra training to master our craft.

Or, in the worst-case scenario, we'd end up in a situation where our master arcanist got us killed because he didn't know how to assess the danger.

"Allow me to explain," Atty said, pushing Zaxis to the side. "New arcanists who wish to join a guild will register with the guildhall. You'll give them any letters of recommendation and anything else they request before consideration."

"I see," I said.

"If you're chosen, you will train with a master arcanist, working for the guild and earning leafs until your debt is paid."

"What debt?"

"The payment for the master training you, of course."

"R-right," I muttered.

She continued, "Once you pay your debt, and you're proficient enough in magic, you'll be given the title of *master*. Then you're expected to give a small portion of your earnings to the guild from there on out."

"Forever?" Illia asked.

"Typically, but not always."

Zaxis shot me a quick glare. "And they don't take criminals, liars, or gravediggers," he added.

"Good thing I'm not any of those things," I quipped.

"Yeah, whatever. I heard about how you wove some fantastical tale of the white hart in the mire." His voice grew angrier and louder with each word. "That was my brother's creature. He could've been here with me if it weren't for—"

"Look," Atty said, cutting him off before he could unload his whole prepared tirade.

We had reached the crowded gates of Fortuna and had to stop. Sailors, tradesmen, and merchants stood in massive lines, their conversations and grumbling masking the crash of the waves on the beach.

"What's going on?" I asked the nearest trader woman.

She tightened her jacket and shook her head. "Some famous arcanist came to town, apparently."

Nicholin hopped up and down on Illia's shoulder. "They heard of me and Illia, obviously!"

The woman cocked an eyebrow. "I don't know the likes of you, lady arcanist. I apologize. I think the man they're clamorin' to see is none other than Gregory Ruma."

"What?" I asked, holding back a gasp. "*The* Gregory Ruma? He's still alive?"

"Course."

Shock paralyzed my mind. I knew arcanists had prolonged lives—hundreds of years, thanks to the magic flowing freely in their veins—but last I heard, Gregory Ruma disappeared while on the hunt for pirates, never to be heard of again.

And now he was in Fortuna? In the flesh? The man who founded my home island? The man known for his good deeds and epic adventures? The man I always imagined I would become?

I almost convinced myself I was dreaming.

"You admire this man," Luthair whispered from the shadows.

I nodded, my heartrate rising with anticipation as I glanced into the crowd, looking for a way to sneak by. "He's the best arcanist of all time," I said. "I have to meet him. If only for a second."

Zaxis forced a sarcastic laugh. "You *have* to meet him? Why? So you can ask to be his apprentice? He'd never take someone like you."

I came to a halt, my mind jerked into a state of overthinking.

I hadn't even considered asking him to be my mentor. That was a brilliant idea. If anyone could teach me about magic, it was Gregory Ruma, the Legendary Swashbuckler. Why hadn't I thought of it?

Pushing my way through the crowds, I headed for the main gate, Luthair slipping through the shadows with little difficulty. I had to speak with Gregory Ruma. I just had to.

10

THE FRITH ARCANIST GUILD

"Volke, wait up!"

I slowed down, my sights still locked on the city. I didn't want to leave Illia behind. She grabbed my shoulder and twisted her fingers into my shirt to keep her grip.

"C'mon," I said. "We should hurry."

"Rushing to meet him probably isn't the best idea."

While I continued to move through the crowd, I gave her a quick glance over my shoulder. "Why would I wait?"

"Think about it. Tons of people want to see him. You won't get much time to speak with him if you're one voice in a massive crowd. You should plan this better. Plus, we just got off a boat. You're covered in saltwater and sweat. Maybe we should get an inn room and you should don some new clothes. You know, to make a good impression when you see him."

I gritted my teeth, irritated Illia would imply I was scraggly and grateful she had taken the time to think of the details. Of course she was right. I should make myself presentable before I threw myself at Ruma's feet and asked him to become my mentor.

"What's so great about this guy?" Nicholin asked. He crossed his little arms. "Did he do something amazing?"

"What didn't he do?" I asked with a laugh. "He fought infamous pirates, charted maps, saved whole ship crews from terrible storms—he's the epitome of what an arcanist should be."

We walked through the gates of Fortuna while the city guard gave us the once-over. When he saw our arcanist marks, he allowed us to pass.

I smiled once we entered the less crowded streets. The Isle of Ruma had three carriages, max, but the streets of Fortuna flowed with horses, carts, and carriages—as though they outnumbered people. It took me a solid minute to get my head under control. I just wanted to stare at everything, and it was hard to pick a direction.

Fortuna had buildings made of stone and wood, wrought-iron streetlamps, trees strategically laid out for shade, and an abundance of orange poppy flowers. The poppies grew everywhere, some even from the cracks between the cobblestones, like a marvelous weed intent on making the world a more beautiful place.

People carried tools of their trade. Some even had flint-lock rifles. The Isle of Ruma had three firearms in total, but here I could see the guards carried pistols on their hips. They were powerful weapons from what I had read, and favored by pirates for their distance. I pushed those thoughts aside, however. I didn't want to dwell on pirates.

After a deep inhale, I took in the scent of the air...

It stank of horse droppings and sweat. The Isle of Ruma smelled like the ocean. Always. Even if I didn't enjoy the scent of Fortuna, I delighted in the difference. The mainland was so much different than the islands.

Zaxis and Atty walked through the gate, not even bothering to take in the scenery. Their phoenixes flew over the city wall and circled overhead before following one of the long city streets. Zaxis headed in the birds' direction.

Atty motioned for us to join her. "This way to the guildhall."

We joined her on the walk, my attention still on the surroundings and my thoughts consumed by tales of Gregory Ruma.

It didn't take long to reach our destination.

The guildhall itself wasn't opulent or gaudy, although in my imagination it had been a palace. No, it barely stood out from the other buildings around it. It was just a government office—far larger than anything on the Isle of Ruma—made of red bricks, dark wood, and thick glass windows that stifled the light. It was single-story and the sign outside had the symbol of a shield and twisted staff. The two phoenixes landed on the roof and settled into a comfortable position.

When we entered, I took note of the dim lighting and cool temperature despite the dozens of people inside. More than half of them were arcanists—I could tell by the star marks on their foreheads.

"H-hello, fledgling arcanists!" a man in black robes said.

He stood behind a wooden counter, his glasses reflecting the lamp lights on the wall. They were large glasses, too. Round like plates.

He continued, "I'm a representative for the Frith Arcanist Guild. Are you looking to apprentice?"

A giant toad sat on the counter next to him—a toad with a bright neon-blue belly and glossy, ebony skin. It must have been four feet at the shoulder, and much thinner and more muscular than normal toads. The counter didn't strain with its weight, however. It stared as Illia, Zaxis, Atty, and I approached.

"What is that?" Nicholin asked with a tilt of his head.

"An *ogata toad*," I said, unable to restrain a smile. "Mystical creatures with a poisonous touch. I've read a few stories about people riding them through dangerous waters. I can't believe I get to see one so big."

The toad had to weigh as much as a full grown man, perhaps more. When it turned its golden gaze to meet mine, I froze. Supposedly, ogata toads could spit venom so potent it melted skin. I didn't think the toad would attack, but a part of me wondered what I would do if it did. Stories told of ogata toads blinding their victims. And some ogata toads had magic to make it permanent, even though arcanists could heal themselves.

Other arcanists stood behind the counter, each representing a different guild. There must have been fifty positions behind the counter, though only ten of them had people manning their station. Two mortal men, no arcanist marks on their foreheads, busied themselves with paperwork.

"Welcome to Fortuna," the man in the black robes said. "Please, allow me to introduce myself." The arcanist mark on his forehead had an ogata toad woven between the points of his seven-tipped star. "I'm Journeyman Arcanist Reo." He motioned to the ogata toad. "And this is my eldrin, Finn."

"Does Gregory Ruma still belong to your guild?" I asked. It was the only question that mattered.

"Of c-course. Ruma was one of the founding members."

Thank goodness. I breathed easy, ready to join the Frith Guild no matter what.

Reo combed back his black shoulder-length hair with his fingers and fidgeted with the edges of his robes. He appeared five years older than me, maybe a little more, but he was gaunt in a way I wasn't.

"Why are the other guilds so busy?" Zaxis asked as he glanced around.

"Ah, well," Reo said with a frown. "Pirates have infested the a-area. And the plague has popped up in a region to the north. Merchant ships are hiring p-protection through the guilds. They want arcanists to protect their wares."

Atty nodded. "That makes sense."

"Yeah, yeah," Zaxis said. Then he ran a hand over his arcanist mark. "I'm a phoenix arcanist, in case you couldn't tell. Which guild has the most phoenix arcanists? I'd like to train with others like me."

"Oh, uh, I'm sorry to be the one to tell you, but all the phoenix arcanists I know are dead."

"Huh? Why?"

Reo's frown deepened. "Remember the pirates I just told you about? They've killed several phoenix arcanists already, including the last three to come from the Isle of Ruma. It's t-treacherous out there."

The information settled over us like a wet blanket. I knew the world could be harsh and cruel, but I never expected to hear such unsettling news the moment I reached Fortuna. All the previous phoenix arcanists had died? Phoenix arcanists were so powerful...

Illia pushed past Zaxis and handed over her letter. "We're not going to die at the hands of a bunch of lowlife pirates. I want into your guild. We have these."

"Thank you," Reo said. He took her letter and then mine.

Atty and Zaxis didn't offer anything.

"We have multiple letters," Zaxis said as he crossed his arms. "We intend to look around for a bit before deciding.

Since there aren't any phoenix arcanist guilds, I'll have to think about what I want."

Reo nodded. "The Frith Guild will only be taking people until the end of the week. After that, we'll be making our way to the next city. You'll have to make up your mind soon."

Illia narrowed her eye. "The guild is leaving town?"

"T-that's right. The Frith Guild travels the world. Since the plague problem has popped up in the north, that's where we'll be headed next."

"And if we join your guild, we can meet Gregory Ruma?" I asked.

It was perfect! If I belonged to the same guild, I would have a chance to speak with him personally.

"I'm sure Master Arcanist Ruma would be willing to speak to new members of the guild, of course."

Illia crossed her arms. "And our letter is all you need?"

"O-oh, uh, no." Reo pushed his glasses up higher on his nose. "We require one letter of recommendation and one *star moth* in order to be considered for apprenticeship. So, uh, you'll also need to bring us a star moth before the next step can occur."

"What's a star moth and where do we get one?"

Reo withdrew scraps of paper from the sleeve of his robes. He handed one to each of us and then pointed to the printed words. "You simply need to show up at the edge of the northern woods right as the sun sets. Our arcanists will be there to assess your skills while you catch the insects."

Oh, I understood.

There was always a Trial of Worth when magic was involved, even with the damn guilds. I should've known. The guilds couldn't take everyone—arcanists had to prove themselves to their potential mentors, just as mortals had to prove themselves to their potential eldrin. A piece of me hated the constant judging, but another piece of me wanted to demonstrate my capabilities for all the world to see. If it was a competition, I would be there in the winner's circle, no matter what.

"You're going to do this?" Zaxis asked me.

"Yes."

"All for Gregory Ruma? You know you could attempt to join another guild."

"Why would I do that?"

"So you have a better chance of getting in. You should shoot for something your level. Low. Forgiving. I hear there's a guild that specializes in tending plants. That's like tending dead bodies, right?"

I shot him a glare. "Thanks for looking out for me, but the Frith Guild is the only place for me."

"Heh. Still a child at heart. You probably read all of Ruma's old swashbuckling stories before bed, right? Or maybe you had William read them to you, is that it?"

Illia took my shoulder and turned me away. Probably for the best. What I wouldn't have given to punch Zaxis square in the nose.

"Do we even need a guild?" Nicholin whispered. "We could learn magic on our own. How hard could it really be?"

Of course we need a guild, was the first response on the tip of my tongue. Well, *I* needed a guild. My magic had already hurt me on the boat. I needed someone to guide my learning process. Maybe Illia and Nicholin could develop magic on their own—she already seemed good at it—but I wasn't as lucky. I never was.

I glanced at the scrap of paper Reo handed us. "The assessments don't happen until night. Why don't we get an inn room and relax?"

Illia smiled. "I like the sound of that."

"Thank you, Journeyman Reo," I said. "I appreciate you taking the time to inform us of the tests."

He nodded. "My pleasure."

Zaxis huffed and didn't offer any sort of goodbye.

Atty, on the other hand, bowed her head. "Good luck."

I returned the gesture.

It occurred to me then that a bow of the head was a sign of respect between equals. Did she see me as an equal? The urge to ask her to join us was high, but the words didn't feel natural. She turned away and spoke with Zaxis afterward, killing my opportunity.

As Illia and I made to leave, Finn lifted his head, his toad eyes blinking with see-through eyelids.

"Hopefully we'll s-see you later tonight," he said with an oddly echoed voice.

To my surprise, and fascination, there were dozens of guilds, all with different purposes and goals. Some arcanist guilds specialized in building things—magical items, homes, walls, weapons—while other guilds were formed around medicine and healing. Obviously some guilds wouldn't take arcanists who didn't have magics suitable for their goals. The healing guilds, for example, wanted people bonded with phoenixes, unicorns, or a caladrius, but not people bonded to gorgons, who turned people to stone, or ettin asps, the two-headed snakes known for their terrible venom.

Obviously they wouldn't take a knightmare arcanist either, so those were out of the question for me.

But no matter how many guilds I learned about, or how many wonderful things they claimed they would do for their new arcanists, I couldn't stop thinking about the Frith Guild.

I learned the Frith Guild undertook dangerous tasks more often than any other guild. If there were storms, their arcanists would quell the rage of nature. If there were pirates, their arcanists would be among the vanguard, fighting the scoundrels of the sea. If there were outbreaks of plague, they would be among the investigators, looking to snuff out the source.

They were well known to the point that everyone in Fortuna spoke highly of them. The whole guild traveled the world. I didn't know how they did it—I didn't ask, either, it was low on my priority list—but it reminded me of Luthair's statement.

You cannot see the whole tapestry if you stare at a single thread.

I wanted to travel the world. I wanted to be a hero arcanist of legendary status. In all ways, I was convinced the Frith Guild was the only guild for me. Besides, Gravekeeper William liked them. They had to be amazing.

As the sun set, I silently thanked Lyell for his coins. Illia and I both had new clothes, boots, and satchels—and that only required a small portion of one gold leaf. Now all my clothes fit. The quality jacket, slacks, and shirt felt soft and smooth against my skin, nothing like the coarse material of William's hand-me-downs.

I washed my face as the last of the sunlight disappeared outside the inn room window.

"Volke," Illia said, smiling. "You're ready to get a star moth?"

"Yes." I turned away from the window. "Are you?"

"Of course."

"You seem like you're in a good mood. You're not

nervous? No second thoughts? You sure you don't want to be a crafter or something?"

Illia threw herself onto her tiny bed, Nicholin clinging to her shoulder the entire way. "Do you really think I want to join some other guild? That's not for me." She glanced away, her expression slowly transforming into something melancholy. In a quieter voice she continued, "I didn't want to become an arcanist to do any of that."

"When did you realize you wanted to become an arcanist?"

"When the pirates took my father's ship," Illia whispered. She rubbed at her face. "I wanted to stop people like them from ever hurting anyone else."

Nicholin hopped off her shoulder, scurried around the bed for a few half-second laps, and then jumped into her lap. "And that's what we're going to do!"

Illia petted his head, her smile returning in full force. "That's right. And the Frith Guild sounds like a perfect fit."

I exhaled, unaware I had been so tense. I was glad Illia had no reservations.

"I've heard many amazing tales involving Frith Arcanists," Luthair said, his disembodied voice shaking our inn room.

Although I knew it was him and he wasn't going to harm us, his out-of-nowhere commentary did startle me from time to time. It took me a moment to relax enough to say, "Was your old arcanist a member of a guild?"

"Yes. The Steel Thorn Inquisitor Guild."

Nicholin snickered. "Sounds so pleasant! Perfect for a creepy creature like you."

"What do they do?" I asked.

"They investigate occult matters, especially the misdeeds of other arcanists who abuse their magic. My old arcanist and I put an end to many wicked men and women after hunting them across the seas. Some villains use their powers for ill gains, some even killing mortals or destroying the land, and the Steel Thorn Guild wouldn't stand for it."

"No wonder your arcanist got himself killed," Nicholin quipped.

I shot him a glare. "Hey. Not many people have the stones to face down an arcanist."

Luthair chuckled. "Mathis never faltered when it came to evil. You reminded me of him when you faced the white hart in the mire."

"Wait," I said. "Was your old arcanist *the* Mathis Weaversong?"

"Yes."

"I can't believe you remember every story from William's old books," Illia said, her eyebrow raised. "There were hundreds of stories in there. Maybe thousands. You remember some guy named Mathis?"

Unable to control my smile, I said, "Of course! Mathis Weaversong outsmarted Galli the Pirate King on his ship the Crimson Scourge. Don't you remember the tale? They were caught in a storm, and their boats were pulled into a whirlpool. Mathis cut down the pirate and his whole crew before steering his vessel straight out of the hurricane!"

Illia rolled her eye. "I can't believe you think that's all real."

"Much of that is exaggerated," Luthair dryly added.

"He did fight Galli though, right?" I asked.

"Yes."

"And there was a storm?"

"Yes."

I clapped my hands together to punctuate the facts. Still,

Illia stared with a bored look on her face, as though my fawning was completely unwarranted.

"We had help," Luthair said. "His guild had sent three other arcanists with us. We had a total of four ships to trap Galli and his men. And there was much talking. Mathis wanted to parley in an attempt to avoid violence."

Stories of Mathis spun in my head. I couldn't believe I had bonded with his eldrin. My chest tightened when I realized his death came at the hands of a villain. It wasn't the proper end for a man of his caliber.

"I've heard enough about *Mathis Weaversong*," Illia said as she stood.

She wore a pair of sturdy leather hunter's trousers, a long coat, and a button up shirt. In all ways she reminded me of the sea-savvy merchants who would travel to Ruma with exotic wares. She kept a tangle of hair over the scars on her face, however. And when she pulled a cap onto her head, she secured it into place to keep her hair from flowing everywhere with the wind—creating a permanent curtain over her injuries.

It didn't matter. It wasn't like the hair was impairing her vision. But sometimes I wished she wouldn't worry about it so much. She didn't need to hide her scars from me.

"Let's go," Illia said. Then she held out her arm so Nicholin could hop on. "We have a couple of star moths to capture."

The woods north of Fortuna were open and inviting. The oak trees didn't bunch up, and there were glades scattered throughout the area. My inner child wanted to explore the region and climb the trees, but I kept such urges suppressed.

Illia, on the other hand, insisted on getting a lay of the land by climbing the tallest tree. She leapt up to the first branch, pulled herself to the second, and climbed the rest until she disappeared, hidden by the leaves.

Seven other arcanists were gathered by the edge of the woods, most of whom had small and difficult-to-see arcanist marks, meaning they were fledglings, like me.

"Welcome!" Reo called out over the small crowd. "I will give you instructions momentarily." He held a stack of papers and shuffled through them.

I examined the other arcanists.

One arcanist was bonded to a pixie. Those pixies had magic of illusions, sleep, and confusion. Mischief makers— that was what all the books called them. The tiny humanoid creature fluttered around his arcanist, his bird-talon feet and tiny feathery wings an interesting sight.

Another arcanist had a cockatrice eldrin. Cockatrice magic involved turning objects to stone, setting things on fire, and flight. Even though most of its magics sounded dangerous, I couldn't help but find the cockatrice nonthreatening. She was a young silver chicken with a snake tail and feathers down her legs. Every time her arcanist walked around, she hustled to keep up, her wings outstretched, her breathing coming out as clucks and huffs.

The largest eldrin in the group was a yeti—a large snow creature with an ape-like body. A yeti offered their arcanist magic over ice, wind, and invisibility, but I thought they only lived in regions far from Fortuna. Nowhere near the isles, at any rate.

I stared at the beast for a while. It was about the size of a human teenager, but in a few years it would be a monstrous beast, perhaps two-stories tall.

The yeti arcanist, a thick guy with a neck made of

muscle, crossed his burly arms and glared at everyone around him. He huffed whenever the pixie got close and growled something rude when a girl ran into his elbow.

What a pleasant guy.

All the other arcanists wore fine robes, some with silk, silver, or gold. I silently thanked Illia for stopping me from rushing to Gregory the moment I entered town. I would've come across as a kook touched in the head and not as a respectable potential apprentice. Although my clothes weren't as nice as the ones around me, they were still tailored and high-end.

"Ah, so here you are."

I turned around, my excitement draining faster than the water in a bottomless barrel.

Why did it have to be Zaxis? Didn't he say he was going to apply to other guilds? Couldn't he just leave me alone? And Atty was nowhere to be seen. At least when she was around, sometimes he behaved.

"What're you doing here?" I asked.

"Frith arcanists are known across the world," Zaxis said.

He walked over to me, his phoenix perched on his arm. He wore a leather gauntlet to protect his flesh from the coal-black talons of his eldrin, just like Atty did, but I imagined his arm had to get tired from time to time if he kept the phoenix there often.

Zaxis smiled as he added, "And I heard Gregory Ruma doesn't have any apprentices right now."

"Why do *you* want to apprentice with him? Weren't you the one calling me a child for fawning over him?"

"You were so excited, it got me thinking. Ruma *is* famous. Legendary, even. I would make our whole island proud if I trained under him."

I gritted my teeth, my blood pumping hot enough to

burn. Zaxis only became interested in Ruma after I mentioned it. He wanted to take this from me—he wanted to compete, just like we had competed for the phoenixes. The worst part was his smug smile. It told me he didn't consider this a challenge. In his mind, the competition was already over.

His phoenix tilted his head. "I hope Gregory selects you as well," he said to me.

Zaxis glowered. "Why would you say that?"

"Arcanists can have more than one apprentice. And Volke hasn't done much to convince me he'd be like his parents. I watched him closely on the boat, just as you wanted, and he never attempted to steal from the sailors or—"

"*Forsythe*," Zaxis hissed. "Have you forgotten about Lyell?"

"Even that story makes me wonder. Parts don't line up. And Lyell did rush to Volke on the docks."

Zaxis huffed. He turned away from me, the soot of his phoenix—Forsythe—sprinkling to the ground. "Just stay out of my way, Volke. I'm going to become our island's most famous and powerful arcanist. You might have everyone else fooled, but not me."

I watched them walk away, my irritation still high. I felt sorry for the phoenix. Someday Forsythe would be just as arrogant and confrontational as Zaxis. That was how it worked, after all. But right now I still liked him. I think we would've made a great team if Forsythe had become my eldrin.

"Remember: anger and envy build nothing," Luthair said.

His advice reminded me of the Pillar. Step thirteen. *Tranquility. Without it, we cannot control our rage.*

Reo stepped up to a small podium and waved the arcanists over. I searched for Illia, but found no trace of her. Was she still in the tree? Hopefully she could hear everything.

Reo's ogata toad leapt to his side and let out a rough ribbit, silencing the whispers in the crowd. Once the arcanists were completely quiet, Reo smiled.

"H-hello," he began. "I'm honored to see so many of you tonight. Allow me to get straight to the point: this is an assessment. There is only one goal. You will have until dawn to bring me a star moth. Those of you who are successful will be considered by the Frith Arcanists to become apprentices, but it is ultimately up to them to decide who they will mentor. If none of them are impressed by your performance, then the Frith Arcanist Guild will have to reject you, even if you managed to secure a star moth."

"What's a star moth?" someone in the crowd blurted out.

Reo snapped his fingers. "I'm g-glad you asked. A star moth is not a mystical creature—it is simply a normal moth imbued with ambient magic. It glows in the moonlight, which is why our assessment takes place at night."

"Are they dangerous?" another arcanist asked.

"While, uh, they're typically harmless, star moths are extremely attuned to corrupted magic. When it's near, they shift forms and grow slightly larger. But that shouldn't be a concern."

"Corrupted magic?" I whispered.

Luthair shifted through the shadows around my feet. "Like the plague-ridden white hart in the mire."

"Hm."

"That's all you want us to do?" another arcanist blurted out. "Catch bugs? Do you think we're children? Why not base acceptance on a game of *ring toss*? Or hide-n-seek?"

His sarcasm got the crowd chuckling. I joined in, a little

nervous about the assignment myself. It sounded easy enough. Maybe too easy. Why had he given us all night to complete such a simple task? Perhaps they were grading us on something they didn't mention.

Finn croaked, jarring me out of my thoughts.

"You may begin," Reo shouted, his arms in the air.

11

STAR MOTHS

The other arcanists headed into the woods, some hustling, but most taking their time, much to my surprise. Did they think their victory assured? The pixie flitted between the branches of the trees, leaving a sparkle behind him as he flew. The yeti arcanist stomped off on his own, his eldrin lumbering behind him.

It wasn't hard to keep track of Zaxis. His phoenix glowed with an inner fire, much like a beacon or a torch. And when Forsythe took to the sky, he left a faint trail of embers.

Illia leapt down from the branches of her tree. She landed next to me, a few leaves caught in her wavy brown hair and hat. "There are so many star moths in these woods," she said.

"Really?"

"Reo said they glow in moonlight, right? I saw hundreds of them! They twinkle like stars caught on land. C'mon. This way."

She took my arm and hurried between the trees, her excitement greater than it had been in years. Nicholin clapped his paws together as we ran, like he didn't know what to do with all his extra energy.

We came to a clearing, and my jaw nearly hit the dirt. Illia had been right—hundreds of blue glowing dots filled the area. Some on the grass, some in the trees, some flying about. Everywhere I looked, I noticed more. How was it even a challenge to gather them up? I would be lucky if my clothes weren't covered in moths by the time I finished strolling through the woods!

"Don't be deceived," Luthair said from the shadows. "These are not what you seek."

"What're you talking about?" Nicholin said. "Look! They're glowing, just like the toad arcanist said."

Illia crouched down and scooped up a handful of the glowing insects. She stared at them for a long moment, her one eye scanning each before moving to the next. "Oh, no."

"What's wrong?" I asked as I walked to her side. I stared at her palm, and my throat seized.

They weren't moths. They were glowing beetles.

I turned my attention to the insects bobbing in the air.

Fireflies. Dragonflies.

But no moths.

"Does everything glow in these woods?" I asked.

"Yes," Luthair said. "These are the Night Sky Woodlands. The insects are known far and wide for their beauty."

"And you couldn't have said something sooner?"

Luthair didn't answer.

Illia released the beetles back on the grass and slowly made her way to the floating clouds of glowing blue dots. She and Nicholin captured them one by one, examined them, and then let them go.

I glanced around the clearing. Even if I didn't count any of the insects on the ground, there were hundreds of bugs, perhaps thousands. And most flew away whenever Illia or Nicholin reached for one. It would take hours to search this clearing alone, and what if there weren't any moths here? Until daybreak suddenly didn't seem like enough time.

Nicholin jumped from Illia's shoulders and searched across the ground. He kept his nose hovering over the grass until he came to a patch of clovers.

His eyes went wide and he gasped—a powerful enough inhale that a blue speck got sucked straight into his throat. He coughed and hacked and flailed around, startling the other insects and creating a small flurry of blue that wafted around us.

I shielded my eyes. Illia ran to Nicholin and patted his little back. He coughed up a glowing blue dot and kept his tongue hanging out of his mouth.

"Eh..."

Illia scooped the tiny thing into her hands. "Volke! Come look. I think it's a moth."

I jogged to her side and examined the insect. Sure enough—even if it was covered in saliva and not moving—it was a moth. A tiny moth. Maybe the size of the nail on my little finger. Much smaller than a normal moth, which meant it would be even harder to spot in a swarm.

"Congratulations," I said. "You got one."

"I'm not going back with it until you have one too," she said. "C'mon. I'll help you look."

I nodded. At no point did Reo say we couldn't help each other. He just said we were being assessed. I scanned the area, my gaze unable to pierce the darkness. How, exactly, were they watching us? I didn't see any judges or scholars. I didn't even see any other mystical creatures, just the ebony ink of night, the shine of the waxing moon, and the glitter of magical insects.

One by one, I searched.

Beetle.

Firefly.

Ant.

Aphid.

Cricket.

Mayfly.

Beetle, again. Thirty more ants. A whole nest of earwigs. A tree full of aphids. A centipede. Another beetle. There were so many insects in this damn forest, it practically rivaled a museum. Where were the spiders when you needed them?

Patience. Without it, you cannot see a seed grow into a tree.

I tried to repeat the words to myself as I worked, but it was difficult, especially after the third hour.

We moved to another clearing. And then another.

"I found one!" someone shouted a few trees over. "Finally!"

I stared between the trees, jealous of the pixie arcanist who had found something. Then the yeti arcanist lumbered out of the forest, twice the size of the pixie arcanist, and with three times the muscle.

"Didn't you say you'd give me your first moth?" the yeti arcanist asked, a cruel smile on his face.

The pixie arcanist, thin like a reed, forced a smile. "O-oh, uh, sure. H-here." He handed the moth over with a shaky hand.

"Good," the yeti said, his mouth filled with fangs. "Now we'll find a master to train with, my arcanist."

The yeti eldrin and his arcanist laughed as they headed toward Reo. Illia glanced to me and then resumed her search, her precious moth tucked away in her jacket pocket, Nicholin acting as its guard. I had no idea there would be thuggish tactics employed by the others. Was that even allowed? I didn't see anyone stopping it...

Another two hours.

Dawn approached.

Really? I couldn't find one? What kind of test was this? Some people just got lucky and others didn't? That wasn't fair!

I jumped when Illia placed her hand on my shoulder.

"Don't worry," she said. "We'll find one."

"Y-yeah," I muttered. Then I stepped away from the tree I was examining and exhaled. "Maybe we're going about this the wrong way. Where would moths normally go? You got lucky and found one in the grass, but surely there's a place that—" I stopped myself short, already aware of the answer.

Illia's eye widened. "Light," she whispered.

"Yeah," I replied. "Where's the most light?"

"When I was up in the tree I noticed the city had a lot of lamps. And the woods go all the way to the city wall."

"Yes! Illia, that's perfect! We should head in that direction. I'm sure that's where all the moths have to be."

She nodded along with my words.

Nicholin stroked his chin. "Yes, clever indeed. But we should hurry. There isn't much time."

Struck with a wave of energy, I ran toward the Fortuna walls. Although the timing would be tight, I was confident in our strategy. A moth would definitely be in the area. All I had to do was find it.

The sting of smoke filled my nose. I slowed my pace and covered my mouth with the sleeve of my coat. What was on fire?

"Forsythe, stop!"

"I'm sorry, but I can't."

I wove between a grouping of trees and found Zaxis

standing beside a smoldering fire consuming the shrubs of the woods. Forsythe waited above him, perched on a tree branch, his head hung low.

"You're killing all of them," Zaxis said as he ran both his hands through his fiery hair. "Can't you just lower the flames of your body for a little bit?"

"They *are* me," Forsythe replied as he stretched his wings. The feathers lay overtop a body of flame, and with each motion the flash of light lit the area. "I really can't help it."

"That's five dead moths. I can't return with ashes."

"I'm sorry, my arcanist."

"*Damn.*" He slammed a fist into the bark of a nearby tree, bloodying his knuckles. He pulled back his hand and held it close to his chest, but it didn't seem to quell his anger. He continued to curse under his breath.

Neither he nor his phoenix had acknowledged my presence, so I took a step back and hid in the shadows. While Zaxis huffed and glared at the fire, I made my way around the clearing as quietly as I could. Illia followed suit, giving Zaxis a quick glance before keeping pace with me.

I could tell Zaxis my plan. Then again, why would I help him? Well, Lyell had asked me to keep an eye on his brother. But did Zaxis really need any assistance? Apparently his phoenix was drawing moths to him. He'd get one eventually. Right?

"Illia," I whispered as I stopped a good distance from Zaxis.

"Okay," she said.

I lifted an eyebrow. "I haven't asked you anything yet."

"You were going to ask me to tell Zaxis what our plan was." She met my gaze and smiled. "Right?"

"I..." I almost wanted to deny it, simply because I was

afraid of how she would judge me. "Do you think we should just leave him?"

"I think we shouldn't be hostile with each other. We're all from the same island. Maybe this will make things right."

I nodded.

"Why don't you go tell him?" she asked. "He likes you the least."

"Huh. You don't say."

She responded with a sarcastic glare.

"C'mon," I said. "He won't believe me. I could be pulling him from the riptide, trying to save his life, and he would think I was secretly out to drown him. But you—he hasn't said much about you. I think he'll listen if you tell him."

"Guys, guys," Nicholin said, holding his front paws in the air. "*I'll* go talk to him. Everyone likes me."

Illia half-laughed as she patted his head. "We'll go together. Volke, we'll meet you at the wall." She turned, but stopped herself halfway. "Hey. If you run into another white hart or plague-ridden creature, you don't fight it without me, okay?"

Her request got me smiling. "All right."

"I mean it."

"It's a promise."

She headed back for Zaxis. I continued toward the wall, Luthair's shifting through the shadows more noticeable than before. He moved like a fish in the water, flitting from one dark puddle to the next, avoiding the moonlight that streamed down between open patches of leaves.

Then we reached the wall. I stopped a few feet from it and stared up. The stones, stacked together in perfect fashion, stood fifteen feet high. Torches sat on top, casting orange light into the edge of the woods.

But I didn't see any glowing insects. Not a single one.

I searched, my eyesight horrible thanks to the poor lighting. How could hundreds of bugs dwell in the wood a few feet away, but none were here?

I had been so certain this would work. I continued, regardless of my growing doubts. Maybe, because of the lighting, I just wasn't seeing them properly.

The crunch of leaves heralded Illia's approach. I turned around to tell her the bad news, but I stopped once I saw her panicked face. She flailed her arms. "Volke, look out!"

"Huh?"

A giant moth crashed out of the tree next to me, breaking branches as it fell toward the ground. The shock prevented me from moving, but Luthair coalesced into his armored form and grabbed me by the shoulder just in time to yank me from the moth's path.

The insect had to be as large as I was, and its wings, when opened, stretched a good twenty feet from point to point. Although it hadn't been glowing before, the moment it started beating its wings, a bright blue light emanated from its fat, fuzzy body.

To my horror, it opened its mouth, revealing a twisted tunnel of teeth—no order to it, just a spiral of sharp fangs all the way down its throat, like a meat grinder.

It screamed and flapped, twisting to get into the air.

It was a star moth, however, no doubt in my mind, even if it was hideous.

"We need to stop it," I said.

Illia glanced up as the insect continued to fly, almost reaching the tree line. "But—"

"Leave it to me," Nicholin shouted.

He leapt out of Illia's pocket and disappeared in a flash of light and sparkles. When he reappeared, he was above the moth and fell straight into its face, just above its giant black eyes. Nicholin poked one and the moth thrashed about, letting out another scream. Then it plummeted back to the forest.

"Stand back," Luthair said.

He stepped in front of me and drew his sword. Like his armor, the blade seemed to be made of shadow itself, black and with a luster that reflected the orange torch fire.

The moth hit the ground in a puff of bright blue dust. It washed over us in a wave, prickling my skin like a sunburn. The moment I inhaled, the sensation spread to my throat. I wheezed, but I could still breathe.

What was this?

Nicholin cried out and fell to the ground. He shivered and sobbed under the blue dust, completely incapacitated and writhing as though in pain. Luthair grunted and fell to one knee, his sword clattering to the ground.

They were stunned and unable to move.

Although the dust stung, it didn't render me defenseless. Illia took a step back as the moth forced itself up onto its six legs and screeched. Its oddly circular mouth remained open, the throat undulating, its many teeth scraping together.

"My blade," Luthair growled, his voice coming out strained. "Use it."

"I don't know how," I replied. Never once had I trained with a weapon.

"I'll help you."

When the moth approached Illia like a rabid dog, she waved her hand out and touched one of the insect's antennae. The limb disappeared with a flash, ripped from the moth's head and reappearing a few feet over, twitching. She had teleported it right off its body, just like she had teleported the breadfruit. The creature backed away and faced Nicholin.

I picked up Luthair's longsword. Like ink on a quill, some of the darkness slid from the blade and enveloped my hands, coating my skin and creating gloves up to my shoulders. As I lifted the weapon, my grip was controlled for me, the shadows guiding my hands.

The moth lunged for Nicholin, its mouth open, spittle flying out in bursts.

I raced forward and swung, unsure of a stance even though my arms moved with the muscle memory of a seasoned warrior. The blade sliced into the moth's neck with ease. The insect sputtered out a wet cry and then staggered to the left, its bright green insides spilling across the grass. I pulled the blade out and swung again, this time into the body. The moth toppled over and collapsed, its wings going limp and the blue dust settling onto the foliage.

It took me several deep breaths to calm my pounding heart.

It was dead.

I couldn't help but smile.

"That was amazing," I said.

Illia glanced at me, utter disbelief written across her face. "Are you serious?"

"Yeah. We killed a giant star moth. You don't think that's amazing?"

"We clumsily messed around with a giant corrupted moth and barely killed it before it bit one of us. This is an assessment, remember? We shouldn't act like amateurs. Stop celebrating."

"R-right." I straightened my posture and restrained my smile. How should I react? Most stories about Gregory

Ruma involved him going to the tavern afterward and winning a drinking game.

Then an odd thought hit me. Why was there a giant moth in the first place? Reo said they got larger near corrupted magic. I didn't see any other insects nearby, and certainly no other monstrous moths. I also didn't see any plague-ridden mystical creatures.

"Urg," Nicholin groaned.

Illia rushed to his side and scooped him up into her arms. "Are you okay?"

"Better now..."

I jogged to Luthair. He hadn't gotten out of his kneeling position, his helmet low and his tattered cape hung heavy over his shoulders.

I handed him his sword. "Thank you. I didn't know you could lend me your strength."

He managed to take it and return it to his scabbard. "Knightmares often fight as one with their arcanists. I *am* a suit of armor."

"You could be *my* armor and weapon?"

"Yes."

The thought of wearing an entire suit of shadow armor intrigued me, but the shifting colors of the sky warned me that dawn would soon be upon us. I didn't have time to daydream.

I jogged to the moth and kicked it to make sure it was dead. When it didn't move, I grabbed a leg and dragged it across the forest floor. The insect was surprisingly light-weight, despite its size. It made sense. How else could it have flown?

Illia tucked Nicholin in her jacket pocket and walked over to help me. "Here."

Luthair melted back into the shadows, no longer frozen

in place. Together, we hustled through the trees, creating a shallow furrow through the dirt as we dragged our catch. A moth was a moth, after all. Surely they wouldn't be upset with a giant one.

We arrived back at the starting point right as the first rays of a new day shone over the treetops. Reo stood in the clearing, Finn at his side. He held his hands together on the small of his back, chatting with his eldrin as we approached.

"I hope we're not late," I said. "But this guy was difficult to catch."

Reo's eyes widened as we approached. "Oh, my. Is that your star moth?"

"Yeah."

"It's so... large."

I didn't know what else to say so I repeated, "Yeah."

Illia reached into her pocket and pulled out her tiny moth. It was half-crushed and falling apart, but it was still technically there.

Reo took hers. "Very good. Both of you." He stared at the giant moth for a long moment, his eyebrows tightly knit together. "I'll... handle this. No n-need to worry."

I rubbed at my neck. "Okay. So, uh, can we join the Frith Guild?"

"You'll have to return to the guildhall at the end of the week. If one of our master arcanists was impressed by your skills, you'll have a letter waiting for you."

"That's it?"

"That's it."

Illia and I exchanged glances. She returned her attention to Reo first.

"How many new apprentices will they be taking on?" she asked.

"Six."

I caught my breath. There were already seven arcanists here tonight, and that wasn't even counting the other nights of the week. They were going to narrow their choices down to six? How would they decide? Obviously the assessment would play a part, but what were they looking for? Would turning in a giant moth net me extra points or would that upset them?

The uncertainty of the situation ate at me.

"You t-tried hard," Finn said. "Don't look so glum. You should be proud."

"Thank you," Illia said.

I took a step back and sighed.

There wasn't much I could do but wait.

12

REVENGE

"Here," Illia said. "Let me wipe your face."

Nicholin held still while Illia rubbed his nose and head with a damp towel. His white fur ruffled under her touch, and once she was done, Nicholin licked his arms and used them to smooth everything into place. The blue dust from the moth lingered on his legs and tail, and Illia took her time wiping away each speck.

Our inn room had two oil lanterns and one candle, enough to see, but heavy shadows lingered in the corners. Although Luthair typically remained out of sight as disembodied darkness, he stood in the far corner, his helmeted gaze on the floor. The cracks of his armor were visible with the flickering of the candle, some deep and jagged.

"Do you still feel the effects of the dust?" I asked.

He shook his helmet.

Satisfied he wasn't in pain, I took a seat on the edge of my bed and removed my boots. Illia and I didn't share a room in William's cottage, but the space had been so cramped that it didn't really matter. I knew how much she cared about tidiness. She had yelled at me time and time again about keeping my boots free of dirt and out of walkways. She and William both. So, I took the extra time to shove the boots under my bed, hiding any excess dirt on them.

Luthair walked out of the corner and approached me, his armor suit body clinking with each step. I glanced up at him, his helmet a void of darkness with no eyes to lock on to.

"I must apologize," he said.

"For what?" I asked.

"For failing you. A simple star moth never should've incapacitated me."

"It's fine. I didn't get hurt."

Luthair said and did nothing. It was difficult to understand him sometimes, like trying to read the emotions of a wooden plank, but I could tell he wasn't satisfied with our conversation.

I shrugged. "It really is okay."

"I was incapacitated when Mathis died. Frozen by fell magic and forced to watch as he was cut down." Luthair placed a gauntleted hand on the hilt of his sword. "I should've learned my lesson then. In difficult situations, I should take point."

"Oh, yeah," Nicholin added. "I remember all that ice. You couldn't move at all."

Illia dried his legs and tail. "You were there when Luthair's arcanist died?"

"Uh-huh. I was on an island, along with a few other mystical creatures. I was born there! The researchers and caretakers told me all about how rare rizzels are, and it was really nice for a while, but then the plague broke out."

Luthair kept his attention on Nicholin, and I did the

same. I was curious about their past, especially how they ended up on our island.

Nicholin continued, "But when we were all organizing for an evacuation, something happened. There was fighting."

"Who was fighting?" Illia asked.

"I don't know. One of the researchers hid me and a white hart on a small boat in the harbor. Two arcanists said they were there to save us. One was a knightmare arcanist, and the other was a golem arcanist."

"Yes," Luthair added. "Mathis and I were on a mission. We had been following signs of the plague for weeks, and our search led us to this remote island of breeders. They kept rare creatures, but someone was infecting them."

Nicholin nodded. "Yeah! And then a storm broke out! Ice everywhere. Our boat couldn't leave the dock, cuz it was trapped, and Luthair was practically a statue—separated from his arcanist. I hid in the hold of the ship, and the golem smashed the ice so we could get away. I think he saved Luthair, too. But even though we escaped... something was wrong. The arcanist who saved us said we couldn't touch him. We couldn't even be near him. And we didn't have much of a crew. We crashed, and the arcanist left us in that mire. He said we had to wait for him and not go near the town."

I turned to Luthair. "Is that right?"

"Yes," he said. "I never should've separated from Mathis. If we had been merged, perhaps our combined strength could've saved him from that fiend."

Illia scooped Nicholin into her arms and scooted to the edge of her bed. "Who was he? The man who killed Mathis."

"I don't know his name. All I know is that he was a

master of his magic. The storm and ice were all his. We knew he was the spreader of the plague. He captured so many mystical creatures. None of them could escape his hoarfrost. Even the researchers and breeders... He kept most of them alive. Collecting them. Mathis was a master swordsman, and he tried to stop the fiend, but even that was useless."

"I'm sorry," I said.

Luthair remained quiet.

I continued, "Wait, the killer was also the one spreading the plague? Why?"

"I'm not sure. Pirates use it to spread chaos before they attack a port or town, but some arcanists believe corrupted magic makes you stronger. Mathis was convinced the man we were hunting wanted to test out the plague on mystical creatures—that was why he targeted a place of rare and exotic breeds."

"He sounds like a lunatic," I said. "Dastardly in every sense of the word. We'll definitely find him and stop him one day."

"For everyone's sake, I hope you're right."

I knew I had made a promise to Luthair—and I would keep it, even if it took me to the blackest waters of the abyssal hells—but I didn't want to throw my life away either. Perhaps, since I knew this arcanist wielded magic of water and ice, I could think of a way to counter his tactics. William always said naval officers studied their opponents before engaging in combat. This was a similar situation. I had time to plan, so I shouldn't waste it.

"Don't fret," Luthair said. "You should focus on learning magic first. Then we can deal with that monster in human flesh."

I could practically feel the hate, regret, and sadness rolling off Luthair's midnight armor.

Arcanists and their eldrin were partners. They were bonded for life, or until one died, but even then they typically died together. And since the eldrin became like the arcanist, it was as if they were one and the same—two beings woven together through magic. It had to be painful losing his arcanist, more than I could even imagine. I wanted to see Luthair's unfinished business set right, if only to give him peace of mind.

And it was the least I could do for Mathis. He deserved to be avenged.

I stood from my bed, heat coursing through me. "We'll stop this man no matter what."

Luthair chortled.

"What?" I asked.

"You have an amusing—and naïve—enthusiasm to fight the evils of this world."

Nicholin nodded. "Yeah. Calm down. You can't even wield magic yet."

I deflated a bit and retook my seat back on the bed. "One step at a time, I suppose."

"You really are similar to Mathis," Luthair said. "He had a strong sense of justice. He became excitable whenever he heard about a person or place that needed saving."

"It's good to hear we're similar."

"Indeed."

The closer I was in temperament and personality to his old arcanist, the less likely Luthair would succumb to madness. If I was different, it would guarantee that Luthair would crack further.

Before anyone could further our conversation, a light knock on our door echoed throughout the room. Luthair shifted back into the shadows, and Nicholin hunched his back, his ears flat against his skull.

I walked over and opened the door.

"Zaxis," I said, half-shocked, half irritated. We never told him where we were staying. How did he find us?

He stood stiff, with long dark robes of black and indigo. The symbol of the charberry tree was stitched onto the chest in shimmering gold thread. It wasn't the outfit he had worn to the assessments. Had he dressed up afterward?

Zaxis smoothed his outfit as he narrowed his gaze into a glare.

"What're you doing here?" he asked. "I thought this was Illia's room."

"What do you want with Illia?" I asked.

"I have business with her, obviously." He glanced past me and gave Illia a quick smile. "Do you mind if we speak? In private."

Illia stood from her bed. Nicholin dropped all hostility and watched her go with wide eyes, almost as if he felt he was being abandoned. Illia gave me a quick *don't worry about it* look as she stepped out into the hall and shut the door.

I cursed under my breath.

What did Zaxis want with Illia? Nothing good, no doubt.

Curiosity got the better of me. I pressed my ear against the door.

"Oh, good idea," Nicholin said. He scampered off the bed and did the same, his furry ears erect.

The hallway didn't have much activity. It was a small inn, no more than four rooms, and most of the residents had long since gone to bed. The quiet atmosphere made it easy to hear Illia and Zaxis, despite their hushed voices.

"You don't have the coin for your own room?" Zaxis asked.

"That's not it."

"You don't have to stay with Volke now that you're an arcanist. Why don't I get you a separate room? It's the least I could do."

"No, thank you. I don't mind sharing."

"You're not actually siblings. No need to act like it."

I clenched my jaw, half-tempted to storm out into the hall and throw him from the building. Who did he think he was? It wasn't enough to harass me, now he had to badger Illia as well? Or was he trying to court her by offering her a fancy room? Ha! Like that would work. Never. Not Illia.

I huffed, my pulse high and my hands gripped tight into fists.

Illia didn't want someone like Zaxis. Had he ever even had a pleasant conversation with her before now? Of course not.

"A knight gives a woman her privacy," Luthair growled from the shadows.

Although I wanted to tell Luthair to shove his advice straight into the abyssal hells, I knew he was right. Illia wouldn't appreciate me spying on her conversation. I stepped away from the door.

Nicholin didn't care. He kept his ear to the door, nodding along with a conversation I could no longer hear.

I waited, my thoughts dwelling on them and unable to move forward.

When Illia returned, I jumped to her side, expecting her to be just as frustrated as I was. "Are you okay?" I asked.

"Yes," she said. "I'm fine. He just wanted to thank me for the information about the moths." She shut the door and walked back to her bed.

Ah. That made sense. Not that I was worried. Still, I didn't like him coming around. And it made me uncomfortable that he had found our inn. And what did it matter if we shared a room? It wasn't like I was crowding Illia or bothering her.

Nicholin leapt up in her arms, and Illia held him close. She smiled.

Then again, I had never asked her opinion on the matter. I had just done it to save money.

"Uh," I began. "Illia. It doesn't bother you that we're sharing a room, right?"

She shot me a glare. "Were you listening to my conversation?"

"Not all of it," I quickly said. "Just... the first part."

"I don't care about sharing a room."

"Yeah." I paced along the far wall, still unable to think of anything else. "But you're a woman now. You had your coming-of-age ceremony, and I'm—"

"*Volke*. Stop." She threw herself against the bed, Nicholin held tight in her arms to the point he looked like he had trouble breathing. In a whisper she said, "Don't make this awkward. We've never had to talk about this kind of stuff before. Everything is fine between us."

Illia didn't look at me. She didn't even move. She just stared at the wall, her back facing me, Nicholin squirming in her arms. This was her *I don't want to talk right now* mood. I wanted to make things right between us, but I knew if I pressed the issue, she would grow angrier and more frustrated.

So I dropped it.

Well, I dropped it verbally. That didn't mean I let it go. It was all I could think about for the rest of the night. We were adults now. Things were different. I couldn't continue acting as though we were still orphans taken in by Gravekeeper William.

Small details floated into my thoughts, and added to my enlightenment. Illia had insisted we purchase clothes separately. She changed while I was at the market, avoiding all possibility of us seeing each other. I hadn't given it much thought before, but she obviously had. I should've paid more attention, but I was so focused on the guild and the assessment, I hadn't even thought about anything else.

The guild.

I mulled over the situation. Would we be accepted? I liked thinking about that a lot more, so I rolled onto my bed and tried to block out the rest.

13

THE ATLAS TURTLE

The end of the week came faster than a storm on the ocean.

I woke with the sun, jittery and unable to stay still. I didn't want to wake Illia or Nicholin—they were curled up together in their blankets—so I exited our room and headed for the guildhall. Would there be any news? I couldn't wait to find out. I ran the whole way there.

To my disappointment, no one had arrived yet. I decided to head for the marketplace to purchase breakfast.

I enjoyed exploring the local produce. The fish in Fortuna weren't as good as the fish around the Isle of Ruma, but their breads and red meats were ten times better than anything I had ever tasted before.

After eating a hearty sandwich, I made my way back to the guildhall. When I arrived, the doors were open and arcanists were thronging inside. The pixie arcanist kept his eldrin in his pocket, and the cockatrice arcanist held his puffy chicken creature in his arms.

The yeti arcanist shoved his way into the building. I waited until they were all in before I entered.

I walked over to the Frith Guild counter. Reo stood waiting, a bright smile on his face. When I approached, he turned to Finn. The toad lashed out his tongue and grabbed a letter inside a cubby on the back wall. The sticky appendage retraced back into Finn's mouth, the letter in one piece, although marked with a dot of saliva. Reo detached the paper and handed it over.

I broke the wax seal so fast I didn't even see what insignia the Frith Guild had used.

Dear Volke Savan,

I stopped reading, struck by the name. Savan was William's last name, not mine. Had his letter of recommendation introduced me as his son? I cherished the thought for a moment longer before continuing.

I am pleased to inform you that your performance in the Night Sky Woodlands impressed a master arcanist within our guild. Everett Zelfree has trained many talented apprentices and looks forward to mentoring you. If you accept his offer, please arrive at our guild headquarters before sunset. Failure to do so will result in a retraction of the offer.

I look forward to seeing your progress.
    Guildmaster Liet Eventide

While I was overjoyed I had been selected to join the guild, the name *Everett Zelfree* took me by surprise. I had read about him before. He was once a prominent arcanist, known for his ability to infiltrate pirate crews and disguise himself as anyone. But like Gregory Ruma, the last I had read, he was injured in a terrible battle against sea raiders near the Crescent Islands.

I was starting to see a pattern. All of William's books were out of date. Clearly, I didn't have the latest information.

"Is there a letter for Illia?" I asked.

"That's private," Reo replied. "I'm not allowed to give out such information."

I held my letter close, my chest tight. If I got one, surely, she would as well.

"Did you receive an offer?" Reo asked.

I nodded. "From Master Arcanist Zelfree."

Reo and Finn exchanged narrowed glances.

"Is something wrong?" I asked.

"Oh, it's n-nothing. He just hasn't taken apprentices in a while."

"Why?"

Silence. His refusal to answer almost caused me to jump straight to anger. Did he think I couldn't handle the truth? Why mention something and then keep it from me?

Finn turned his toad head. "His last apprentices died. Killed by pirates. Since then, he hasn't accepted anyone else, even people who b-begged him to be their mentor."

The news settled into my thoughts. Did that mean I impressed him so much he had to have me, or was this just a coincidence now that he felt comfortable with having new apprentices?

"I didn't get in?" the yeti arcanist said. He tore his letter in half and threw it on the floor. "What nonsense is this? I got you a star moth!"

Reo shook his head. "I'm sorry. No master arcanists wanted to offer you a mentorship."

"None of the master arcanists were even there!"

No answer. The yeti huffed, exhaling ice all over the floor. His arcanist stormed out of the guildhall, but I didn't care. Someone like him didn't deserve the majesty of the Frith Guild. It did make me wonder, though... How had the master arcanists come to their conclusions?

Before I could leave, Zaxis sauntered through the guildhall doors, soot on his shoulders. He patted himself clean before approaching Reo.

"I'm here for my letter," he said.

I half-laughed. "Are you that certain you got one? I just saw some guy storm out of here because he got a rejection."

"They would be fools not to accept me."

Finn used his tongue to retrieve another letter hidden in the back cubbies. Reo unstuck it and handed the paper over. I waited with bated breath, wondering what it would say.

But Zaxis's smile only widened.

Of course. I never had much luck.

"Look at this," he said as he handed it over.

Dear Zaxis Ren,

I am pleased to inform you that a master arcanist within our guild wishes to mentor you. Gregory Ruma is a man who needs little introduction. He has had centuries of magical experience and traveled the world over. If you accept his offer, please arrive at our guild headquarters before sunset. Failure to do so will result in a retraction of the offer.

. . .

I look forward to seeing you in our guild.
    Guildmaster Liet Eventide

I almost didn't finish reading the letter.

Gregory Ruma took *him* as an apprentice? I bit back all my commentary. What did Ruma see in Zaxis? What had Zaxis even done? The letter didn't even mention it! It sounded as though Ruma already wanted Zaxis before the assessment. How was that fair?

Dammit.

I swore the heavens were plotting to give everything I ever wanted to Zaxis and he took some sort of sick delight in allowing it to happen.

Zaxis snatched back his letter.

"Congratulations," I forced myself to say, though I didn't mean it. This entire situation was my own fault. I never should've suggested Illia help him. Maybe Forsythe would've burned all their moths, and then he would've been rejected.

"Well," Zaxis said as he turned on his heel. "Looks like I should be on my way. I wouldn't want to waste this glorious opportunity. Perhaps Forsythe and I will see you around."

He exited the guildhall, his head high and his stride long. I watched him go with my jaw clenched tight. William always told me it was a fool's game to compare lives with other people. *Envy is for small-minded people*, he'd said.

It was hard sometimes to apply such lessons to real life, however. How was I supposed to ignore everything that had happened between us? We were the same age, from the same island, with the same goals—it would be insane *not* to compare.

And everyone already compared us. If I didn't keep up, I could already hear what they would say.

He's just not as talented as Zaxis.

Of course, he would fail. It's in his blood.

It's cute he had dreams, but we all knew he would never accomplish them.

Their phantom judgments drilled into my thoughts, killing my desire to face the world and continue trying.

Atty walked into the guildhall, pulling me from my whirlpool of doubt and misery. She swished her long golden hair over her shoulder and smiled. "Good morning."

"Good morning," I replied in a quiet voice.

"Were you accepted?"

For a moment I didn't know what she was referring to. Then I held up my letter. "O-oh, uh, yes. Here." I showed her the text.

Atty scanned the words and smiled. "Ah, so you impressed Master Everett Zelfree? I read about his travels with Schoolmaster Tyms."

"He's impressive."

"You're lucky to have someone like him as a mentor."

The words eased my doubt. I *was* lucky. Everett Zelfree wasn't some chump to be pushed aside, even if his last apprentices had died. He had been an arcanist for over a century. And I had impressed him—legitimately impressed him.

While I convinced myself I wasn't a failure, Atty got her own letter from Reo and Finn. She opened it, thanked the two of them, and then returned to my side. I was surprised when she came back, though I didn't let it show. I straightened my posture and motioned to the paper.

"Did you get accepted?" I asked.

"Yes," she said.

But she didn't show me her letter. Instead, she tucked it away in her pocket, safe and secure. Although I wanted to ask, I kept the question to myself. I shouldn't pry, though I did wonder when she went to take the assessment. I hadn't seen her the night the rest of us went to get our star moths.

Atty touched my shoulder. "I'm glad we're in the same guild, Volke."

"O-oh, thank you. I mean—it'll be great to have you in the same guild as well."

Not the smoothest sentence I had ever delivered, but I saved it at the end. I hoped.

Then Atty left.

I rubbed my upper arm, dwelling on the short moment of contact. I had never seen her touch Zaxis's shoulder. Or anyone's shoulder.

The winds outside picked up. I jogged to the front door and glanced to the sky. It had been cloudless earlier. In a flash, the sky swirled and darkened. Clouds piled together like a herd of black sheep, blotting out the sun and lacing the winds with a cold chill.

I stepped out onto the street. "What's going on?" I asked a passing man with a bag full of carrots.

A flash of rain pelted the entire city, but only for a few seconds, as though the heavens coughed and forgot to cover their mouth. The man secured his pack shut, protecting his vegetables.

"Oh, this again," he said.

"Does this happen often?"

"Storms happen frequently enough," he replied. "This ain't no storm, though. It's those flashy arcanists. They like makin' a show. Just you wait. You'll see somethin' good yet."

Making a show?

I headed toward the docks. Despite the creeping chill, I

moved with energy and purpose. Crowds of people clogged the roadways, making travel by foot damn near impossible, even for an arcanist. Frustrated, I jumped onto the wheels of a nearby carriage and used the extra height to pull myself onto the roof of a building. The A-frame roof made for a steep trek, but the tiles were easy to grip, even when wet.

Once on top, I turned my attention to the nearest pier.

A tremendous flash of lightning lit the sky. Thunder chased after, strong enough to rattle the windows and pierce straight to my bone. Luthair shifted through the shadows as another round lit the sky. I knew some arcanists could control the weather, but I had never seen a demonstration so showy before.

A flurry of snow soon followed, but like the rain, it lasted only a few seconds. People lifted their hands in the air, trying to catch the snowflakes as they approached the earth. Most evaporated before anyone could hold them, but I managed to catch a few on my tongue.

The ocean waters beyond the docks swirled into whirlpools. Two cyclones of saltwater rose upward, forming pillars of ocean as thick as forty oak trees, each stretching straight to the sky.

Rapt by the show of magic, I almost didn't notice the massive leviathan snaking through the ocean. Its shiny scales glistened with each new flash of lightning. The serpent-like body must've been as long as ten galley ships and as thick as a three-mast sailing ship. Although the mystical creature never lifted his head out of the water, I already knew who he was.

Decimus—Gregory Ruma's legendary leviathan.

Which meant the storms had to be his doing.

As fast as the clouds had gathered, they dissipated, each breaking apart and smoothing into wisps of their former selves. The water hanging in the air mixed with the sunlight and created rainbows throughout the city.

The citizens of Fortuna cheered, shaking the city more than the thunder had.

I leapt down from the roof and nearly collided with Illia.

"What're you doing here?" I asked as I stumbled back.

"Collecting my letter," she said. "I can't believe you left me at the inn!"

I rubbed the back of my neck and stared at the ground. "I didn't want to wake you, but I couldn't wait either."

Nicholin snorted. "Next time you better not ditch us! We're the stars of the show, for crying out loud. You need to have us in your life at all times."

"I think Ruma is at the docks," I said, trying to switch the subject. Especially since it was all I could think about. "We should go see him."

Illia crossed her arms. "We should get to the guild first. Didn't you read the letter? Besides, we'll get to speak to him there. We'll never get to talk to him out on these streets." She motioned to the congested roads, every inch jam-packed with people.

"What did your letter say?" I asked.

She handed it over.

Dear Illia Savan,

I am pleased to inform you that your performance in the Night Sky Woodlands impressed two master arcanists within our guild. Everett Zelfree, a talented man with a penchant for rare mystical creatures, and Gregory Ruma, an adventurer known the world over. If you accept either of their offers, please arrive at our guild headquarters before sunset. Failure to do so will result in a retraction of the offers.

I look forward to seeing your progress.
   Guildmaster Liet Eventide

Both Ruma and Zelfree? Amazing. And unlike Zaxis's letter, which got me angry, Illia's filled me with earnest enthusiasm. We would be in the same guild, training with famous master arcanists. Life couldn't be better.

I went to hug her, but I stopped and moved my arms around as though I had always intended to cross them over my chest. We were adults. No need to make a childish display. No need to make physical contact. I was a man. She was a woman.

Gods, it was so awkward.

"Congratulations," I said. I handed her back her letter.

Illia shoved my satchel into my arms. It contained my clothes—something I didn't want to be without—and I slung it over my shoulder. I hadn't even noticed she had been carrying it.

"We can celebrate later," she said. "Right now, we need to get to the guild."

"Where is the guild?"

"I asked Reo the same question. And you'll never believe this. Remember that mystery island when we arrived in Fortuna?"

"Yes."

"That's the guild's headquarters."

The way she said it—with a slight smile and a tap to the

side of her head—I already knew she was hiding something else from me.

"What is it really?" I asked.

"You'll see. Follow me."

Nicholin clapped his paws. "Yeah! Follow us!"

It took us a while to weave through the crowds, but we eventually made our way to the far eastern dock. Several skiffs waited to take the new apprentices to the mysterious island out in the bay. Illia and I were the first to arrive. No sign of Zaxis and Atty, but I suspected they would join us soon enough.

No sign of Gregory Ruma, either. I was sure he would be on the dock, but perhaps he was at the island.

We wasted no time in departing. Illia and I squeezed onto a skiff and headed straight for the island, the ocean breeze rushing over us with an energizing presence. The waves rocked out tiny boat. Perhaps some people would get seasick, but not me. Islanders never got seasick, that was what William had said.

The moment we neared our destination, I understood what Illia had been hiding from me.

It wasn't an island.

It was an *atlas turtle*—a massive mystical creature from epic tales of old. Their shells created lush dirt capable of growing delicious produce and supporting all types of wildlife. They grew to gigantic proportions. The Frith Guild was a manor house built on a single corner of the vast creature's shell. There was even a small lake on the opposite end, its clear water shimmering under the morning light.

I thought atlas turtles had gone extinct. It was so massive! How old was this one?

The turtle's fins moved under the ocean water, creating waves with each slight gesture. Its head rose above the surface as we sailed toward it, the giant eyes larger than the skiff we rode.

"Whose eldrin is this?" I whispered.

Illia giggled. "You sound like you're in shock."

"Do you see this? It's... gargantuan."

"It's the guildmaster's eldrin—Liet Eventide's."

Although I had seen Liet Eventide's name in several books, I couldn't remember much about her. She was an ancient arcanist, one of the few I remember reading in the front of every history book.

"What's her eldrin's name?" I asked.

"Reo said the atlas turtle's name is Gentel. She's very nice. At least, that's what Finn said."

Gentel's green scales glittered, even while underwater.

While most normal turtles had dome-shaped shells, atlas turtles had flatter shells, easy to mistake for land. I wanted nothing more than to speak with Gentel and ask her about all the adventures she must have been on. She was too huge to really speak with her, however. Maybe one day I could venture onto her head and shout, but otherwise I doubted she would hear anything I said from the boat.

We arrived at the small pier on Gentel's shell and found two individuals waiting for us—one man and one woman, both with long, flowing coats and shiny silver pendants.

The woman's coat, long enough to reach her knee-high boots, had scales and feathers stitched into the fabric. Dragon scales? Pegasus feathers? They worked as patchwork, mending what would otherwise be tears or holes. Her hat rustled with the wind, two phoenix tail feathers hanging off the side, their peacock-like extravagance easy to identify.

"Welcome," she said. "You must be our second and third new apprentices. Volke and Illia, I assume? I'm so happy to finally meet William's children."

Guildmaster Liet Eventide. It had to be. And the silver pendant around her neck glittered in the daylight, the design of a sword and shield plain on the face.

Her arcanist mark—it was an atlas turtle—glowed with a gentle inner light. I had never seen a mark do such a thing. I had never read about it either.

I stared, transfixed, wondering what caused such a phenomenon.

Up close she appeared advanced in age, perhaps in her early sixties, though I knew she had to be centuries older. Her silver hair was tied back in a tight braid, some strands glistening in the morning light, shining with the brilliance of polished metal. Her eccentric coat fluttered in the wind, adding to the sight.

"Thank you for meeting us out here," Illia said. "It's an honor, Guildmaster Liet Eventide."

Illia elbowed me, and I snapped out of my awe.

"Yes," I muttered. "It's an honor to meet you, Guildmaster Eventide."

The guildmaster smiled. "Please, call me Grandmaster Arcanist Guildmaster of the Frith Arcanist Guild, Liet Helvinair Eventide the Second."

Both Illia and I stared at her for a moment, my tongue already twisting just thinking about saying that name.

The guildmaster smiled wider and laughed—a full-body laugh that highlighted the lines on her face. She must have laughed often, with more lively energy than people half her age.

"It never fails," she said. "Young arcanists are always so serious! Don't worry. You may call me Liet or Eventide. If you must be formal, for some reason, Guildmaster is also acceptable."

"O-okay," I said, half-laughing myself.

Illia joined in the chuckling. She gave me an *I like this lady* kind of look.

The man next to the guildmaster stepped forward. His coat was a mix of pirate clothes and armor—thick with leather, worn with age. His hair fell to his shoulders, and his beard was kept trim. When a strong ocean wind washed over the rest of us, it didn't seem to affect him. On the contrary, he was caught in his own personal breeze that kept his coat fluttering, his hair flowing back, and his shirt slightly open—all a magical show to heighten his appearance. And his silver pendant, with the same sword and shield design, sat right in the middle of his bare chest.

He had been the one controlling the faux storm earlier.

And I already knew who he was. His reputation preceded him.

Gregory Ruma.

"It's a great honor to meet you," I said, still dazed he was only twenty feet from me.

His smile reminded me of William—easy-going, charismatic, no hint of malice—and when he relaxed, he hooked his thumbs into the belt loops of his trousers.

The leviathan mark on his forehead was so prominent and extensive that it went into his hair, wrapped around his neck, and disappeared beneath his shirt. Did it cover his body? I had never seen an arcanist mark get so large. Both his and the guildmaster's marks intrigued me like no others.

Ruma swept back his shoulder-length brown hair.

"While I was eager to see the phoenixes, it's nice to finally see a rizzel. Haven't seen one of those in decades."

Nicholin held himself up on Illia's shoulder. "Why, yes. I am super special. Thank you for recognizing that."

A sharp pain filled my shoulder. I stifled a cry and whipped around. It hadn't been Illia and there was no one else around. But the shadows on my clothes revealed my attacker. Luthair tightened his grip, even though he opted not to take full form.

"Luthair," I hissed under my breath. "What're you doing?"

"It's him," Luthair whispered straight into my ear.

"What?"

"His voice. I would recognize it anywhere. And the magic... it all fits."

"What're you talking about?"

"The man who killed Mathis. It was Gregory Ruma."

14

MENTOR

The information didn't register for a long moment. Gregory Ruma? A murderer? No. It had to be a joke. Some jest Luthair made up to deceive me. No matter how many times I replayed his accusation in my head, it was the only rational conclusion I could reach.

Luthair had to be mistaken.

Guildmaster Eventide smiled and motioned to the stone path that led to the manor house. "Please, allow me to show you to the map room. Once you get settled, I'm sure Master Zelfree will be awake enough to introduce himself."

She headed for the building, but my legs remained frozen in place. Luthair's shadowy grip tightened on my shoulder. What was I supposed to do? Surely Luthair didn't want me to attack Ruma. Not here. Not on the docks of the atlas turtle.

Even if I had promised to bring Luthair's former arcanist's killer to justice, if I acted now it would be tantamount to suicide. Ruma had vast magical powers, and one quick glance around the guild's grounds revealed dozens of other arcanists nearby who would surely rush to his aid.

Not that Ruma would need aid, but still.

Illia touched my elbow. "Let's go," she whispered, her one eye searching my gaze. "No time to get cold feet."

Luthair released me.

I didn't know what to say, so I remained silent. After a deep inhale and exhale, I took a step toward the path. I would have to talk to Luthair in private to really understand the situation. Until then, I would just pretend I hadn't heard the information.

Ruma placed a hand on my shoulder, stopping me dead in my tracks. My heart leapt into my throat, cutting off my breath.

"You're not lookin' so good, son," he said with a half-chuckle. "Seasick, is that it? We're gonna have to break you of that before the week is over."

I had to relax. He wasn't attacking me.

Up close, I noticed he had a few scars on his chin—deep enough hair didn't grow—but his face, golden after baking in the sun, was marked with laugh lines similar to the guild-master. Although centuries old, he appeared no more than forty, perhaps forty-one or forty-two. Still a man in his formidable years. Again, I was reminded of William. Even the jovial tone in his voice put me at ease.

Luthair had to be wrong.

Ruma patted me on the back and returned his gaze to the ocean. "No response? You're an odd one, aren't ya? That's fine. I haven't met a man worth knowin' who wasn't a little odd himself."

Illia motioned to the tiny pier mounted to the turtle's shell. "Master Ruma, are you staying here?"

"I'll be in after a moment. I like the crowds I can draw with my sorcery. Winds, sleet, rainbows—the people of Fortuna always love a good show."

Sure enough, people overcrowded the Fortuna docks, some with kites, long banners, or ribbons. When Gregory lifted his hand, a powerful gust rushed past the jubilant crowd, catching all the windswept toys and swirling them around.

His leviathan, Decimus, rose close to the surface of the ocean, his blue and aqua scales shimmering just beneath the waves. Each twist and movement barely disturbed the water as he swam under the atlas turtle and disappeared. The citizens of Fortuna replied with thunderous cheers.

Illia and I took the path to the guild. She practically dragged me along the path. Once we were out of earshot from Ruma, she asked, "What's wrong with you?"

"Everything is fine," I muttered.

"No, it's not," Illia said with a huff.

"Why do you say that?"

Nicholin stared at me with a sarcastic glare. "Are you daft? You've been talking about Gregory Ruma for seven days straight. Then he's right in front of you and all you can manage is a *nice to meet you*? Hmph!"

"Thank you," Illia said as she patted his head. "That's exactly what I'm trying to say. It isn't like you."

I hadn't said much to him? Of course not. What would I have said? *Hey, did you happen to kill some innocent arcanists in your many travels? I have a knightmare who claims you did.* Yes, I could see it all clearly. Everything would've gone over smoothly. It was a common question he had no doubt heard millions of times.

"I'll talk to you about it later," I muttered.

Without another word, Illia continued on the path, walking faster with each step, her wavy hair trailing behind her. Her reaction didn't surprise me. She had the same narrowed stare and slight frown that told me she was irritated beyond speaking.

She did surprise me, however, when she slowed and turned around. "Volke."

"Y-yes?"

Silence settled between us. I stopped and waited, but she never continued.

"Forget it," Illia muttered.

The rest of our walk remained stuck in an awkward quiet. What did she want to say? Should I have revealed Luthair's accusation? No. First I had to talk to Luthair. I couldn't go throwing around a bunch of misinformation. What if someone heard?

The guildmaster stood by the door of the manor. Had she been waiting long? Hopefully she didn't think we were wasting her time.

We reached the manor house and allowed ourselves a second to absorb the massive building.

The red bricks and pale white ivory contrasted perfectly with the ivy growing up the lattice fencing. All three stories had pristine windows and decorative clay designs interlaid with bricks. Etchings of mystical creatures—from the phoenix to the sphinx—were hidden in every detail. Even some of the shrubs in the garden were cut to appear like unicorns, harpies, and bugbears.

And, of course, there was a bird bath with a statute of an atlas turtle holding up the dish, larger than three grown men.

"Frith Manor has stood for one hundred and twenty-two years," Eventide said. She smiled, and with a flick of her wrist, the giant double doors opened to the main room of the manor. "The last manor house was destroyed by a stubborn pirate lord who swore vengeance on me. Interesting story, that one. But never fear, I've taken precautions to make sure the grounds are safer than ever. Your training will occur without incident."

"Do you fight many pirates?" Illia asked as we both walked inside.

"Plenty. A few smaller nations have practically turned pillaging, plundering, and piracy into a profession."

"No one stops them?"

"Well, *we* stop them," Eventide replied with a laugh. "But we aren't an army. I can't defeat entire nations and tell them to change their ways. We simply come to the aid of communities who call for our services. That's why we're heading to the Crescent Isles."

Illia held her head a little higher and smiled. "I can't wait until we find some deserving pirates."

I glanced around the front room. While I had been impressed with the exterior, I found the interior to be a place made of my wildest fantasies. Scrolls hung long on the walls, written in an ancient language I had only heard of. The stairway banister was carved wood, every inch depicting dragons, leviathans, and undines, all spun together in a serpentine twister. A chandelier hung overhead with glass orbs filled with eternal fireflies—undead insects that glowed with a pale white light, much like the star moths.

"Amazing," I whispered.

Illia offered me a knowing smirk. "There's the Volke I know."

Nicholin swished his tail from side to side. "Jeez. This place even rivals my greatness."

Several arcanists and their eldrin strolled the halls of the building. They all stopped and greeted the guildmaster with a deep bow and an excitable tone in their voice.

"It's a pleasure to see you, Guildmaster," one woman said.

A man added, "Back from your overseas trek already? I thought you wouldn't join us again for another fortnight."

"I wanted to meet the new apprentices," Eventide answered. "Once we leave Fortuna, I'll be on my way again. Only for a few months. Maybe more."

Guildmaster Eventide would be leaving us for a while? The news saddened me.

The woman and man nodded and shared a smile.

None of the arcanists appeared to wear uniforms. This man wore black slacks and a button-up shirt, while the woman wore robes and a thick hat with a large brim.

They did have one thing in common, however. They all wore pendants around their necks with the same ornate sword and shield design, but theirs had a crack running through. Plus, instead of silver, their pendants were bronze.

The symbol was that of the Frith Guild—a token that marked the wearers as members.

As if the guildmaster could read my thoughts, she reached into her coat pocket and withdrew several pendants. She handed a bronze one to me and then one to Illia. "Wear these. They mark you as apprentices to the guild. When you become a journeyman, you'll receive a copper one, and when you're a master, you'll be given our guild's silver pendant."

"Thank you," I said.

I flipped it over and found words engraved into the metal. It read:

Knightmare Arcanist Volke Savan
   Frith Guild Apprentice

. . .

It was official. I was a knightmare arcanist.

Illia put her pendant on. "Thank you."

Guildmaster Eventide waved away the comment. "Come, come. We have much to go over." She pointed to a door tucked between two bookcases. "That's the library. It's run by Master Arcanist Vala and holds all our research." She pointed out a window. "Those are the gardens. We grow our own vegetables, with the help of magic, of course. Master Arcanist Sillvia can make anything grow, trust me."

She disappeared through a door. I jogged to keep up, and Illia did the same.

We entered another room just as breathtaking as the last. I almost didn't have enough excitement and shock to adequately express my fascination anymore. It was like expecting a tour of a house, only to discover three palaces of opulence lay within. Everything about the Frith manor intrigued me. Its beauty washed away my dread from hearing Luthair accuse Ruma of murdering his old arcanist.

"This is the map room. Gentel, my eldrin, is in charge of navigation."

The map room, practically a ballroom in terms of size, had a single circular table, massive enough that it took up the entire space. A topographical map was carved into the top, showcasing the mountains, oceans, rivers, valleys, and islands of our world. Some mountains rose several inches high, each jagged on top, some rather pointed. I ran my hand along the edge, mesmerized by the craftsmanship.

"We chart maps here," Eventide announced with her arms raised. "And this table is where I set our destination. We also use this space to conduct meetings between the master arcanists. The map you see before you is much more than it seems. I communicate with Gentel from this table. She can feel the graze of a fingertip across the surface."

I pulled my hand away and shoved it into my pocket. "Oh. Incredible."

"Once we know where we want to go, we move our location."

Eventide pointed to the city of Fortuna. A small turtle figurine sat next to the tiny docks, idle in the blue-painted portion of the map that represented the vast ocean.

"And Gentel will take us there?" Illia asked.

"Yes. And don't be fooled into thinking she's slow. Gentel moves with surprising speed."

"But the map looks so small. I can see the island nations, and the Isle of Ruma, but it doesn't extend far."

The guildmaster smiled. "That's because the map changes as we move. It only shows the radius around Gentel. Well, unless I change a few settings." She ran a finger over the edge, spinning cogs built into the table. The whole thing trembled with movement. Before my eyes, like a clockwork toy, it shifted and "zoomed out" of the area, showing oceans, mountains, and land beyond what we had seen earlier. The turtle figurine stayed the same size— almost the same size as the city of Fortuna now.

"Wow," I said.

Eventide scanned our surroundings. We were alone. No one else besides Illia, Nicholin, myself, and the guildmaster. It gave the room a cold, lonely feeling.

"Zelfree should've been here," the guildmaster said as she walked around the map table. "I'm sure he's eager to meet the newest apprentices." She waited a moment more, tapping her boot on the polished wood floors.

The brilliance of the crimson phoenix feathers hanging from her hat caught my attention. She wasn't bonded to a phoenix. Where had she gotten them? I was on the verge of asking when she turned back around.

"Why don't I go fetch him?" She gave us a quick nod and then left the room at the opposite end.

The second she left, Nicholin leapt from Illia's shoulders and landed on the map between two huge mountains. Illia tried to snatch him back, but he disappeared in a flash of white and reappeared on the opposite end of the map. He scurried over the modeled landscape, his feather touch barely leaving a scratch or a sound.

"Nicholin," Illia said. "Don't touch the map! Didn't you hear the guildmaster? Gentel can feel that."

"I'll be careful, I swear."

He crossed his heart over his furry chest.

Illia pursed her lips. It amused me how much his slight disobedience irritated her. Illia had never been one to follow the rules. Was this the first of her personality rubbing off on him?

"I'm like a giant creature on this map," Nicholin said with a laugh. "Just like Gentel! I was wondering what it would be like to be so big." He stopped running and stared down at the Isle of Ruma. "Eh. Kinda boring. All the fun stuff happens with people. At this size I would squish them." Nicholin perked up, his ears erect. "Oh! I could make them bring me offerings! I'd be a god."

I snorted back a laugh. "Power goes to your head quick, doesn't it?"

"Huh? No, no, no. I'd be a benevolent god." He brushed off his white fur. "I would declare thirty-six new holidays."

The door to the map room opened. A man wearing scraggly clothing shuffled in, his eyes half-lidded and marked with dark rings of sleeplessness. His long black hair hung to his shoulders, disheveled and matted in clumps. In one hand he carried a cup of tea, with his other hand he poured the contents of a flask into the drink and swirled it all around.

The sting of hard liquor dominated his odor. When he got close, I lifted an eyebrow, confused by his presence.

"Uh," I said. "Sir, are you in the right place?"

He cocked an eyebrow and threw back a gulp of his drink.

No answer.

The man wore a black button-up shirt—though most of the buttons weren't properly secured—along with a pair of trousers, a loose fitting belt, and worn boots. A pair of gold bangles hung on his wrist, but the most interesting accessory was his silver guild pendant hanging around his neck, marking him as a master arcanist.

No. Not him. It couldn't be.

Did the Frith Guild accept drunkards into their ranks?

I glanced up at his forehead. He had a seven-pointed star arcanist mark—and nothing else. No mystical creature. No other indication of where his powers came from or what his eldrin looked like.

And if his eldrin had died, the mark would've disappeared completely, so that wasn't the reason. How was it even possible for him to have a blank one?

Illia walked to my side, her good eye on the stranger, her hand covering her missing eye. "Can we help you?"

The man rubbed at the stubble on his chin as he gave us the once-over. "Who are you two?" he asked, his voice gruff and rusty, as though he hadn't spoken in a long time.

"I'm Volke Savan. This is, uh, my sister. Illia. We're new apprentices."

"Uh-huh. Where's your guild pendant?"

I held it up. "Here."

"Are you slow, boy? You hang it around your neck."

I gritted my teeth, holding back commentary. But I did as he directed. I threw the pendant around my neck, and my frustrations melted away. This proved I belonged. No more being an outsider.

The man glared at us for a moment longer. "I'm Everett Zelfree, a master arcanist of this guild."

He lifted his cup in a sarcastic *cheers* before downing the second half in a powerful swig. A shiver washed over him a moment later. He let out a contented exhale before placing the cup onto the edge of the map.

This was the man I had read about? The infiltrator and spymaster extraordinaire? My new mentor? He wobbled like the only place he ever infiltrated was an alehouse. And even then, it was the alehouse infiltrating his coin purse, not the other way around.

Nicholin scurried over to the edge of the map and examined Zelfree's tea cup. He dragged a paw along the inside and then tasted the residue. I held back a laugh as Nicholin locked up, his hair on end and his eyes scrunched shut.

"Gross," he muttered in his squeaky voice.

Illia pointed to the back door. "I think Guildmaster Eventide is looking for you."

"She'll find me soon enough," Zelfree said with a grunt.

Illia gave me one of her *what is even happening* looks. I wanted to agree with her, but I still hoped it was all a joke. Or maybe we were meeting the man at a bad time.

Without warning, Zelfree walked over to me. Although I normally didn't care about someone's proximity, Zelfree crossed the line of decency and went straight to invasive. He got up close, pushed my hair aside, and stared at the arcanist mark on my forehead, his brandy-breath the only thing I could smell.

The shadows flickered and moved until Luthair rose from my shadow, his sword drawn.

"Calm down," Zelfree said. "I was simply lookin'." He removed his hand from my hair and backed away. "And it's just as I thought. Second-bonded. That's unfortunate. For you."

I reached up and rubbed my head. "You can tell that by my mark?"

He didn't respond.

Luthair placed a gauntleted hand on my shoulder. His grip reminded me of outside. Would he soon tell me Zelfree was a murderer as well? Was the whole damn guild nothing but villains?

"You're the one with the rizzel, right?" Zelfree asked, glancing over at Illia.

"Yes," she replied. "He's right here."

Nicholin jumped into her arms and smiled.

"I've always wanted to see what powers rizzels possessed."

Zelfree removed the bangles from his arms and placed them on his shoulder. The metal twisted and writhed together until it formed the shape—no, *an exact copy*—of Nicholin. Even the white fur, silver stripes, and blue eyes were the same. And not a statue either! A living, breathing rizzel.

Zelfree's arcanist mark shimmered for a second before reforming anew on his forehead with a rizzel interwoven with the star.

"Interesting," the fake rizzel said as it patted itself down. "So limber and mobile. I bet I could hop around all over the place in this form."

Illia's mouth hung agape. "But—"

Zelfree's new rizzel leapt into the air, disappeared in a

puff of light, and then reappeared on the other side of the room with a pop of air. One more flash and the rizzel was back on Zelfree's shoulder, seemingly unfazed by the sudden teleports.

"Interesting," Zelfree said. He leaned against the side of the map table and stroked the fur of his new companion. "Now show me some evocation."

"Certainly," the fake rizzel said.

Luthair yanked me by the shoulder. "Stay back!"

The rizzel opened his mouth, and a bright shine collected between his sharp teeth, much like a dragon gathering flame for a massive breath of destruction.

15

GUILD APPRENTICES

The fake rizzel breathed onto the edge of the map table. White and sparkly flames washed over the wood without any heat. Instead of burning the table, the white fire teleported pieces away, but not in large chunks. It teleported tiny fragments away—splintering the wood and scattering it all over the room—in effect, ripping it apart from the inside out, all in a matter of two seconds.

A giant portion had been blasted into the map table, the destruction all around us, punctuated by tiny pops of air, like fireworks. The turtle figurine remained in place, but a mountain was gone, along with Zelfree's teacup. Bits of porcelain lay intermixed with all the wood.

Nicholin laughed. "Wow! I can do that? I need to flex my magic a little more."

The fake Nicholin chuckled and waggled a clawed paw. "Not as well as I can. But maybe one day."

"Hey! I won't be outdone by an imposter!"

Illia ignored the argument and took a step closer to Zelfree. "What is that?" She pointed to the rizzel on his arm.

"You don't know?" Zelfree asked with a huff. "I thought

the arcanists on the Isle of Ruma valued education before bonding."

"We know what it is," Nicholin snapped. Then he swished his tail for a moment and added, "We just... can't think of it right now."

Zelfree narrowed his eyes. "This is my eldrin. A mimic. She's difficult at times. Say hello, Traces."

The fake rizzel shifted her form again, melting together like clay and then shaping into a feline. The short fur, sleek enough to shimmer, had no markings. She was a pale grey, with a tail three feet in length. Her eyes—one rose, one gold—stared straight at us.

I had read about mimics. They fell into the same category as all other shapeshifting mystical creatures. Most books said they were difficult to comprehend and their magic unwieldy. Doppelgängers could shift into people and copy their magical abilities. Mimics, on the other hand, could become other mystical creatures or inanimate objects, also copying the magical abilities therein.

"You're not the most impressive bunch," Traces said, a fine feminine voice that contrasted harshly with her arcanist's, even if her tone was just as dry and sardonic as Zelfree's. "Maybe you made the wrong choices, my arcanist."

I had long grown tired of people talking down to me or thinking I was worthless. I stepped forward, my pulse hot. "You don't think it's a little pathetic for a master arcanist to insult his newest apprentices?"

Illia flashed me a bizarre look, but she remained quiet.

Zelfree chuckled. "Oh, I'm sorry. I shouldn't have set my expectations so high. Don't worry, though. I won't do it again in the future."

Was he trying to rile me? I knew what a mimic was, but most books William had didn't include many pictures. All I had for descriptions were ambiguous firsthand accounts. And I would be damned if I did all that studying just for my first mentor to think I was an uneducated island bumpkin!

"Mimics are unique," I said. "They draw on all types of magic, but when they transform, they limit themselves to whatever creature they're copying. I'm sure Traces is much more powerful than Nicholin, simply from having an arcanist for a longer period of time, but she can't use any magic beyond what Nicholin is capable of in his young form, even if an older rizzel would have more tricks up their sleeve."

Illia lit up. "Oh, just like the tale of Scarlet the Burglar. In the story, she used her mimic to fight the dire wolf of the city guard. It was an exact mirror match, despite the fact she was much more accomplished as an arcanist."

I nodded.

Although the way I remembered the story, Scarlet deserted her eldrin in favor of making off with enchanted jewels. I never much cared for her after hearing that story. I liked stories about heroes who fought the injustices of the world, not arcanists who used their vast powers and gifts to make it worse. I always secretly hoped they caught her, but I never read the tale of where she was found.

"Oh, so you do know a few things," Zelfree said with a shrug. "Fantastic. I guess I won't have to tell the guildmaster I made a mistake."

He turned and wobbled a bit before shuffling toward the door. His mimic transformed back into bangles and slid into place on his wrists.

Had Zelfree been planning to reject us simply because he thought we didn't know what a mimic was? Or was that his sarcastic way of insulting us again? Either way, I could barely believe the situation. He conducted himself like a slob, not like the legendary arcanist I had read about in William's books.

Zelfree glanced over his shoulder. "What're you waiting for? Come on. I have better things to do than wait for you to piece everything together."

I motioned to the destroyed map table. "We're just going to leave this?"

"It'll get fixed."

Illia and I exchanged questioning looks. She shrugged. Uncertain of what to do, I opted to follow along.

Luthair, who had been silent for some time, simply melted back into the darkness and followed me through the shadows. Together we exited the map room and headed to the large staircase.

For the second time in one day, my chest tightened and my throat locked up. Gregory Ruma stood at the base of the steps, his thumbs still hooked in his belt loops, his casual stance anything but threatening. He gave Zelfree a cheerful smile.

"Already up, eh?" Ruma said with a chuckle. "Isn't before noon early for you?"

To my shock, Zelfree didn't acknowledge the other man, even though they were peers. He simply walked by as if nothing had happened between them.

Illia followed Zelfree onto the steps. She gave Ruma a quick bow of her head before she continued upward. It took me a moment to remember what I was even doing—was this awe? No. Too many of my thoughts were consumed with dread. I still didn't know what to say to him, or what to do with my situation.

I stared at Ruma as I slowly shuffled past. He returned my stare with a lifted eyebrow.

"Why so nervous?" he asked with a grin.

My mouth went dry. "I, uh, was born on the island named after you."

"Oh, it all makes sense now." Ruma placed a hand on my shoulder and stopped me from climbing the stairs. "I take it the people on the island still tell tales about me?"

"Yeah..."

"How am I in person? Probably disappointing, right?" Ruma poked his stomach and then tugged at his belt. "I used to have a six-pack, and now here I am. Hopefully I haven't let you down too badly."

I almost laughed. "You're still very impressive. The magic at the pier—it was incredible. I've read all about master leviathan arcanists and how they control water and weather. You're among the best."

"Volke," Illia called from the tenth step. "C'mon." She turned and leapt up the next couple until she reached the second story.

"You two look out for each other," Ruma muttered.

I held my breath. What did he want me to say to that?

"I saw the both of you working together in the Night Sky Woods," he continued. "Cherish a friendship like yours. Few people will ever experience it."

I swallowed my breath before saying, "You saw us?"

"That's right. The master arcanists of the Frith guild were out in the woods during the assessments. Master Arcanist Freeya is bonded to a sylph—a creature proficient in invisibility."

A part of me couldn't believe there so many arcanists out in the woods that night, but I knew it had to be true if Ruma saw me and Illia helping each other. And it would explain why the yeti arcanist had been denied. They saw the way he manhandled his way into getting a star moth.

"How did you all determine who you would mentor?" I asked.

Ruma lifted an eyebrow. "Everyone handles that challenge differently. Some use magic. Some rely on others. Some help others. Some scoff and say it isn't worth their time—it's too whimsical. You can see a person's true demeanor in moments when they think no one is watching."

"I see..."

"Go," Ruma said, motioning to the staircase. "She's waiting."

I hustled past him, right up the stairs, unable to say anything further. He never gave me the impression he was hostile or deranged. Zelfree gave me more anxiety than Ruma. There was no way Ruma murdered anyone. Absolutely not.

Although I had taken my time at the bottom of the stairs, I caught up to Illia and Zelfree with little trouble. Zelfree didn't seem to appreciate the many steps up to the third story. He grumbled the entire way, muttering *all these ridiculous stairs* before yanking most of his weight up using the banister. I easily kept his pace. The staircase was small-time compared to the Pillar, and once we reached the top, I understood where he was taking us.

Everyone lived on the third floor.

Each room we passed was a cozy bedroom—at least three times the size of my dinky closet back home. The arcanists were given a bed, a dresser, a small desk, and a bookshelf pre-stocked with learning essentials. Apprentice arcanists had to learn the fundamentals of magic, after all. While I learned arcanist history and magic lore as a child, now I would learn the essentials of magic itself, and how to develop it within myself.

Zelfree stopped and pointed down a hallway. "This side of the manor is for women. Illia, your room is at the end on the left."

Illia stroked Nicholin's head and answered with a curt nod. She walked down the hallway, her steps slow, her attention drawn to each new door. When she reached her room, she gave me one final glance before entering.

Part of me wanted to go with her, especially after Ruma's words telling me to cherish our friendship. But I knew it was inappropriate. We were adults. We couldn't do everything together.

Zelfree continued to the other side of the manor. I walked alongside him in silence, my attention drawn to his bangles. Did his mimic prefer that appearance or was it for a tactical advantage? No one would suspect the bracelets to be a mystical creature.

Zelfree stopped in front of an open door. I stood next to him, waiting for the moment he would tell me I could call the guild home.

"Second-bonding is dangerous," he said as he leaned against the wall. He rubbed at his eyes and pinched the bridge of his nose. "I wondered why your knightmare was so grown when you were hunting the star moths and figured you would need special training to control it."

I mulled over his statements, my eyebrows knit together. What did he mean by *control it*?

"Unlike other arcanists, your creature may have a different agenda than your own," Zelfree continued. "Especially a knightmare as grown as yours. He's embedded with the personality and goals of his last master. You understand, right?"

"Yes," I said.

"Good. Then you'll understand why you need to train more than anyone else."

"W-well, how will I do that?"

"By doing everything that I say, to the letter. When I assign the others tasks, you'll need double their requirements. The more magic you channel through your body, the more your knightmare will gradually fall into line. If you slack off, or allow the creature to control you, it can become messy."

I opened and closed my hands, dwelling on my memory of me moving the shadows on the Sapphire Tide. Channeling magic had hurt. *Physically hurt.* And now Zelfree wanted me to use my powers twice as much?

"All right," I said.

Whatever it takes. That was what I told myself before ever becoming an arcanist.

"Good." Zelfree motioned to the bedroom. "You'll sleep here. Meet me at the edge of the lake by dawn."

"Will you even be awake at dawn?" I quipped. I probably shouldn't have asked, but his condescension had worn away my manners.

Zelfree half-smiled and waved away the comment. "Kid, I don't sleep. You never know who will come callin' in the middle of the night."

I waited for him to follow up his ominous statement with a jest or a laugh, but it never came. He simply turned and shuffled back down the hall, his hands in his pockets.

When I imagined mentoring with a master arcanist, I had always imagined someone like Gravekeeper William. Someone disciplined, caring, world-wise, and dedicated to their craft. Zelfree was... not those things. At least, not that I could tell. He seemed like an eccentric drunkard.

Perhaps there would be books about his exploits here at

the guild. If I reread stories about him, perhaps I would have a better understanding.

But first I had to speak with Luthair.

The manor halls of the Frith Guild were lively with conversation. All the apprentices wanted to meet and greet, but I shut myself in my room before anyone could corner me for an introduction. I didn't want to be social, not when I had so many heavy questions to deal with.

Luthair formed in the corner of my room and remained still. He reminded me of a decoration more than a creature —an old suit of armor from a castle hallway.

"We should wait until night to speak," he said.

Although I thought that was a bit long, I didn't argue. My thoughts sped through a million scenarios, grappling with the odd situation and facts. I paced the room until my feet hurt, my gaze on the floorboards the entire time.

Day transformed into night with a cascade of orange, red, and purple. The islands always had an amazing view, but sunsets and sunrises were my favorite. The ocean acted as a second sky, bleeding into the colors of the evening. Nothing compared.

Once the talking outside my door died down, I slowed my pacing, trying to think of a compromise to my terrible situation. My feet hurt.

Finally I said, "Ruma couldn't have been the one who killed your old arcanist."

"It was him," Luthair stated. "There is no doubt in my mind."

"How are you so certain?"

"Very few could rival the magic displayed that night."

"It could've been someone else. It could've been—"

I stopped myself short, my breath caught in my throat. I hadn't thought of it until then, but the moment I did, I knew I could cast doubt on the situation.

"What if it was someone with a mimic?" I asked.

Luthair turned his helmet to face me, but his expressionless silence wasn't the shock I was hoping for.

It could have happened. Someone *could* have impersonated Ruma. In theory. However unlikely.

"Let's assume that is a valid possibility," Luthair said. "Where would you suggest we go from here?"

"Well... I hadn't thought of that."

"I understand you admire the man, but he's a villain and needs to be brought to justice."

"Don't say that so loud." I lowered my own voice to a whisper. "If there's doubt, we can't go around saying he's a criminal. *If* he's a villain, *then* we'll bring him to justice."

"Are you suggesting we investigate the man?"

I ran a hand through my hair, my palm coated in sweat.

Damn. I said I would do this—I said I would catch the killer—but why did it have to be Gregory Ruma? I stared at the ceiling.

If we investigated Ruma and found nothing, Luthair wouldn't be upset if we dropped the issue. And what would we even be looking for? It wasn't like Ruma would have a note in his bedroom explaining all his evil deeds. There was a higher likelihood we would find nothing rather than anything incriminating.

Then again, if I was caught snooping around Ruma's personal belongings, I would get in trouble. And if a psychotic murderer found me snooping around his belongings...

No.

Ruma was innocent. If we investigated, I could prove it. If I proved it, Luthair wouldn't insist on killing Ruma. I had to do this.

"Yes," I said. "We'll investigate Ruma. He lives here on Gentel, right? And we'll be training alongside his apprentices? We'll have plenty of opportunities to look for evidence."

Luthair nodded. "Very well. But when we find incriminating evidence, we must take it to the guildmaster straightaway."

"*If* we find evidence."

"Again, I see little reason to doubt. That man's voice haunts my thoughts and reminds me of my failings."

I jumped at the sound of tapping at my window. With my heart beating against my ribcage, I walked over and opened it. Illia hung on the lattice fencing used for the ivy growing up the building. We were three stories up!

"Are you okay?" I asked as I reached out and helped her into my bedroom. "What're you doing?"

"I came to see you," she said. "I thought that was obvious."

Nicholin poked his head out of her coat and glanced around. "Ah. It's the same boring bedroom as Illia's."

"It couldn't wait until morning?" I asked.

Illia shrugged. "What does it matter? You're still awake, aren't you?"

"Isn't it against the rules for you to be here?"

"What?" She gave me one of her sly smiles. "Are you going to report me?"

"Look, I just don't want to get into trouble. And you shouldn't either. We haven't even been here for twenty-four hours. Now doesn't seem like the time to start a bad reputation."

"I need to speak with you, though." She glanced away and smoothed the hair over the scars on her face. "What you said about Zelfree being our mentor."

"What about it?"

"I thought we were going to train under Gregory Ruma. Didn't you get an invitation from him as well?"

I caught my breath. I hadn't shown her my letter. Zelfree was the only one who offered to take me as an apprentice, and I just figured Illia would join me. What a stupid assumption. Obviously she would pick the best arcanist as her mentor. Who would pick Zelfree over a living legend?

"I didn't get an offer from Ruma," I said.

"You didn't?"

"No."

Illia fidgeted with the cuffs of her coat.

I shook my head. "Don't change your decision based on me. It would be an honor to train with Ruma. I don't want to hold you back."

The last sentence hurt. It dug into my chest, worse than the cut of a blade. I couldn't selfishly demand she stay with me. What kind of arcanist would I be then? It might be painful now, but Illia needed to make her own decisions.

Luthair put his hand on my shoulder and squeezed tight.

Did he fear sending Illia to Ruma? That made sense. If Ruma was a killer, I should at least warn her. But if I said that now, would she think I was lying just to manipulate her choice?

"Volke."

I glanced up and met her gaze.

"I'm going to train with Master Zelfree."

"Really? But why?"

"Loyalty," she said. "Without it, we cannot know true friendship."

I never thought I would hear her recite a step from the Pillar. I almost didn't know what to say. "I thought you said you didn't want advice from a centuries old staircase."

Illia crossed her arms. "Don't ruin the moment."

We both shared a chuckle.

She took my hand. I wanted to cling to it, but doubt held me back. She continued, "We started this journey together with an unconventional bonding. It's only fitting we have an unconventional mentor as well, don't you think?"

Illia...

Damn. She always knew what to say. I wanted to thank her, but even that seemed wrong somehow. Not enough. But what could I do?

Nicholin leaned heavy onto the edge of her pocket. "C'mon. You can't deny any of that. Stop looking so sad and celebrate already."

Ha! If only Luthair were as jovial.

"Tomorrow we're supposed to meet at the edge of the lake," I said.

"All right." Illia headed back for the window. "What time?"

"Before dawn."

"I'll see you there. Oh, and Volke."

"Yeah?"

"Don't make me come all the way over here to wake you up, got it? I don't know how much more of this lattice I can climb."

16

EVOCATION, MANIPULATION, AUGMENTATION

I stepped outside before the dawn, prepared to study magic, but unprepared for the frigid ocean winds. I had lived on an island my entire life—the breeze was more of a companion than my shadow—but riding on an atlas turtle wasn't the same as island weather.

Gentel glided through the waves, away from the mainland, out to the coldest reaches of the ocean. And without the sun, the morning chill added a whole new depth to the temperature. I shivered as I made my way to the edge of the lake, my coat and button-up shirt far too thin.

I didn't even need to ask if the breeze bothered Illia. The chattering of her teeth could be heard from the docks of Fortuna.

Four others waited by the water's edge. I recognized two of them, especially when their phoenixes flew in circles overhead. Zaxis and Atty both turned when we neared, but only Atty offered us a slight bow of her head.

"I still can't believe you're here," Zaxis said to me with a huff.

I replied by patting his upper arm. "Good morning to you, too."

"Don't touch me."

He jerked away from my hand and sneered.

I don't know why, but it amused me to no end. I had to stifle a round of laughter at his over-the-top rejection of my proximity. Maybe I could get him to leave me alone by causing him nothing but slight irritation every time we interacted.

"Oh, wow," a girl said, her eyes wide. "Look at the scars on her face!"

Illia's cheeks flared a deep crimson. Her hand flew straight to old injuries, covering them in an instant.

The girl who spoke—short, with her cinnamon-colored hair tied up in a clump on top of her head—had the audacity to point. Then her freckled face lit up in delight. "Those scars looked deep."

"*Hey,*" Zaxis barked. "Leave her alone or I'll give you some burn scars everyone will talk about." He shoved the girl away.

She was half Zaxis's size, with freckles on her nose and cheeks, but she didn't back down. The girl puffed out her chest and clenched her teeth. "I'd like to see you try. Have you ever seen someone crippled by hydra venom? You're about to experience it first-hand!"

A mystical creature slithered around her feet—a baby hydra with a single head and four stumpy lizard-like legs. Its scales curved at the tips, giving it a pokey appearance, and when it opened its mouth to hiss, it displayed a row of fangs all the way to the back of its throat. It cuddled close to the girl, its gold eyes flashing with rage.

Zaxis's phoenix swooped down and landed on his forearm, his fire flaring and his feathers puffed. "Threats don't scare us."

Atty stepped between them, both her hands held up. "Please, everyone. We should take a breath and calm down."

"After she apologizes to Illia," Zaxis snapped.

A small piece of me wished *I* had been the one to demand an apology, but another piece of me was surprised Zaxis cared so much. Since when did he care about Illia's feelings? I thought he and his whole family said she was *ugly and uncooperative.* Maybe he just wanted to throw his weight around or something.

"I'm sorry," the girl said to Illia without an ounce of remorse in her voice. "I just thought they were awesome, okay? I didn't know all you weirdos would get upset about it."

"You thought they were *awesome*?" I asked.

"Yeah. Where I come from, everyone has scars."

The girl took off her coat and tossed it to the ground. She wore a sleeveless shirt, exposing most of her shoulders and both her arms. They were, in fact, covered in scars. Some faded—no doubt over a decade old—but others were still pink. And some were deep.

"What happened?" Atty asked as she covered her mouth in a dignified gasp.

The girl huffed. "I'm from the canyon town, Regal Heights. If you want to become an arcanist, you have to prove yourself to the hydras. They always want to fight, so everyone ends up getting scuffed up a bit." She grabbed her coat and wrapped herself back in it. "The people with the best scars impress the best hydras. Isn't that right, Raisen?"

Raisen, her hydra, stopped hissing and glanced up at her. "That's right, my arcanist."

Illia lowered her hand and rubbed it on the front of her trousers. "Uh, what did you say your name was again?"

"My name is Hexa d'Tenni," the girl said with an energetic wave of her hand, her speech a tad faster than what I was accustomed to. "And you, girl with the scars, would be really popular back in Regal Heights. Our city founder—who's still there, by the way—lost his eye while fighting a plague-ridden hydra and saving the canyon."

"Well, we aren't a bunch of barbarians," Zaxis said. "We don't go around trying to scar ourselves. Keep that in mind when you interact with all the other arcanists around here."

Hexa fluffed her cinnamon hair. "Yeah, yeah. I got that. You islanders and seaside-folk do all sorts of bizarre stuff around here. I thought you'd have thicker skin." Then she pointed to Illia. "Wear an eye patch if you don't want people to make comments!"

Atty let out a quick sigh. "Please. There is no need to antagonize each other."

"I agree," said a boy who stood off to the side. He had a matter-of-fact tone to his voice and a stiff posture. And while it was probably petty to compare heights, I was an inch or two taller than Zaxis and a good half a foot taller than this new guy.

The boy—probably my age—had long black hair pulled back and secured with a metal ring to create a loose ponytail. His clothes, however, were the most interesting part. He wore a shoulder cape with a gold chain link, and his trousers were stiff and creased so perfectly they could cut someone.

"Fighting among ourselves is unbecoming of Frith arcanists," the boy said. "Why don't we try this again and introduce ourselves? My name is Adelgis Venrover."

"I'm Atty Trixibelle," Atty chimed in. "But you should all consider yourselves on a first name basis with me."

Zaxis motioned for Forsythe to take to the sky. Then he gave everyone a quick glare. "I'm Zaxis Ren."

That was it.

Illia shrugged. "Call me Illia."

"I'm Volke Savan," I said.

Hexa, who had already introduced herself, replied with a sarcastic clap. "Wow. You islanders are *way* different than I imagined."

"I am not an islander," Adelgis said. "I hail from Ellios, the city between mountains. A white jewel, with many quarries and *fascinating* trees."

Zaxis half-laughed. "Did you just get excited for trees?"

"Of course. They're not ordinary trees, but evergrow trees. The kind of trees that sprout and spread like weeds. They make for excellent paper, which is why the city of Ellios is the birthplace of the library and the university. It's a beacon of knowledge for the world."

"So, we have a barbarian and a book nerd? Perfect." Zaxis rolled his eyes. "You all know this guild is known for swashbucklers and heroes, right?"

Adelgis held up a single finger. "And researchers. I know that's not as glamorous as *swashbuckling*, but it provides us with much needed information on magic and mystical creatures. My father is a researcher and arcane zoologist, and I intend to follow in his footsteps."

It dawned on me then that Adelgis enjoyed talking. He had a voice built for it too. Somewhat loud, but articulate, like he was leading a lecture. I bet if no one interrupted, he would tell us his whole damn life story.

Adelgis had an interesting arcanist mark. Some sort of seashell was behind his seven-pointed star. A conch shell, perhaps? I couldn't really tell, and he didn't have any mystical creatures near him. What was his eldrin? Maybe he would get around to telling us at some point.

I stared at Hexa for a moment. A hydra's many heads were wrapped around the star, some with fearsome fangs and others calm and thoughtful. Hydra's were like phoenixes—powerful and world-renowned. I remembered reading stories about their lairs. Phoenixes were drawn to charberries, but hydras were drawn to canyon prawns, which are land crustaceans with a thick exoskeleton.

"What?" Hexa asked.

I rubbed the back of my neck. "Nothing. Sorry."

She walked over to me. "Your name is Volke, right? My brother's name is Valtem. Kinda the same."

"Uh, yeah, I guess."

She had a distinct look—a cute button nose and blue almond-shaped eyes. And even though she had to be the shortest of the group, I was willing to bet she had the most energy. The tight curls of her hair bounced with each move of her head, practically alive.

Hexa pointed to my arcanist mark. "I read stories about knightmares. Scary things, those. Not as scary as liches. My mother used to say liches ate unruly children. I had literal nightmares for weeks."

"Well, Luthair isn't—"

Wait, she recognized the mark on my head as a knightmare? She was the first. A cape and sword were more ambiguous than the blatant picture of a hydra, rizzel, or phoenix.

"Luthair isn't scary," I finished.

"Huh."

Silence settled over the group. The sun crept over the horizon, a sleepy speed to its rise into the sky. Where was

Zelfree? Didn't he want us here before dawn? I didn't see him.

Zaxis walked over to the shivering Illia. He slung his coat off and draped it over Illia's shoulders.

She tried to hand it back. "It's okay. Won't you be chilly?"

"Take it. Ever since I've bonded to Forsythe, I haven't felt cold."

Part of me wanted to rip his coat off and give Illia my own. What was he playing at? He never would've been like this back home, and I seriously doubted he had changed overnight. The moment he did anything that even slightly displeased Illia, I would—

"Ahoy, there."

We all turned at once.

Gregory Ruma walked over, his hands in his pockets, his coat flowing behind him. The wind swirled in such a way as to flutter his shirt and hair, prominently displaying his guild pendant. He nodded to each member of our group.

"Ah, I see everyone made it. My apprentices, along with Zelfree's." He offered a shrug and a smile. "Let me be the first to welcome everyone."

"Hello, Master Ruma," Atty replied.

"No need to be so formal. We'll be spending a lot of time with each other. If you're stiff and rigid, you won't learn as much."

"Where is Master Zelfree?" I asked.

Ruma glanced around. "He's not here, I take it? No surprise there. Seems the drink's gotten to him again. Don't fret. He's got a buccaneer's spirit. I'm sure he'll pick himself up."

I took a step back, my palms sweaty. We were going to be alone with the man? I didn't want to believe Luthair, but what if he was correct?

"I take it the rest of you are here for me?" Ruma smiled. "I've never had five apprentices before. It'll be a challenge, but I've made a name for myself by tackling challenges."

Adelgis lifted his hand. He stepped around Zaxis and swept back his long black hair.

"Excuse me, but I'll be apprenticing with Master Zelfree. He and my father have a long history, and mimics were the subject of his latest research. I think, given the oddity of my eldrin, I would benefit from his insight."

"Rejecting my invitation for apprenticeship?" Ruma asked with a laugh. "That's a first. Fortunately, I've got an ego that can handle it."

Illia wrapped her two coats tight around her body. "Uh, well, I was also going to apprentice with Master Zelfree."

For whatever reason, Ruma didn't reply right away to her statement. He stared for a moment, the words obviously leaving an impact on his thoughts. Just before the silence curdled into a state of uncomfortable, he nodded.

"I see," he said. "Didn't expect that, I'll be right honest with you. Zelfree's more popular than I suspected."

Three of us with Ruma. Three of us with Zelfree. An even spread.

Wait...

Ruma offered the other five a chance to apprentice with him, but not me? Why? He had been impressed with everyone else's performance, but mine wasn't worthy of his attention? I gripped the collar of my coat, frustrated with my string of last-place achievements and determined to prove everyone wrong.

Ruma clapped his hands together and rubbed his palms. "Well, since Zelfree is three sheets to the wind, why don't I take this opportunity to introduce you puppies to the basics?"

The two phoenixes swooped to the ground and landed next to Zaxis and Atty, their bright golden eyes fixated on Ruma. He regarded them with smiles as he walked into the lake until the water reached up to his knees.

Ruma stopped and turned back around, a cocksure smile on his face. "Think of magic like water. Water can be many things. Liquid, solid, mist, rain, snow—it depends on outside factors. *You* are the outside factor to your magic. You shape it with your force of will, and while there are many ways to do this, we'll focus on the three easiest to master. Evocation. Manipulation. Augmentation. Got it? 'Course you do. Watch here."

He turned and held up his hand. In an instant, a bolt of lightning emanated from his fingertips and crashed on the opposite shore of the lake, the flash of the light almost blinding. The strike left a small crater and a couple fires spreading to the nearby grass.

"Evocation," Ruma said. "That's when you create something with your magic. Fire. Lightning. Whatever. It depends on your eldrin."

Before any of us could ask questions, Ruma swirled his hand around, and the water in the lake seemingly jerked to comply with his motions. Ripples formed, then a whirlpool, then a monstrous wave. It rose out of the lake and crashed into the tiny fires he had created with his lightning, snuffing them all out.

"Manipulation," he said. "That's when you control the elements associated with your eldrin. Leviathans draw their magic from the ocean, obviously, so I command the waters. Phoenixes from fire, and so on."

We remained silent as Ruma tapped on his chest. A burst of wind twisted around him. He jumped with unrivaled speed and sailed over the lake like a leaf caught on the gale winds of a hurricane. He landed on the muddy bank and then leapt again, crossing the vast expanse twice—at least a thousand feet each way—until he landed next to us with a puff of wind.

"Augmentation," he said. "That's when you alter something with your magic, be it yourself or an object. Jumping. Flying. Teleporting. You get the picture. All three of these basics are useful as salt. Every arcanist should know the difference and how to effectively use them."

Ah! It all made sense then.

Atty used evocation when she created fire on the boat. Illia used augmentation when she teleported the apple. And me—I had attempted manipulation when I shifted the shadows around like a sad clown. We were all using different forms of our magic without even realizing it.

"I want you all to practice evoking," Ruma said. "When you channel your magic, you'll want to project it outward. Like a belch from your soul."

Zaxis, Hexa, and I chuckled. Atty frowned.

Ruma rubbed at his beard, half-covering his smile as he stared at the group. I swear he glanced in my direction for a long moment before looking away, but perhaps I was paranoid.

Atty stepped forward.

"You gonna try first, lass?" Ruma asked. "Focus on pulling the magic from within."

She nodded. "I'd like to demonstrate what I've accomplished so far."

"Oh, you're already accomplished, are you? Then use your heat on me. I wanna see how hot your flames can be."

Atty's eyebrows shot straight for her hairline. She rubbed her knuckles for a moment, her gaze fixed on Ruma. She didn't move.

"Don't worry about me," Ruma said with a chuckle. "I doubt you'll even singe my beard hairs."

The blatant taunt took me by surprise. I exchanged a half-smile with Illia, curious to see the legend himself tackle phoenix fire. All arcanists could heal their injuries so long as they weren't killed outright, but his beard would definitely get singed if he wasn't careful.

Atty held up her hand and waved it through the air.

On the boat, her flames had been noticeable, but tiny. Now they popped through the air, like she had been practicing for this moment. She created a rainbow of fire that scorched the last of the early morning mist and flew straight for Ruma.

He lifted a hand and water rose out of the lake to follow his gesture. A torrent splashed in front of him, quenching the flames and snuffing them from existence. Once the steam died down, everyone could see Ruma wasn't harmed.

"Good attempt," he said. "That's exactly what I want from my apprentices."

Atty offered him a deep bow. "Thank you, Master Ruma."

Everyone else clapped as she took her spot in the group.

Ruma pointed to Zaxis. "What about you, lad? You're the other phoenix arcanist, aren't you? Let's see you beat Atty's performance."

Zaxis cleared his throat and stepped forward. "You want me to attack you as well?"

"That's right. Don't hold back."

"And you want us to burn you?"

Ruma laughed. "If you can! I'd be impressed then, boy."

For a long moment, Zaxis hesitated. He inhaled and exhaled, his gaze slowly drifting to the grass underfoot. What was he waiting for? A second invitation? With his jaw clenched, Zaxis lifted his head and then held out his hand.

Fire erupted forward, but Ruma was ready. Again, the water rushed up with a mere flick of the wrist, blocking the attack completely. Zaxis's flames weren't as prominent as Atty's, and the steam that resulted wafted away within moments. While the others in the group responded with gentle claps and wide eyes, I could see the hard look on Zaxis's face.

He didn't have the excuse that his eldrin was weaker—Atty and he both had phoenixes born at the same time, from the same place—so if he couldn't match Atty's flames, it was all on him. Either he hadn't practiced as much, or perhaps his very soul was weaker than hers. Regardless of the reason, I'm sure everyone judged him for it. He didn't want to be second best.

I knew the feeling well.

I almost felt bad for him. Almost.

"You'll get better," Forsythe said.

"Let me try again," Zaxis demanded, ignoring his eldrin altogether.

Ruma cocked an eyebrow. "What's that?"

"I can do better." He tightened his grip into a white-knuckled fist. "Let me try again."

"Fine. Let's see it."

The second Ruma ended his statement, Zaxis lifted both his hands. A small inferno washed forward, the bright orange, yellow, and red flames lighting up the area like only a bonfire could.

Ruma almost didn't react in time, but the lake water still responded to his movements as though they were one of his limbs. This time, however, Zaxis leapt to the side and created yet another pyre, no doubt trying to catch Ruma off-guard.

More water rushed out of the lake, stopping the surprise attack with little difficulty. At no point did Ruma even move from his position. He remained at the edge of the lake, smiling wide, a jovial casualness to his stance, as though amused by the brazen attempt.

When Zaxis held out his hand for a third strike, Ruma waved his hand, sending a wave of water crashing over Zaxis and his phoenix. They tumbled back through the grass, unable to steady themselves in the torrent. Then Ruma summoned the water back to the lake, chuckling the entire time.

"Good attempt," he said. "You've got spirit, that's for sure."

Zaxis slowly got to his feet, his soaking wet clothing hanging heavy on his body. He kept his teeth gritted and glared at no one directly, but the hate could be felt from three feet away.

Forsythe shook the water from his feathers as steam wafted from him like a boiling pot, and said, "Zaxis, don't push yourself. Ruma is a master arcanist."

Zaxis didn't respond. He scrunched his eyes shut, water dripping from his red hair. Then he turned back to Ruma. "Thank you." He offered Ruma a quick bow and walked back to the group, his steps slow and shoulders trembling.

No one said anything to him.

Perhaps it was because I knew the situation all too well, or perhaps it was Lyell's letter, but I couldn't stand around and do nothing. I walked over to his side, slid off my coat, and offered it to him.

"Are you okay?" I asked.

Zaxis replied with an icy glare. "I don't need anyone's pity," he hissed under his breath.

His phoenix landed next to him and rubbed his heron-like head against Zaxis's soggy slacks. It genuinely seemed to soften Zaxis's mood, but not by much.

I donned my coat again and shrugged. I made the attempt to help, if he didn't want it, what else could I do?

Ruma pointed to Hexa. "Let's see your hydra evocation. To be safe, though, everyone should step back and cover their mouths."

Hexa leapt forward, her smile dominating her face. The curls of her hair bounced with each step. "Do you want me to use my magic on you?"

"Go for it."

"It's hydra magic."

"I'm aware, lass."

"Okay."

She held up a hand, and the rest of us backed away.

Hydra's were known for their poisonous breath and deadly blood. Inhaling even a small mouthful of their toxins could cause people to become nauseated or pass out.

Hexa waved her hand and a pale green fog wafted in front of her. Anything it touched—the grass, flowers, the leaves on a nearby tree—withered and died in a matter of seconds. Hydras were powerful creatures. I was certain, given enough time and practice, she would be able to clear a small forest if she wanted to.

Wind flared to life around Ruma, controlling the deadly fog and sending it over the lake with little difficulty. He smiled as he stared at the dead vegetation.

"Impressive."

"Thank you," Hexa said. "My mother said I should be

prepared for whatever my mentor would ask of me, so I've been practicing since I've bonded."

"Smart girl."

She bowed deep, turned on her heel, and jumped back into the group. Everyone clapped, and Atty even gave her a gentle touch on the shoulder.

"So, who's next? Rizzel girl? Let's see what you've got."

While Illia took her position in front of Ruma, I stared at my feet. The shadows moved with a slight unnatural sway. Luthair lingered around me, and I knew I *could* attempt using magic, but it had gone so poorly last time. What if it went just as terribly? I would make a fool of myself in front of the others—in front of Gregory Ruma, the man who already judged me as unimportant. They assumed I would fail, and I was about to prove them all correct.

And it would be worse than Zaxis's attempt. He at least tried and accomplished something. If I tried and *nothing* happened, it would be laugh-worthy.

Illia's evocation was a small demonstration of Zelfree's blast to the map table. A wave of white mist destroyed the dead grass of the surrounding area, fragmenting it like only a thousand tiny teleports could.

Again, Ruma seemed to deflect the teleporting flame with powerful gale winds. Once Illia's demonstration came to an end, she returned to the group. I clapped and gave her a quick smile, but I wasn't paying much attention.

Then Ruma asked Adelgis to try.

My vision and my hearing tunneled. I didn't want to be the sad sack they all assumed shouldn't be here. I had to show them I belonged. I *had* to.

Adelgis held up a hand and a beam of light shot forth, like an arrow made of the sun itself. It flashed forward at impossible speeds, but Ruma managed to leap out of the way with his wind-assisted jump. The beam of light continued across the lake in a streak before fizzling out, much like a firework.

"Not bad," Ruma said.

"I, too, had been practicing before I got here," Adelgis said. "My father will be disappointed if it takes me long to master my craft."

"The Frith Guild isn't one for slackin'. Trust me, you'll master your magic or die tryin'."

The statement had the others chuckling and exchanging nervous glances.

"It's your turn," Ruma said to me.

I walked in front of the group, my heart pounding in my ears.

What would I even evoke? I didn't have fire or poison or anything like Adelgis. Knightmares were creatures of shadow. Was I supposed to throw shade at my enemy? What would even happen?

I held up my hand and gritted my teeth.

17

PLAGUE SHIP

I would rather run up the Pillar and answer Tyms's questions than channel my magic in front of the group for the first time. At least back on the island I knew what I was getting into and I wasn't mired in doubt. A small part of me—the worst knot of fears tangled in my gut—figured I would botch this no matter what I did.

Hadn't I messed up at every step of my journey? I wanted to prove myself to the citizens of Ruma. I wanted to bond with a phoenix. I wanted to be mentored by Gregory Ruma himself.

I... hadn't done any of those things.

Sure, I left the island, and I bonded with Luthair, and I was in the same guild as Ruma, but all of those were just concessions and half-ass acceptances of my failings. I set out to do something great, and then I settled for mediocre. How could I possibly hope to use my magic at the same level as everyone else?

Maybe I didn't belong here.

"Is he going to do anything?" I heard Hexa whisper, her boisterous voice distinct even when she tried to keep it low.

I kept my arm up, my hand trembling.

What was I supposed to do? What if I couldn't do it? How could I even face them knowing everyone else could do it but me?

"Don't be a fool," Luthair hissed from the shadows, his voice so faint I almost didn't hear it.

I wanted to argue, but I didn't know what to say.

He continued, "If you aren't willing to try, just give up now. You can always return to your tiny island home and dig graves. Is that what you want?"

Of course not.

"The world doesn't create furrows for the rivers," Luthair said. "The water cuts its own path—through mountains, rock, and forests—not with sheer power, but perseverance. Ruma was right. Imagine the water is your magic. You must persist, no matter the obstacles."

I closed my eyes and focused. Forcing magic sounded difficult, but once I let go of my thoughts, it came naturally, like ice on my bare skin. I grimaced. The longer I concentrated, the more the chill turned into a slow burn, stinging my insides and charring my bones. It was my magic. I knew it.

When I opened my eyes, I half expected to see something—a grand evocation worthy of the suffering I felt in my body.

But I saw nothing.

Wait, *nothing*?

No. I could feel the magic. There had to be a mistake. Or maybe I wasn't channeling enough? I held my breath and wrestled with the burning sensation at my core. The small fire of pain gradually became a pyre that rose to my head and stung the back of my eyes.

Something was wrong. My legs threatened to buckle. Tears welled at the corners of my eyes.

But still—I saw nothing. Ruma stood only twenty feet in front of me, his arms crossed, his gaze narrowed.

I refused to walk away without having evoked *something*. I would do it. Even if it was just a small display of magic.

So I closed my eyes and forced it again.

"Stop! Make him stop!"

I let go of the magic coursing through my veins and took in a ragged breath. Was that it? Did I fail? The burning sensation from the magic lingered, but I never saw anything.

I turned around and found the rest of the apprentices either on their knees or drenched in a cold sweat. When I glanced back at Ruma, even he appeared to be shaken—his hand on his face, his eyebrows crushed together. They took several moments to pick themselves up and shake away their trembling.

Ruma huffed. "I should've known."

"I don't understand," I said.

"Knightmares evoke fear, lad. Actual nightmares. Probably should've started you with something else rather than evocation."

Adelgis stepped forward without prompting, almost like he couldn't keep himself quiet even if instructed. "Knightmares are so interesting. My father said they were born from slain kings, forever walking the Earth to torment those without honor."

"Wait," I said. "I did it? I evoked something?"

Ruma nodded. "Aye. You did. Good job." He patted me on the shoulder and pushed me back toward the group. "Now let's all move on to some manipulation."

It took me a few seconds to calm down. Illia gave me a smile, and I responded with a nod. At least I hadn't walked away as a failure, even if it felt like I jumped over an erupting volcano in order to do it.

Adelgis helped Zaxis stand. Zaxis offered him a muttered thank you before turning his attention back to me. Why did he always have to give that look? Like he hated anything I accomplished, no matter how much I struggled. At least he had also struggled this round.

Before we could get into the next lesson, a bell rang out across the atlas turtle island. While Illia, Atty, Zaxis, Adelgis, Hexa, and I exchanged confused glances, Ruma stared at the highest point on the guild manor, his eyes narrowed.

"Guess today will be cut short," he muttered. "You all head inside. Seems we have company."

"Company?" Zaxis asked. "As in, people are approaching us? Who would try to intercept a moving island?"

"Don't know. But Decimus and I will handle it. The rest of you can practice your evocation and report back tomorrow. Perhaps Zelfree will have recovered enough to stumble out here and give you three some training of his own."

Ruma ended his statement with a chuckle. Then he headed for the far end of the turtle, right near the head. I watched him go, curious as to how often anyone would approach an entire guild of arcanists. Surely they had flags up that indicated they were merchants?

"It's not even noon," Hexa said as she glanced up into the sky. "I'm surprised we didn't get more time with our mentor."

Adelgis shrugged. "Eventide said it would take a week to get where we're going. We've got plenty of time to learn some of the basics."

Even though he didn't have his coat and he was still soaked, Zaxis showed no sign of chill. He hadn't been lying when he said his phoenix somehow kept him warm, simply from bonding. Could it be a form of augmentation? Heat ran through his veins? It made me wonder what a knightmare would do for his arcanist. I already looked forward to the lesson.

Adelgis approached me. "Your evocation was, by far, the most intriguing. Do you mind if I see your knightmare? I've only ever read about them in books."

I rubbed at the back of my neck and glanced down at my shadow. Although Luthair kept himself hidden most of the time, I feared Ruma might recognize him. Of course, if Ruma *did* recognize Luthair, it would be damning evidence in favor of Luthair's claims.

But Ruma had already left...

"Luthair," I said. "Do you mind?"

For a second, he didn't respond, but finally he formed in the darkness of my shadow and stood. Although I considered phoenixes majestic, I did still catch my breath whenever Luthair stood out of the void. His armor shone in the early morning light, his cracks and torn cape a little less noticeable when I was busy admiring him.

"I see," Adelgis said as he stroked his chin. "You really are second-bonded."

"This is what you bonded with in the Endless Mire?" Zaxis asked.

I nodded.

"Why was it there?"

"A ship crashed," I said.

"Yeah, but why were a bunch of mystical creatures on a boat to begin with?"

"We should be getting inside," Illia interjected. She motioned to the manor.

Happy to escape the conversation, I nodded. My joints flared with more pain than the rest of my body. The need to rest dominated my thoughts, and even the short walk inside seemed too long.

Luthair walked alongside me, however, which was a surprise. I didn't want to hobble next to him, so I gritted my teeth and forced a normal gait until we reached the manor house.

The evening winds brought with them a slight drizzle of rain. Gray clouds stretched forever in every direction, creating the perfect recipe for a storm. I waited at the window, staring out across the atlas turtle island, my body still irritated by the forced use of magic. Gentel had come to a stop in the middle of the ocean.

Although most of the arcanists had retreated inside, a small contingent remained near the atlas turtle's head. Five ships had drifted near the island, no flags or sails. Two were three mast vessels, large and sturdy, but they were all unmanned. None of the Frith arcanists attempted to board them, either.

How had five vessels drifted together and not run aground? Why was everyone afraid to handle them? Even Decimus didn't swim close.

They readied skiffs and kept them tied to the pier. Their hesitation intrigued me more than the vessels. What were they afraid of?

But I didn't want to think about that. I pushed away from the window and paced my room. "Luthair," I said. "Come out. I want to practice magic."

The shadows came together in the next split-second, forming Luthair a few inches from where I walked. He stood still and silent, and I almost felt bad for commanding him. He wasn't my slave—we were partners.

"Sorry," I muttered. I stopped pacing. "I just wanted to try some of the other things Ruma mentioned. Augmentation or manipulation. What could Mathis do with those things?"

Luthair pulled his black sword from the scabbard and held it out, hilt forward. "You've already seen augmentation. Mathis and I would fight as one. Take my blade. I can guide you."

Although I hadn't thought about wielding Luthair's sword since the star moths, the idea intrigued me. I took the hilt and watched in fascination as the inky shadows crawled up my arms and created pseudo-gauntlets. But the moment the shadows latched at my shoulders, I lost control of my arms, much like in the woods.

With no command from me, my arms twisted the blade and held it in a combat-ready position.

"O-okay," I muttered. "What do I do?"

"Nothing," Luthair said. "I am a master swordsman. I trained for years with Mathis. You can let me take care of things."

I forced a chuckle. But Luthair didn't laugh. He was as stoic as a brick wall.

"I can't let you do everything," I said. "I have to learn too."

"If you try to take control of the shadow, it'll burn you, like any other magic."

"So... this isn't actual augmentation? You're just controlling me?"

"Correct."

I glared at him. This wasn't what I meant! I wanted to train my magic. Zelfree said I had to do it twice as well as anyone else. I had to practice, and even if I was injured, I couldn't let up. I didn't want to make an embarrassment of myself.

Despite Luthair's warning, I moved my arms. Instantly, I felt the pain—the shadows burning my skin. I eased up a bit and the darkness on my arms swung the sword a few times with grace and ease.

"What's the point of coating me in shadow armor?" I sarcastically asked. "If you're going to do everything, you might as well leave me in the room and do it yourself."

Luthair shook his helmet. "I want to protect you. Also, once you master some magic, you can use it while we are augmented together. We will be an unstoppable fighting force."

"Then I need to learn my magic as soon as possible. Help me do that."

"Protecting you comes first."

"I won't need protecting if you help me with my magic."

There was a long stretch of silence. Did he feel the need to coddle me because Mathis had died? Luthair said he blamed himself. But how could I show him I wasn't Mathis?

Then the shadow gauntlets eased up, practically going limp. I could move my arms, even if it hurt.

"The first lesson to swordsmanship is to keep your wrist straight," Luthair said. He stepped around to the side, his armor body clanking. "When you strike an opponent, the force of the blow must travel through your arm. If your wrist is bent, you risk injuring yourself or dropping your blade. Do you understand?"

I nodded and straightened my wrist.

"Keep your dominant knee pointed forward. Allow a slight bend. Never lock up. You must be nimble and capable of movement. A stiff stance invites your opponent to strike."

"Got it," I muttered as I loosened my knees.

"Always aim to cut *through* your target. If you aim to cut *into* your opponent, your strike will be weaker and less effective. Imagine your target is right behind your opponent's back, if that helps you remember. You want to kill him as fast as possible—so that he cannot use his sword or sorcery against you."

I almost dropped the blade as his words sunk into my thoughts. Yes. I would have to kill people. I knew that. The world could be harsh. Pirates plagued the seas. Brigands pillaged villages. The occult plague drove mystical creatures insane. In order to save innocent people, I would have to cut down the wicked.

But I hadn't really grasped it until that moment. *Cut through my enemies. Kill them fast.* I had to keep these things in mind.

"Are you okay?" Luthair asked.

"Y-yeah," I muttered. "Sorry. I just needed to think that through for a moment."

"Perhaps we should take a break. Look out the window."

The ink of my arms receded. I handed Luthair back his sword and glanced out to see what was happening. Despite the rain, the Frith arcanists were lighting the five mystery boats on fire. The flames didn't die in the water—some mystical creatures were strong enough to defy nature—but *why* were the boats being burned? What was on them? Anything?

Ruma was among the group near the pier. What was *he* doing?

"Most of the arcanists are preoccupied," Luthair said.

"Yeah."

"Perhaps now would be a good time to investigate the guild manor."

"What?"

I turned around, my eyebrows knit together. Luthair wanted to investigate *now*? It made sense, I supposed. With so many arcanists outside, we wouldn't bump into them. And Luthair did want to investigate Ruma's quarters or perhaps even his study area—anywhere for evidence of his past deeds. I doubted there would be anything incriminating in the man's dresser, but the sooner I got this out of the way, the sooner I could go back to focusing on my training.

It wouldn't hurt to wander around and map out the manor, even if I didn't necessarily dive head-first into Ruma's personal belongings. I wanted to know the layout of the guild manor, after all.

"All right," I murmured.

Luthair melted into the shadows, and I walked out of my room.

Eternal firefly lanterns lit the hallway. I glanced in both directions, wondering if anyone else was up at this evening hour.

I made my way downstairs and into the main room. As I reached the bottom steps, Reo came rushing up, books and papers held tight in his arms. Although I tried to avoid him, he slammed into me, knocking some of his materials out of his arms.

"I'm so s-sorry," Reo said as he stooped to gather his books.

"It's fine."

I picked up a couple pieces of paper, stunned by what little I read on the page.

OCCULT PLAGUES – RESEARCH – DAY 32

Effects on Mystical Creatures – Transformations
Some creatures have become stronger after being infected. Their magic doubles in strength, and their body grows in size, similar to how a mystical creature grows when bonded.

Reo snatched the paperwork from my hands and tucked it away into one of his books.

"Is everything okay?" I asked.

"You should stay inside. The derelict ships are carrying plague corpses. Until they're destroyed, we should all be careful."

"Where're you going?"

Reo took a few more steps up and shook his head. "Everything w-will be fine. Just stay inside."

"Why would anyone spread the plague? Why wouldn't they set the ships ablaze?"

"It's a tactic for pirates." Reo frowned. "They send out plague ships, and after the plague has spread to a town or island, they swoop in during the panic. Have you seen mystical creatures who are affected? They... aren't r-right in the head. It creates chaos."

The white hart certainly didn't act right in the head.

Reo continued up the stairs, his books gripped tighter than ever. I watched him go, my mind fixated on the boats. I had heard about this horrible tactic in the past. Pirates truly were the scum of the world, and I started to share Illia's intense dislike for them.

Another thought struck me. Had Gregory Ruma used the same tactic when he attacked the island of rizzels? It all made sense. He sent the plague to the island, causing everyone to panic and prepare to leave, only to step in and catch them at the piers.

But why? What did he get for killing them all? It still didn't make sense, and I refused to believe Ruma would turn into a coldblooded killer. I had to be missing something—there had to be someone sullying his name.

"What do you know about this occult plague?" I whispered to the shadows.

Luthair shifted around my feet. "It rots the mind of mystical creatures who contract it."

"What about arcanists?"

"I don't know. Those who carried the plague didn't become laughing madmen like their eldrin."

"Anything else?"

"Mathis was no researcher. We hunted villains together. There was never much time for studying."

Perhaps I needed to change that.

Knowledge. Without it, we fear our surroundings without hope to understand.

I hustled away from the staircase, my thoughts turning inward. I walked into the map room, pleased to see the table in one piece. I didn't know how, but I suspected someone had repaired it with magic. Perhaps a mystical creature capable of mending.

As I continued my walk, I found a chart room, complete with a map archive and a small library. The compasses reminded me of William. He told me it was good luck to carry one on the ocean, and Illia pointed out it was just common sense. No sailor worth his salt would set sail without a compass.

I smiled as I recalled the memories. I leafed through the books, examining the spines and taking note of each one William had in his own tiny library. When I moved onto the maps, I wasn't really seeing anything. Illia loved helping

William mark up maps with notes and places of interest, especially shipwrecks and merchant routes.

I examined the maps, intrigued to see some were centuries old. They, too, had marked points of interest. Someone had made notes next to their marks, highlighting the homes of mystical creatures, natural resources, caves, crystals, and turbulent water. Pirate attacks and terrible storms had also been catalogued.

While I found it all nostalgically interesting, sifting through maps wasn't really investigating Ruma. I placed the maps back in a pile, making sure to stack them just as I had found them.

"Wait," Luthair said.

"What is it?"

"Look at that map again."

The shadows on the walls and ceiling shifted around in the corners. I pushed the top map aside and stared at one with a collection of islands dotted throughout the ocean to create a triangle. One island was circled, but there weren't any notes or indications why it was of importance.

"That's the island," Luthair muttered. "The location Mathis was murdered."

"Really?"

I ran my hand across the longitude lines. Why was there a map with this circled in the Frith Guild?

Luthair shifted around the room, disturbing the otherwise motionless shadows. "We should keep searching. Perhaps the Frith Guild had been called to investigate Mathis's murder."

That was a possibility I hadn't considered.

"It could be a coincidence," I said. "You said this was an island for research on rare mystical creatures, right?"

"Its presence brings up questions I don't know how to answer, but I feel it only points to my ultimate conclusion."

I tucked the map back into the pile and exited the room.

The quietness of the manor unnerved me a bit, almost like I was being watched, but every time I glanced back, I saw nothing. It wasn't like we had found anything definitive, but the simple unmarked circle on a map had left me questioning.

I wandered, lost in thought, until I looped back to the main room. The rain came down in torrents, filling the manor with a melancholy song of nature. Rain didn't bother me. Our island had its fair share of random downpours. I quite enjoyed the rain at times, but it did little to help my mood after what I had seen.

"That way," Luthair whispered. A part of my shadow pointed to a far door on the opposite wall.

I walked over, trying to act casual, but I glanced over my shoulders more times than I blinked. I grabbed the handle and shook. Locked.

"We can't," I said.

"Wait."

Luthair slipped under the tiny crack between the door and the floor, as thin as any normal shadow. After a few moments of anxious waiting, the familiar click of an unlocked lock reached my ears. I opened the door and stepped through. Luthair stood on the other side, having formed after he slipped in.

"I didn't know you could do that," I whispered.

"I rarely use my gifts for thievery."

Although I wouldn't want to do that either, I did think it was a shame. The ability to slip into anywhere as a shadow was beyond useful, and my mind was already spinning with possibilities.

"What're we doing here?" I asked as I shut and locked the door behind us.

"You don't keep garbage behind locked doors."

Huh. That was true. Something important had to be here if they kept it behind locks.

We had entered a hallway with several more doors. Was I even allowed to be here? No one had told me I *couldn't* explore the manor, but I knew the moment someone caught me I would be in trouble.

"We can't stay long," I said. "We won't find anything if I'm thrown out of the guild for trespassing."

"Then we shouldn't waste time."

I headed down the hall, the terrible feeling of being watched burning the back of my head.

18

HIDDEN WINDOW

We walked down the corridor, each door as tightly locked as the first. Without a real understanding of where I was going, I picked the door with a handle that was more worn than the others.

Luthair shifted underneath, just like before, and opened the way. Together we entered a large sitting area that stole my breath.

Ripped pirate flags hung on the walls, cracked stone statues sat on shelves, and the remains of a stained glass window were arranged on the center table. They weren't flotsam dug up by fishing nets—they were trophies, and I recognized them all.

I walked over to the wall, my eyes wide. "Are you seeing this, Luthair?"

One pirate flag had two skulls with a single sword piercing through them. It was the flag the infamous Tang Brothers used on all their ships. They raided towns, fought the imperial navy, and even ran prohibited items across borders. Both brothers had bonded with sirens and their ability to lure merchant ships was unrivaled.

Gregory Ruma put an end to their dastardly deeds. Their fight on the open waters was said to have created a typhoon the likes of which had never been seen before or after—sirens had control of water as well, just not as strong as leviathans. I gently touched the edge of the pirate flag, shocked to see a piece of history.

"You recognize these ornaments?" Luthair asked.

"They're legendary. Haven't you heard of all the amazing things Ruma has done?"

Luthair didn't answer.

"Look at the stone statues!"

I jogged over to the shelves and held my breath as I gazed over each one. They came from the mystical Fini Isle. Arcanists on that island bonded with sibyls and could predict the future. They carved statues of events yet to come, each with a special meaning that could only be revealed in time.

Three statues had been gifted to Ruma when he saved the isle from a disturbance at sea. One statue looked like a boat—the High Riser, Ruma's personal vessel. The second appeared to be two leviathans locked in combat. The third was a phoenix. It took me a moment to really appreciate the detail of the statues, what with all their tiny sculpted scales, feathers, and planks. I stared longest at the phoenix. Why would Ruma have a phoenix statue? The leviathans made sense, though I didn't know why they were fighting each other, but Ruma wasn't bonded to a phoenix.

I supposed he did discover an island of phoenixes. That made sense.

I pushed the thoughts from my mind and focused on the broken stained glass window.

"And this is from the cathedral where Ruma wed his wife," I said as I walked over. "Apparently it had been

wrecked by pirates a couple decades after his wedding ceremony, and he traveled back to it in order to collect this very
window."

I didn't dare touch the glass itself, opting instead to lean
in close and examine everything with a critical eye. The
shards had been polished to a fine luster.

"Are you looking at all this stuff, Luthair?" I asked.
"Don't you think you could be wrong? Ruma isn't the kind of
man who would do all these marvelous things and then
secretly be a killer."

Luthair examined the room, his void helmet empty. "You
already convinced me there could be doubt. None of these
trinkets prove I'm wrong, however."

"Then how do you explain all his great deeds?"

"People change. These are objects from decades ago.
What has he done recently?"

I turned away from the stained glass and ran a hand
down my face. I didn't know what Ruma had been up to
lately. I had only recently discovered he was still alive.

"He returned to the guild to take apprentices," I said.
"That's... commendable."

"If you're done fawning over Ruma's baubles, perhaps
we can continue."

His chastising tone got to me. I took a step back and
looked at the four doors around the room. No labels or
plaques.

"Why don't you take a peek into each and tell me where
we should be going?"

Luthair replied with a curt nod before disappearing
under the door to the first room. While he wasn't looking, I
went back to examining the stained glass. The picture on
the window was the gold ring of eternity—the everlasting
paradise where lovers were destined to reunite once their

lives were over. It was meant to look like the sun, shining bright in a cloudless sky, reflected on a smooth ocean surface. I had never considered William a romantic, but he said the story of Ruma's devotion to his wife moved him more than any other.

What was her name? Acantha. She had been born on my island, before it came to be known as the Isle of Ruma. When Ruma met Acantha, the stories say, they both knew it was love at first sight—fate had brought him to the island, and she stole his heart with a mere glance.

For a brief second I wished I could see the stained glass window in the cathedral. It must have been magnificent. I vowed to write William and tell him everything I saw in the room, even though I would have to omit the sneaking-in part.

Luthair shifted out from the first room and explored the other three, slipping from one shadow to the next like a silent snake. When he returned, he pointed to the second door.

"These are all personal quarters. Ruma's living space is through there."

"How can you tell?"

"More of his accomplishments are on display."

I stared at the other three doors. "So this is the common area for four people? Probably master arcanists—this is a common room for them. So why aren't there any trophies from the others?"

"Perhaps Ruma doesn't like to share in the glory of others."

I had never thought of that.

With a shake of my head, I headed for the room Luthair indicated. I opened the door to find a study and a short staircase to the second story. The study, poorly lit, contained very little. Blank paper, ink wells, books on the ocean and seafarers codes. I headed up the stairs and admired the many trinkets on display. Maps, paintings of treasures found —even beautiful limpet shells collected from odd islands.

When I got to the bedroom, I took note of the lavish accommodations. The bed could swallow three people and the pillows were so numerous it was as if someone had raided a whole island for them. The window had heavy curtains, shrouding the room in thick darkness despite the wall lamps.

"It's just a bedroom," I said.

"We should search everything."

"What're we looking for? A signed confession?"

"We won't know until we find it."

With a sigh, I walked over to the bed. The sheets were strewn about, some twisted over the pillows. I detected a slight musk as I looked under the bedframe.

Before I could search between the mattresses, the unmistakable sound of a door slamming shut echoed from the common room. Icy dread overtook me. Frozen in place, I listened to the heavy steps of someone milling about. Had we locked the doors behind us? I didn't remember. Had Luthair? Did it even matter? What if the newcomer was Ruma? What if he found me in his room?

I had to focus on breathing in order to get any air.

"Calm yourself," Luthair whispered. "We can leave out the window."

Could we?

I got up, careful not to disturb my surroundings, and inched my way across the room. Whoever was in the common room continued walking around, almost like they were pacing. Once I reached the curtains, I pushed them aside, cringing as the metal curtain rings scraped along the steel rod.

If I made it out of this situation, it would be a miracle.

The door to Ruma's room opened down below.

Was the thumping in my ears the sound of someone walking up the stairs or my own heart on the verge of exploding? I grabbed the window latch and opened it, my hands shaking.

A half-second before I climbed through, my attention landed on a small white object sitting on a desk near the sill. Although I only had a fleeting moment to analyze the object, I recognized it as the pelt of a rizzel. The silver stripes were unmistakable.

But it was dead. Skinned. Without bones or meat. Just the husk of fur. It haunted my thoughts for a prolonged moment as I stepped over the sill. Didn't Nicholin say they were breeding rizzels on the island where Mathis died?

My foot slipped on rain water, and I almost fell, but I kept a grip on the window. The drizzle hadn't let up, and it made everything thirty times more difficult. A tiny beam of wood had been built into the wall of the manor house, but otherwise I had no foothold—just a two-story fall to the bushes below. I clung to the wall, my palms sweaty.

Dammit.

Luthair shut the curtain and window behind me and then slithered outside as a weightless blob of shadow. When I glanced back, I almost did a double-take. I couldn't see the window. It had disappeared. An illusion? It had to be. The room was protected from outside people looking in.

But I didn't have time to dwell. I leapt without a second thought, hoping the bushes would ease the pain of the fall. Much to my surprise, shadows shifted around, taking a soft physical form that blunted my descent. It still hurt to tumble across the mud, but it wasn't as bad as I expected.

When I got to my feet, I patted myself off. We were in a garden of some sort. I shielded my eyes from the droplets of water and returned my attention to where the window should've been. Although I couldn't see it, I knew it was there. I decided to make a mental note of its location. Perhaps I would need to return.

"Luthair," I whispered. "Did you see what I saw?"

The pelt of the rizzel brought so many questions to mind, it almost caused me to forget where I was. Maybe Luthair was right.

"Well, hello there."

Somehow, my already iced-over body locked up again—even my heart stopped beating for a moment. It wasn't Luthair's voice.

I forced myself to turn around, my thoughts blank. What lie could I possibly tell to explain what I was doing? I couldn't even claim I was lost, not when I had jumped out of a window!

"Uh," I began, my throat tight.

My mentor stood only a few feet away, half-illuminated by the dim lanterns all around the garden. He, like me, was half soaked from the light drizzle.

"Master Zelfree," I said.

He pushed back some of his disheveled black hair and lifted an eyebrow. "What're you doing?"

"I, uh, well... it's complicated."

"Is it?"

His hint of amusement didn't help me remain calm. He saw right through me! Of course he did. A blind man would see right through me. I had never been an accomplished liar.

"I can explain," I said. "I was exploring the manor. No one said I couldn't. And then I got lost."

Zelfree took a few steps closer, into the lantern light, as he nodded along to my words. When he stood a few feet away, he muttered an *uh-huh* but otherwise refrained from any commentary.

"I got paranoid when I came to this room," I said, grasping for anything even slightly plausible. "And I wanted to exit as fast as possible so, I, uh, took the window. It was an honest mistake. We only have one-story houses on the Isle of Ruma, so, uh, going out the window is pretty common, actually."

"Hm."

Honestly, it was the worst lie I had ever come up with. It would've been more believable if I had said I was sleep walking. Or maybe I should've feigned temporary amnesia. By the abyssal hells—*running* probably would've been a better answer than the poor excuse I offered.

Before I could dig myself a deeper hole, Zelfree's mimic leapt down from the wooden beam above us, right from the spot the window should've been.

Wait. Had Traces been following me? Was that the terrible feeling I had the entire time I was in Ruma's room? Did Zelfree already know everything that was going on? And he was just letting me spin a lie? Why? For his own amusement?

I stopped talking, my body unresponsive.

Zelfree petted the shimmery gray cat and offered me a smile. "Well, I knew you were going to be a handful, but I hadn't expected this kind of behavior on your first day."

"You... knew?"

"It was obvious from your history."

My history?

In an instant, the ice in my veins burned with an unbearable intensity. Was he trying to imply I would be trouble because of my mother and father? I wasn't here to steal or damage things! I wasn't acting out simply because I was predestined to do so! If anything, I was on a quest to discover the killer of a noble arcanist!

"You don't know me," I snapped.

Both Zelfree's eyebrows rose.

"I'm not who you think I am. I barely even knew my parents, and I certainly won't become like them. I've worked too hard to get here. Do you understand?"

Zelfree chuckled.

For some reason, that angered me even more.

"It's true! I'll show you. *I'll prove it.* I'm better than that."

He snapped his fingers, startling me a bit. I cringed back, but he simply smiled.

"First off," he said, "sneaking around the manor isn't helping your case. Secondly, I don't know who your parents are, and I wouldn't have even considered them had you not brought it up. I was referring to William's letter of recommendation. He mentioned you were the type to power through all your problems—not following the rules when you thought they were stacked against you. Makes for an unpredictable apprentice, he said."

I opened my mouth and then closed it, my shock twofold. Zelfree didn't know about my parents? And William said I was an unpredictable apprentice? I thought everyone would know about my history—I figured Zaxis would've proclaimed it to the sun and back.

"William also said you were the most dedicated and hard-working young man he'd ever known," Zelfree said. "Which means even your mischief will be thorough."

"I, uh..."

"You know what would prove you're a well-mannered apprentice?" Zelfree asked. "If you headed back to your room and got a good night's sleep. You have more training to do tomorrow."

And would Zelfree even be there?

I didn't ask the question. Obviously, since he was letting me go without much scolding, it would be too snarky to point out his own questionable behavior.

"Can I ask you a quick question first?" I muttered.

Zelfree nodded.

"Why would anyone, uh, have the pelt of a rizzel? I mean, most societies I know about have laws against harming them, and—"

"Long ago," Zelfree said, cutting me off. "Rizzel were used to lure other mystical creatures. They smell tasty and have a powerful musk. It stays in the pelt long after they're dead."

"Oh." Was that why Ruma had one? Was it an innocent reason, or had he harvested it from the rizzel island where Nicholin was born?

Zelfree waved my comment away. "I wouldn't worry about that. Or mention it to anyone. Ever."

The harsh edge to his voice startled me a bit. "R-right," I muttered. "I won't."

Before I could walk away, Zelfree threw his arm over my shoulders. He pulled me close, his odd scent of liquor clinging to the air. "Oh, and don't go sneaking around this portion of the manor anymore, got it?"

"Y-yes, sir."

He turned to me, a cold look of seriousness that hadn't been there before stared back.

"I mean it," he whispered. "Don't mention anything you saw in that room. Next time you might not be so lucky."

Was he... threatening me?

I shivered as I stepped back.

Then Zelfree patted my shoulder. "Good night then." He turned on his heel and headed in the opposite direction as though nothing odd had happened between us.

What was that?

"Luthair?" I whispered.

"He may be Ruma's accomplice," Luthair said.

That was the most believable thing Luthair had said since we started this investigation. But I still didn't understand why. And what if more Frith arcanists were somehow in on this? What if the whole guild really was a band of murderers?

No. Absolutely not. There had to be another explanation.

Luthair snaked through the darkness. "Come. The evening grows old."

I hung my head and followed the movement in the shadows, occasionally glancing back at where the window should have been.

19

ABSENT MENTOR

To avoid getting lost in the manor gardens, I kept close to the building as I made my way around. When we had first entered Ruma's quarters, I thought we would discover he wasn't the killer. But the presence of the rizzel pelt—coupled with Zelfree's odd warning—made me less certain than ever.

The light sprinkling of rain coated everything in a fine layer of water. I almost slipped on a stepping stone in the garden, but my years of living on an island had trained me for unexpected water in all sorts of situations.

As I carefully made my way around the corner, I almost slammed face-first into Zaxis and his phoenix, Forsythe. I stumbled back, my eyes wide.

"Zaxis," I said aloud, so shocked I couldn't contain my words.

Forsythe flew from Zaxis's arm and landed on the branch of a nearby tree. He scooted under the leaves, protecting himself from the drizzle.

Zaxis wiped his red hair out of his eyes, but the rain

brought it back every couple seconds, no matter how hard he shoved it away.

"What're you doing here?" he demanded.

"*Me*? I could ask you the same thing."

"I was sent to check the grounds."

"Out in the rain?"

"Of course," Zaxis snapped. "Why are you out here?"

"Well..."

It was complicated. Even the truth would require an inordinate amount of explanation. But what could I say that would be halfway believable? Nothing.

"Master Zelfree knows I'm out here," I eventually said. "Everything's fine."

"That doesn't answer my question."

"It doesn't matter."

I tried to walk around him, but Zaxis grabbed my upper arm and jerked me back. His grip acted like a flint, igniting my anger. It took all of my willpower not to punch him across the face.

"This is the kind of thing Schoolmaster Tyms was talking about," Zaxis growled. "You don't care about anyone but yourself."

"What're you saying?" I asked, just as heated and curt as Zaxis.

"You're making us look bad! You're out here, skulking in the shadows, no doubt up to suspicious activity, sullying the name of our island."

I ripped free of his grip. "I'm not—"

But I caught my breath.

I *had* been up to suspicious activity. I broke into Ruma's room and searched his things. But I wasn't planning anything devious. I couldn't really tell that to Zaxis, however. Still, the situation, and guilt, killed my righteous indignation.

After a few calming breaths, I said, "I'm not going to harm the reputation of our island."

"You already have."

"How? By being here?"

Zaxis shoved my shoulder, and I staggered back. "Every ungraceful step you've taken toward becoming an arcanist has angered someone. You irritated the whole town when you failed to impress a phoenix."

"So?"

"You snuck out into the Endless Mire without permission!" Zaxis's voice grew louder with each word. "You messed up Lyell's opportunity to join me here. And now you're struggling to do even the most basic of magical tasks while showing a complete lack of respect for the guild!"

I shoved him back, my anger trapping me like quicksand.

What did Zaxis even know, really? Ruma could be a killer and a spreader of the plague. I could be the one saving the whole guild!

"Leave me alone, Zaxis," I said through clenched teeth. "I won't give up on my dreams because it upsets other people. What I'm doing is none of your damn business."

He grabbed me by the collar of my shirt and twisted his fingers into a tight grip. "We'll see about that once I bring you to the guildmaster for traipsing around the grounds when everyone was told to stay inside."

I knocked his hand away, and without much consideration, focused on the sorcery I had felt earlier in the day. It happened in a matter of moments—the hot pain of magic scorching my veins, the terror released from my evocation. Zaxis and I hit the mud, him on his knees, me rolling onto my side. My legs had buckled under the agony, and although I wanted to stand, I couldn't bring myself to do so.

Zaxis gripped at his head, his eyes scrunched together. Forsythe opened his wings, but he, too, collapsed and fell to the ground. He chirped, not unlike a normal bird, the high-pitched cry enough to tell me he felt genuine fear.

"S-stop!" Zaxis shouted, his voice on the verge of cracking. "*Stop!*"

The magic left me as fast as I had created it, but my legs still wouldn't function.

Trembling and unable to fly no matter how he flapped his wings, Forsythe's cry became weak sobs. My terror magic had frightened him enough that tears streamed down his heron-like face.

Zaxis ground his teeth and waved his arm outward in a large arc. Flames blazed toward me, and I covered my head in a futile attempt to shield myself from the heat. Luthair sprang from the shadows and blocked the brunt of the attack by physically stepping between me and Zaxis. He wrapped his tattered cape around to shield himself, but it didn't stop the destruction of the fire.

Luthair grunted and fell to one knee, but otherwise saved me from the attack.

"Are you okay?" I asked as the last of the fire dissipated in the evening drizzle.

While I forced myself to stand on wobbly legs, Zaxis dashed over to Forsythe's side and gently touched his crimson feathers.

"I'm here," Zaxis whispered. "Everything will be fine." He scooped the phoenix up into his arms and cradled him close.

Luthair faced me, smoke wafting from the singed shadow armor and half-charred cape. "Are you hurt?" he asked.

I shook my head.

"Thank the heavens," he muttered.

Then Luthair offered his shoulder. He supported my weight and half-carried me to the front of the manor. Zaxis didn't follow. He stayed with Forsythe, patting the phoenix's head until the crying stopped.

"In the future," Luthair muttered, "perhaps you should allow me to speak for you."

"Did you hear what Zaxis said, though?" I asked. "He was implying—"

"A knight doesn't resort to attacking others over petty arguments. You're both arcanists in the same guild. Now isn't the time to make enemies of each other."

How was Luthair both the voice of reason and the cause of trouble in this situation? It was *his* urging that brought me to Ruma's room and got me caught in the first place. Yet here he was, trying to scold me for not acting proper.

"You're confusing, you know that?" I said.

"I've thought the same thing of you," he drawled.

I chuckled to myself, though the effort hurt. I wished my magic didn't have such a terrible price. What if I had been fighting a pirate? Or an enemy arcanist? I would've been prone after one attack. I had to practice. It was the only way.

Right at the edge of sleep, before my eyes sealed themselves shut, a light tapping echoed in my ears. I shot up, sweat coating my skin. Where was I? A single lantern flickered in the corner of my room, dimmed to a low glow, but it was enough to see by.

Oh, right. I was in the guild. In my quarters. But what woke me?

Luthair swirled around the foot of my bed. He had recovered from the earlier attack, even though he remained cracked and tattered.

While I tried to orient myself to my surroundings, my window opened, and in came Illia with Nicholin. Although the drizzle had upgraded to full-blown rain, she had somehow climbed across the wall of the manor house to reach my room.

"Illia," I whispered. "Are you crazy? You could've hurt yourself."

"I'm sorry, Volke. I just couldn't wait for tomorrow." She tapped the window sill and whispered, "This way, Hexa."

I threw my blankets over my shoulders as Hexa also crawled through my window, my heart rate rising with each breath. In the past, I slept without any clothes, tightly wrapped in blankets, but since living in the manor house, I kept a pair of pants on, even at night. I had a gut feeling Illia would barge in on me at some point, and I wanted to avoid any awkward situations.

And for some reason, I didn't want Hexa to see me without my shirt. It was momentary, and I knew it was a foolish response, but still. I kept my blankets close as I stood.

"Are you two okay?" I asked. "What's happened?"

Illia stifled a laugh as she walked over to me, both her hands over her mouth. "Nothing, nothing. Calm down." She guided me back to my bed. "We just had a good day."

Nicholin slumped off her shoulder and fell onto my mattress, his shimmery white fur sparkling, even in the dim lighting. "Oh," he groaned. "I ate so much." He patted his protruding belly and let out a quiet belch. "Illia," he whined. "Carry me gently."

"We had so much food," Illia said.

She patted my shoulder as I took a seat next to her.

Hexa took a seat on my other side, her freckled face slightly flush. "So, this is your room, huh?" She wore her sleeveless shirt, displaying her many scars for the world to see. And for some reason she smelled like that drink Zelfree had in his tea cup.

"Have you two been drinking?" I asked.

"Shh," Illia said with a giggle. "The Pillar doesn't say anything about *drinking*."

"Abstinence. Without it, we act like drunkards."

Illia shot up straight, her one eye wide. "W-wait, really?"

"I was joking." But I wished it were true.

Hexa scrunched her eyebrows together. "What're you two talking about?"

"They're quoting an ancient staircase from their home island," Nicholin said with a burp. "It's weeeiiiird."

"Islanders are bizarre."

"Ha! I'm sure you have weird habits, too."

"We eat scorpions where I'm from." Hexa leaned back and then gave me a sideways glance. "Hey. Why're you wearing a blanket? Stop that."

"I can't believe you," I said, ignoring Hexa. "Both of you. We'll be training tomorrow."

Illia held up a hand. "We didn't go crazy." Then she pulled her hair to the side, exposing the rest of her face. "Listen, Hexa said that after a few drinks I wouldn't feel so self-conscious, and she was right. Normally I don't like it when you see me like this, but I'm fine now."

"Me?" I balked. "I'm your brother. I don't care that you have scars."

"You're not *really* my brother, though." She looked away. "You don't think of me as a literal sister, right? We just say that to everyone else."

The conversation was taking a turn for the worse. What did she want me to say? We weren't siblings? William basically adopted us both at the same time. I had always thought that... Well, none of that mattered anymore. Life was different now. We were adults, and we could choose what our relationship would be.

"Illia," I muttered.

Then my throat tightened.

Silence. One minute. Then another.

It went on too long.

"This is intense," Hexa said, startling me.

I whipped around, having forgotten she was so close. "Uh, maybe you two should go."

Illia grabbed her hair and fixed it back over her scars, never once meeting my gaze as she got off the bed. "Hexa said the people of her city wouldn't think I was ugly. Maybe I should just go there."

"I don't think you're ugly," I said.

"Don't lie to me," she snapped, her voice heated. She walked over to my window. "Don't... don't ever do that."

Her voice waivered for a second.

I stood from my bed, but didn't approach her. I hadn't been lying. Why didn't she believe me? Even when we were kids—she always said I was lying, so I stopped trying to compliment her appearance. I never wanted to hurt her feelings.

Hexa stood, gently scooped up Nicholin, and joined Illia by the window. "I think we should be going. Maybe one night I'll bring some rum for *you* too, Volke. Obviously you island folk keep too much stuff bottled up inside."

"I don't drink," I muttered.

"Eh, we'll break you of that habit."

"But..."

The two left before I could form a coherent argument.

What had *that* been about? Did Illia want something from me specifically? Why didn't she just say? I would do anything for her, all she had to do was ask. But I couldn't read minds. And having Hexa nearby made everything awkward.

On the bright side, I guess they were becoming friends. I had never seen Illia sneak around with someone, after all.

I would talk to her about it later. In private. Away from everyone, even our eldrin.

A knock on my door woke me before dawn.

I dragged myself out of bed, stretched, and then went to see who it was. To my surprise, Adelgis stood in the hall, dressed in his finest shoulder cape and knee-high boots. His long hair was pulled back in a tight ponytail, and his face had recently been washed. He looked like a soldier attending a parade.

"Uh," I muttered. "Can I help you?"

"Good morning," he said, too chipper for the early hour.

"Yeah. I guess."

"May I come in?"

I opened the door farther and motioned him into my room. Once inside, I closed the door and went for my clothes. While I would've changed out of my sleeping trousers, I didn't feel comfortable doing anything in front of someone who looked like they had taken three hours to prepare themselves for the day. Something about his attire made *me* feel stiff.

"What're you doing here?" I asked as I buttoned up my shirt.

Adelgis lifted his eyebrows. "We're apprentices to the same arcanist. I thought we could get to know each other better."

"Oh. Okay."

He stood straight with his shoulders back, even while I laced up my boots. Silence filled my room as he glanced around. I hadn't put anything personal around, so it was just a standard, barren bedroom.

What were we even going to talk about?

"So, what's up with your shoulder cape?" I asked. It was the single most defining thing about him.

Adelgis laughed. "My sister bonded with a brownie. They specialize in creating things. She designed this outfit." He patted his cape, then his creased pants. "She designed all my outfits, actually. My home city of Ellios rarely sees problems. The weather is nice, we're protected from bandits, and we're miles away from the seafaring pirates. Most arcanists take up the magics of art and entertainment."

"Huh," I muttered as I pulled on my coat.

"What was your home island like?"

"Small. Filled with tradition."

"What did you do there?"

I didn't really want to talk about my past. I shrugged. "All my free time was spent studying our island's oath of the arcanists. It's a bunch of lessons on wisdom that all arcanists should know."

Adelgis's eyes went wide. He took a step closer to me, his hands clasped together. "That is fascinating. Can you recite the oath?"

"It's long," I said. I forced a laugh. "It was written in pieces across one hundred and twelve steps. The first: *Integrity. Without it, we cannot have trust.* And the second: *Passion. Without it, we grow complacent.* Things like that."

"Was there one on knowledge?" Adelgis asked, in a tone way too excited for the information I was sharing.

"Uh, yeah. *Knowledge. Without it, we fear our surroundings without hope to understand.*"

"I'm intrigued. You should tell me all one hundred and twelve steps. Oh, let me take notes."

He reached into his pockets and withdrew a small piece of parchment and a fine stick of charcoal. He wrote down the steps I had told him, and then met my gaze, his hand poised over the parchment to continue writing.

Adelgis continued, "My father told me the guild was the perfect place to learn about other cultures. So many arcanists gather here from around the world."

I wasn't as enthusiastic, but the sun was rising, and I knew we had to be out by the lake. "I'll tell you while we walk," I said.

We headed there together while I recited all the steps— including the two broken ones. I would always remember those two, all the way to my deathbed. The embarrassing moment when I was chased off the stage still haunted some of my nightmares.

Adelgis and I made our way down to the first level. The guild seemed more at ease now that the plague boats were gone. The guild arcanists had been dealing with it for an entire week. During that time, I had swordsmanship and evocation magic training. While the others saw fast results after training together, I found myself struggling. I only practiced with Luthair, away from the others, so I didn't know how effective my terror was becoming. I borrowed a practice stick from the training yard and learned the basic stances for sword fighting.

Maybe someday I could call myself a swashbuckler too.

Still, learning magic hurt. I didn't complain though. I couldn't. If I did, I'd be the ungrateful apprentice who *doesn't want to try hard* and who *expects everything will be handed to him because he's so lazy.* That wasn't the reputation I wanted, not when Gregory Ruma was around.

With a shake of my head, I dispelled the negative thoughts.

"What's the last step?" Adelgis asked, shaking me from my anxiety.

"Justice. Without it, we cannot differentiate from revenge."

"Hm. Interesting. Ellios has a much shorter oath."

We arrived at the edge of the lake, the last two to join the new apprentices. I shivered to keep the chill from settling into my bones. The evening's rain had created a crystal rime that covered everything from the blades of grass to the stepping stones around the lake. It made for a snow-like environment. I had never seen snow, but from what I had read in books, it seemed to match.

Illia and Hexa didn't greet me when I arrived. Illia hadn't spoken to me since she visited late the other night.

"Hello," I said to her.

Nicholin turned his little ferret head and glared. "Seems like someone is late."

I returned his glare with one of my own. "I heard rizzels were formerly used as bait to lure out other mystical creatures."

His white fur stood on end. "Ha! I'd like to see someone try!"

"No one will use you as bait," Illia said, stroking his back. "Volke is just being mean."

I rubbed at my shoulder, hating the fact she was so cold to me. I had never seen her do this before. Not to me, at least. We were closer than this. What could I do to make things right?

"I'm sorry," I said.

Illia and Hexa both turned to me, each with an odd, almost bemused, expression.

"I was talking to Nicholin," I added. "Because I didn't mean to hurt his feelings."

They remained silent.

I continued, "I haven't been myself lately. I mean, we're supposed to be adults now, and I don't think I know what that entails. But I would never hurt Nicholin intentionally."

Nicholin swished his tail. "Are you actually talking about me? Because it doesn't sound right..."

"I'm sure you and Nicholin will *always* be close," Illia replied. "But Nicholin wants some time to think over stuff. Perhaps Nicholin doesn't really know what he wants, and that makes it confusing for everyone."

"Okay. Now I *know* you're not talking about me."

To my shock and surprise, Zelfree emerged from the morning fog and walked toward our group. And I do mean *walked*, no stumbling or drunken stupor about him. He actually seemed confident—maybe on the edge of agitated. He had a stern expression, his eyes narrowed and set directly on us. I straightened my posture as he approached, worrying he would still be upset about my break-in of Ruma's room.

"Where are my apprentices?" Zelfree asked.

Not even a *good morning*.

Illia, Adelgis, and I stepped forward. Hexa offered Illia a

tiny wave before shuffling off to join Zaxis and Atty. It was a shame we couldn't all be together, and for the first time since Illia said she would have the same mentor, I actually felt guilty about her decision. If she had gone with Ruma, she could've trained with Hexa as a friend.

Zelfree motioned with a jerk of his head. "Come with me."

The three of us trailed behind him.

"Don't dawdle," he snapped.

We picked up our pace until we were inches behind him.

Adelgis leaned over and whispered, "Looks like someone missed out on their morning ale."

Illia covered her mouth to stifle a laugh. I dwelled on the statement. Maybe Zelfree was a man who didn't function well without spirits in his veins.

My crazy hair puffed out extra in the morning wind. I tried to keep it down, but nothing worked. After a few failed attempts, I let it swirl with the breeze.

"That's why you should have a hair tie," Adelgis said, pointing to his ponytail. "It's practical and—"

"Are you three done?" Zelfree glared at us over his shoulder. "This isn't social hour."

We exchanged questioning glances but otherwise stopped talking.

It wasn't long before we came to the tip of Gentel's shell and climbed up. Unlike the edges of her shell, which gradually sloped into the water, the portion above the head was lifted, perhaps a good hundred feet above the waves of the ocean. It made for a breathtaking view.

Everyone on the islands knew sea turtles, no matter their breed, couldn't retract their head under their shell like a land turtle could. Even atlas turtles kept their heads out at all times, their thick scales and sharp beaks enough protection.

Standing so high above the water reminded me of sailing on the ocean, and I took a moment to allow the salt-water to swirl into my hair. What would William do if he saw me now? I wondered if he would be proud I made it this far. Had he read my letters? I hoped so.

Zelfree snapped his fingers and then removed the bangles around his wrists. "This is where we'll be meeting for the next week."

Adelgis raised his hand.

"This isn't an elementary school," Illia murmured.

Zelfree glanced over at Adelgis and sneered. "I've only given you a single sentence of instructions and already there're questions? Fantastic."

"What should we do if you don't arrive on time?" Adelgis asked. "Given your attendance last week, I just wanted to know what your stance was on training under Master Ruma."

"You won't ever train under Ruma again. Understand?"

His curt and venom-laced words buried themselves in my thoughts. Had something happened? He hadn't displayed this level of animosity before.

"Hopefully you're all done?" Zelfree asked.

Adelgis lowered his hand and nodded.

"Good. Because I'm going to show you what your magic should look like. Who wants to go first?"

"Go first?" Illia asked. "What're we even doing?"

Zelfree's bangles transformed into Traces, his gray-furred mimic. She purred and smiled wide as she walked across Zelfree's shoulders. "Oh," she said. "We're training the baby arcanists today? Fun."

Zelfree snapped his fingers. "Traces will transform into

your eldrin and I'll wield your magics against you. Whoever can knock me off the turtle using their magic alone will earn a special reward."

I lifted both eyebrows. "You want us to knock you off the atlas turtle? From this height?"

I glanced over the edge a second time, confirming we stood a good hundred feet above the water. A fall from here could result in death, even for an arcanist. Did Zelfree want to die? Was this some sort of pathetic attempt at suicide? I knew he had a drinking problem, but this was ridiculous.

"I don't think this is safe," I said.

Zelfree nodded. "That's the point. Life isn't safe. You need to know how to protect yourself, especially if we're getting close to pirate-infested territory. The more we practice, the better we get. Simple logic." He clapped his hands. "I'll ask again. Who wants to go first?"

No one said anything. I don't even think the other two were breathing.

I was the first to clear my throat with a cough.

Zelfree smirked. "Volke."

My shoulders bunched at my neck. Traces hopped off his shoulder. Before she hit the ground, she blackened into a deep shade of ink and then disappeared into Zelfree's shadow, much like Luthair did with mine.

"Step forward, boy. I've always wanted to see what a knightmare can do."

20

SIREN

I took a step forward, uncertain of what to do with my hands. I shoved them in my pockets, then took them out and fidgeted with the hem of my shirt. Fighting another arcanist had never crossed my mind as one of the first types of training I would do.

"Master Zelfree," I said. "I've never fought anyone before."

He lifted an eyebrow.

"I tussled with other kids on my home island, but I still don't really know how to wield my magic."

"This will help you learn."

"But—"

"Watch me," he growled.

I flinched. When it became apparent he wouldn't back down from his unique training style, I exhaled and took another step forward. Was his plan to beat the information into me? Arcanists could heal, sure, but digging the lesson into my flesh didn't seem like the most efficient teaching method.

Zelfree waved his hand. "Summon your eldrin. You're wasting our morning."

"Luthair?"

The shadows at my feet wrapped around in front of me and rose into a solid mass of plate armor. Luthair brushed aside his cape and offered Zelfree a formal bow before pulling his black sword from its scabbard.

And what was I supposed to do? I awkwardly stood behind Luthair, half-shielding myself with his body and half glancing around him, trying to keep my eyes on Zelfree.

"Come on," Zelfree said. "I know you two have been practicing with the sword. Show me what you have."

He knew?

Luthair lowered his weapon and then handed it to me. I took the hilt and allowed the inky darkness to cover my arms. I still hadn't managed to do much with it. Sure, I practiced with the stick, and I knew the basic stance, but that wouldn't save me from Zelfree.

"Attack me," Zelfree commanded.

But he hadn't summoned his mimic-knightmare. He just stood there. No weapon. Not even a fighting posture, just with his arms crossed and his eyes narrowed into a glower. He even took a few more steps toward the edge of the turtle shell and glanced over the edge. The ocean waves crashed against the atlas turtle, creating a pleasant melody.

I walked forward, sword at the ready.

Zelfree didn't move.

"Go on," he said. "Knock me off."

"You sure?"

"I'm not going to repeat myself anymore. Either you pay attention, or I'll throw *you* over."

"All right..."

I swung my sword, the magic of Luthair's shadows

burning my forearms. When Zelfree dodged to the side—barely dodged—I swung again. He took a step back. Too close to the edge for comfort, but I wasn't swinging particularly fast or strong. Zelfree could go to either side if he wanted.

I swung a third time. He stepped back again.

Then Zelfree slipped on the edge. And went over.

Illia and Adelgis both gasped.

By the abyssal hells, I even gasped!

"Is he okay?" I asked as I dropped Luthair's sword. The black gauntlets disappeared from my arms.

"I can't believe you killed our instructor!" Adelgis shouted.

"I-I didn't mean to!"

Before I could look over the side, Luthair grabbed my shoulder and pushed me back. "Careful. He's planning an attack." He picked up his own sword and held it at the ready.

"While falling to his death?" I asked, waving my arms at the sheer drop to the ocean.

"Shadows don't fall. Be on your guard."

What? Shadows? Falling? What was he trying to tell me?

Inky snakes of darkness slithered up over the edge and traveled across the ground with lightning speed. They circled around behind me and coalesced together, much like Luthair. They formed into Zelfree and Traces—Traces having assumed the perfect duplicate of a knightmare. She appeared to be a suit of midnight armor, not cracked or tattered, gleaming in the early morning light that pierced the fog.

I stood frozen, my mouth agape, my eyes wide.

How did they do that?

Traces pulled her sword and swung in one blinding motion. Luthair stepped between me and the mimic, his sword clanging against the imposter's. While Luthair held Traces at bay, Zelfree melted back into the shadows and disappeared as though he had sunk into the ground.

I watched him go—what else could I do?—and backed up once I noticed the shadows slipping toward me once again. I couldn't go anywhere, however. I backed up to the edge of the turtle's shell, my heels hanging over the side, the ocean's waters far below me.

Would Zelfree attempt to knock me off? He had threatened it.

Zelfree appeared in front of me, rising from the shadows in a matter of half a second. I nearly jumped to my doom, but I held my ground, my mind scrambling to come up with any way to fight him.

I shoved him back and did the one thing I had practiced —I evoked the terrors, even though it burned my insides. The pain almost caused my legs to give out, which would have sent me plummeting a hundred feet, but I managed to stagger forward.

Zelfree didn't react like the others, however. He shook his head and sneered.

"Really?" he asked. "Pathetic."

He waved his hand, and I swear my mind twisted into a state of stagnation.

Before I could voice my concern, my thoughts went back to my time on the Isle of Ruma. Specifically, back to when the crowd threw stones at me, right at the moment Tyms had told me to go home. The memory wouldn't go away. I grabbed my head, trying to focus on the present—Zelfree was still right in front of me!—but I couldn't make the images go away.

And then the memory changed to something worse than reality.

I ran home to the cottage and...

And William disowned me. So ashamed, so disappointed—he wanted nothing to do with me, like a piece of trash he threw me away. He told me the cottage was no longer my home.

I scrunched my eyes, the false memory playing so fast I didn't have time to recover or think.

William had been the only person who wanted me after my father was taken from the island. He taught me everything I knew, patched all my scrapes whenever I fell near the tide pools, and held birthday celebrations for me, even when he couldn't afford it.

He was my real father, even if we shared no blood.

And I had disappointed him.

Where was Illia? She always helped me. Always stood by my side. Even when I messed up or made a fool of myself, there she was, pulling me back onto my feet, reassuring me everything would turn out for the better.

But when I went to the graves in our cemetery... her name was etched on the newest one. Somehow, I knew the pirates had gotten her. Like in a dream where the information just came to me, even out of order.

My visions weren't real, yet I couldn't help but feel all the agony as though they were my *actual* memories. How could I have lost both William and Illia? What would I ever do without them? If I had just tried a little harder—*if I had done a little better*—would they still be with me?

"Stop!" I shouted. "Stop!"

I couldn't take anymore! Hot tears burned my face.

Then the false memories stopped, and I managed to catch my breath.

That had been *my* magic—the terrors *I* could create. Zelfree had used it against me.

He stared down at me, his look of disappointment plain as day.

I gulped down some air and wiped at my face. What did he want from me? This was his first day training us as his apprentices! My first day under William didn't involve him pushing me into a grave and throwing a corpse on my face. He gradually built up to what I needed to know.

Luthair and Traces clashed with their swords one last time before breaking apart. Once finished, Luthair bowed again and sheathed his weapon before returning to his shadow state around my feet.

"Knightmares are masters of terror and shadow," Zelfree said. "They have the ability to ward themselves from fear attacks—from any mind-altering magic, to be precise. You should never attempt to evoke terrors on a knightmare or his arcanist. It was foolish to use it against me."

"Well, I didn't know that," I said, half-shouting. I motioned to our surroundings. "I didn't even know you would make it back up after falling off the turtle!"

"Shadows have fluid movements."

I waited, but he didn't offer any more elaboration.

"That's it?" I asked.

Zelfree huffed. "What did I say? As a knightmare arcanist, you have mastery over the shadows. I see you can use the terror, but you can't forget the basic element your eldrin represents. Think of yourself as a shadow now. What can they do? They don't fall, boy. They don't fly, either. Understand?"

"I think," I said, trying to grasp the abstract statement.

"I got back up the ledge by slipping into the shadows. As long as shadows have a surface, they can go anywhere. Even the slightest of cracks will allow a shadow to slide through."

Although I said nothing, it reminded me of when

Luthair made his way under doors to unlock them from the other side. Not even the tiny crack between the door and the floor had prevented him from getting through.

Could I do that? Zelfree had done it with no problem. He became a shadow and used his magic to snake his way up a sheer cliff.

"You need to embody your magic," Zelfree said. "It *is* you, got it? Make yourself and the shadows one and the same. That's the essence of augmentation magic."

I nodded, probably more than necessary.

He pushed me back toward the group. "You stand over here and practice before you embarrass yourself further. I have other apprentices to help while the rusty gears in your head mull all this over."

I took my place next to Adelgis. Zelfree motioned Illia to join him near the edge of the turtle shell. She and Nicholin rushed over and Traces took the form of a rizzel once again.

I didn't watch their fight. Illia was capable, I had seen her teleportation, and I wanted to focus on my own magic so I didn't fall behind. While she faced our master, I closed my eyes and tried to imagine embodying my magic.

After a few seconds, the terrible burning built up under my skin, replacing my focus with agony.

Damn!

I stopped and rubbed at my nose. I pulled my arm away to find it covered in blood. When did that happen? I glanced over. Adelgis hadn't noticed. He watched the practice bout between Illia and Zelfree with rapt attention.

"Why isn't this working?" I whispered. But I already knew. I had to overcome the second-bonding if I was ever to move forward. "I just need to try again."

Closing my eyes, I tried to claw my way through the pain.

While most of my attention went into embodying the magic, a small piece of me dwelled on the problems I constantly faced. Was there any way around this? Could I somehow turn the second-bonding to my advantage?

For some reason, my mix of hatred and frustration helped me stay focused through the biting pain. My nose bled, but I ignored it. Inch by inch, magic crept into my veins, down my arm, into my fingertips, all the way to my toes. Zelfree had managed to become a shadow in mere seconds to avoid falling—I had probably taken over a minute.

And then, in the last of my hair and tips of my ears, I sensed the completion. When I opened my eyes, I sank into the shadows around my feet, disappearing from the physical world and plunging into a realm of darkness. No sight. No sound. How could anyone navigate like this?

And I couldn't breathe.

No problem. I would just resurface.

But when I released my hold on my magic, nothing happened. I waited. My heart beat, even in the realm of pitch black void. Each thump of my heart only added to my panic. Without air, the beating became louder and louder, filling my ears and drowning out my thoughts.

I flailed around—or, at least, I *thought* I was flailing around—trying to find an escape.

Odd sounds penetrated through the noise as I reached the edge of my breath.

Singing. Both beautiful and soothing, but without lyrics. More like humming. A woman? Who was it?

I gasped the moment I emerged from the shadows, much like breaking the surface of the ocean and finding the sky again. What in the abyssal hells happened to me? I was on my back, staring up at a ceiling. In a cave? Water lapped over my shoulders and onto my body.

Somehow, I had left the edge of the turtle shell.

Despite the lingering pain, I sat up. It took a few minutes for my eyes to adjust to the morning light streaming through the cave's mouth.

No, not a cave.

This was part of the atlas turtle—the opening for one of its many limbs. Gentel's fin stretched out into the ocean for several hundred feet, resting idle.

I sat on top of one of her fins, tucked inside the shell.

How did I get here? Through shadow shifting?

The same singing I heard before echoed throughout the crevasse. Gentel was so large, a fat fold could be considered a canyon, so when I stood and glanced around, I wasn't surprised by the size of her.

"Hello?" I called out. With a grimace, I rubbed at my face.

Blood everywhere. My nose might as well have been a crimson waterfall. I snorted to clear my nasal passages, but that only made it worse. It looked like a murder had taken place on my shirt.

At least I had used my magic! That fact perked me up. I knew I hadn't used it properly—or even in a manner I would want to replicate—but using it at all was still a success.

"Luthair?"

No answer.

The humming grew louder. And lovelier.

"Anyone here?"

Then the humming stopped.

"Hello?" a delicate voice answered back.

I walked toward the source, squinting as I made my way into the light. "I'm coming."

Ocean waves washed over the turtle's limb, splashing onto the fin and coating me in saltwater. Perched at the highest point of the fin sat a glorious white bird—who appeared owl-like—with legs and talons shaped like human hands. She was the size of a small dog, perhaps a little larger.

A siren.

I had read so many books on mystical creatures I knew them well. Song birds with the voices of women who ruled the rocks of the ocean coast, their kingdom secured from all others and marked with bones. They were one of the few mystical creatures that rarely sought to bond.

But weren't they supposed to have the faces of women? This one had the face of an owl.

"Are you lost?" I asked. "I didn't think we were near siren territory."

"I... need to *tell* you something. It's very... *important*."

I lost my breath for a moment, struck by the bizarre cadence of the siren's speech. It was only then that I noticed its eyes were closed and that its talons were buried in the fin of the turtle, red with blood. The creature had been pecking past the scales, digging into the soft flesh just underneath.

With shaky movements, I took a step backward. But where would I go? I didn't see a way up onto Gentel's back unless I jumped into the ocean and swam for the side.

"Where are you... *going*, Volke?"

How did it know my name?

"I'm not going anywhere," I muttered.

The water splashed up again, half-soaking the siren and washing over me completely. The blood of the atlas turtle mixed with the sea foam, creating a pink swirl of water that disappeared into the ocean. The bird didn't seem to mind the waves. She spread her wings, and much to my horror, her feathered face split down the middle and then peeled outward, revealing a woman's face underneath.

There it was.

Her lifeless eyes bulged from their sockets, jiggling and gray, much like a dead fish.

Plague-ridden. No doubt in my mind.

"Stay," she said in a sing-song tone. "*Stay*. I need you. Soft. You smell good. *So good*. Let me quell that bleeding."

Then she fluttered and hopped closer, her hand-like talons gripping tight into the scales of the atlas turtle. Once she had moved, I could see the pumpkin-sized gouge she ripped into Gentel. Was she eating the turtle? Could Gentel feel it? Maybe not—it was small when compared to the massive size of her whole body.

The points of the siren's talons were needle-thin and several inches long. The crash of the ocean waves reminded me I was out in the middle of nowhere, without Luthair, Illia, or Nicholin.

The siren advanced closer, her human face twisting with a giant smile, her teeth sharp, and her eyes glancing in all directions.

21

LAND HO

"What're you doing here?" I demanded.

"I need magic." The siren laughed. "I need magic to transform!"

Just as another wave washed over the turtle's fin, I lunged and collided with the siren, throwing us both down. She cackled as she twisted in my grasp, her talons sinking right into the tender flesh of my thigh, slicing through muscle with ease. I flinched, but as long as she didn't hook the soft bits between my legs, I would keep fighting. Fortunately, the siren didn't act with much rhyme or reason.

"Fool," she said with a giggle. "I grow... *stronger.*"

A second set of wings burst from the siren's body, both covered in red mucus and membrane, like a newborn infant emerging from its mother's womb. The wings, fully feathered and soaked in blood, flapped with a powerful rhythm. Unable to hold the creature, I let her go and stumbled back, slipping across the fin.

The siren took to the air, her four wings a distinct sight.

"What in the abyssal hells?" I murmured.

Sirens never had four wings. And the new set was horrific, especially when coated in fresh blood. Ragged feathers, bulbous muscles, a twisted thumb protruding at the top —disgusting and nightmarish in every sense of the words.

When the beast flew back around, she didn't go for me, she went right back to the bloody mess she had made on Gentel's fin. The siren, using her human face, chewed on the flesh of the turtle, gnawing at the exposed insides, all while smiling and laughing.

I couldn't allow the monster to hurt Gentel. Despite the fact that my left leg barely responded to my demands, I hobbled forward. A wave splashed over us, filling my mouth with saltwater, stinging my injury, but I coughed it back and leapt forward, missing the siren and tumbling onto my hands and knees.

The siren cackled. "I need... *more magic*. Give it to me."

"No one is giving you anything," I said as I forced myself to stand.

"I will take it. *I will take it!*"

I grew numb and stiff, almost unable to move. The chill of the water, mixed with the burn of my lingering injuries, played with my perceptions. The world spun. I'd fall off the fin sooner or later, I knew it in my gut.

If I didn't stop the siren now, no one would.

"You're nothing, *insect*," the siren said, the woman's face smiling wide, blood on her lips and between her teeth. "You'll die *alone and forgotten!*"

I lunged for her again, but when I collided, she kept her razor talons embedded in the turtle's flesh. I thrashed and yanked, but it only tore more flesh. How could I get her off? In a split-second decision, I channeled my magic—creating terrors. The siren screamed, half-laughing, and her talons loosened. I rolled off the side, taking us both to the ocean below.

We crashed through the waves, my heart pounding in my ears. The siren didn't claw me, no doubt still shaken by my magic.

Sunlight shimmered into the water, bright enough to see, but also creating an enchanting aura of sea-greens, water-blues, and sunrise-golds. The siren swirled in the undertow, her disgusting secondary wings thrashing about as if operating with a mind of their own.

But using my magic harmed me further. I couldn't move. I tried, I really did, but the agony from the injuries made everything difficult.

I had learned to swim when I was two years old—I had never been afraid of the water—but I knew what would happen if I let the currents have their way. I flailed about, pushing my arms to their limits, directing myself to the surface, if only to breathe.

When I threw my head above the waves, I gasped. A second later, I was tossed back under, more saltwater rushing into my mouth.

I wouldn't make it.

No, dammit! No!

I refused. I wouldn't die here.

I kicked and flailed, grinding my teeth together so hard they hurt. I managed to grip the side of the turtle, my nails digging into the soft flesh between scales. The moment my head got above the water, I snorted and wheezed, coughing up the sea still trapped in my lungs.

But I couldn't drag myself from the waves, not with my failing strength. I just hung onto the turtle shell, the chill seeping into my core.

Someone grabbed the back of my shirt and yanked me

from the ocean. I clung to the arm, and for a brief moment, I wondered who could've possibly found me. Zelfree? Illia?

"What're you doing over here?" Ruma asked with a laugh.

I coughed and hacked another round of saltwater, unable to respond.

Ruma dragged me up the turtle's back until we were once again on soil. Then he set me down and patted my back. Once the water had cleared from my lungs, I glanced up at him, my eyebrows knit together. How did he even manage to find me?

He stared down at the gash on my thigh. "What happened?"

It took a moment for me to breathe. "A plague-ridden siren attacked me..."

"Here?"

I nodded.

Ruma grabbed my shirt and I widened my eyes. "*Here?*" he asked again, like I hadn't already answered him.

"Yeah," I said. "It was on Gentel's fin. I threw it into the water."

"What was it doing?"

"I don't really know. Eating her?"

"Wait here," Ruma said.

He stood and walked back to the water's edge, a crackle of electricity swarming around his body. Ruma waited until a series of bubbles popped along the ocean waves. The siren emerged from the depths, flapping her four wings with enough power to break free of the water's hold.

"Over here," Ruma called out. He withdrew a knife from a hidden pocket on his slacks and sliced himself down his forearm. "Come get me."

I stood, but collapsed to the ground when pain flared

from my thigh. I wished I could heal myself faster. Magic seemed to take its sweet time knitting the flesh together.

The siren shot straight for Ruma, her wild laughter and wide smile more chilling than the fact she had survived the undertow of the ocean. She was inches from plunging her talons into Ruma's chest, but he lifted his hand and created a powerful bolt of electricity. His evocation, far beyond anything I had seen before, tore through the siren, burning and destroying it in a single fell blast.

The charred corpse hit the edge of the turtle shell, still twitching, and then rolled into the water. Bits of feathers, mucus, and blood were all that was left.

Ruma walked over to the mess and knelt in front of it.

Someone placed a hand on my shoulder. I whipped my head around, shocked to see Zaxis.

"You okay?" he asked.

"I think so," I said.

"You're bleeding. You sure you're okay?"

I had never heard Zaxis so concerned. It almost worried me.

"Let him catch his breath," Ruma called out. He stood and jogged to me. Then he knelt and examined the wounds on my thigh. "She got you good, lad."

"What's going on?" I asked.

"Do you know how this occult plague is spread?"

I shook my head. I honestly hadn't thought much about it. I just figured it jumped from one mystical creature to the next, like a flu or a disease.

"It travels through the blood. Magical blood. So through arcanists, their eldrin, mystical creatures, and even animals who have absorbed ambient magic, like the star moths."

My hand shot down to the injury on my thigh.

Arcanists? It could spread to arcanists? Was the siren

bleeding when I fought it? Did our blood mix at any point? I could barely think, let alone remember such details. Would I go insane, like the mystical creatures? Was there a cure? What would I do if—

Ruma grabbed my shoulder, freeing me from the whirlpool of dreadful thoughts I had trapped myself in.

"The siren wasn't bleeding," he said, his voice low.

"I... I fought a plague-ridden creature before. A white hart."

"Was it bleeding?"

"It bled all into the mire. Everywhere."

I had to be infected. I ran a shaky hand through my hair, my nails cutting at my scalp.

"Wait," Zaxis said. "The one my brother was trying to bond to?"

"Y-yeah."

He went quiet after my response and crossed his arms. Did he believe me? I didn't care either way, but I wished he would let the incident with Lyell go.

Ruma narrowed his eyes. "Were you an arcanist then?"

"N-no, but I became one at the end, and when Luthair killed the white hart, its guts spilled into the mire water."

"It doesn't matter. It couldn't have infected you if you had just turned."

My breathing came easier. Ruma patted my back and stared out at the ocean.

"How would I know if I was infected?" I whispered.

He turned to face me again. "The occult plague warps magic. Since mystical creatures are entirely magic, it infects them throughout. But arcanists are more than just magic."

Before I could ask anything else, Zelfree appeared in the area—teleporting in with a flash of white, much like

Nicholin. He shook himself off, and Traces leapt from his shoulder. He and Ruma shared a quick glare.

"I'll take care of my apprentice," Zelfree said. He knelt next to me. "He needs medical treatment."

"He needs rest," Ruma said.

"Like I said—*I'll* take care of my apprentice."

Zaxis took his place next to Ruma and shrugged. "Sounds good to me."

Ruma gave me a long look. I didn't know what to say to him. I wanted to thank him. He pulled me from the ocean, after all, but I couldn't get the words out. After a few seconds, Ruma nodded, and then headed back to the training grounds with Zaxis by his side.

Once alone, Zelfree placed his hand on my knee. I flinched, but he quickly tied a cloth around my injury, keeping it from bleeding. After he finished, he offered his shoulder. I took it and we both stood.

"Master Zelfree," I muttered. "Doesn't an arcanist's magic come from their soul?"

"Yes," he said.

"If the occult plague infects magic, does that mean it could infect an arcanist's soul?"

Zelfree sneered. "It doesn't just *infect* things. The plague corrupts. And yes, it'll corrupt a person's soul. No doubt in my mind."

"W-what happens then?"

"The arcanist's perceptions become warped and tainted. Most discard empathy. Why do you think so many arcanists are becoming pirates? It's not *just* to earn a quick coin. They're falling victim to their own dark tactics."

The information stunned me like a blow to the gut. I figured most arcanists became pirates because they were knaves. Some were, no doubt, but imagining them as once-decent people unnerved me.

"I fought a siren," I whispered. "It had the plague. Ruma said I wasn't infected, but... could you somehow check?"

Zelfree stared at me. After a few minutes of walking, he finally said, "You don't seem infected. But you should be careful from here on out. We don't have a cure. Understand?"

"I'll be careful."

"Where was the siren harming Gentel?"

"On her fin. O-over there." I gestured to the front fin out in the ocean. I still couldn't organize my thoughts, but I knew I still had one burning question I couldn't answer on my own. "If the plague really is so terrible, why did anyone begin spreading it in the first place? Why risk getting infected just for a quick attack tactic?"

Zelfree huffed. "Some people think it makes their magic stronger."

"How?"

He stopped at the door to the manor home. "It transforms eldrin, and corrupted magic does have the edge when in a conflict. It breaks down normal magic, like a disease."

"No kidding." I caught my breath. "What about Gentel? Is she—"

"Calm down," Zelfree said. "Gentel is highly resilient."

I leaned on his shoulder. "You don't think she'll be infected?"

"I will check on her while you head back to the manor. And if you see something like this again, you come straight to me, understand?"

"S-sure."

"And no one else," Zelfree quickly added.

"Not even Ruma?"

"I want to be the first person to know. Before Ruma can kill or destroy anything. *Me*. Got it?"

No one else? Why? It seemed more efficient to let everyone know rather than keeping it quiet, but I was injured and not in the mood to think.

"Okay," I said.

"Good. Now head inside."

It took me two days to recover from my injuries. The wounds from the white hart hadn't taken as long, but Zelfree insisted I wait until even my bruises had healed. Other than waking from several nightmares, all of which involved me contracting the occult plague, I slept fine.

During my forced recovery, I explored more of the guild's manor house. I enjoyed the many mystical creatures most of all. When I was younger, I daydreamed what it would be like to bond with all sorts of creatures. Dragons had been my favorite, but they were nearly extinct outside of the northern coast, so only the raider arcanists who lived there bonded with them.

One journeyman arcanist in the guild, I think he said his name was Gavus, had bonded with a hellhound. His magics involved fire and stone manipulation. He and his eldrin had been a friendly pair, which amused me, considering how sinister a giant black dog with horns appeared to be.

Another journeyman, Yellis, had bonded with an orthrus—a two-headed dog with bulging muscles and exceptional scent. She said her enhanced strength came in handy when out in most towns or fulfilling guild contracts.

I explored everything. A dining hall with a chef—a man with a fairy eldrin who prepared some of the most delectable foods I had ever tasted. A commons area for the arcanists to congregate in on long travels... Oh! And a substantial library run by two arcanists bonded to satyrs.

By the end of the two days, I had investigated most of the manor. Locked doors had prevented me from searching the remaining areas, and I had refused to allow Luthair to sneak me in. After getting caught the last time, I dreaded any further reprimands.

I had also written Lyell and William. The guild had a post system and a few mystical creatures who could deliver our messages. I wanted to hear from both of them, but I knew it would be more difficult in the reverse. No letters yet.

Just as I recovered from my injuries, Gentel reached land.

The master arcanists asked the journeymen and novice apprentices to wait in the guild manor house while they disembarked into the city of Tallin. We had no training scheduled. Our only order had been to wait.

How long would we be stopped at Tallin? No one knew. Some said a week.

I waited in my room watched from the window as the master arcanists gathered outside. Once they headed to the pier, I took a seat on my bed and relaxed back. Two seconds later, someone knocked on my door. I leapt up to answer, confused.

Atty stood outside, smiling. For a brief second, I didn't know what to say. Her blonde hair hung loose, her outfit hugged her in all the right places. And her phoenix stood by her side, majestic and grand all by itself.

"What're you doing here?" I asked. Then I immediately regretted it. What was I thinking? How could I be so rude?

"I wanted to see if you had gotten better," she said with an apologetic tone. "Should I come back at a different time?"

"What? No, no. I'm sorry. You just surprised me. Come in."

I opened the door to allow her and her phoenix into my room. I tried to shut it once they entered, but Adelgis stopped me by raising his hand. I lifted an eyebrow, unaware he had been standing behind Atty.

What was *he* doing here? I thought I would finally get some alone time alone with Atty, and now Adelgis was barging in? Just my luck. He walked in and took a seat on the foot of my bed.

"We came to see how you were doing," he said. "You look better."

Atty stood by the window, the sunlight sparkling on her golden hair, highlighting the arcanist mark on her forehead. She stroked the head of her phoenix eldrin. "Oh, I don't think I've ever introduced you. This is Titania."

I nodded to the phoenix. "Hello."

"Good day," Titania said.

Luthair rose up from the shadows around my feet. He stood over six feet, his empty helmet rather ominous. I wasn't shocked when everyone's eyes went wide. Why had he come out? Probably to be social.

But when was he ever social?

"You all remember Luthair, right?" I asked.

As if to give everyone space, Luthair stepped into the corner of the room. He really did look like a suit of armor in an old castle. He said nothing, playing the role of a shadow.

Adelgis swished his long black ponytail over his shoulder. "Since everyone else has introduced their eldrin, I should show you mine. I'm bonded to an *ethereal whelk*, creatures made of light and dreams."

"That sounds interesting," Atty said.

I shrugged. "Yeah. They're rare. Almost extinct."

"My eldrin's name is Felicity."

I waited, but Adelgis didn't move. Was she going to get here or what? Then the light in the room started to flicker, much in the same way the shadows moved when Luthair took form. I held my breath, wondering what could possibly emerge.

22

ARGUMENTS

The light coalesced into crystals that formed together into a spiral seashell.

I had seen thousands of whelks growing up as a child. The sea snails always fascinated me, specifically because of their shells. They ranged in color and shape, some with an iridescent sheen, much like a soap bubble. But the ethereal whelk had a crystal shell unlike anything I had ever seen before. It sparkled with a whitish-pink inner light.

When the whelk emerged from her shell, she moved in a slow and deliberate manner. While sea snails typically had soft slug-bodies of a green or red color, hers had the same soap bubble iridescence as a seashell. She appeared neither slimy nor porous, but smooth and half-glowing.

She had four tiny tentacles hanging from the underside, like she was the byproduct of a squid and sea snail. She floated through the air, the tentacles dangling, flowing as if caught in an invisible current.

"My arcanist," she whispered in a delicate voice. "It's quite an honor to meet other arcanists of your guild." She moved through the air like a dandelion puff caught on the breeze, seemingly without any weight.

"Felicity can hear thoughts and manipulate light," Adelgis said with a smile. "And she's good at entertaining company."

Felicity's eye stalks lifted out of her slug body, the eyes shimmering with an inner luster. "I do enjoy the adventure tales. And romances. Anything with a happy ending."

"I've never seen anything like an ethereal whelk," I muttered. "Nice to meet you, Felicity."

She shimmered as her eye stalks lifted up and down.

Atty smiled and clapped her hands together once. "Oh, if we're all going to socialize, I know how we could do it. Wait right here while I go get the cards." She hurried from the room with her phoenix, but not before giving me an extra glance.

My heart rate increased. The moment she closed the door behind her, I let out a long sigh.

"I hope you don't mind us visiting," Adelgis said.

"It's fine," I replied. I wanted to tell him to leave—Atty and I could play games alone—but that wasn't becoming of an arcanist. "We should get to know each other better."

"Well, I suggested we visit you so that you and she could have more time together, so I'll probably duck out halfway through our game, if that's okay."

I whipped around and faced Adelgis. "Wait, what?"

"You two," he said, motioning to me and then the door. "I figured you should spend some time together, so I suggested to Atty we come visit."

"Er, really? But..." I rubbed at my neck. "Atty is sweet, and kind, and knowledgeable. You wouldn't want her to yourself?"

Adelgis brightened to a glowing crimson. His eldrin, Felicity, giggled.

"You two are from the same island," Adelgis said, louder than usual. "And she talks about you nonstop! She isn't interested in me. I have, well, other things to preoccupy myself!"

Felicity floated through the air, dreamlike in all ways. "Don't worry, Arcanist Volke. Adelgis reacted in a similar fashion when his mother proposed an arranged marriage."

"D-don't tell him that!" Adelgis said. He waved around his arms until he grabbed his eldrin. He held her close. "That's private information. I'm perfectly capable of picking my own bride!"

I laughed, amused by their whimsy. And the news of Adelgis's gesture lightened my mood. He wanted to help me? We barely knew each other, yet here he was, thinking of ways to improve my relationship with Atty. I had thought him nothing more than a weirdo, but perhaps I had been wrong.

Atty and Titania rushed back into my room. The soot of the phoenix left a slight trail, but I didn't mind.

"I have the cards," Atty said. "We can play on the bed." She hopped on next to Adelgis, more playful than I had ever seen her. "Look at these."

She set down an entire deck of wax-covered cards and then fanned them out to show the seven suits: ships, anchors, griffons, kirins, crystals, sea serpents, and stars. Each had obviously been hand-drawn with careful attention to detail, especially in the swirl of the numbers.

"What card game should we play?" Atty asked.

There were all sorts of games I had played as a kid that I wouldn't mind teaching Atty. Then again, it would be childish to teach her *three pigs, two bakers*. I doubted anyone besides a seven-year-old would be interested. I turned to Adelgis, hoping he had something a little more mature.

He released Felicity, and she floated up to the roof.

"We'll divide the deck up between us," Adelgis said. "Then we'll each pull a card off the top at the same time. Whoever has the highest suit and number gets to ask a question to the whole group and everyone else has to answer."

"That's it?" I asked.

"Did you want something more complicated?"

"N-no."

It made for a simple ice-breaker game. Good enough.

I took a seat on the bed, and we all scooted closer. Adelgis dealt the cards.

Atty's phoenix, Titania, stayed off the bed, but she poked her heron-like head up to watch the events with large golden eyes. Luthair didn't move. I suspected cards weren't his thing.

Adelgis pulled his first card, and I followed suit. Atty pulled hers last.

I had the three of sea serpents. Not a good start.

Atty won with the ten of stars.

"I can ask a question?" she asked.

We nodded.

She replied with a sly smile. "Have either of you been in love?"

My face heated, and I rubbed at my nose to hide any sort of color change. Did she know why Adelgis brought her here? Or was I that obvious? Or perhaps the question was random. Yes. Random. She just wanted to know more about us.

Adelgis shook his head. "Never."

"Why not?"

"Tell them about your arranged marriage," Felicity said.

Adelgis returned to his shining red color. "I... have had a wife lined up since I was born. My mother... didn't let me mingle with girls because of this. She would escort me places, or my father would keep me in his lab. Then I went to an all-boys school."

Ah. He was embarrassed by his lack of control in life. Well, that was what I guessed, anyway. And maybe his lack of experience.

"I see," Atty said. "I've never felt that way about anyone either."

"Really?" I asked. "Even though everyone on our island loved you? I overheard tons of boys talking about you constantly. Some wrote love letters."

Atty's face flushed—an event I had never seen. She turned away and pulled most of her blonde hair forward, as if trying to hide behind it. "My mother wasn't controlling like Adelgis's, but she did say swooning over someone was a sign of weakness."

Titania flapped her wings. "It's your turn, Volke."

"I've never been in love," I said.

There wasn't any time for relationships when I was younger. I either helped William or I studied to impress a phoenix. When would I court anyone? Then again—I shot Atty a quick glance before turning away, my gut a tangle of knots—I had always admired others. I don't think that counted, however.

"Next round," Felicity said, her voice sing-song.

We each drew new cards. I pulled the king of kirins—the highest scoring card in a seven-suit deck—and flashed it to the group. "Guess I'm asking a question."

The others stared at me with slight smiles and nervous expressions. I hadn't thought of a question, however. What would tell me more about the others? What would strike at the core of their person?

"I think I have one," I said. "When you die, what do you want to be remembered for?"

Adelgis stroked his chin "A little morbid, but I appreciate the insightfulness of it." He thought for a long moment. "I suppose I want to be remembered for discovering something. A new mystical creature or a way to wield magic. Something everyone would talk about for generations to come."

"That's amazing," I said.

I had never imagined something like that. I wanted to be a legend—like Gregory Ruma—known throughout the world for my great deeds and epic adventures. It didn't matter how I got there, so long as everyone knew me as a hero and not a know-nothing criminal. But Adelgis cared about the method and had passion revolving around magic itself.

We both turned to face Atty. I must admit, I eagerly waited to hear her response. Would it be as interesting as Adelgis's answers? Would we secretly have a similar goal we could commiserate over?

"My mother told me a legend once," Atty said, her gaze on the table. "Powerful arcanists could change their eldrin into their *true form*." She half-laughed. "My mother said only those pure of soul could do it."

Adelgis perked up. "I've heard that legend. Some arcanists grow so powerful, that when their eldrin matures, it gains untold power. Atlas turtles capable of moving islands. Dragons capable of creating volcanos."

"Or phoenixes resurrecting the dead," Atty added in a whisper.

Adelgis and I laughed. But we both stopped when we realized Atty had been serious.

"Is that what you want to do?" I asked.

Again, Atty's face reddened. Her gaze drilled a hole in her lap as she said, "My mother has told me that since I was young. *Phoenixes resurrect the dead, sweetie. You need to become powerful.*" Atty stared at my blankets. "One summer, my grandparents died in a terrible boating accident out at sea. And then the next year, my mother's brother, my uncle, died of illness. Then my younger sister... she..."

"Perhaps we should move on," Luthair said from the corner, startling everyone, myself included.

Atty nodded. "Yeah. I always hated talking about that with my mother." She sighed. "I had to be perfect, or else I didn't have the *pure soul* needed to see a phoenix's true form, so she would yell a lot." Then she forced a smile. "Let's talk about something else."

Her mother had forced her to be perfect? No wonder she acted the way she did. I bet that had been an unbelievable amount of pressure. No one was perfect. William had told me that time and time again.

My bedroom door opened. We all turned to face the newcomer. I expected Illia—who else would enter without knocking?—but I wasn't that lucky.

Zaxis.

"What're you three doing?" he asked.

"What're you doing in my room?" I snapped.

"Reo said he saw Atty run in here after borrowing a deck of cards." He gave me a glare. "I wanted to check it out."

"We're playing a game," Adelgis said. "Just asking each other questions."

"Tsk. Like what kind of questions?"

Oh, please no. Why was Adelgis engaging him? Zaxis

needed to be thrown from my room as soon as possible! Nothing would go right for me and Atty if he was around.

But Adelgis didn't seem to comprehend. "Volke just asked, when you die, what do you want to be remembered for?"

"Easy," Zaxis said as he threw himself down onto my bed, crowding everyone with his presence. "I want to be a world-renowned arcanist, like Gregory Ruma. A swash-buckler without rival."

I huffed and wanted to make a sarcastic comment, but then I'd be a hypocrite. How did we have the same goal? We were leagues apart in personality, and it felt like he was only after my ambitions because he had some sort of vendetta against me.

Forsythe, his phoenix wandered into the room, his talons clicking on the wood floor.

So many people in my tiny room. I swear it felt like a petting zoo.

"You guys are just playing games?" Zaxis asked, his eyebrows knit together. "Why? Wait. Let me guess. *Friendship. Without it, we become crazy cat ladies.* Or something like that."

I hated every second of his presence.

Atty perked up, her eyes wide. "Oh. Wait. I forgot I had to do something." She leapt from my bed and rushed to the door. "Come, Titania!" She stopped in the hall, turned around, and gave me a deep frown. "I'm sorry, Volke, Adelgis, Zaxis... I said I would meet Master Ruma and I need to go. We can play again though, okay? I was having fun. Really." She dashed off before anyone could offer her a response.

Perfect. Could this afternoon get any worse?

"We should continue our conversations," Adelgis said as he gathered up the custom-made cards. "My mother kept a watchful eye on me as a child. I never knew many people within my peer group. I'm sure our masters will take us to different locations during our studies, but when there is a sense of kinship between—"

"We get it," Zaxis snapped. "You're lonely. Use shorter sentences. Maybe then you'd make more friends."

"You certainly have a confrontational attitude."

"And? What of it?"

Adelgis shrugged. "It'll be hard to become a world-renowned hero like Gregory Ruma with your demeanor."

Zaxis opened his mouth but stopped himself before he said anything. He huffed and turned away, his shoulders stiff and his hands clenched into fists. Although I had money on him exploding, he said nothing.

Felicity floated down from the roof and landed on Adelgis's shoulder. "Perhaps it's best if we do something else *other* than talk."

"Actually," Zaxis said. He loosened a bit and rolled over to face me. "I've been meaning to talk to you about Illia."

"Why?" I snapped.

"I'm just curious about a couple things. Like why do you two give each other a lot of... odd glances?"

"We're siblings. Siblings have their own language between each other."

But maybe she doesn't want me saying that anymore.

"Is that all?"

"How about we talk tomorrow?" I said. "I'm not in the mood to discuss this."

Although he didn't answer, the tension in the air thickened. Adelgis stroked his eldrin's shell and forced a smile whenever he caught our eye.

Zaxis glanced around my room. He pointed at the bare walls. "You're a simple man of simple tastes, I see."

"It's chic," I quipped.

He got off my bed, walked to the window, and stared across the fields growing on the atlas turtle.

Adelgis stood. "I like his room. No distractions from decorations or games." Then he turned his attention to me. "I bet you're good at studying."

I shrugged. "Yeah. I guess."

"We're more similar than I originally thought."

"What is this?" Zaxis asked as he reached into the drawer to my nightstand.

He picked up the box Lyell had given me—the Ren family crest was stamped on the top, no doubt catching Zaxis's eye. I walked over to grab it from him, but he shoved me back.

"You stole this?" he asked.

"No. I didn't steal anything."

I reached for it a second time, and he responded with a quick burst of flame. It startled me more than it hurt, and I stumbled backward, an arm over my face to protect my eyes. Adelgis rushed to my side and patted away the singed edges of my clothes. The shadows shifted at a fierce rate, but I held up my hand and shook my head. I didn't need Luthair to fight this for me.

Zaxis ripped open the box and dumped the coins to the floor, a sneer across his face, like he had proven his ultimate point. Then Lyell's note floated out, and he snatched it out of the air. Although I wanted nothing more than to throw him from my room, I allowed him time to read the damn note—just so he could know how wrong he was.

He read over each sentence at a slow pace until he came to the end. Then he read it a second time, his eyes scanning the page. When he lowered the letter, he didn't have much of an expression.

He didn't say anything either.

Adelgis glanced between us. "What's going on? Did you steal something, Volke?"

The silence persisted.

Zaxis slowly knelt and collected the coins. He placed them back in the box, along with the letter, and returned everything to the drawer. For a long moment, he tapped a single finger on the top of the nightstand, his gaze vacant.

"You saved Lyell in the Endless Mire?" he finally muttered.

"Yeah."

Adelgis took a step back. "Oh. You two have history."

I nodded.

"Hm," Adelgis muttered. "I'm not so good with awkward confrontations." But instead of leaving, he took a seat on the edge of my bed and watched, almost as if he wanted to learn from the experience by observing.

Zaxis turned to me. He looked like he wanted to say something—to yell something like he always did—but nothing came. Instead, he glanced at the floor, silent and hardly breathing. Did he want me to say something?

A full minute passed between us, adding to the awkwardness of the moment. I crossed my arms.

"Zaxis, it's no big deal."

"That's my brother," he said. "Of course it's a big deal. Why didn't you say anything? All this time I've been calling you out on something that never happened. Are you just a masochist? What's wrong with you?"

Zaxis had a gift. He could turn anything into a confrontation, even a moment where we both knew he owed me an apology. I wouldn't force it though. I didn't help Lyell because I wanted something in return. Even now, as Zaxis floundered, I just wanted things to be good between us.

Despite the tense moment, Adelgis shot to his feet. He held Felicity close to his ear, his eyes wide. "Quiet," he said.

Both Zaxis and I glared. What did Adelgis want now? But he didn't say anything else. He kept hold of his ethereal whelk and closed his eyes, like a child listening to the sounds of the ocean in a seashell. We waited for a full minute, no one uttering a word.

"Master Zelfree and Master Ruma are returning from the city," Adelgis murmured. "They're coming into the manor house. And... they're arguing."

Zaxis and I exchanged questioning glances.

"What's he talking about?" Zaxis whispered.

I shrugged. "You don't know?"

"He's your fellow apprentice. You haven't seen this before? Open your damn eyes when you're training together next time."

"I swear you make it difficult for people to like you," I muttered.

Adelgis stepped forward, cutting our conversation short. He glanced between us, his eyes wide, his breathing shallow. "Felicity can hear thoughts. I told her to inform me when Master Zelfree returned, but I never thought he'd be in such a heated argument with Master Ruma."

Heated argument? What if Zelfree was in danger? If Ruma killed other arcanists in the past, he could kill again, especially if Zelfree had discovered something about his illicit activities.

"Where are they?" I asked.

"I told you. They're coming into the manor."

I pushed my way past Adelgis and dashed out into the hallway. The shadows darted along the walls, Luthair keeping my pace with little difficulty. I didn't care if the others followed me—all I cared about was helping out if something terrible happened.

The front door to the manor house opened and closed with a heavy slam. I made it to the top of the stairs in a matter of moments, but I stopped when I heard the angry voices of Ruma and Zelfree echo up to the third story. They were anything but quiet, the heated sting of their words was enough to make me hesitate.

"—the guildmaster hasn't returned yet," Zelfree shouted. "She would never approve of this."

"You're one to talk," Ruma replied, his shouting just as loud. "Why don't you worry about your own apprentices?"

What were they arguing about? When I turned around to speak with Luthair, I held back a gasp. Adelgis and Zaxis were inches from me, leaning close to listen as well. Even Felicity leaned her eye stalks closer.

"What're you all doing?" I whispered.

Zaxis huffed. "Listening. Keep it down."

Doors slammed. Zelfree's and Gregory's voices disappeared behind the barrier of walls. Unable to hear them any longer, I sighed.

"You said Felicity can hear thoughts?" I whispered. "What are they arguing about now?"

Adelgis shook his head. "There are too many people in the manor house. She could hear their thoughts when they were separated, but now she can't. Besides, Zelfree told me not to use it on arcanists in the manor house."

"Of course he would say that," Zaxis said with a smirk. "Master Ruma told us all about Zelfree's shady past. I bet he doesn't want you hearing any of his thoughts."

"Past?"

"His last two apprentices died. *Phoenix arcanists*. He said pirates got them on the Crescent Isles. No witnesses, just

Zelfree and his mimic blaming pirates. Master Ruma said he reported Zelfree's behavior to the guildmaster, but they never got any hard evidence. Master Ruma and Zelfree have been at each other's throats since then."

That all made sense then. But it was worrying to hear that Zelfree was somehow involved in the disappearance of the last phoenix arcanists.

I had to know what they were arguing about if I was going to get to the bottom of everything. It mattered to my long-term stay at the guild. But how would I figure it out? The answer came to me immediately. The illusionary window. I could sneak into Ruma's room. If they were still arguing, it would definitely be in the common area between the master arcanists' rooms.

I headed down the stairs. I traveled two steps before Zaxis grabbed my shoulder and jerked me back.

"Where are you going?" he asked.

I pulled away. "It's none of your business."

"Are you going to speak with Master Zelfree?" Adelgis asked. "If you are, please take me with you. I want to know what's going on."

"Er, well, that wasn't the plan."

Zaxis snorted. "He's not going to speak to them. He's going to *spy* on them."

Adelgis and his ethereal whelk both turned their attention to me. I caught my breath, unable to think of an excuse. How did Zaxis know? It didn't matter. They couldn't stop me. This was too important. Something was going on, and I needed to get to the bottom of it.

23

PIRATE-INFESTED WATERS

"Please take me with you," Adelgis said.

I caught my breath. "Even though I'm going to spy on them?"

"I'm a fan of information, not secrets."

"All right. But it might be complicated. I know where they'll be, but getting inside is an undertaking."

"I'm coming too," Zaxis said.

I shot him a glare. Him, too? But what else could I do? He knew what I was planning, and he already heard me say I'd take Adelgis. If I didn't want him to report us as an act of revenge, he had to come along. But would either of them be a liability while sneaking around? Neither seemed stealthy.

Illia never had trouble sneaking around.

"I'm going to get something from my room real quick," I said. "Then we'll go."

I ran back to my room. Luthair slithered around near my feet, offering no commentary. The moment I reached my door, I threw it open and ducked inside. It was late afternoon, so I knew Illia wouldn't be waiting for me, but I had hoped.

"Luthair," I said. "Can you tell Illia I need to speak with her? But don't let anyone know."

"Yes, my arcanist."

He shifted through the shadows, right out my window, and across the wall. I paced while I waited, staring at the floor as I went back and forth. Although I worried about her telling me this was a bad idea, I never doubted she would at least hear me out.

I stopped walking the moment Illia pushed open my window and leapt into my room.

"Where's the emergency?" Nicholin asked, his tail swishing. "Your heroes are here to rescue you!"

"Shh," I said as I walked over to Illia.

She gave me an odd look, her eyebrow up. "Volke, what're you doing?"

"It's about my eldrin, and Gregory Ruma." I shook my head. "But that needs to wait. I need your help. Ruma and Zelfree are arguing. I want to know what they're discussing. So... I'm going to sneak into Ruma's room."

I probably rambled and sounded like a madman, but Illia never missed a beat. She offered me a sarcastic smile. "Isn't there a step about privacy on that Pillar? Or at least no trespassing?"

"This is important."

She dropped all joking mannerisms and hardened her expression. "All right. I'm in."

"Oh, we're playing the scoundrels today," Nicholin whispered with a smile. He rubbed his paws together. "I like it."

We crossed my room, and I threw open the door. Zaxis stood in the hall. He gave Illia a quick glance before turning his attention squarely on me.

"She was in your room?" he asked. His face brightened to a shade almost as red as his hair.

"It's not like that," I hissed. "It's complicated. And also, not so complicated."

Illia nodded. "Yeah. Don't mention anything, okay?"

Although I suspected Zaxis would be difficult no matter what we said, he huffed and glanced away. "Fine. I won't say anything."

"Thank you." She tried to walk around him, but when he turned to follow, she shot him a glare.

"He's coming with," I said.

Illia snorted. "Really?"

"Yes," Zaxis snapped. "Let's go."

We headed to the end of the hall, down the stairs, met up with Adelgis, and then made our way outside. The sun was setting in the distance, drowning the room in deep oranges and reds, leaving the manor house with only its lanterns and chandeliers for light inside. Although I had never spoken with him about it, Luthair seemed to prefer the night hours. He moved a bit more and stirred around my feet with each step.

Zaxis's phoenix took flight.

"Good thinking, Forsythe," he said. "Stay up high, and let me know if anyone finds us, okay?"

"As you wish, my arcanist," Forsythe called down.

With a body that burned as vibrantly as the sunset itself, Forsythe flew to the roof and perched himself at the edge, his crimson tail feathers dangling off the side.

I brought the group to the garden outside the illusion-covered window. Although I didn't remember the exact location, Luthair did. His shadowy form guided me all the way back to the location where I had landed when I leapt from Ruma's room.

"There's a window up there," I whispered. "Illusions."

Unlike the dark night I had snuck around Ruma's quarters, tonight's setting sun provided an ample amount of light. I pointed to the location of the window, even though it appeared as nothing more than a wall of brick and beam of wood.

The others stared for a moment, examining the height. The room sat on the second story, and the window was at least fifteen feet above the ground. Although the floating whelk could make it up with little problem, the rest of us didn't fly.

"Rizzel arcanists can teleport," Adelgis said matter-of-factly. He turned to Illia. "Can you get us up there?"

"I'm not that good yet. If you were an apple, maybe I could help you, but you're too big as you are."

"I can get up there," Nicholin said.

He leapt off Illia's shoulder and disappeared midair in a flash of sparkles and light. I didn't see where he appeared, but I hoped he had gone inside. Seconds turned into minutes while we waited.

"My father said rizzels are mischief makers," Adelgis said. "Is there a possibility he's not returning?"

Illia shook her head. "Of course he'll come back. He's just... doing something."

"Did you know Volke saved my brother, Lyell, in the Endless Mire?" Zaxis asked out of the blue.

Illia nodded. "Yes."

"And you didn't say anything either?"

What was Zaxis's problem? Why dwell on that fact? He almost sounded offended—like he couldn't believe it happened.

"Volke was also behind me helping you during the star moth trial. He asked me to deliver the information because he figured you'd never trust him."

"W-what?"

"Yeah. Maybe you should think about that."

I ran a hand down my face. Why did Illia mention the star moths? Whatever problem Zaxis had with me, I was certain this would only make it worse. I didn't really understand him, but it had become clear that anything I did was a personal affront he couldn't ignore.

"So, you all *aren't* friends," Adelgis commented, like he enjoyed puzzling out our relationships. "I thought you were cohorts through and through, but I guess I was mistaken."

The window popped open above us, cutting the conversation short. The illusion broke once the window opened, but I suspected it would fall back into place the moment it shut.

Nicholin leaned out, his blue eyes bright in the sunset light. "Psst! Watch out below." He tossed down a rope and then clapped his paws together.

Where did he find a rope? Then again, Ruma kept so many trophies from his past exploits in his room that it didn't seem unlikely one would include a rope.

Illia grabbed ahold and tugged. Once satisfied it was secured, she yanked herself up and climbed through the window. Zaxis followed, his gaze distant. Adelgis struggled a bit more than the other two, awkward in every regard. He placed his feet in weird positions, made odd grunts with each inch he traveled upward, and his ethereal whelk muttered bubbly encouragement.

I waited until they had all made their way inside. I wasn't afraid of climbing a rope—I had done it tons of times on boats and around the Isle of Ruma. I wanted to test out my magic again. Last time I shifted through the shadows, I ended up on Gentel's fin, but this time would be different.

"I should be able to shift through the shadows and enter the room, right?" I whispered.

Luthair slid across the wall of the building, his shadow-form uninhibited by gravity. "You should be able to shift up any surface."

I closed my eyes and focused.

"Don't," Luthair said. "Keep them open. You need to see where you're going. You need to visualize it. That was your problem last time."

Illia leaned over the window sill and frowned. "Are you okay?"

"I'll be up in a second," I said.

"Hurry. Adelgis says they're still discussing things, but we don't know how long this'll last."

She ducked back into the manor house.

With the pressure mounting, I took a deep breath and then exhaled. Calmed and ready, I focused my magic through every fiber of my being. It didn't happen as fast as I wanted, especially since the others were waiting for me, but I did manage to do it at a steady rate. And it didn't hurt as much. There was still a burning sensation, similar to a whole-body fever, but I could focus despite the feeling.

Once certain I had enough magic in my being, I tried visualizing my destination.

I sank into the shadows, the darkness covering my eyes and squeezing my chest, adding to the pain. Again, I couldn't breathe, but I didn't panic. This had happened before, and I reassured myself it would end soon. When I moved, it felt like water rushing over me—warm, thick water—but I refused to dwell on it. I visualized Ruma's quarters and nothing else.

Then my magic failed me.

I ejected from the shadows, gasping for air, the pain fading. I hit the floor of Ruma's room on my hands and knees, sweat dripping from my skin.

"Quiet," Adelgis whispered.

Illia jumped to my side. "You can shadow-shift? Why didn't you come in here instead of Nicholin?"

I gave her a sarcastic glare. "Yeah, I nailed this. I definitely should be the one everyone counts on to get into places."

She slapped me on the shoulder. "Don't be a whiner. You'll be shifting all over the place soon enough." Then she helped me to my feet.

Once steady, I followed her, Adelgis, and Zaxis down the stairs to Ruma's study room. Halfway down the steps, blood poured from my nose and spilled onto my shirt. I didn't care about my clothes—I could always get more—but if I left blood everywhere in Ruma's room, he would know someone had broken in. I pressed my palm against my nostrils and breathed through my mouth.

Zaxis stopped walking. "What's wrong with you?"

"My magic," I muttered. "It... hurts me."

"Because you're second-bonded?"

I nodded.

He walked up a couple steps and grabbed my forearm. At first, I thought he was going to throw me down the staircase —irrational, I know, though I wouldn't put it past him. Instead, his palm grew warm and a tingling sense of magic crept through my arm and then spread to my chest and head.

When Zaxis pulled away, he huffed. "C'mon."

I removed my hand from my nose and realized I had stopped bleeding. "You healed me?" Arcanists would eventually heal themselves, but added magic made everything easier.

"Phoenix arcanists can mend wounds. Everyone knows that."

"But—"

"You can't get your blood all over the damn place," he hissed. "And I saw your injuries from the siren. I knew I'd have to learn this one day. Now keep quiet and c'mon."

He... worried about me? And he learned healing magic because he thought I would be injured all the time? I didn't know if I should be honored or insulted. Why would I get injured all the time? I wasn't *that* bad.

But maybe I should just see it as a compliment. It was nicer that way.

We met up with Illia and Adelgis in the study room. Sure enough, Zelfree and Ruma were still arguing, their voices so loud it wasn't difficult to hear everything.

"—which is exactly why these rules were put in place," Zelfree shouted.

"I'm not waiting for the guildmaster," Ruma said, his tone heated but not to the point of yelling. "You saw all those requests and bounties. The pirates are going insane. *They're the ones who sent out those plague ships.*"

"That entire area is a death trap. Something is going on near the Crescent Islands and you know it. Those pirates are all infected. Every last one."

"Just because you lost your old apprentices in the Crescent Islands doesn't mean I will."

I caught my breath. What had happened? And why were they discussing going there again? Obviously, pirates needed to be dealt with—and the Frith Guild specialized in such tasks—but I agreed with Zelfree. Why take inexperienced apprentices on such a dangerous mission?

"Every phoenix arcanist who has sailed near those islands has gone missing or died," Zelfree stated. "You and I know that better than anyone else. It's too much of a risk.

Just leave your apprentices with me if you want to handle the situation. Why are you fighting so hard to take them?"

"I won't leave any apprentices in your care."

"*Ruma*," Zelfree hissed.

Ah. It all made sense now. Ruma was trying to protect us since Zelfree had a questionable history.

Someone smashed something against the wall. A glass? It sounded fragile.

"You're just as unstable as those pirates," Ruma barked.

"*This* is insanity. Your apprentices would be safer in the midst of a storm than out there with murderers!"

"I can handle them," Ruma replied in a curt tone. "No harm will come to my apprentices, and they may be the key to luring the captain out. He's been hunting phoenix arcanists for years. This needs to end."

Zelfree cursed something fierce.

Although none of us had moved much, Adelgis shot us all a concerned look.

"You're planning on using them as bait," Zelfree stated. "Is that it?"

"They'll be safe."

"I won't allow you to go."

For a moment, no one said anything. I held my breath, and so did the others. Even Nicholin held still. Perhaps Ruma's reasons weren't as noble as I once thought. But was Zelfree safe? I didn't really know who I should trust. Perhaps they were both bad.

"You can't stop me," Ruma said, so quiet I almost didn't catch it.

The finality of his statement sent a warning straight to my thoughts. I grabbed Illia by the arm and motioned back to the stairs. Zaxis must have felt the same way because he yanked Adelgis back by the shoulder cape.

Heavy footsteps headed for Ruma's door. My heart seized, my breathing shallow.

For a split second I thought shadow-shifting would be a safer and faster escape method. It was silent, I could move without getting in the way of the others, and no one would see me, even if someone were waiting in the garden outside. But I couldn't use my magic fast enough, not in this situation. I needed a good minute of concentration ahead of time in order to do anything.

"Don't walk away from me," Zelfree growled.

The footsteps stopped.

Illia and I headed for the stairway and made our way up, Adelgis and Zaxis close behind. We reached Ruma's bedroom and I pointed to the rope.

"Where did you get this?" I whispered.

Nicholin saluted me. "I'll take care of it once you guys are out of here." He hopped off Illia's shoulder and dashed around the floor, his bouncy run surprisingly quiet.

Again, Zaxis and Illia went for the rope first. Adelgis followed afterward, murmuring to himself the entire way, like his head was so full of thoughts he couldn't contain them all. I waited until the others were outside before leaning over the sill and climbing down.

"Other phoenix arcanists?" Illia whispered to the others.

Adelgis nodded. "That's right. Zelfree had two phoenix apprentices a decade ago. They died."

Once I hit the ground, Nicholin rolled up the rope.

"Do you think Zelfree's dangerous?" Zaxis asked, his arms crossed.

"No," I said. "Well... maybe."

"Master Ruma thinks he's crazy," Zaxis said. "Maybe Zelfree doesn't want us to go to the Crescent Islands because we'll find evidence of his crimes."

Although I hadn't been planning on telling anyone about my situation, I knew the time had come. I tapped everyone on the shoulder and motioned away from the manor house. The moon lit up the gardens, and I led them down a stone walkway between rose bushes. Nicholin joined us halfway through, teleporting with a pop of light. Once we reached the edge of the shrubbery, Illia grabbed my arm.

"What's going on?" she asked.

I lowered my voice and leaned close. "Luthair believes Ruma murdered his last arcanist, Mathis Weaversong."

Zaxis scoffed. "What is this? You like Zelfree so much you're gonna lie about Master Ruma?"

"Volke wouldn't lie about that," Illia said. She searched my gaze with her single eye. "Is that why you've been so distant?"

I nodded.

"Do you have any proof?" Adelgis asked.

I shook my head. "I've been looking, but I haven't found anything definitive. All I know is something strange is going on. I keep finding odd coincidences or items." I slumped my shoulders and turned away from the group. "Luthair didn't get a good look the night his arcanist died, so there's a chance he's wrong..."

"Maybe it's Zelfree," Zaxis said.

"No. Luthair recognized Ruma's voice."

"Zelfree has a *mimic* eldrin. He could imitate voices if he wanted, and his eldrin could transform to look like a leviathan."

"He doesn't seem like that kind of man," I said.

"Neither does Master Ruma."

That was true. I didn't want either of them to be a blackheart.

Illia turned to me. "What're we going to do about this, Volke?"

Nicholin nodded along with her statement, like it was somehow my responsibility to solve this.

I shrugged. "I doubt Ruma will take Gentel and the whole guild to these pirates, so he'll probably captain his ship."

"And he'll be taking his apprentices to pirate-infested waters," Adelgis said, drawing out each word as he stroked his chin. "If something were to happen to Zaxis or Atty, no one would be around to see. Ruma could claim anything."

"He wouldn't do anything to us," Zaxis growled. Then he faced me. "Right?"

I straightened my posture, a little shocked he wanted me to back him up. "I'm not his apprentice."

"But you admire the man. You know everything about him. I can't believe you would even say this. Do you hate him now because he didn't pick you as an apprentice?"

"N-no. I meant what I said. He could be a murderer. I don't want him to be, but he could. You should be careful."

Adelgis's ethereal whelk shimmered in the darkness, drawing all our attention.

"What are his motivations?" Felicity asked.

"I don't know," I said.

"Without that, it's hard to say whether he'll strike again or not. Perhaps he held a grudge against Luthair's old arcanist, which means he would have no reason to attack Zaxis, Hexa or Atty. We're lost in the dark unless we know the answers to these basic questions."

"I just..." I gritted my teeth. "I need more time. If I could just investigate longer..."

Between magic training, dealing with Zelfree, and recovering from attacks by plague creatures, I hadn't done as much as I had wanted. But what could I do now?

"We should sleep on it," Adelgis said. He patted Zaxis on the shoulder. "Don't worry. We'll get to the bottom of this."

Zaxis jerked away and shot him a glare. "I'm not *worried*. I think this is all crazy. It's more likely Zelfree is a kook than anyone else here. He drinks himself to sleep every night, and he's already lost his apprentices."

Without any new leads, I didn't know where else to go. So, I instead mulled over the comments. Sleeping on the new information was probably for the best. We could discuss everything tomorrow.

24

THE CRESCENT ISLANDS

Too bad I couldn't sleep a damn wink.

I tossed and turned, the chill in my room making it difficult to get comfortable. I stared at the moonlight streaming through my window, hoping Illia would emerge and discuss the situation with me. She never appeared, however, and I wondered why.

I hadn't told her about Luthair's accusation the entire time we had been here.

Gulls heralded the sun with their constant cawing. I sat up and exhaled. A knock at my door drew me out of my thoughts. I stood, pulled on a shirt, and crossed the room.

When I opened the door, Journeyman Reo stood in the hall, his glasses sliding down his nose. He pushed them up as he said, "Ah, Volke. I'm here to inform you that Master Zelfree wants you to prepare to depart. You will be t-traveling with him while he completes a few contracts on the guild's behalf."

Finn, his giant ogata toad, tilted his head to the side. "Sorry for waking you."

"It's fine," I said. "What did Zelfree say about his tasks?"

"They're dangerous, and you should pack light. You're heading to the Crescent Islands."

The information shocked me, but I recovered. "Are all Zelfree's apprentices going?"

Reo nodded.

The Crescent Islands... Did that mean Zelfree planned on following Ruma to the islands that swarmed with the plague and pirates? Zelfree seemed upset Ruma would endanger his apprentices, yet now we were all going?

"I'll pack my things," I said as I rubbed at my neck. "Thank you, Reo."

He nodded before continuing down the hall. He had a small piece of paper in his hand, and he muttered a few names to himself as he went.

Luthair appeared from the shadows and stood in front of the window, his dark form silhouetted by the sunrise.

"Something is happening," he said matter-of-factly.

"Oh?"

"You're in danger."

I glanced around my cold room. "Right now?"

"Perhaps not this moment, but this turn of events is ominous—a terrible omen. I had the same feeling when Mathis wanted to continue pursuing our target, even when we discovered that target was a powerful arcanist."

The information settled on me like a pile of rocks. What would I do if we were attacked by pirates? Or by Ruma? My magic just wasn't strong enough. No matter how I looked at it, if something happened, I wouldn't have the power to protect us.

Luthair pulled his sword from the scabbard. "My arcanist, if something happens... if you're in danger..."

"You want me to use your sword?" I asked.

"I think I should protect you like only armor can."

I raised both my eyebrows. We had never done that before. "Won't it... burn me? Like when I use the sword?"

"If you allow me to control—"

"No," I said. "No. If we do this, we do it together. I don't care how much it hurts or strains me. We'll be a team."

"Volke..."

"I have to learn to deal with this at some point," I said, my voice heated. "Especially if we're going into dangerous territory. I'll be fine."

Luthair sheathed his sword. "Very well. We fight together. But I should warn you, when a knightmare merges with their arcanist, they will live and die as a single being."

Live and die as a single being? I held my breath.

Luthair could use his own magic freely. He shifted through the shadows, he controlled the darkness—but if we were merged, he wouldn't be able to do that anymore. *We* would have to do it. In theory, an arcanist's magic was stronger, so we would be better as one, but since I was so bad at magic...

I'd be limiting him. And if we messed up and died, we'd both suffer for my mistakes.

"I won't let us down," I said. "I promise. This is too important."

I had no idea what Zelfree and Ruma were planning, but I had to stay on edge if I wanted to avoid getting caught flat-footed. It meant my life—and Illia's—and the lives of Zaxis, Atty, Hexa, and Adelgis.

The next day, I couldn't believe it. There it was, sitting in the port of Tallin.

The High Riser—Gregory Ruma's personal vessel. Fourteen glorious white sails and a single blue jib fluttering in the wind. The flag at the top of the crow's nest depicted the Frith Guild seal, a sword and shield, along with a leviathan.

I had read hundreds of stories involving his vessel. It was the fastest ship on the ocean. Decimus would clear the way while the High Riser rode the wake, propelled by Ruma's magic. I took it all in, from the mizzenmast to the bowsprit, admiring the dark oak of keel and frames.

Illia elbowed me in the ribs. I grunted and rubbed at the spot. "What?"

"You look like a gawking child."

"S-sorry."

Zelfree and Ruma hadn't wasted any time. It wasn't even noon, and already they were preparing to set sail. I wished I knew what changed Zelfree's mind about heading toward the Crescent Islands. He had been so against it before. Did Ruma change his mind after we all fled into the gardens?

If only I had mastered shadow-shifting. If I were a shadow, I could've listened to the conversation without risk of getting caught.

Illia took my arm and guided me to the edge of the dock, clearing the way for everyone else. Sailors carried provisions onto the High Riser, walking up the gangplank in groups of three to carry the larger crates.

Zelfree walked over to the bottom of the plank. He wore a heavy coat long enough to reach his ankles and kept his collar up, shielding his skin from every ray of sunlight. The bags under his eyes told a long story of sleepless nights and tall mugs of ale. He glanced between the busy sailors and the crates of provisions.

He snapped his fingers. Traces transformed from a pair of bangles into a bright white rizzel. With a wave of his hand he teleported a crate onto the deck with a pop of sound and light. It slammed down into position next to the others.

The sailors clapped and gave a few thumbs up.

Illia lifted her eyebrow. "Wow."

"Your turn," Zelfree said, curt.

She pointed to herself. "Me? But I've never teleported anything larger than an apple. That must weigh more than two men."

"It wasn't a suggestion. You need to push yourself."

Illia rubbed her forearms as she stepped forward. Nicholin whispered something in her ear, but I couldn't hear. She nodded and took her place next to one of the crates. Zelfree hadn't touched the crate at all, and she placed her hand on the side, her palm flat. She closed her eye and exhaled.

The crate shimmered for a moment, but never did it pop or flash away.

Nicholin clapped his paws. "You can do it!"

I held my breath. Should I cheer as well? Would she be embarrassed if I shouted to encourage her?

I didn't know, but I remembered the moment Illia quoted the Pillar to me.

Loyalty. Without it, we cannot know true friendship.

"C'mon, Illia!" I said.

She flinched and glanced over her shoulder, her eye wide. I smiled, and she replied with a nod. Then she returned to her concentration. The crate shimmered a second time—and then popped away.

Reappearing two inches to the left.

I snorted and stifled a laugh. If I burst into a chuckle now, she'd be pissed, so I gulped down my breath and forced a neutral expression.

To my surprise, Illia laughed aloud. "I did it," she said. "Impressed yet?"

Zelfree narrowed his eyes at the crate. "Eh. I suppose that was better than I was expecting." He snapped his fingers and the crate joined the others on the ship. "Now get aboard. We'll be doing more impromptu training sessions like this as we travel."

He stomped up the gangplank as Traces shifted back into her gray cat form and landed on his shoulder. She wrapped her tail around Zelfree's neck like an odd scarf, purring the entire way.

Illia and I followed him onto the ship.

Zaxis, Atty, Hexa, and Adelgis were already aboard. They stood by the port side railing, staring out across the ocean at Gentel. The massive atlas turtle held her head above the waves, waterfalls pouring from the corners of her mouth as she stared up at the cloud-spotted sky.

Both Forsythe and Titania flew circles overhead, their soot wafting onto the ocean breeze and sailing away. Felicity held onto Adelgis's shoulder cape to keep from floating away.

But Hexa's eldrin wasn't as majestic and beautiful as the others. She held a young hydra tightly in her arms, a wide smile on her face.

Newborn hydras were small, about the size of a medium dog, with all the adorableness of a rabid alligator. The hydra's python-face made it seem both cunning and sinister, its gold eyes observing us all in a matter of moments.

Ruma leapt down from the top of the mainmast, a hundred and seventy-two feet above the deck. He landed with a whoosh of wind, cushioning his fall and preventing any harm. He cocked half a smile as he swished his shoulder-length hair off his shoulders.

"It seems you're all here," he said.

I had to admit, I was impressed. As a child, I had always imagined he would be bigger than life, and I wasn't wrong. He had the kind of charisma everyone envied.

Ruma walked up to the group, his thumbs hooked in the belt loops of his trousers. "Are you all wondering why we're here?"

Illia gave me an odd glance. I held my breath.

"The city of Tallin has had a problem with pirates near the Crescent Isles," Ruma said. "Not only are they pirating things, but their eldrin are afflicted with the plague, and they spread it wherever they can."

Hexa rubbed her hands together. "I heard the Crescent Isles are vast. At least thirty isles and some in storm territory."

"You needn't fear, lass. I know my way around them."

"How so?" I asked. Could he be incriminating himself?

"I was married on the Crescent Isles years back," Ruma said with a grin. "They're a lovely place when they aren't swarmin' with pirates."

"Really? That's where you married Acantha?"

The mere mention of her name erased the smile from Ruma's face. He glared, his whole body visibly tense. I took a step back, a little shaken by his sudden change in demeanor.

"You know her name?" he asked.

I forced a chuckle. "I've read hundreds of stories about you."

"Then did you read the one where she died?"

I bit back the rest of my commentary. What could I even say to that?

Ruma exhaled. "Pirates. She was killed by pirates.

Which is why we need to go to the Crescent Isles. I won't have them polluting this world any longer."

"There's nothing more we need to know?" Illia asked.

"No, lass," he said. "People need help, so the Frith Guild will deliver. It's as simple as that."

He wasn't going to mention Zelfree's missing apprentices? Or the mysterious targeting of phoenixes? Or the danger of the region? I suspected it was to prevent us from panicking, but it still surprised me. Traveling to the Crescent Isles would put our lives at risk, yet he didn't want to say a word.

"What's that?" Nicholin shouted. He pointed at Ruma's belt, his fur puffed out and his fangs flashing.

I caught my breath the moment I spotted the pelt of a rizzel on his belt, tucked behind him, half-hidden by his jacket. It was the same pelt from his room, I was sure of it, but I hadn't expected him to wear it like an accessory.

"This?" Ruma pulled the pelt out and rolled it around his hand. "It's a lure. I want to find the pirate captain—the lord ruling these scum. Don't worry, this rizzel died centuries ago, but the magic in its fur still works enough for the task at hand."

Nicholin stiffened, his tail twice the size I had ever seen it.

"It's okay," Illia said. "Calm down."

But I thought he told Zelfree he would be attracting the pirate captain with the phoenix arcanists? Was he lying to us so that we wouldn't know?

Ruma smiled and motioned to the accommodations of his ship. We had everything we could want. Food. Water. A second cabin for officers all to ourselves.

"Get settled in," Ruma said as he hopped onto the railing. "Zelfree and I will sleep in the captain's cabin. We'll be traveling for a few weeks around the islands. Hope y'all have your sea legs." He leapt into the air, flying straight up to the top of the mainmast.

I turned around, intent on exploring, but flinched when I realized Zelfree had been standing behind me. "Uh," I began.

Zelfree snorted. "On edge?"

"I, um, have never traveled to pirate-infested waters before."

He eyed me for a long moment. "Have you been practicing your magic?"

"Well, I was resting for a few days because—"

"That's what we should be doing. Get your eldrin ready. From now until sunset, we'll be going over your augmentation."

25

PIRATE RAIDS

Drenched in sweat, I threw myself on my cot. The rocking of the High Riser soothed me a bit as I closed my eyes and exhaled. Practicing magic all day had taken its toll on me. While the others continued their training, I had to return to my room. After a few minutes of even breathing, I glanced to the porthole window and stared out into the darkness of the night.

The room I shared with Zaxis and Adelgis was spacious for a boat, but smaller than the rooms we had at the guild. Each of us had a cot pushed up against a different wall, but even then, they almost touched at the corners. We shared a single trunk and a cabinet on the wall.

Luthair stepped out of the shadows and stood at the foot of my cot. "We should practice more before you go to bed."

"I need to rest."

"Your master specifically said you should be more dedicated. You need to get up."

No one knew how much it hurt me to use my magic. Sure, they'd seen me grimace from time to time, but they couldn't experience it like I did. I don't think Luthair knew how much it harmed me.

I sighed.

What would William say if he saw me? He'd be disappointed. I closed my eyes again, my teeth gritted. Even imagining his disappointment reminded me of the terrors Zelfree used when he mimicked my magic. I couldn't stand it. I had to keep trying. No rest—not until I was just as good as the others.

I forced myself to sit up.

"Okay," I muttered. "Let's go. We'll train some more."

Luthair nodded. "You have the spirit of a knight, Volke. I know you can overcome this obstacle."

I half smiled. Luthair didn't compliment me much. "Thanks."

He offered his gauntlet, and I took it. With his help, I stood, my legs threatening to buckle. Luthair kept me up all the way to the door, steadying me long enough to recover.

Day four and we ran across the wreckage of a ship plundered by pirates. The ruined hull stuck up above the waves. It had been impaled by a sharp rock just beneath the ocean's surface, the tattered sails fluttering in the wind like a grave marker.

A handful of ships from the imperial navy sat on the waves not far from the destruction. They had arrived too late to prevent the attack and instead searched the area for any drifting survivors. The presence of the navy reminded me of William. He had rescued plenty of people from shark-infested waters, and I admired the unsung work of those who swore a duty to their nation.

Ruma's leviathan, Decimus, swirled around the sharp rock, his glittering scales transfixing as he smashed the wreckage off and pushed it under. He was so gigantic that I never saw all of him, just the midsection of his serpentine body.

Illia stood on one side of me, her white-knuckle grip tight on the boat's railing. Adelgis stood on the other, his gaze fixated on the wreck, his ethereal whelk pointing with a long tentacle.

"Have either of you dealt with pirates before?" Adelgis asked, clearly oblivious to Illia's anger.

Before I could steer the conversation, Illia replied, "Pirates took my parents and my eye." She lowered her voice before adding, "So, yeah. I've dealt with them before."

"I, uh, didn't know. Forgive me. I shouldn't have been so callous."

"I'm fine."

Felicity turned her eye stalks to her arcanist. They remained silent for a moment, and I wondered if they could communicate through ways other than words. He did say ethereal whelks could read thoughts, but did they have telepathy?

"Do you remember Atty talking about a mystical creature's true form?" Adelgis asked out of nowhere.

I nodded. "Yeah."

"Do you think Decimus has changed into his true form?"

"I don't know. He looks like any other leviathan. He's a little larger, but that's just because he's older."

Adelgis stroked Felicity's shell. "Leviathans are said to control the currents of the ocean. If Ruma had achieved Decimus's true form, our boat would've been traveling faster. I think he's still straining. Not yet powerful enough."

His odd statements reminded me of the siren I found on

Gentel. It had sprouted a second set of disgusting wings, and claimed it was transforming into something more powerful. Why did the plague do that? Perhaps it was a kind of reverse leprosy. Instead of losing skin and body parts, those affected would grow new limbs—though they'd be bulbous and vile.

"I wonder what a rizzel's true form would look like," Illia said, her grip looser than before. "And what it would do."

I gave Adelgis a slight smile. He had managed to get Illia's mind off the pirates. I hated when she dwelled on them, if only because it caused her distress. Hopefully we wouldn't run across any on the trip, but my gut said we wouldn't be so lucky. I was never lucky, after all.

"We should get back to training," Illia whispered. She turned away from the floating bits of wood planks on the waves and motioned to the deck. "C'mon."

"*All hands on deck!*"

I awoke with my heart in my throat, my mind reeling to recover from unconsciousness. It was the dead of night after a long day of training, but I jumped from my cot regardless, adrenaline acting as a powerful fuel.

Adelgis and Zaxis leapt from their cots as well, each dressed in their long johns, their eldrin next to them—Forsythe so puffed up he glowed like a beacon. Our sole lantern swayed on its chain from the ceiling, moving in time with the waves, but it felt like the midafternoon thanks to the phoenix.

"What's going on?" Zaxis demanded.

"I don't know." I motioned to the door. "It came from outside."

I yanked on my shirt and boots before dashing out the

door. The deck swarmed with sailors. I danced around them until I caught sight of a fire out on the ocean, perhaps four hundred feet away. No, not the ocean—a merchant ship. Smoke billowed from cannon holes on the side, and its two masts had been broken in half; one floated on the waves next to it.

Another ship sailed around the first, one with no flags or crests of a nation. It was a pirate's ship, no doubt in my mind. Their cannons blasted at odd intervals, the iron balls smashing through the wooden hull of their target.

"Decimus!" Ruma shouted from the mainmast. "The merchant ship!"

The wind howled, carrying his voice like the boom of thunder. The massive leviathan swirled in the water and headed straight for the merchant's ship. When the pirates shot their cannons again, Decimus lifted his tail and shielded the ship. His steel-like scales protected him, and when he whirled around, the wake and waves of his movements jostled the ships.

Two wyverns took flight from the pirate's ship and headed straight for us.

"Volke!"

I turned to see Illia run to my side, Nicholin on top of her head. "Pirates," she said, her voice surprisingly steady. "We should stick together."

I nodded. Where were the others? Where was Zelfree? The panic and chaos of the sailors made it difficult to locate anyone. They loaded the High Riser's cannons and prepared to fire.

Once the two wyverns got close, I noticed they had riders.

And I heard their laughter.

The cackling—the insanity—like the death and destruction was all a joke.

"They're plague-ridden," I said. "Illia, be careful. It's in the blood!"

Wyverns were deadly creatures, even when they were sane. All wyverns had the body of a dragon, the leathery wings of a bat, two legs with talons the size of knives, and a diamond-shaped stinger at the tip of their tail. William's books said they dominated the skies with their iron hides and fiery breath. The perfect eldrin for pirates.

When both flew overhead, they giggled with unparalleled excitement, their haunting laughter echoing off the waves and all around us. A quick belch of flame lit the deck on fire. Wyverns could cough up an odd oily fluid that clung to everything, and their flames sprouted from the same bizarre oil.

Ruma jumped from the mainmast and flew with the winds toward the pirate ship. He waved his hand and black clouds gathered within a moment. Seconds later and we were awash in rain, the bullets of water beating down the wyvern's fire, though it didn't extinguish it. Gregory continued away from the High Riser, and I wondered if he left us to contend with the attackers.

One wyvern circled back and landed on the edge of the boat with a heavy crash, its giant claws puncturing holes in the deck. The beast had to weigh as much as three horses. The pirate on its back—an arcanist with a wyvern mark—held up a flintlock pistol and fired at the sailors. The burst of light from each shot seemed like magic itself.

"Burn," the wyvern said through its incessant laughter. *"Burn!"*

It vomited another round of flaming liquid. The rain

kept it from spreading, but the middle of the deck transformed into a pyre. Sailors who got splashed caught fire.

Illia dashed around the flames. I followed behind, barely thinking. She went straight for the wyvern and slammed her palm on its side, just under the wings. A flash of light emanated from her touch and she teleported a hand-sized chuck of flesh from the monster's ribs. The meat landed on the deck with a wet splatter.

The wyvern whipped its head around, the creature's eyes bulging and jiggling, its mouth twisted upward in an unnatural smile.

"Magic! I need *magic!*"

The pirate rider turned his pistol on Illia.

Nicholin held his paw up. "No!"

The bullet hit a veil of light created by Nicholin and then disappeared.

I hadn't even realized until I got close, but I had been focusing on my magic the entire time I ran over. Although it normally hurt, I felt nothing. I heard my heart beating in my ears, I felt the shake of the boat underfoot, but there was no pain or anxiety.

When I unleashed my terror, the wyvern and pirate rider both locked up. So did Illia and Nicholin, however, but they managed to stumble away and collapse to the deck, shaken.

To my surprise, the wyvern's reaction was much more pronounced than his rider's. It shrieked and trembled as its eyes swirled in all directions.

"*Help me,*" it screamed. "I can't... remember..."

A brilliant explosion of light blanketed the ocean. Torrents of lightning flew down from the clouds and obliterated the pirate ship in a matter of seconds. Gregory Ruma had a reputation for utter destruction, and he lived up to his legends.

The shock of the lightning distracted me. My magic failed, and the pirate shook his head.

"Take the eldrin," the man yelled as he loaded his pistol. "Kill the arcanists!"

"Luthair!" I yelled.

The shadows came together in an instant and formed into armor. Luthair swung his sword and met the wyvern, cutting deep across its wing, crippling it. The monster thrashed its head and struck Luthair. When Luthair swung again, he aimed for the wing and sliced down the middle.

The second wyvern swooped in close, his rider waving around an arm. "This is Ruma's ship," he shouted. "We need to go!"

Before the pirates could get their act together, a stream of fire hit the injured wyvern, and then a beam of light hit the one in the air. Adelgis and Zaxis had joined the fray—Forsythe even took to the sky and lunged at the massive flying wyvern. He screeched and cawed as he hooked his talons into the monster's neck.

The wyvern giggled, even as it bled. "Tasty…"

Then it bit at Forsythe with its massive dragon jaws, clipping Forsythe's wing and ripping out a handful of crimson feathers. Forsythe fell, flapping hard with his uninjured wing, but it only made things worse.

Titania swooped in with all the ferocity of a sibling defending her family. She attacked the wyvern at the eyes. Once she dug her talons into the sockets, she locked up and remained clinging to the wyvern's head, even when it thrashed—even while it continued to laugh.

Atty stood near the bow of the ship, overlooking the chaos.

She waved her hand and the fire on the deck diminished. Then she turned her attention to the sailors with flames on their shirts and manipulated the fire until they were all snuffed out.

The wyvern fighting Luthair managed to bash him off the side of the boat. I caught my breath, but then I remembered—*shadows don't fall*. During the half-second Luthair was incapacitated, the wyvern stomped toward Forsythe. When the phoenix crashed onto the deck, the wyvern cackled, its mouth wide, its saliva thick and sticky.

"Forsythe!"

Zaxis jumped over his phoenix and shielded him from the rabid wyvern.

I unleashed another round of terror, desperate to prevent the pirates from doing any more damage. I stopped the wyvern—it screamed again, tears at the edges of its eyes.

Illia leapt at it. She touched its side, teleporting bits of flesh off the monster's body. It whipped its diamond-point stinger around and slashed her across the arm. Blood splattered to the wood of ship.

Luthair formed back on the deck and caught her before she fell backward.

"Look after her," I shouted. "Don't let the Wyvern's blood anywhere near her injury!"

Hexa ran up—I never even saw her arrive—and she threw her hydra onto the wyvern's back. Raisen vomited on the open wounds, his poison invading the injuries. The screaming could be heard the next nation over.

The panic, the chaos, the noise...

It was so damn hard to focus on a single person or thing.

So when a *third* wyvern joined the fight, I turned my terror on it.

"Enough!" Zelfree shouted.

I didn't see him until he grabbed my shoulder and shook

me. My magic failed, and the third wyvern flew forward and killed the injured wyvern with a swift stab of its tail—the stinger ripping right through the throat and ending the creature's life.

It was Traces. She was fighting in wyvern form.

And then Gregory Ruma returned to his ship. He landed in the middle of the fire, but his wind whipped the flames off into the ocean with a powerful burst that almost knocked me over. He held up his hand and lightning struck the wyvern in the sky.

It gasped in one final half-screech of death. The pirate rider fell to the deck.

Ruma turned his palm toward the man.

Zelfree tried to get in the way. "Don't!"

But Ruma didn't listen. He let loose a bolt of lightning and killed the man in an instant. Then he turned to the last pirate and wyvern.

"We need to question them," Zelfree shouted.

The pirate's eyes widened. "W-wait, Gregory!"

Another crack of lightning and the whole fight was over —it struck both the wyvern and the man, ripping through them with an unparalleled amount of magic, even damaging part of the deck.

No one moved. The silence that followed was unnatural for the ocean. The tension of a real battle didn't disappear when the threats vanished. It took me a moment of controlled breathing to even get my thoughts in order.

The sailors were the first to act. They clapped and cheered, some of them chanting Ruma's name. They holstered their weapons and shook each other in glee.

My hands trembled, but I knew we had all come through the fight. Illia, Hexa, Atty, and Adelgis were all with their eldrin, exchanging glances with each other. I offered

Zaxis a hand up, and he took it, but he never let Forsythe out of his arms.

"Thank you," he muttered.

"Don't mention it," I said.

"No, I mean it. You saved me. Just like you did with Lyell."

I didn't know what to say. I shrugged. "It's what arcanists do, right?"

"R-right."

"Look after Forsythe. If plague blood gets into his injuries, he'll..."

Zaxis nodded and held his eldrin close. "I'll heal him."

Traces transformed back into her cat form. She leapt onto Zelfree's shoulder and hissed in Ruma's direction. "We don't know where they're hiding," she said. "Did you have to kill both of them?"

"They were dogs," Ruma said. He patted his hands together. "They would've killed us if they'd had the chance. And we'll find their hideout soon enough."

Zelfree and Ruma stared at each other for a long moment before turning away. The sailors went about cleaning up the mess, and Ruma went to the edge of the ship to command Decimus. Although it hadn't ended in a shouting match, it felt like they were still arguing about something.

I agreed with Zelfree. Why wouldn't we use them to find the other pirates? But it was too late now. Their corpses littered the High Riser, and the sailors were busy mopping up the carnage.

Luthair appeared at my side. The fight replayed in my head over and over again. I couldn't believe how much my magic came as an instinct. I just used it, even though it would harm me. I preferred that outcome—I'd hate myself if I locked up when someone truly needed me.

Zaxis and I walked over to the other four apprentices. They whispered until we drew close and then stopped. Illia, Hexa, and Atty all turned to Adelgis.

"Tell them," Hexa whispered.

"Tell us what?" I asked.

Adelgis shook his head. "The pirates... Felicity heard some of their thoughts."

"What did they think?"

"They didn't want to anger Master Ruma."

"Of course," Zaxis said with a laugh. "No one would."

"No, you don't understand. They didn't want to anger him because they would be meeting with him on an island not far from here." Adelgis stared down at the deck. "They were... planning something together."

The information unsettled me, but nothing surprised me anymore.

Although it seemed like Luthair would be proven correct, I still didn't understand Ruma's motives. He hated pirates! Especially if they killed his wife. What did Ruma have to gain by working *with* them? He was wealthy beyond his wildest dreams and respected throughout the world. He had a powerful eldrin —and vast magical powers—what more could he ever want?

The others stared at me for a long moment.

"You warned us about this," Adelgis whispered. "What do you want to do with this information?"

"I don't know," I said. I turned to Hexa and Atty. "Do you know everything?"

Hexa nodded. "Illia told us all about your knightmare accusing Ruma of bein' a murderer."

Good. We were all on the same page.

Zelfree, Gregory, and the sailors moved to clean up the mess and I motioned to join them.

"Act like nothing happened," I whispered. "I need time to speak with Luthair."

Even if I confirmed Ruma's misdeeds, I still couldn't do anything about it. He destroyed an entire ship of pirates all by himself. What could I hope to do against him? Nothing. What I needed now was either a lot more magical control or information. If I knew Ruma's motives, perhaps I could stop him in another way.

We broke apart and went about helping patch up the ship.

Luthair remained in my shadows. We'd talk later, when it was safe to do so.

26

DESERTED ISLAND

The ship creaked as it rocked back and forth on the waters. The evening waves didn't jostle us too much, and for that I was thankful.

Although the girls had a separate room, they had all snuck over to ours with Illia the moment Ruma retired. Six people cramped in a small area made for a stuffy environment, even with everyone's eldrin out on the deck of the ship. The smell of body odor mixed with salt stung my nose. I scooted to the edge of my cot before summoning Luthair.

He rose from the shadows—a seventh body filling the tiny room—and took a step back against the wall.

"What all did Felicity hear?" I asked.

Adelgis, still dressed in his formal attire, cleared his throat. "I told you everything. The pirate's thoughts were panicked right before he died. He didn't meticulously review his plans as he was being electrocuted by Ruma."

I crossed my arms. "Well, considering our relative strength compared to Ruma's, I suggest we continue on as if we never heard anything."

"That's it?" Zaxis barked. "That's your plan? We waited all day to hear this?"

"What do *you* suggest we do, then?"

He huffed. "We should tell Zelfree. Demand answers from Master Ruma. If he doesn't answer, Zelfree and us can handle him."

The others exchanged nervous glances.

"On his own ship?" I asked. "In the middle of the ocean? You actually think we stand a chance?"

Zaxis mulled over my comment. Had he not considered Ruma's natural advantage? While on the ocean, Decimus could drag us below the waves, and the storms alone would prevent anyone from escaping, even if we took control of the ship. We needed more arcanists, perhaps the guildmaster, before we escalated into a confrontation.

"We have to do something," Illia said.

I snapped my attention to her. "Really? You too?"

"We're in danger. Ruma is in cahoots with the pirates, and it's obvious they want mystical creatures, whether they're eldrin or not." She narrowed her eye and lowered her voice. "And other apprentices already went missing in this territory. There's no doubt in my mind that Ruma intends to do something with one of us. Perhaps *all* of us."

Damn. She was right.

Atty fidgeted with the hems of her sleeves. "Should we escape?"

"How?" Adelgis asked. "The Crescent Isles are far removed from any major port."

"Convenient," Hexa muttered. "This is why I hate the ocean. If we were on land, we wouldn't be trapped on this damn boat."

No one said anything after that.

The High Riser had dinghies, but that wouldn't take us

far across the ocean. Running wasn't an option. What other choices did we have?

"One of us should claim we're sick," I said, the words flowing with my stream of thought. "Then we'll have to go to a port. Even if it's a small one. We could form a plan then."

Illia nodded. "Yes! I like that."

"I agree," Adelgis said.

The others didn't join in.

"Who will do it?" Zaxis asked.

Hexa lifted her head. "I will. Raisen has venom that'll affect me. He accidently bit me a few times, so I know I can live through it."

"And you can pull this off?"

"You can count on me," she said with a wide smile.

I awoke to sounds of vomiting. Zaxis, Adelgis, and I left our room to find Hexa out in the hall. Her skin had gone yellow, and her eyes sunken in overnight. Illia stayed by her side, patting her back.

"It'll be okay," Illia muttered.

Both Ruma and Zelfree entered our cabin. Their disheveled clothes, still spotted with blood, betrayed the fact that neither of them had slept. They regarded each other with neutral expressions before walking over to Hexa.

"What happened?" Ruma asked.

"Raisen..." Hexa managed to mutter.

Zelfree shook his head. "That kind of poison can be deadly."

"I know of a talented apothecary on the Isle of Luna," Ruma said. "We'll stop there."

Zelfree gritted his teeth. "That's exactly where we're

already heading! We're not far from Rock Town. We should stop there."

"Why do you keep trying to change my course, Zelfree? I told you none of the cities outside of Luna have anything of interest. I've searched them already."

"Why won't you ever listen to any of my suggestions?" Zelfree growled. "Why is it so important we go straight to the Isle of Luna? There are plenty of places for pirates to hide at port!"

"Rock Town doesn't have any healers," Ruma said as he strode down the hall, passing us with powerful strides. "Trust me. We need to see Madam Jaysa. She'll be able to heal hydra bites, I promise."

Before Zelfree could offer another counterpoint, Ruma exited the cabin onto the deck. He slammed the door behind him, shaking the ship. Zelfree cursed loud enough his voice echoed around us.

"Put her on a cot," Zelfree said, curt. "I'll get us somewhere if I have to put a bullet through this damn man's head." He chased after Ruma.

Atty and Illia complied with his demands. Although Zelfree and Ruma continued to argue out on the deck, the course never changed. We headed for the Isle of Luna, a medium-sized island deep within the Crescent Isles. Although Rock Town could be seen in the distance, we passed that too.

I rubbed at my neck, dwelling on the terrible situation.

Perhaps we had already fallen into a trap.

After a morning of training, I rested on the deck railing, my gaze on the small dots of green in the distance. Illia and

Adelgis continued their training with Zelfree, but I needed time to gather my thoughts. My quiet contemplation was interrupted by Zaxis, however.

He sauntered over and leaned against the railing next to me.

"Hey," he said.

I turned to him with a lifted eyebrow.

Zaxis ran a hand through his red hair, combing it back with his fingers. "I'm worried about Forsythe."

I straightened my posture. "Is he okay?"

"He's fine. Right now. But phoenixes and their arcanists have gone missing near here."

"Yeah."

"I don't want to lose him." Zaxis shot me a glare. "And not just because I'm afraid of losing my magic. I'm worried about *him*."

"I wasn't going to accuse you of anything," I said. "I understand. I wouldn't want anything to happen to Luthair either."

Zaxis relaxed a bit. "I just wanted to make it clear."

"Okay. So why tell me?"

"We grew up on the same island, didn't we? We're apprentices in the same guild. We're both trying to expose Ruma's dastardly deeds. Stop being obtuse—of course I would tell you."

Of course he would tell me. Like we were friends. Were we now? I didn't really know, so I shrugged and went along with it.

"We won't let anything happen to Forsythe," I said.

Zaxis huffed. "We can't stop Ruma if he decides to do something."

"That's why we have to outsmart him. Stay alert. You're

his apprentice. You could probably stay two steps ahead if you played your cards right."

He pushed away from the railing. "I know that," he snapped. "That's what I've been doing all along."

Had he? He never mentioned it before.

Zaxis walked away with a dismissive wave of his hand. "I have to get back to training." He slowed his walk as he added, "Oh, and thank you." But he hustled away before I could reply or ask him for what.

We arrived at the Isle of Luna, but the High Riser was too large a vessel to dock at the tiny pier. The sun set on the horizon line of the ocean, but a lighthouse shone bright in the distance, keeping larger ships at bay. The chill of the evening winds brought more than an icy drop in temperature. Tension mounted as the sailors loaded up one of the dinghies.

"Zelfree and I will head into town," Ruma said. "The rest of you will wait here. We'll bring the apothecary back before dawn."

He jumped into the tiny boat, and motioned Zelfree to join him.

Zelfree hung back for a moment. He turned to me and glared. "Don't leave the High Riser."

Nothing else. No *stay safe* or *I'll be back*. He simply took off with Ruma on the dinghy and sailed across the dark waters until we couldn't see them anymore.

Minutes passed. The moon hung high in the sky. Would they be gone until sunrise? I wouldn't be able to sleep until this whole damn mission was over.

Decimus circled around the High Riser, like a shark

closing in on a bleeding victim. The sailors didn't talk much, and the howl of the breeze over nearby rocks made for an eerie symphony. While these details were harmless on their own, everything added together made even the shifting shadows of rats scurrying across the deck enough to get me jumping.

Illia approached me, her gaze flitting around from sailor to sailor. "Are you nervous at all?"

"I know I am," Nicholin added, his fur so puffed he looked like a snowball.

"I'm not sure what we're going to do about it," I muttered.

"I think we should get off the boat," Illia said. She grabbed me by my upper arm and pulled me close. "Right now. We still have a dinghy."

"Decimus is right there." I motioned to the water. "If we really are being set up for something, there's no way we're getting past a leviathan."

"He might leave the boat," Illia said with a sly tone. "If he were chasing a lure."

My first reaction was to argue. Where would we find a lure? But then it struck me. We had a living lure right here.

"I can teleport myself," Illia whispered. "If I got away from the boat and Decimus followed me, maybe the rest of you could escape with the dinghy."

"You can teleport yourself?" I asked. I had never seen her do that!

She flushed a slight red. "I can... do it a little bit."

"You'll be putting yourself in danger if you do that, especially if you can't teleport far. Send me instead. I've always been a good swimmer."

Illia shook her head. "Nicholin is the lure, and I'm his arcanist. We should do this together. Even if I can't go far, I can keep teleporting myself over and over again. And if something goes wrong… I don't want to hurt someone else, okay? You've seen what I can do when I don't teleport the whole person."

She was afraid of dislocating parts of our bodies? "You won't hurt yourself, right?"

"No. Of course not." Illia pointed to a mountain of rocks jutting out of the water. "I'll head there. I can swim between the littler rocks until I reach the island. Or hide in places Decimus is too large to search."

Did we really need to do this? No. But if we were going to do *anything*, we didn't have many other options. And if we made it to the island and nothing happened, it wouldn't tip our hand. We could claim we were just worried—it had taken them too long—and then we could at least meet this *wonderful* apothecary that Ruma spoke of.

"Okay," I said. "Let me tell the others."

Illia nodded. I grabbed her shoulder before she left, her eyebrows knit.

"Don't get into trouble."

She smiled. "Never."

I stood next to the release for the dinghy, my hands on the rope. Atty and Adelgis had the rope ladder ready, each whispering to the other. Zaxis and Hexa stood nearby. Although Hexa was still wan and wobbling on her feet, Zaxis kept his hand gripped tight on her arm, his healing magic working wonders on her condition. It was a good thing Gregory didn't realize how accomplished Zaxis had become. It didn't surprise me, though. Zaxis had the determined spirit to be the best at everything he did.

Illia waited at the bow of the ship, her eyes on the glistening rocks in the distance, the clear night sky a boon for our endeavors. Forsythe and Titania sat on the railing of the boat, their glowing bodies adding light to our situation.

With Nicholin in her arms, Illia disappeared with a pop.

The two sailors on deck gave each other quick glances.

"Hey," one called out. "What happened?"

"Nothing," Zaxis said. "Mind your own business."

"What're you doin' with that dinghy? You're not allowed to leave!"

"Really? Because I don't think anyone is going to stop us."

The two sailors hustled over, but Atty stepped between them and our escape vessel. She waved her hand and fire blazed out in front of her. The flames didn't quite wash over the men, but her magic did singe their clothes. They jumped back, their eyes wide.

"We don't want to hurt you," I said. "But we're not going to stay on the boat either."

The men took a moment to mull over my words before heading to the hold. Would they alert the rest of the crew? It didn't matter. None of them were arcanists, and we would be long gone with the last dinghy anyway.

Decimus swirled around the High Riser one last time before turning toward the distant rocks. Had he sensed Nicholin? Was he chasing the lure? My chest tightened when I thought of Illia fleeing from a gargantuan serpent. But I shook my head, dispelling the fear.

"Let's go," I said.

I lowered the dinghy as Adelgis lowered the rope ladder. Once situated, we each climbed into the small boat, Hexa's hydra being the trickiest part. He flailed around in Hexa's arms as she got closer to the ladder, to the point she couldn't hold him properly.

"I got him," Zaxis said.

He grabbed the wiggling hydra with one arm and climbed down the ladder, the scales of the creature scraping his side. He grunted down each rung, his teeth gritted.

Once everyone was aboard, we each grabbed an oar and headed for the island. With the moon shining bright, it wasn't difficult to keep track of Decimus. He crashed through the waves and slammed a portion of his serpentine body against the distant rocks, his scales harder than anything he was striking.

Forsythe and Titania flew overhead, their glowing forms akin to fireflies, they were so high up.

"Will Illia be alright?" Adelgis whispered.

"Of course," I snapped.

Why did he have to remind me that Illia was somewhere over there? All I could do was watch the dark swirl of the leviathan beneath the surface, circling the rocks. At one point, Decimus lifted his head out of the ocean, but I couldn't get a good look—I heard his screech, however. It sent a chill straight to my bones.

"He's letting Master Ruma know," Atty muttered.

Damn.

Salt water splashed into our boat as the waves grew larger. We rowed faster. My arms burned by the time we reached a sandy shore. I took deep breaths as I leapt out of the dinghy and sloshed through the shallow waters up the beach.

The lighthouse stood watch not far in the distance, the flames of the light burning bright.

I trudged through the water, slowing when I reached the beach. Luthair appeared and pulled me the last bit onto the sand. I stared up at him, thankful for his help and surprised I hadn't noticed his arrival from the shadows.

Zaxis, Atty, Hexa, and Adelgis walked up the beach and toward the town. I followed behind, Luthair trailing after me. The island had tall trees with leafy canopies that blocked out the moonlight, creating a void we had to trek through. No one spoke as we stepped over exposed roots and wove through the sparse woodlands.

We reached the edge of town, but I almost gasped the moment I got a good look around.

The broken walls, the shattered glass of windows—everything had a fine layer of dust and a fresh dress of cobwebs. I took a few steps forward, glancing between the ruined buildings.

This place had been destroyed. Years ago, by the looks of things.

Yet the lighthouse still operated? What had happened here? Why did Ruma insist on bringing everyone to this location?

We walked along the main road; no one said a word. I caught my breath when we reached the town square. An old cathedral stood at the far end. The stained glass of the windows matched the shards in the master arcanist's common area in the Frith Guild. This was the cathedral where Ruma married his wife. The same one wrecked by pirates.

This place was deserted.

Atty frowned. "I don't understand."

"It's a ghost town," Hexa said. Her hydra curled around her legs as she stared at a dilapidated wall. "Someone destroyed it. Look. Bullet holes. Burns. Arcanists were here."

Zaxis huffed. "Damn. There's no apothecary here. You were right, Volke. Something is happening."

"What're we going to do?" Adelgis asked. "Should we wait for Illia?"

I held my breath, my heart beating so hard it echoed in my eardrums.

Why had Ruma brought us here? Where was he? Where was Zelfree?

"We should look around while we wait for Illia," I muttered. "Quietly. Ruma and Zelfree have to be around here, but I don't think it's a good idea to let them know where we are."

The others nodded.

Luthair stepped up to my side, his black armor shining with the moonlight. "My arcanist. I said we shouldn't merge unless it was absolutely necessary, but now is the time. Something is amiss, and I fear we won't be leaving this island without a fight."

I agreed. Something was wrong, and we needed all the strength we could get if we were to get to the bottom of the mystery.

"Let's merge," I said.

SECRET IN THE STAINED-GLASS CATHEDRAL

Shadows crept up my body, lacing together into hard plate. When the dark tendrils reached my head, I closed my eyes and held my breath. The cool touch of shadow settled onto my skin. When I reopened my eyes, I stared through the slit of a full helmet. Although actual heavy armor would have weighed me down and restricted my movement, Luthair's form didn't hinder me at all.

I stared down at my hands, glancing between my palms and forearms.

The inky armor fascinated me, but not as much as my movements. Everything felt odd, like someone or something had an invisible influence over what I did. My sight had also improved. The dark of the night no longer troubled me, I saw our surroundings as well as I could have during the midafternoon hours. Every shadow, every shade, every nook of darkness—nothing hid from my new vision.

We need to stay alert, Luthair said, speaking through thoughts.

I caught my breath. *What is this?*

I told you. We'll live and die as a single being. We are one.

The knowledge startled me, but not for long. Steeled to my role, I turned to the others. They stared, no doubt having watched the entire time Luthair merged over me.

"Interesting," Adelgis said. "I've heard of such sorcery, but I've never seen it."

Zaxis swept his arm in an arc. Forsythe swooped down and landed on the road next to him. "Light the way for us," he said. "We should get to the bottom of this."

I pointed to the cathedral with the broken stained-glass window. "That's where we should start."

"Why?"

"I recognize this place. It's where Gregory Ruma married his wife." The others nodded and stuck close together. But before we could move out, I motioned to the beach. "I need to get Illia. You all can go without me."

Atty called down her phoenix. "Do you want Titania to go with you?"

"No. I'm fine."

I dashed away from the group, the shadow armor burning my legs as I did so. That was why I didn't want anyone to follow me. I knew I would have to deal with the pain, and I didn't want anyone to know. Fire licked my skin and pierced my muscles.

Are you sure you can handle this? Luthair asked.

Yes, I replied. *Let's go.*

The armor clanked with my movements. It also enhanced my speed and strength. When I moved, I did so with purpose, fueled by a new source of energy I didn't have before.

Illia said she would swim from the rocks to the island, so I ran to the closest rocky shore. I leapt over the tide pools and trudged out into the shallow waters. The pull of the waves wasn't enough to move me, and I realized my armor did add to my weight, even if I couldn't feel it.

I waited.

When Illia didn't arrive, I went out farther, my throat tight, my entire body tense. Far out at sea I heard another shriek—something bordering on a laugh—and I couldn't help but imagine Illia's dead body washing up on shore.

She'll make it, Luthair thought.

I swallowed hard, forcing my anxiety down with my saliva. *You're right. She wouldn't let this stop her.*

No way I could swim like this, but I gave it a thought. The pain would eventually stop me, though. And then I would drown.

A pop of air and a few splashes later, I finally relaxed. I waded out farther, until the waves lapped at my chest, and spotted Illia between a pair of rocks jutting out of the ocean. Nicholin clung to the top of her head, his eyes scrunched closed. If he weren't pristine white, he'd look like a drowned rat.

"Illia!" I called out.

I bit back the rest of my words.

The tone of my voice was a mix between mine and Luthair's. It disturbed me for a moment, to speak with someone else's timbre.

Illia perked up and hurried toward me, one arm after another, her breath coming in gasps.

"Volke," she murmured in a soft voice.

I waded into the water until it came to my chin, and I reached out to help her. She took my hand, and I pulled her close as I helped her to shore.

"Are you okay?" I asked—again, my new voice foreign to my ears.

"Yes," she said, breathless. After she gulped down a few

breaths, she stared up at me with a smile. "You all made it? I... I did it?"

"We're all here. But there's no one on this island. It's deserted."

"What?"

"We need to find Ruma and Zelfree. I think something has happened."

"Decimus," Illia muttered. "I think he was trying to catch me at first, but then he started talking... I couldn't understand him. And then he tried to kill me."

"The ocean tried to kill me," Nicholin wheezed. He coughed up a ferret-sized lung's worth of water. "Rizzels aren't designed for swimming."

I guided Illia through the dark and pointed her toward the abandoned town. "This way. Follow me."

Although she traveled at a slow pace, Illia never complained. We made our way along the winding path until we reached the edge of town. I wasn't tired, but Illia had to stop to catch her breath. Water dripped from her clothes, and it was then I realized she no longer had her coat.

I pointed to the cathedral in the town square. No need to speak between us. She knew what I wanted.

The main street led us straight to our destination, and I shivered. It felt as if destiny itself wanted us to go to the cathedral. There was nothing in our way, and the island grew silent. Even the wind calmed down, as if the world held its breath. We climbed the steps up the slight slope to the cathedral and found Hexa, Adelgis, Zaxis, and Atty.

They hadn't entered. I already knew why. Light shone through the cracks of the large double door. Someone had smashed it and the wind howled as it swept into and out of the building between those cracks.

"Should we sneak around?" Adelgis whispered.

Before I could answer, a low moan echoed inside the building. Everyone froze. We waited for a long moment until the sound rang out a second time. A terrible noise—half a cry, half a gasp of pain. Who was it?

Zaxis squared his shoulders and walked to the front door. Although the cathedral had been ruined years ago, the walls still supported most of the roof, and the large double doors remained hinged in place. Zaxis pushed one door in, the creak louder than anything we had heard so far.

We all jumped back as a stream of light cut through the night.

Another agonizing moan.

Zaxis finished opening the door.

"Gregory..."

The name lingered at the end of a groan.

"I think someone needs our help," I said.

The others nodded. Zaxis held the door open, and we stepped in as a group. The long front room of the cathedral greeted us with a cold gust of wind. The pews had been knocked over or destroyed, and the once grand walls were stained with salt water and blood.

"Gregory..."

Light emanated from lanterns hung on pillars. Someone had to have lit them recently.

A slight bit of movement caught my eye. Something shambled on the pulpit, and I moved closer, curious about what lay ahead.

"Hello?" I called out.

"Gregory..." it answered. Then it sobbed, feminine and anguished.

She was suffering.

I ran forward, intent on taking her from this place.

"Volke!" Illia cried. "Don't!"

I made it all the way to the pulpit before I saw what had been moaning this entire time. A woman. No. Not a woman. Not anymore.

A corpse. A shuffling, rotted corpse. It jerked around, its skin yellowish green and sloughing off like a snake shedding skin, only with a slick slime. The stench of maggot-infested meat reached my nose and I gagged.

The corpse wore clothing, but the trousers and shirt had long soaked up the stinking vital fluid, tarnishing them black and yellow. The hair—likely once long and lustrous—now flowed in the wind, white and wispy, so fine it nearly flew off with each new gust. There were no eyes. Just sockets devoid of organs with clumped blood pooling at the bottom.

Illia rushed to my side. "What is it?"

Nicholin puffed up and hunched his back. He hissed and urged Illia away. "W-what is that?"

The second cathedral door swung open. We all turned, and I lost my breath.

Gregory Ruma stood in the doorway, his gaze locked on us. He stared for a moment before walking inside, allowing the busted door to shut behind him. Each of his boot steps echoed as he made his way to the pulpit. Zaxis, Atty, Adelgis, and Hexa stepped aside to allow him to pass. He never acknowledged them.

"Where's Zelfree?" Zaxis asked, his anger obviously substituting when courage failed him.

"He's no longer with us," Ruma casually replied.

His pants were splattered with fresh blood.

"Gregory..." the corpse moaned. It reached out its skeletal arms, its fingers unable to escape their twisted-claw position.

"I'm here," Ruma said, his voice tender and soft as he

stepped onto the pulpit and reached out for the cadaver. "Don't worry, my love. I haven't left you."

To my disgust, he laced his fingers through the wispy hair and cradled the disgusting body close. Even though the flesh stained his coat and shirt with puss and coagulated blood, he didn't let go. The corpse stopped moaning and crying. It leaned against him and settled down, like any good corpse should.

I chanced a glance at Illia. She stared, her one eye round in shock.

"Master Ruma," Atty muttered, her soft voice echoing. "Why have you brought us here?"

Ruma broke his embrace, but he kept the corpse close as he said. "Acantha isn't feeling well."

I almost laughed, no doubt from knotted nerves twisting throughout my gut and chest. *Not feeling well*? I never heard anyone say that about the dead, and I had once worked as a gravedigger.

"She's dead," Illia said, parroting my thoughts.

Ruma stroked Acantha's sunken cheeks, his eyes filled with nothing but adoration, even as some of her skin peeled away. "No. She's getting better. Each day, each month, each year. A little better. The more I feed her eldrin magic, the more Acantha recovers. Soon she'll be just like she was."

"How can you say that?" I asked.

"Because I've seen it," he snapped.

"S-seen it?"

"She died in my arms, but look at her now! Talking and walking. Improvements. I swore I wouldn't stop until she smiled again." Ruma chuckled as he glanced between us. "That's why you're here. To help me."

He's a fiend of the highest order, Luthair spoke in my mind.

A man who thinks he's doing justice when, in reality, he's destroying everything he touches. There can be no mercy here.

To my shock, the corpse still had an arcanist mark on her forehead. If an arcanist's eldrin died, or *they* died, the mark was supposed to disappear.

How had her eldrin stayed bonded after she died? I asked Luthair.

Some people and mythical creatures can't let go. Obviously that's what happened here. They're all deranged.

Hexa took a step back. "You're touched in the head."

"Am I?" Ruma said with a laugh. "You've obviously never known true love. Some things are worth more than anything —more than wealth and fame and glory. Acantha didn't deserve the fate she got. I'll correct that and bring her back. I just need a little more magic."

"For what?" Adelgis asked. "You can't resurrect the dead! It just can't be done."

Ruma whistled, the sound so piercing it hurt my ears.

A few moments later, the fire from the lighthouse moved on its own. It swirled and thrashed and took to the sky. Everyone watched as it drew closer and closer to the cathedral, sailing straight for the shattered windows. Would it collide with the building? What was happening?

I braced when it got close, but then I realized it wasn't a fire.

It was a phoenix. A giant, monstrous, phoenix.

The bird crashed through the last of the stained glass, screeching as it forced itself into the cathedral, its body so massive it had trouble squeezing through the stone frame of the window. It smashed down on a pile of pews, its black talons sharp enough to cut stone.

But something wasn't right. It had six wings—four terrible wings made of bulbous limbs, broken feathers, and hand-like claws. Although Forsythe and Titania had gold eyes, this giant phoenix had nothing but sockets that wept gold, as if its eyes were liquefying and running down its heron-like face as tears.

Then it laughed. Louder and louder until the sound transformed into a cackling.

"I need... *more* magic..." it screamed, its voice filled with mirth and horror.

"Yes," Ruma said with a smile. "I've brought you more phoenixes and rare creatures, Falvala."

"Yes, *yes*, yes!" Falvala answered with more laughter than before. "I must... transform... I must become perfect! I need... phoenixes!"

"Consume them," Ruma commanded. "Show me a phoenix's true form. Show me you have the power to resurrect the dead!"

The phoenix flapped four of her six wings, washing the cathedral in a wave of flame. I leapt behind a broken pew, Illia teleported behind a pillar, and the others shielded themselves with rubble. The heat swept overhead, catching the edge of Luthair's cape, but nothing more. Then the monster phoenix, Falvala, leapt to the front door and landed in front of it. She giggled, even as golden tears streamed down her face.

She was at one end of the cathedral, and Ruma stood at the other.

"This is insanity," Atty called out. "Please, listen! This isn't how you go about perfecting your magic. You need a pure soul and—"

"Don't lecture me," Ruma said with a smile. "It's already working. Don't you see? Acantha is right here! The plague is the key to a mystical creature's true form. *This*—what Falvala has become—is what all phoenixes aspire to be."

I didn't believe it. I couldn't. Whatever had happened to Falvala, it couldn't be natural or right. When she laughed, my skin crawled. When she moved, she jerked around as if on strings held by an amateur puppeteer. Nothing about her could be what a phoenix truly was.

Falvala moved forward, her giant talons clicking against the stone floor of the cathedral. She glanced behind the rubble and breathed white flames. Zaxis and Adelgis dove away, but they weren't fast enough. Zaxis's trousers were burned, and Adelgis rolled through some of the fire, his body smoking.

I ran down the cathedral walkway and held up my hand. Although I hadn't mastered my tricks, I knew I could pull off one without fail. My terror flooded the cathedral and the phoenix screamed. She staggered backward, shaking her head, splashing the gold eye fluid on the walls.

"No!" she cried. "Help me!"

I turned to the others. "Run! Hurry, before it's too late."

As the others forced themselves to their feet, Ruma lifted his hand and let out a bolt of lightning. It struck me in the back and my vision flashed a bright white. I lost all consciousness. When I awoke—how long had I been out?— I was on the cathedral floor, my mind buzzing, my muscles twitching.

Up, Luthair urged. *You must get up.*

I staggered to my feet, my vision returning in waves, despite the pain of moving in the shadow armor. Then again, if I hadn't been wearing Luthair, I *definitely* would've died when Ruma struck me with his lightning.

I realized then the others were fighting with Ruma, each using their limited magical abilities in an attempt to catch him off-guard. But we had done this before in training.

Ruma blocked their attacks with ease, his mastery of magic far above ours.

Falvala cawed and trembled near the front door. She muttered to herself, lost in some imaginary conversation where she giggled every other sentence. Could we get by? Not with Ruma around. He could shock us or knock us down with wind—any number of his abilities enough to kill.

Atty and Zaxis combined their fire, but Ruma blasted it away with wind, sweeping it across Adelgis and Illia. While Illia popped and teleported away, Adelgis crumpled to the floor, his arms and face badly burned. When Ruma held up his hand, no doubt to finish him off, Felicity floated between them, shielding her arcanist with her crystalline body.

"We're not dyin' without a fight," Hexa shouted as she released a wave of noxious gas.

Zaxis ran to Adelgis's side and used his healing to perk him up. They shuffled behind a broken pillar, each ragged and drained.

We didn't have the skill or the power to beat Ruma or his plague-infested wife.

"Everyone get down!" someone shouted from outside the cathedral.

I recognized the voice, but I couldn't place it, not with the haze over my mind. I didn't care. The others obviously hadn't heard, so I shouted it again.

"Get down!"

A CLASH OF TWO LEVIATHANS

Although I hadn't explained myself, the others threw themselves to the floor without a second guess. A moment later, the upper half of the cathedral was blown away by the swipe of a leviathan's tail. The top of the building came off so cleanly it was as if it had been sliced with a razor knife. Each wall stood only three feet high and the roof tumbled into the next building over, smashing glass and creating a pillar of dust and debris.

It took me a moment to realize I wasn't breathing. As the wreckage settled, I pushed myself to my feet, confused as to who had attacked.

Ruma had ducked and taken his corpse bride with him. He stood and helped Acantha to her feet, even going so far as to smooth her hair over her head. "It'll be okay," he whispered. Then he turned his attention to the front door, his expression angrier than I had ever seen. "Zelfree. Why can't you ever stay dead?"

A leviathan waited outside, so massive and gigantic it could crush the whole town if it rolled around for half an hour. Zelfree stood on one of its fins, clinging to the scales on its serpentine body. His arcanist mark bore the symbol of the leviathan.

One of his arms was mangled—he couldn't even move it —and blood soaked his shirt and pants. He didn't look well, but he laughed regardless.

"You thought you could throw me to the ocean?" Zelfree asked, his voice much weaker when compared to Ruma's. "I'll make you pay, Ruma. Now that I know it was you..." He shook his head, his teeth gritted. "How could you do all those killings? The phoenix arcanists? My apprentices?"

"I needed them," Ruma growled. "*Acantha* needed them."

"You tried to pin your evil deeds on me!" Zelfree glared. "You told me it was *my* fault my apprentices had been captured by pirates—yet here you were, orchestrating the whole damn thing!"

"You should've run while you had the chance," Ruma shouted. "By coming back here, you've guaranteed your death."

"The plague has gotten you, hasn't it? The Ruma I know never would've done such heinous things."

"You don't know what it means to love. I made an oath. To protect her. *Cherish her.* And that's what I intend to do."

In a gentler tone, Zelfree said, "We could find a cure."

"There is no need for a cure! *This is what I want.* I want my Acantha back!"

Ruma unleashed another bolt of lightning.

Zelfree's mimic-leviathan—Traces in disguise—blocked the attack with her scaled tail. We hadn't heard a giant leviathan approach because she had simply transformed outside the door of the cathedral. Seeing her and Zelfree stand strong lifted my spirit. If Zelfree could keep Ruma busy, perhaps we could get away.

Falvala emerged from a pile of broken stones and shattered support beams. She screeched and spread her six wings, fire washing off her in small waves.

"I must have *magic*," she said with a giggle.

"Adelgis," I said. "Can you hear me? Break more of the wall. We have to get away."

He stood from the debris and held out a hand. A beam of light flew out and collided with one of the half-busted walls. A loud cough could've knocked it over, but his firework-like magic exploded and sent it toppling. While the others gathered to flee, I hustled toward the deranged phoenix.

Careful, Luthair said.

When I was close, I used my terror again. The phoenix struggled in the rubble, screeching and crying, tormented by horrors I couldn't see. It was enough of a distraction to let the others escape, however, and that was my entire goal.

The ground quaked, breaking my concentration. A second leviathan—so large I could even see it from inside the broken cathedral—smashed its way into town. There could be no doubt as to who it was.

Decimus.

With the speed of a cobra, it snaked through town, a concertina movement that smashed the remaining houses and destroyed the last of the streets. When he drew near, he lifted his head and laughed—the same bone-chilling laugh as all the other plague-infected creatures.

"I'm here for you master," Decimus said, his voice a rumble that shook the stones on the ground. "We must... *kill them all*."

I had never seen Decimus up close, and now I knew why. He opened his eyes—not a pair of them, like a normal leviathan—but hundreds of them. They littered his body

344

like chicken pox littered the skin of a child. They swirled and undulated, their dead fish appearance the thing of my nightmares.

Zelfree leapt from Traces, and the two behemoths collided with one another, the force of their physical confrontation on par with hurricanes. Electricity and ice rolled off them as they snaked together, each no doubt attempting to wrap their massive body around tight enough to strangle the other. It was a mirror match between goliaths. One wrong move and they could crush everyone in the cathedral.

The deranged phoenix hissed and laughed. I turned back to her, having forgotten I'd dropped my terror magic. She breathed flame and knocked me over, the heat of her attack searing my skin and scorching my eyes, even with Luthair as my armor. I rolled behind a pew and curled in on myself, angry I had lowered my guard.

Luthair gave me a mental urging. *If we fall here, all will be for nothing.*

I know.

Someone touched my shoulder. I glanced up and smiled as Zaxis used his healing to wipe away the pain of the burns. "You're so weak," he said. "If I weren't around, you'd have died here for sure."

"Thank you," I muttered as I got to my feet. I pulled out the sword at my side, my body moving with Luthair's expertise.

Zaxis ducked behind one of the far pillars, no doubt staying close, just in case he was needed. But his fire couldn't hurt Ruma, and it definitely wouldn't hurt a phoenix made of flame.

Ruma waved his hand and blew away another portion of wall. He leapt outside and iced over the surroundings, even under my own feet—even under Falvala's. He pulled his own sword as he approached the wounded Zelfree.

Much to my surprise, Zelfree stood his ground. He wouldn't win, though. His dominant arm looked shredded, as though a monster had gnawed on it. How did he hope to duel one of the best swashbucklers in the world?

"Run!" Zelfree shouted to me. "Get the others to safety!"

Ruma leapt for him, his sword up. Both had the speed and the grace of wind. It was clear Zelfree wasn't as strong though. He created ice and lightning, but Ruma dodged each attack and came in with the blade. Zelfree would get cut, but he wouldn't stop his magic—always on the defensive.

What was Zelfree's plan? To die fighting Ruma? Just so we could escape?

I wouldn't allow it. If I could help, I would. And I knew what I needed to do.

Although I stood too far away to catch Ruma with my terror, I used it anyway. The phoenix fell victim again, and it cried as I approached with hesitant steps, careful not to slip and fall. I held my sword, ready to cut into the bird and end its miserable life.

"Gregory..." the corpse moaned from the pulpit. "Gregory..."

Her calling stilled my hand, and I knew her "life" was tied to Falvala. If I cut the phoenix down, I cut her down as well. And perhaps Ruma was right. Perhaps he could resurrect her with enough blood, magic, and arcanists. Perhaps this was a phoenix's true form—I didn't know.

But I did know that sacrificing hundreds of lives to bring Acantha back couldn't be tolerated, even if I understood. Perhaps I would've gone to similar lengths in his position, but the Gregory Ruma I knew, the one I had read about—

the one I idolized—wouldn't have stood for this. He would've waited until he could meet his love again in the heavens beyond. He would've treasured her memories and honored the things she stood for.

He wouldn't have kept her as a rotting corpse in a collapsing cathedral.

As leviathans raged across the town, shaking the island with their fury—and as Zelfree and Ruma exchanged blows with mirror-like magic—I approached Falvala, my sword raised.

"Magic," she whispered, her golden tears flowing down her entire body. "It hurts me... so..."

With expert skill, I plunged the black sword into the chest of the giant phoenix, cutting deep through her breast bone. I pulled back the moment the blood began to gush, but my aim had been true and straight to her heart. She laughed and sputtered, but her wings drooped and she collapsed to the floor.

Acantha also collapsed, her body writhing as it went, her voice stolen from her.

"No!" Ruma screamed.

He stopped fighting with Zelfree, threw down his sword, and wind-leapt back into the cathedral, all the way to Acantha's side. With unsteady hands, he lifted her from the floor and cradled the corpse in his arms. He muttered soothing statements and rocked her back and forth.

"You'll be okay," he said. "Everything will be okay. I'm here for you. I've never left you. Just like I promised."

Zelfree stood in the cathedral doorway, the massive clash of leviathans not far behind him. He took a moment to breathe deep, his skin so pale it had almost become translucent. He held his one hand over his mangled arm, holding the injuries as if to quell the blood flow.

"Volke," he said. "Bring me Ruma's sword."

The adrenaline of the confrontation slowly left me as I walked outside to retrieve the weapon. Pain flooded my being and I gritted my teeth to push through it. Ruma hadn't moved by the time I returned to Zelfree's side.

Zaxis had rushed over and offered some strength to Zelfree. He also healed me a bit, erasing some of the ache lingering in my muscles. It wasn't much, but it would keep me going.

Zelfree took Ruma's sword and let out a long exhale.

"You two should get to safety," he said. "Find the others. If anything happened to them, I don't think there's enough drinks in the world to help me recover from that."

I almost wanted to laugh, but instead I offered him a nod.

Zelfree hobbled through the cathedral, the chorus of battle echoing outside. He reached Ruma and although I couldn't hear what he said, I knew he spoke as he lifted the sword.

I figured Ruma would do something—fight him, or attack at the last moment—but he neither moved nor acknowledged Zelfree's presence.

For a long moment, neither moved. Had they been friends at one point? Zelfree seemed hesitant to act, even though Ruma was a fiend. A terrible blackheart. Someone who had killed others. There was no need for Zelfree to hesitate.

Although I wanted to see the conclusion, I left the cathedral with Zaxis, just as my master wanted. I ran into the streets, my breath shallow as I struggled to keep going. It didn't take me long to find the others. They stood on the rooftop of a house that had yet to be destroyed. Adelgis held up his hand and shot a beam of light. It sailed for some distance before colliding with Decimus and rupturing one of his many eyes.

Atty and Hexa tried to do the same, but their evocation wasn't up to it. Illia teleported from the roof of the house and made her way to my side.

Decimus didn't care about his ruptured eye. He likely didn't notice.

Instead, he continued his struggle with Traces until he finally seized up and screamed.

In that moment, Traces struck. She coiled around, used the ice and lightning to help her trap Decimus in place. Then she squeezed—hard enough to crush the leviathan's insides and still his beating heart. When Decimus collapsed, it shook the island again and brought down another row of walls that had been left standing.

The Isle of Luna grew still and quiet.

Illia hugged me, and I hugged her back.

SIX APPRENTICES

Illia, Hexa, Atty, Zaxis, Adelgis, and I stood in the map room of the guild manor house, each with new robes and guild crests, fresh from a long week of rest. Zelfree, Reo, Guildmaster Eventide, and Library Master Vala also joined us, each at a position around the giant map table. We had our eldrin next to us. Everyone but the guildmaster, anyway.

The guildmaster cleared her throat with a cough and glanced between everyone. "We're gathered here to discuss both wonderful accomplishments and grave circumstances. Let's start with the good news, on the off chance we don't have enough time to make it to the bad."

She smiled at her own joke as she continued, "I'm impressed with our newest apprentices. From what Zelfree reported, you managed to pull through even when the odds were against you. If you had stayed on the High Riser that night, Ruma's crew would've killed you in your sleep. If you had tried to sail on the ocean in a dinghy, you undoubtedly would've been lost to the waves. You confronted destiny head on, and for that I commend you."

Nicholin scurried up Illia's clothes and hopped onto her

shoulder. "We'll always take destiny head on, thank you very much."

"I appreciate your kind words," Illia said.

Adelgis bowed his head. "Yes, thank you."

Atty, Hexa, and Zaxis each followed suit.

When it came to me, I bowed and said, "I've been lucky to have such good role models in my life." William, Zelfree —even Ruma, back in the day. None of them would have run from destiny, so neither would I.

Guildmaster Eventide smiled. "I'm glad to hear it." Then she turned to the other master arcanists. "But unfortunately, we have the terrible news of Ruma's passing. Thank you, Zelfree. I know you likely didn't want to be the one to end his life."

Zelfree stroked Traces behind the ears. He had deep wounds across his body, and although arcanists could heal, some magical injuries could leave scars. He didn't seem to mind, though. He wore his shirt half-open, exposing the bandaging.

"What will become of Ruma's apprentices?" Zelfree asked.

"I can take some," Library Master Vala said. "That's why I came here today. We shouldn't lose these fine arcanists simply because Ruma endangered us all."

Zaxis raised a hand.

The guildmaster pointed. "Yes?"

"I want to train under Zelfree." He gave the man a quick glance. "If he'll have me."

"That will be for him to decide."

"I'm going to get saddled with all the difficult ones, aren't I?" Zelfree quipped.

Atty stepped closer to the map table. "Only if you consider me to be among the difficult ones."

"And me," Hexa chimed in.

"Six a-apprentices?" Reo asked. He turned to the guild-master. "We've never done that before."

"Then it's settled," Guildmaster Eventide said.

"I thought I got to decide?" Zelfree asked.

"Oh, no. That was just for show. Of course you'll take them all. I expect great things, too. My plan, as it stands, is to create a specialized force of arcanists who handle issues involving the occult plague." She motioned to all of us. "Everyone in this room has dealt with it in one way or another. Can I count on you all to fight against it still?"

"Yes, guildmaster," everyone answered in unison.

I had never considered becoming part of a specialized team or force meant to fight the plague, but it felt fitting now. I had seen so many mystical creatures become mad beasts. And I had seen firsthand what would happen to a man who lost himself to the corruption. The plague was a curse that we needed to rid the world of.

Luthair faced me. Although I could no longer hear his thoughts, I already knew he agreed.

I had held up my end of the bargain—I had avenged Mathis.

THANK YOU SO MUCH FOR READING!

Please consider leaving a review—any and all feedback is much appreciated!

The Frith Chronicles continue with
The Dread Pirate Arcanist

While protecting the newborn griffins on the Isle of Landin, Volke Savan and his adopted sister Illia run afoul of the Dread Pirate Calisto, the same cutthroat who carved out Illia's right eye. As a master manticore arcanist, Calisto's strength and brutality are unrivalled. When Illia suggests they bring him to justice, Volke wonders if they'll have what it takes to fight the corsairs on the high seas.

Get the book now to join them in their next thrilling adventure!

ABOUT THE AUTHOR

Shami Stovall grew up in California's central valley with a single mother and little brother. Despite no one in her family having a degree higher than a GED, she put herself through college (earning a BA in History), and then continued on to law school where she obtained her Juris Doctorate.

As a child, Stovall enjoyed every portal fantasy, space opera, and magic series she could get her hands on, but the first novel to spark her imagination was Island of the Blue Dolphins by Scott O'Dell. The adventure on a deserted island opened her mind to ideas and realities she had never given thought before—and it was the moment Stovall realized that story telling (specifically fiction) became her passion. Anything that told a story, especially fantasy series and military science fiction, be it a movie, book, video game or comic, she had to experience.

Now, as a professor and author, Stovall wants to add her voice to the myriad of stories in the world. Everything from sorcerers, to robots, to fantasy wars--she just hopes you enjoy.

To find out more about Shami Stovall and the Frith Chronicles, take a look at her website:

www.sastovallauthor.com

If you want to be notified when Shami Stovall's next book releases, please sign up to her newsletter here:

https://sastovallauthor.com/newsletter/

Or contact her directly at:

s.adelle.s@gmail.com